THE IMMORTAL KING RAO

THE IMMORTAL KING RAO

A Novel

Vauhini Vara

W. W. NORTON & COMPANY

Independent Publishers Since 1923

Copyright © 2022 by Vauhini Vara

For information about permission to reproduce selections from this book, write to Permissions, W. W. Norton & Company, Inc., 500 Fifth Avenue, New York, NY 10110

For information about special discounts for bulk purchases, please contact W. W. Norton Special Sales at specialsales@wwnorton.com or 800-233-4830

Manufacturing by Lake Book Manufacturing
Book design by Brooke Koven
Production manager: Julia Druskin

Library of Congress Cataloging-in-Publication Data

Names: Vara, Vauhini, 1982– author.
Title: The immortal King Rao : a novel / Vauhini Vara.
Description: First edition. | New York, NY : W. W. Norton & Company, [2022]
Identifiers: LCCN 2021061979 | ISBN 9780393541755 (hardback) |
ISBN 9780393541762 (epub)
Subjects: LCGFT: Dystopian fiction. | Novels.
Classification: LCC PS3622.A7235 I46 2022 | DDC 813/.6—dc23/eng/20211222
LC record available at https://lccn.loc.gov/2021061979

W. W. Norton & Company, Inc., 500 Fifth Avenue, New York, N.Y. 10110
www.wwnorton.com

W. W. Norton & Company Ltd., 15 Carlisle Street, London W1D 3BS

2 3 4 5 6 7 8 9 0

For my mom, Vidyavathi Vara,
and my dad, Krishna S. Vara

Once the choice has been made to organize economic, commercial, and property relations at the transnational level, it seems obvious that the only way to transcend capitalism and ownership society is to work out some way of transcending the nation-state. But exactly how can this be done?

—Thomas Piketty,
Capital and Ideology, 2019

When the superior man has no choice but to oversee all under heaven, there is no better policy than nonaction.

—Unknown Author,
The Zhuangzi, circa fourth century to third century BCE

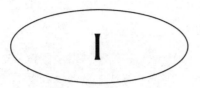

I

King Rao left this world as the most influential person ever to have lived. He entered it possessing not even a name.

In the beginning, his mother-to-be stood at the little general store in the center of her village, eyeing the tins of soap piled neatly on the countertop facing the road. It was 1951. Radha had seen this brand before, on excursions to Rajahmundry with her father and sister, but finding a stack of soap tins at their shop, three high and two wide—

PEARS PEARS

PEARS PEARS

PEARS PEARS

—was something else altogether.

Radha was eighteen, and she hated Kothapalli, this hot, wet nothing of a village, nestled in the elbow crook of one of the many canals delivering the Godavari River east to the Bay of Bengal. Its name meant, simply, "new village," the equivalent in Telugu of all the Newtowns scattered around the English-speaking world. Several variations on the name could be found in the region. This particular village was distinguished, if that word could even be used, by the arrangement of its small center around a circle where the roads converged. In the middle of the circle stood a peepal tree, under which men congregated in the shade, sitting on over-turned wooden crates borrowed from the general store, while stray mutts made languid tours around them, hoping for food scraps. Around the circle were the government school, the offices of the tax collector and the village council president, the vegetable and fruit vendors with their carts, a shop selling farm tools, and the general store before which Radha stood.

International products such as Pears, a British brand, did not often appear in Kothapalli's store. The shopkeeper, one of the most reviled men in the village, was a mean, eagle-eyed miser when it came to his customers, but sycophantic toward the politi-cians whose favor he required. He was a fat, sweaty man, with the skin of a dead tamarind tree and big, curling lips, black at their edges and pink inside, which he pressed together in a grotesque way that reminded Radha of a fish. He sat behind the counter, perched on a high stool. When customers weren't around, he passed his time reading or filing his nails with a scrap of sandpa-per, his nostrils narrowed in concentration. Behind him was the storehouse where he kept most of the goods: groceries, toiletries, housewares. Under the counter in front of him were the grain and jaggery, in big jute sacks, and the cooking oil, in an alumi-num tin.

On the countertop, he displayed items meant to draw the attention of people passing by. He kept his jars of sweets there, for instance, and now that school had ended, children pushed past Radha and lingered in front of the counter, ogling the treats that sat just out of their reach. "Are you going to buy some?" the shop-keeper wheezed at them. He never stopped wheezing, a condi-tion that, because he was a mean man, inspired revulsion rather than compassion. "If not, get out of here!" But a curly-haired boy produced a scarred little coin and asked what he could get for it, and the shopkeeper sighed and began haggling. The rest of the children crowded around, offering their advice about the best use of the coin. And now Radha swiftly grabbed one of the soap tins, stuck it in her armpit, where no one could see it, and ducked around the corner. Once out of the shopkeeper's sight, she ran past her house, which doubled as her father's school for Dalit children, to the Muslim graveyard. The roofed, four-arched stone structure in the center had always been her secret hiding spot.

Most people avoided the graveyard, that deathful place, but Radha feared nothing. She was a wild-haired, big-boned, dark-skinned girl. She intimidated people; she knew this. It was partly because Appayya, her father, was a headmaster, and partly because she had brains and an inborn imperiousness. The village store, with its occasional imports from other lands, was the closest Radha had gotten to a more cosmopolitan life. But soon, she had determined, she would move to Rajahmundry. She had applied to the teacher's college there. For someone like her to be accepted—a girl, a Dalit—would be unusual. But her father had connections, and she was sure that when she told him of her plans, he would help execute them. She would leave him behind, and her sister. They both doted on her, but her father and sister had never understood each other. She imagined them living, after she left, in embarrassed silence, neither able to begin a conversation that wasn't about her. Still, it gave her only a slight pang of guilt. She'd always had the feeling greatness was in store for her. She was, after all, King Rao's mother-to-be.

So the air of death that lingered in the graveyard did not faze Radha. She and her younger sister, Sita, had grown up playing there. Now, crouching in a corner of the structure and making as little noise as she could, Radha unboxed the soap and carefully peeled off its paper wrapping, so she could get a better look and feel. She'd never committed such an act as this, but what had she done, exactly? She didn't consider it stealing, because she planned to return the item. The soap was cool and light in her palm. It had rounded sides and the loveliest color, clear but with a deep amber tint, like an amulet that belonged at the breast of an ancient queen. She turned the soap around in her hand, enthralled. It was the advertisements on the radio and billboards, promising that Pears could turn bad skin good, that had made her so desirous. When she lived in a hostel in Rajahmundry, she decided, she would bathe with one of these.

What Radha wouldn't have realized—but I can't help but remark upon—is that Pears had been selling its soaps across the British Empire for a long time. In 1899, at the height of British colonialism, one advertisement had read, "The first step towards lightening The White Man's Burden is through teaching the virtues of cleanliness. Pears' soap is a potent factor in brightening the dark corners of the earth as civilization advances." By the time the Lever Brothers, William and James, acquired Pears toward the end of World War I, it had established impressive markets around the world, including in India. Several years later, when Indian soap sales fell, William Lever suspected that Gandhi's Swadeshi movement was to blame, so he purchased a little soap-making plant in Calcutta to help him position his products as just as indigenous as the local stuff. The move proved prescient. Soon afterward, in one of the world's first transnational mergers, Lever Brothers combined with the Dutch margarine producer Margarine Unie. When India gained independence and codified its economic nationalism, the Calcutta plant meant Unilever's Indian subsidiaries could operate under the same terms as any Bombayite competitor. At first, the nationalists resisted. But as Radha entered high school, their opposition was fading. Hence the arrival of Pears at Kothapalli's store.

Radha noticed someone coming into the cemetery. She froze. It was Pedda Rao, a boy in her class at school, and he was coming toward where she hid. Pedda's father, the richest Dalit landowner in the village, was a friend of her father's. Pedda had an identical twin brother, Chinna, but their personalities were nothing alike. Chinna was confident, ambitious, and popular, friends with Brahmins and Reddys as well as Dalits; Pedda was bitter, lazy, and friendless. Pedda peered into the structure, then stood looking at Radha as if expecting something. "Hi," she said, standing. She had meant to shoo him off with her tone, but her voice, when it came out, surprised her: wet, soapy.

He must have heard it, too. He didn't answer, but he didn't leave, either, and after a moment he sidled inside and stood facing her. She supposed he had come there for some private business of his own. But she had been there first. He should wait his turn, she thought, and she gave him a look of annoyance meant to convey this. She was holding the soap at her side, feeling its good, cool weight.

"Is that the soap you stole?" Pedda said.

She reddened. "I bought it!"

Pedda laughed bitterly. "That's not what the shopkeeper said. I was walking by and heard him telling the children to run and find you. If they did, they'd get a reward. They're wandering all over town. I thought you'd be in your usual spot."

The atmosphere between them was charged. If they were both boys, someone might have spat. Instead, Pedda moved close and made a completely unexpected move. Taking her by the shoulders, he spun her to face one corner of the structure and stood right behind her, his hot breath wetting her neck. A strange pressure, hard and soft at the same time, pushed into the curve of one of her hips. She, with the soap in her hand and her desire—not for him, but for the soap, for the life she had promised herself—went mute. His hands cupped her hips and pulled her to him, and he bucked against her, while she stood perfectly motionless, holding the bar of soap tight in her fist. At one point she thought he had unzipped his pants. She should scream and flee, that would be the correct thing to do. But there was that desire. She was not herself. She cried out, and he did, too, spurting a warm jet of fluid onto her langa.

From down the road came the shopkeeper's voice. "Hey, who's that in there?" At once, he was at the arch, peering in. "What's this? What's this?" Pedda gasped, pulled away, and sprinted out of the cemetery, leaving Radha alone to confront the shopkeeper, who stood there breathing so heavily she could see his gut moving up and down. "The children saw what you were doing in here," he said. "They ran and got me." He took her roughly by the shoulders, and steered her toward the village center, shouting in the direction of her father's school as they passed, "Headmaster, hey, see what your little girl is up to! Master, wait till you find out what I caught her doing!"

Radha's father came out of the school. The shopkeeper called out over his shoulder, "I know she's not a bad girl, but I saw it myself!" In the center, the president of the village council, too, emerged from his office, shielding his eyes from the sun. Radha's face went hot with rage. She wanted to shout that the shopkeeper was lying, but then, there was the semen's wetness soaking through her langa and the soap in her fist. The shopkeeper had not even taken it from her. Drop it, little fool, she told herself. It'll be his word against yours. But she couldn't bring herself to do it. The ridiculousness of the situation—the joke of it, even though the joke was on her—made a strong impression. In her final moment of freedom, my grandmother-to-be held that bar of Pears with a faint smile and did not let go.

THE MORNING OF the wedding, Pedda told his twin, Chinna, that he didn't plan to consummate the marriage yet. It was in fact Chinna who had harbored a crush on Radha ever since her father, the schoolmaster, had combined the boys' class with the girls'. "She's *strong*," Chinna would whisper, late at night. "She's like a horse." Ever since the engagement, the brothers had barely spoken. Pedda's talk of delaying the consummation was his first acknowledgment, albeit an indirect one, of his breach. Chinna flinched. He spat in the dirt. "Don't be immature," he said. "You're going to have to touch her one of these nights." He added, "It's not like you've never touched her," and spat again as if expelling something disgusting.

The wedding took place on the Rao property, which everyone called the Garden because the land was famously fertile: The Raos' livelihood came from a sizable coconut grove around which they had built their homes. It was a good family to marry into. But that afternoon, Radha stood straight-shouldered, as grim and resolute as a political prisoner awaiting her execution. When Pedda, her groom, tied the mangalsutra around her neck and knotted it three times, she did not flinch. She smelled, to Pedda, of sandalwood and sweat. He found her fearsome.

Later on, the feast consumed, the chicken bones and other postprandial debris tossed in a heap for the goats, Pedda and Chinna's room swept clear, their cot strewn with marigold petals, Pedda stood in the middle of the room looking at his wife, who sat on the cot. It occurred to him that he did not know her at all. They were strangers. Radha sat with her legs folded to one side and her back pressed to the wall, tracing the henna designs on her feet with her finger. Pedda murmured, almost as if to himself, "I'm not like other men."

"Men!" Radha said, her lips twitching a little. She spoke precisely, every vowel and consonant standing erect in its place, the verbal equivalent of good posture.

"Other men like to show off about how great they are," he said. "I take action." He had rehearsed these lines, but his words now mortified him—stupid, grandiose. He wondered if Chinna, who was sleeping out on the veranda tonight, since their room had been turned into the marital chamber, could hear the conversation. The horror of it.

Though Pedda was technically the older one, having been born nine minutes before Chinna, he knew he was less impressive by all other metrics. Chinna was handsome and sharp-featured, Pedda soft and lymphatic. Chinna attracted friends and admirers everywhere, while Pedda repelled them simply by entering a room. It must have been Pedda's perverse sense of competition with Chinna—it never left him—that had compelled him toward Radha that afternoon in the graveyard. He had never regretted anything more.

Radha picked up a marigold petal and tore it in half. "Great," she said.

"I mean we'll work together, side by side"—but he was losing his thread—"because you're strong, you're like a horse!"

She laughed harshly. She might as well have slapped him. "A horse!" she said. "But, no, dear husband. I'm going to be a teacher, not a farmer."

Oh God, what had he done to get to this point? But she'd had a part in it, too, hadn't she? She had pressed against him, he could have sworn she had. And hadn't she been the one to steal that soap, to refuse, even, to return it to the shopkeeper once she had been discovered, like some kind of imbecile? Now here she sat frowning on the cot as if she were the victim. His ill will toward her thickened. His arms were spring-loaded; it took effort to keep them at his sides. After a while, she stood and walked just past him to the far corner of the room, where her belongings lay folded in a chest. With her back to him, she reached between her breasts and unfastened the hooks of her blouse under her sari.

A small swell rose in him, some combination of care and lust. He focused on this, encouraging it to expand and displace his anger. "That must feel better," he said.

"Don't look at me," she replied.

He fixed his gaze toward the bed and silently counted the marigold petals there, one, two, three, four, and heard the rustle of his wife undressing, five, six, seven, and was reminded of his childhood, when his cousin sisters used to strip in the rain and splash naked in the shallow pools of water that collected at the edge of the clearing between the house and the coconut grove. The boys sometimes stole the girls' underwear and threatened to feed it to the stray dogs. "Idiots!" the girls shouted, coming at them with clawed hands. "Get back here, we'll break your rotten teeth!" The girls were leaving now, one by one, married off.

His wife moved toward him. She had changed into a plain cotton sari, ocher-colored. She walked past him to the cot, where she sat and undid her braid, releasing her hair into loose waves around her shoulders. Without looking at him, she pulled her legs onto the cot, turned away, and lay curled against the wall. He bristled with desire, but what was he supposed to do? The minutes stretched on forever. From her careful breathing, he could tell she wasn't sleeping. Finally, he sat on the bed and put a hand on her shoulder. When she didn't recoil, he said, "You look like a mendicant, Lemon." It was her father's nickname for her, which he'd overheard. She froze but didn't open her eyes. "They wear those red robes," he said, overexplaining.

"What did you call me?" she said.

He laughed nervously. "I'm going to call you that from now on," he said.

"Don't," she said, and shivered.

"Cold?" he said, rubbing her shoulder, and when she didn't answer, he said, "Lemon, are you cold?"

"No," she said. She gave a shrug so violent that his hand slipped from her.

He moved closer, raising himself on an elbow so that he was propped above her. Her scent was musky and vegetal—mannish. "I can keep you warm," he said, his voice sounding roguish even to himself.

"If you touch me," she said, "I'll scream."

"But I'm your husband." He couldn't understand what his brother saw in this girl.

"I swear this time I'll scream."

The truth was that she terrified him. But he gathered his courage and rolled close to his wife, taking her in his arms. Her breath caught. "I told you, don't touch me," she murmured. He didn't move. "I mean it," she said.

But she wasn't as insistent as she had been earlier, or at least she didn't seem so to him. From behind, he clamped his hand over her mouth, hard. He straddled her, shifting her onto her back and holding her legs down with his own. He had expected her to scream, as she had promised, but now she only stared up at him with wide, wet eyes, as if waiting to see what would happen next. He pulled her sari and petticoat up past her knees and moved into her, and she gulped a couple of times but lay quietly, still staring up at him. He kept his hand over her mouth and pumped on top of her. Radha's breath was hot and wet on his palm. "I love you! I love you! I love you!" he said.

She thrashed her head around. Her hair caught in her mouth, and snot dripped from her nose; she was crying. There was so much fabric between them. All those ocher folds. He pressed himself to her tightly and said, "My wife!" There came a swell of joy and a bursting and, finally, emptiness and shame. When he extracted himself, he found blood on his thighs.

"I'm bleeding!" he said with alarm.

"No, dear husband," she said. "I'm bleeding."

In the middle of the night, he awoke to find Radha in the corner of the room near the chest, with her back to him, fully clothed. She was untangling her hair with her fingers. Now she stood looking at the henna designs lightening on her palms. It was a bad omen, the early oranging.

"Are you all right?" he said.

She turned to him. "The color's fading," she said.

"Come back to bed, Lemon," he told her, and to his great awe and gratitude, she did.

WHEN RADHA RETURNED, six months later, to her childhood home behind the schoolhouse rooms, she insisted to Sita that she had allowed it to happen only once. Sex, she told her sister, was an inherent violation. She had closed herself off to her husband after that one awful night, which was to say she knew for a fact that it had been that night's violence that had produced her unborn spawn.

Sita was Radha's opposite, the kind of girl who saw no gain in asking for more than she was given. When Radha disappeared into the Rao fold after the wedding, neither visiting nor spending more than a couple of minutes with Sita and her father when they came to the Raos' place themselves, Sita had accepted it as the new order of things. She was sitting on the veranda of the school when their father brought Radha home, to spend the rest of her pregnancy there, according to custom, until the time came to give birth. Sita leaped up and led her sister into their father's bedroom, and when her sister had lain down, Sita brought her a glass of lemonade.

Radha, Sita noticed, did not look well. Several months had passed since they had been alone together, and Radha's bulbed stomach made her seem even more like a stranger. Though her stomach was rounded, the fat seemed to have dissolved from her arms and hips, and a fine line had appeared beneath each of her eyes. Sita had expected her sister to seem radiant, like young brides in stories she had read, but the opposite was true. There was a darkness to her sister that she'd never seen. It frightened her. She hoped the real Radha had hidden somewhere inside this other woman and wasn't lost for good. "Those hicks in your new family are overworking you!" she gently teased. She added nervously, worried that her sister's alliances might have shifted since her marriage, "I'm just teasing."

Sita was sitting on the foot of her sister's bed, her knees up, drilling Radha about her life at the Raos' home. Appayya had prepared his room for Radha so she could rest well and wouldn't have to share a bed with her sister. He moved to the schoolroom floor, where he slept on a rolled-out pallet. Still, Radha shunned her father. She was irate with him for forcing her into marrying Pedda. He let people think of him as a progressive man, but he had shown himself to be as spineless as any other.

Even putting aside the horror of the wedding night, Radha admitted, she hadn't wanted a child at all. Once she gave birth, she would have to stop her studies and stay at home. Even though she hadn't had many chores at the Garden because of her pregnancy, she had failed at the ones she did have. She had tried at first—valiantly, even, waking at three in the morning to start the breakfast preparations and wash laundry by moonlight before going to school—but she wasn't used to it. At home, their servants had always done the housework. At the Garden, everyone was expected to pitch in to keep the operation running; for the women, that meant taking care of all the cooking and cleaning. The women of the Garden, it was said, often died before their husbands did.

The smoke from the kitchen fire made Radha's eyes redden and hurt, and she tired so quickly at the big mortar and pestle that her chutneys turned out fibrous and bitter. Once, she caught pneumonia from the nighttime chill and had to spend days in bed. She heard the wives of Pedda's cousins mutter that they'd thought she was strong. Her whole reputation had been for being strong.

But she had not entirely shed the fortitude for which she was famous. When she was alone, she'd privately terrorize the unborn creature. Get out of here, she told it in her mind. Leave me alone. Sometimes she punched her stomach to punctuate the point. When she imagined the creature, she thought of a leech that couldn't be dislodged from inside her. It made her ill. In the mornings, she woke early so the others wouldn't overhear her vomiting in the outhouse. She still had hope that the creature would receive her messages: Get out of here. Leave me alone. The creature ate her food, shared her blood. Wasn't it possible that it could absorb her thoughts?

"Well, what if she can hear and still gets born?" Sita whispered. "She'll grow up thinking, My mother hates me; I heard her from in there before I was born. It'll mess up her whole life! Don't think such thoughts!"

But the creature wasn't innocent, Radha hissed, it was a monster. When she punched it, the monster punched her in return. This was war, it was violent, it wasn't the magical experience people talk about. "Plus, it isn't a daughter," she added. "It's definitely a son."

WHEN RADHA'S CONTRACTIONS STARTED, the midwife came over and climbed onto the cot. Sita watched the midwife part her sister's legs and peer between them. But the midwife gave a short, sour laugh, and said, "Stop being a pervert and go sit next to her."

Chastened, Sita moved to place herself on the floor next to Radha's head.

The midwife chattered as she pressed at Radha's stomach. She made a mean comment about a mutual cousin of theirs who was an albino, and Sita laughed heartily, not out of appreciation but because she wanted to be on the midwife's good side. She held Radha's work-toughened hand and pressed on the veins of her sister's wrist. Soon, she thought gloomily, she would be married herself, find her own belly expanding into a hard, venous balloon with a knotted center, and end up on this same cot with the midwife's fist between her legs. It made no sense. She still felt like she and her sister were children.

She squeezed Radha's hand, but her sister's eyes were shut in pain, and she didn't return the squeeze. The curves of Radha's nostrils flared, and dots of sweat bloomed on her brow and dripped into her hair. She made wet grunting noises. Many hours passed. The contractions narrowed, and Radha began screaming. Then the midwife committed an act of sheer violence. Kneeling, she shoved her hand into the flesh between Radha's legs. Radha mewled and moved like an animal being butchered. Sita gripped her sister's shoulder, but Radha flung out an arm and cried, "Get *off*!"

How could birth so resemble death? The midwife's bony wrist flexed inside Radha. Then out it came, covered in blood and a whitish grease, the infant's head grasped in the midwife's hand like a cut of meat. The whole child emerged unbreathing. The midwife held him upside down by his legs in one fist and, with her free hand, whacked his backside until he wailed.

My father was born with his eyes wide open and crust-rimmed. He had a muddy, eczematous complexion. From his belly, a glutinous rope swayed until the midwife pinched it between two fingers and snipped with the scissors her husband used for barbering. She laid the umbilical cord and the scissors at the end of the cot near Radha's feet. Only then did Sita turn from the spectacle of childbirth and notice her sister. Radha's breathing was labored, and her face was pale. She didn't smile, nor, when the midwife held the child out, did she raise her arms to receive him. She fluttered her eyelids and groaned. Some spit bubbled from her mouth, reddish, like rusted water. Had she bitten her tongue?

Sita wiped the bloody saliva with her thumb and touched her sister's forehead. It was wet and hot. "Is she supposed to be like this?" she asked, and the midwife hadn't yet answered when blood began trickling, then gushing, from between Radha's legs. Sita sprinted down the street to where the doctor, a Dutch man known as the Hollander, lived. But by the time they got back to the house, Radha's lips were purpling. The umbilical cord had fallen to the floor in a pool of blood. Their father was crouched over Radha, clutching her hands and shouting her name. Sita was peering at him, uncomprehending, when the midwife thrust the swaddled child at her. Sita turned to her father. Should she reach out to him? Hand him the child? Radha would tell her, she thought for a confusing moment. Radha would know what to do.

IF RADHA HAD a given name planned, she had kept it secret from everyone, including Pedda. Even the child's surname was up in the air, since it was not clear whether, in the final accounting, he would be taken in by Pedda's family, the Raos, or by his late mother's.

Appayya blamed Radha's in-laws for her death—his friendship with Pedda's father be damned—and wanted to demand a refund of the dowry. But Sita was in the throes of an uncommon fit of willfulness. If she married Pedda and adopted the child, the Raos couldn't demand a new dowry; it would be distasteful. "Your grandson is part of that family, even if you don't like it, and this way you don't have to pay another dowry for me to marry someone else," Sita said. Appayya, normally a man of unbending judgment, had shrunk in his grief. In the end, he didn't agree with his younger daughter's plan so much as he stopped protesting it.

They had been calling the boy only "him" or "the child." Sita wanted to name him as a rebuke to those who pitied him for having been born under a bad star. Raj, she thought, or Raja. It was Pedda's brother Chinna, an Anglophile, who convinced her to use the English version of the name. King. She figured she had better listen to him. She and the baby were to be Raos, and as a wife and a son, their selves would be subsumed into the Rao collective. Pedda and Chinna's father was getting old, and while Pedda should have been next in line to assume the family throne, technically being older, no one expected much from him. Chinna clearly would be in charge.

A big name for a little runt, some of her new in-laws teased. But Sita wasn't in the mood. "He has strong bones," she responded, straight-faced. "He has a regal lip." Sita had hired a neighbor girl to nurse him, and the child drank from her breast with slurpy gumption. "He has a strong suckle," Sita said. "He'll live up to it."

Radha was dead. Long live King Rao.

ut this cold morning, dear Shareholder, King Rao is three days gone. It shouldn't surprise me that all these people whose names he never mentioned to me—religious leaders, mega-influencers, vice presidents of this and that—parade forth to eulogize him on Social. Still, it galls. It galls. The correctional officers on my cellblock must be watching the clips: I can hear snippets of the thirty-second testimonials, just faintly, by pressing my ear to the wall of the cell in which I'm being held. The father of the modern . . . the greatest innovator the world's ever . . . The whole performance, in its pretense, is like a second violence being committed upon my murdered father. I hate them for it. I should be the one publicly celebrating the life of King Rao. Who in the world has a greater right?

It is I, after all, who used to awaken in my crib early in the morning, the sun warming me through my swaddling blanket, screaming a complex and operatic scream—I was never one of those dumb, satisfied infants who blinks herself awake and lies there cooing in idleness—and know King Rao would answer. It is I who, seconds later, would hear the sound of his voice calling out to me, gently, and his sandals slapping the floor as he came toward my room. Entering, he would lean over the crib, untuck the corner of my swaddle, roll me out of it, and kiss me on the forehead, murmuring, "I'm here; Daddy's here."

I had an old man for a father. In my mind's eye, he wears a threadbare, decades-old lungi in blue-and-white plaid tied around his waist. His dark chest is bare, covered with wiry white hairs. His breath is sour, his eyes half-closed, his gray-white hair all mussed up around his head. Pulling myself up to stand, I would run a finger across the pine slats of my crib, one by one, while my father watched, smiling, his eyes bright. The slats were smooth and cool to the touch. On bright mornings, light surged through the east-facing window and bathed the room. I wanted to touch it. I reached out and tried to catch it in my fists.

He sufficed for everything then. He would retrieve me from my crib and sit me on his lap in the big forest-green armchair by the window, feeding me formula from a bottle. I remember his warmth and his strong rancid morning smell. When I finished the bottle, he would put it down beside him on the floor and press his huge old lined palms to my little ones. His hands were dry-skinned and cool.

One morning, as I sat playing with twigs on the floor near my crib, my father dozed off in the armchair. I wanted him to wake up. I used the slats of the crib to pull myself to my feet. He opened his eyes. He put his palms on his knees and sat extremely still, as if I were a deer and he was afraid I would flee. He couldn't have been more than three feet from me. For the first time in my life, I stepped toward him. The wood floor was cool under my feet. To go barefoot across the room, the floor beneath me—miraculous!

I crossed the three feet and fell forward onto his bony knees, across which his lungi draped, then stood hugging them. For a long time, we remained like that. He was physically slight, five-foot-four, shrunken and slender, though not frail. But he still had a big, strong, expressive face—flaring nostrils, thick lips—and a full head of hair. His hair flopped over his forehead; he swiped it aside. He reached down, pulled me onto his lap, and tickled me until I wailed with laughter. "You did it!" he said. "You walked!"

With that milestone complete, he grew anxious for me to learn to speak. He put me inside the yellow plastic laundry basket and pushed me around the room in it. "Let's pretend it's a boat," he told me. "Pretend it's a car." Or, "Look, it's a train, choo-choo, choo-choo." He would repeat certain words over and over. "Door," he said, for example, pointing at the wooden door of my room. The logic of language—attaching words to their particular meaning, putting them in order—came easily to me. I understood what he wanted from me: to repeat after him. But I refused to obey, feigning ignorance. Then, one morning, he said, "Door," and it happened that I had gotten bored with infancy, it was time to move on, and I said it. "Door," I said, and because I liked the sound of it issuing from my own mouth, I said it again. "Door!"

My understanding of the word differed from the actual meaning. When he pointed to the door, I was captivated not with the large wooden rectangle with its small brass knob, but with what it conveyed, a passage to the universe beyond the room. I loved spending time outside my room, in the living room, the kitchen, and my father's bedroom, and I loved being outside the house, too, in the garden and fruit orchards my father lovingly cultivated.

Never, though, did he allow me into the forest beyond. We lived alone on Blake Island, separated from the rest of the world by Puget Sound, and my father impressed upon me, from a very young age, that the wider universe was an unwelcoming place, full of peril. On Bainbridge Island, to the north, lived people who were supposed to be dangerous. Yet I couldn't help but be captivated by the mysteries beyond what I could see. So that first word—what I thought it meant—was infused with promise, and for a long time I had no use for any other, even as he tried to move on. "Room," he tried. "Floor." "Crib." "Chair." "Athena," he said, pointing at me, and "Dad," pointing at himself. "Athena," "Dad," "Athena," "Dad." I only replied, "Door." Door, door, door, door, door, door, door.

I wouldn't give it up, my first and favorite word, the single one I deigned to use.

He only laughed. He didn't take my refusal to mean much. And it didn't, not then. I loved my father completely. I loved the soft cloud of hair that stood up around his head in the morning, and the deep creases in his leather-brown skin. I loved his big, broad-nostriled nose and his clouded, glaucomic eyes, sagging deep in their sockets. When I grew older, I would sit on his lap in the armchair as he read to me, teasing him by licking my fingertip and rubbing the liver spots on his soft hands as if trying to wipe them off. The flesh of his arms and legs hung loose, and I would hold it between my thumb and forefinger and make a pair of scissors out of my other hand. I pretended it was a bunch of loose fabric, and I, a tailor trimming it.

That was around the time that my father dismantled my crib and took it outside. I sat in the room alone, bereft. The space felt sad and overlarge until he returned with the pieces of a twin bed, its frame painted in pale seashell colors, and put it together. My father excelled at gifts. From the big, luscious garden outside he would bring me cut flowers in little mason jars, which we arranged all around my room—on the windowsills, on the furniture, even on the floor. For a long time, I didn't know flowers died after being cut, because he replaced them so often that I never had to see a petal wilt or a stem droop. I demanded that he bring me the particular flowers I most adored—the fierce and big-headed varieties, roses, peonies, ranunculi—and he did.

One morning, though, when I was not quite three years old, I bit into the head of a rose. I was old enough to know better, but I did it still. The petals surprised me with their bitter taste. I didn't tell him what I had done; he didn't notice the dark, scallop-edged mark on the flower's head. But the next time he brought me flowers, I grimaced and told him I didn't want them.

"You love flowers," he protested, hurt. He crouched next to me, his hand around the jar. He reached out with the jar in his hand.

"I hate them!" I shouted. "I don't want them!" Out flung my

arm. It whacked the jar right out of his hand and onto the floor. He stepped back, crying out, more in bafflement than anger. Though the jar hadn't broken, the water had spilled out, the flowers arraying themselves prettily in the puddle. I see it now as an omen, my violent rejection of his gift. The damage both ecstasized and terrified me. "I didn't mean to," I whispered. It was true that I didn't. But I also did. I didn't, and I did. I was becoming a human being in the world. I was becoming myself, a Rao.

THIS MORNING I awoke for the first time in my cell in the Margaret Rao Detention Center to the sound of a soft plop, then another. A pair of pouches had been pushed through the mail-slot-sized opening in the cell door and lay trembling in the tray on my side of the door. I rescued them, wiped them on my shirt, and brought them back to the mattress where I had been sleeping. The cell was cold, small, and eerily quiet. There was the tan mattress on which I had fallen into sleep the night before, no more than four inches thick, which sat on a concrete shelf built into the wall. Besides this, the room contained an aluminum sink and toilet with excellent acoustics: My pee, the previous night, had sounded almost pretty when it landed, birdsong in a coal mine. From the ceiling, a single white bulb glared down as if in judgment. The cell let in no natural light. I couldn't gauge the time; my sense of morningness was limbic. I sat and sucked on each of the pouches in turn. The cola was bittersweet, like underripe fruit, and fizzed on the tongue. The meal, carrot-flavored, had a pasty mashed-potato texture. I got no aesthetic pleasure from either. He is gone.

3

Can I conjure him from within this cell? Dare I attempt it? The main house of the Raos' Garden—where Pedda and Chinna lived, along with their parents, and where King and Sita soon joined them—stood in a clearing between the coconut grove and the rice paddies abutting the road to the village center. The house was surrounded by a veranda punctuated with several square pillars, which held up a generous coir roof. The house's rooms were like train cars, lined up in a row, in the style more common among upper castes than Dalits. To go from room to room, you could either walk through the house or go out onto the veranda from one room and enter another from the outside.

The other Raos lived in modest traditional huts around the property, but the whole clan spent most of their time working together in the coconut grove or gathering in the clearing for meals and conversation, returning home only to sleep. At the edge of the clearing stood three small buildings for communal use—the kitchen, the bath stall, and the outhouse—and beyond them, the thousand trees of the Garden. Some of the trees were strong and fat, others thin like an old woman's legs. Some bore guava, others jackfruit, tamarind, custard apple, or mango. But the coconut trees were the most important, the source of the family's livelihood and pride.

On lazy afternoons, as the young King lay back on the dead leaves in the middle of the Garden, looking up at the treetops, his heart couldn't help but set to thumping. The itchiness of the leaves on his arms; the hard press of the earth against his spine; the heat of the sun and the chill of the shade, simultaneously on his forehead and chest. Up above, the canopy of outstretched fronds overlapped like interlaced fingers. The light came down through the fronds in thin, trembling rays and illuminated the dust and pollen specks that danced in the faintly sulfurous air. The light pressed warm white shapes onto his arms and legs and the earth around him.

When evening came, the mothers would holler into the Garden, "Dinnertime, children! Dinnertime, rascals!" Rubbing his palms together to rouse himself, he would stand and stumble toward the sound of their voices. Running past the coconut trees, past the smaller trees bearing lesser fruits—the guava, jackfruit, tamarind, custard apple, and mango—and past the irrigation tube well and its reservoir, into which a big clear head of water gushed from a spout as wide as his torso, he would arrive at the clearing. At its edge stood the strange, beguiling cashew tree the children all loved, so aslant that its top leaves brushed the Garden's floor and made a perpetually cool, shaded space where they could all shelter on hot afternoons, pressing their bodies together to make room for more cousins as they arrived. Here was the firstborn son of the firstborn son of the firstborn son of the old patriarch. He mattered. "Here comes King," his cousins called. "Move over for King," they called, and when he came to them, the brightness of their eyes and the heat of their bodies provided the answer to a question he could not form in words.

ONE MORNING, not long after the Godavari Delta was declared part of a new state known as Andhra, a bureaucrat representing the Indian Central Coconut Committee came to Kothapalli. The village council president brought the man to the Garden to meet Pedda and Chinna's father, the Rao patriarch. Grandfather Rao sat in the clearing with King, three years old, in his lap. The government, the bureaucrat announced to Grandfather Rao, had big plans for Kothapalli. The republic, nearing a decade of independence, must learn to be self-sufficient. Mother India must stop relying so much on imports, as if her soil weren't fertile enough. Kothapalli, with its rich earth and its placement on the bank of a canal, was ideally situated to help fulfill this goal. The politicians from up north had sent him to the Godavari Delta to persuade citizens to plant their own crops; there he had heard that, in Kothapalli, Rao was the man with whom to discuss coconuts. Grandfather Rao responded to the bureaucrat's flattery with a blast of bombastic untruth. "I tell my grandson this is all for the homeland," Grandfather Rao sang at him. "All these coconuts are here to feed Mother India and keep her strong and free, I tell him. Isn't that right, King?"

The Godavari Delta had once been a benighted, backward place, alternating between flood and drought. It had become a region of significance only when, at the height of the British East India Company's power, the Port of Coringa had been constructed to aid in the passage of goods and bodies throughout the empire. When the Crown took over from the company, the British general and engineer Arthur Cotton had taken it upon himself to build a dam splitting the river into several canals, distributing water throughout the delta while also providing an efficient transportation route. This had turned the delta into one of the most fertile places on the subcontinent—on earth. A child could pluck breakfast from the trees on his walk to school; the bright green of rice paddy fields were, besides coconut trees, the region's most common physical feature; sablefish leaped into nets at the Dowleswaram Anicut where they spawned. No one hungered much.

Now, with the British having departed, more change was coming. The bureaucrat wanted Grandfather Rao to be among the first to hear that the government planned to carve a gravel road running through Kothapalli that would better connect Rajahmundry, to the northwest, with Ambajipuram and the other market towns located eastward where the river and its canals led toward the Bay of Bengal. The bureaucrat encouraged Grandfather Rao to think about the opportunities this might present.

After the bureaucrat left, Grandfather Rao told King to collect three stones. He dropped them in the dirt of the clearing to form a line. The children gathered around. "This is the city," Grandfather Rao said, pointing with a stick to the first stone, representing Rajahmundry. "This is our village," he said, pointing to the middle one. "This is the town," he said, indicating the last. For as long as they could remember, the network of gravel roads in the region bypassed Kothapalli altogether; the village had been accessible only by dirt roads that turned soupy with mud in the rainy season. But the new gravel road going right through their village, Grandfather Rao explained, would make Kothapalli a really important place.

Grandfather Rao decided on a plan. He let it be known that he was offering low-interest loans to Dalit families in Kothapalli who wanted to start small coconut groves of their own. He wouldn't ask them to start repaying the loans until ten years later—a full three years after their trees could be expected to start bearing fruit.

When the road work began, Grandfather Rao took King and his cousins to watch. Near the center of the village, they looked on as laborers poured red gravel and smoothed it with a wheeled machine, creating a new road where one hadn't even existed. The men's skin shone with perspiration. "Go on, help the workers out," said the politicians, who had come to take credit for the project, to the children, and King and his cousins ran to the road and stomped on the hot gravel. The laborers watched, smiling. Some of them took it as an opportunity to catch some rest. They crouched on their haunches, wiping at their faces with brown rags, then stuffing the rags into the waistbands of their pants.

The heat of the gravel bit at King's feet. But he remembered what Grandfather Rao had said. This was the most important event the village had ever seen. He was to remember it well. The gravel. The workers with the rags. The flint-eyed politicians. The village council president, whom people had started referring to as "Mr. President," brought the politicians one coconut after another. "One day, you'll take your own children on a walk down this road, and you'll tell them you helped build it," he told the children. "Come on and use those muscles!"

Little King Rao used those muscles. He stomped till his thighs burned. One by one his cousins left him and stood by the side of the road. The sun set. Only he was left with the laborers. "Does your boy need work?" the politicians teased Grandfather Rao. "We could use someone like him." He stomped and stomped. It grew late. The politicians got into their cars and left. The laborers left. Even his older cousins left. Only he remained, along with his grandfather, who watched as he stomped. His heart throbbed with the effort—a good, meaningful feeling, to be working on a project that mattered, and trying hard.

"Remember this," Grandfather Rao said, pulling King onto his shoulders on the way home. He was old but strong. The sun trembled on the horizon. "Don't ever forget it. It's important that this happened, and we were all part of it. You're like me, like your uncle Chinna. The Garden's going to be yours one day."

FOR GENERATIONS, the Garden had belonged not to their family but to a Brahmin clan. These Brahmins were the original Raos; King's ancestors were known, then, as the Burras. The Brahmins had passed the land from father to son like some treasured antique, their ownership compounding with each inheritance and growing more absolute. King's ancestors had taken care of the Garden all that time, but they had lived in a tumbledown settlement of huts far from the center of Kothapalli, so distant that it wasn't really part of the village at all. This was by design, since they were Dalits and not allowed to mingle with the other castes. People called it a great partnership, that of the Brahmin Raos and Dalit Burras.

But when Grandfather Rao was a child—when he was a little boy named Venkata—the sons of the Brahmin patriarch had moved to Hyderabad, and the patriarch's wife had died, leaving him alone at the Garden. One day the Brahmin told Venkata's father that he had acquired a smaller home in the center of Kothapalli and wanted Venkata's father to take over the Garden, as a tenant and a caretaker, helping him sell the coconuts in exchange for a small share of profits.

Venkata, the oldest of four siblings, was six years old when they arrived, his father shouldering jute sacks filled with their belongings. Venkata's littlest sister, Kanakamma, his favorite among his siblings, had not even turned one. His mother carried her while the middle siblings, Babu and Balayamma, each held one of Venkata's hands.

The Brahmin was standing on the veranda of his house, looking as if he had been waiting a long time. He gripped the keys tightly, and for a moment it appeared he would refuse to hand them over after all. They waited in the clearing for the Brahmin to come and meet them there, and when he didn't, Venkata's mother nudged his father, and his father climbed the stairs, his head bowed as if for benediction. Even when he stood in front of the Brahmin, he didn't raise his head. The Brahmin looked at him and said, "What a damn shame." His knuckles trembled around the keys. Venkata's father put out a hand to receive them, and finally, without a word, the Brahmin let them drop. He walked down the stairs and turned onto the path bisecting the paddy fields, toward the main road.

"Where's he going?" Venkata wondered aloud.

"Home," his father said, but even he looked uncertain.

"I thought Brahmins didn't swear."

"Some do, some don't."

Over at the Burra settlement, people whispered that the Brahmin had anointed Venkata's father because he was obedient, not because he was intelligent, confident, or otherwise well equipped to run an enterprise the size of the Garden. He was short and lean, with thin, oily hair, a scoliotic posture, and the ribs of a stray tomcat. The years passed, and he diminished. Before long, his four children were each at least a full head taller than him and could see the dandruff caught along the widening part in his hair. He wore the same threadbare lungi around his waist every day. He never spoke much, and when he did, he muttered the palest platitudes. He told his children that they had the Brahmin to thank for their fortune, though everyone knew the Brahmin had been forced to let their father manage the Garden because of his own ineptitude. When the children questioned their father, he only hissed at them, "Don't be disrespectful; don't come to me with that talk." He looked afraid rather than menacing, his shoulders hunched and his eyes darting. It was as if he believed the Brahmin would abruptly appear from behind the trees, like some demon.

Because Venkata was the oldest, his father began sending him, at the age of eleven, to visit the Brahmin at his house in Kothapalli's center, to take care of whatever needed doing. His next-oldest siblings stayed behind to help at home, but Kanakamma, being the youngest, at six, and still free of responsibility, liked to accompany him. He never minded. Kanakamma remained his favorite, a small, pliant, doe-eyed little tagalong. He enjoyed taking care of her and having someone to terrorize. During monsoon season, the Brahmin made Venkata arrange big earthen pots on the floor to collect the rain that poured through the leaking roof, and dump them outside when they filled. It was tedious. The Brahmin didn't take care of repairs, and over time the earthen pots multiplied on his floor.

He always left the house when Venkata and Kanakamma came. It would be taboo for him to be seen sharing an enclosed space with untouchables, breathing the air they breathed. Venkata wanted to show he didn't care what the Brahmin thought, and so he made a game of it. He constructed an obstacle course with the pots and had Kanakamma count the seconds it took for him to complete it. Kanakamma, a rule-follower of a child, would wring her hands, glancing at the front door, and whisper, "Okay, but be *careful*." One afternoon, he slipped and kicked a pot; it toppled and broke into pieces. "I told you," Kanakamma said, whimpering. " 'Be *care-ful*,' I said." Venkata told her to toughen up and made her hide the broken pieces of the pot in the folds of her langa. They ran to the Burra settlement where they used to live and buried the pieces there with the help of their distant cousin Kothayya, a gentle boy, who was in love with Kanakamma. Kanakamma cried softly the whole time, while Kothayya consoled her. "Don't be babies," Venkata scolded them both, but he was fearful, too. "You better not tell anyone," he said to Kothayya. If they were caught, they would be beaten, not by the Brahmin, but by their father.

For days, they were afraid. Kanakamma cried at the slightest provocation, and Venkata eyed her with menace, silently warning her not to tell. One evening, the Brahmin appeared unannounced at the Garden while they were all eating dinner, with an unfocused expression in his eyes. Venkata and his siblings sat cross-legged on the veranda, little piles of rice, lentils, and okra arranged before them on bright green banana leaves. Kanakamma, who sat next to Venkata, pinched his arm and tried to meet his eyes, but he shook her off and kept eating, as if the visit had nothing to do with them. Their mother ran and brought out the stool for the Brahmin.

"Please, sir, sit, sit, sit," their father stammered to the Brahmin, gesturing at the stool.

Venkata hated seeing his father abase himself and hated the Brahmin for causing it. The Brahmin lurched up the steps to the veranda and onto the stool and sat there wobbling to and fro. Their father, who stood to the side of the stool, kept thrusting his arms out as if preparing to catch the Brahmin.

"Stop it, I'm fine!" the Brahmin shouted. He added, more quietly, "I know what you're suggesting. First, my sons call me a drunkard, and now my tenants, too."

Venkata looked up from his plate. The Brahmin was a drunkard. What a thrilling revelation—a Brahmin, and a drunkard! He wanted to laugh.

"Those damn kids," the Brahmin said. "I doted on them, and now I'm old, and they've deserted me. I swear, I never took a sip of liquor till they left. But when they deserted me, what happiness did I have left? My wife, I suppose. That stray dog who came around. Then my wife died, and the dog went away. 'We didn't desert him,' my boys tell people. 'Oh no, we asked him to come with us, and he refused.' Well, I call that deserting me! Or they tell people, 'We send our father money. Every month, we send it!' If that's the case, why am I the poorest damn Brahmin you've ever seen?" He looked at Venkata's father as if he expected an answer.

Venkata had seen drunks before—he had uncles who were drunks—but never a drunk Brahmin. He loved the sight of it.

"Your kids are good because they don't go to school," the Brahmin went on. "If you want my advice, here it is: Keep them far from school. That's where I went wrong with mine. Education, education, that's what they all said. But I educated my kids, and what did they do? They deserted me. My roof! My roof!" He turned, for the first time, to Venkata. "You've seen my roof! They won't even fix it! Tell your dad: You've seen it!" Venkata looked up at his father and murmured, "I've seen it." The Brahmin said, "The gods piss on me." He swayed toward Venkata's father and said, "But I came here because I have a proposal." And he leaned in and whispered in the ear of Venkata's father, who nodded, and they went around the corner of the veranda to speak in private.

Did the proposal have to do with the broken pot? Venkata waited to find out. But he didn't dare ask, and he warned Kanakamma not to, either. Days turned into weeks, months, and years. They didn't learn the significance of the visit until decades later, when their father was dying, and he gathered the kids, now grown, around his deathbed. Their mother had died years earlier. The full weight of their adulthood now bore down on them. They stood there, two on either side of the cot, exchanging awkward looks.

"Well, listen," their father said.

Ever since their move to the Garden, the Brahmin had been handing him more responsibility, so that he was eventually better known to coconut buyers than the Brahmin himself. Quietly, he had found ways to reduce his costs, so that he could pocket a bit more of the earnings, and he had been building up these savings. He hadn't thought the Brahmin was aware, believing he would be furious if he found out. But one evening—the one that Venkata and Kanakamma remembered well—the Brahmin had come over, explained that he knew about the savings, and asked for a loan in exchange for a lien on a bit of the Garden.

After that, the Brahmin had kept asking for more loans, until there was a lien on the entire Garden. When the Brahmin died, Venkata's father had written to the eldest Brahmin son about the situation. He had expected a fight, but to his surprise, the son had admitted he and his brothers had wanted to get rid of the land for years. While they had hoped to sell it and make some money, they were Brahmins and therefore highly ethical. "What's fair is fair," the son said.

"So the point is that all this is ours," the old man said, sounding exhausted.

After their father died, Venkata and his siblings sat on the steps of the house as distant relatives squeezed their faces and sobbed condolences into their necks. But their thoughts kept turning to their newly discovered wealth. They pursed their lips and swallowed, trying to push down those selfish thoughts and replace them with virtuous ones. We're lost without him, they said to the relatives. A good, hardworking man. But the truth, Venkata thought, sitting on the steps, was that they hadn't really known their father at all. Venkata, Balayamma, and Babu were in their twenties by now and married. All this time, their father had been hiding their wealth—perhaps for good reason, not wanting them to be corrupted, or worried that if people found out it would be taken from them—but, as a consequence, how could they help but feel estranged from him? A good, hardworking man, they said, and then they ran out of platitudes and thought again of their wealth. Landowners, imagine!

The only unmarried one among the siblings was Kanakamma, the youngest. Their mother had died when Kanakamma was still a child, and their father hadn't known how to take care of her.

Kanakamma's quiet, acquiescent attitude made her easy to forget about. Even Venkata, who loved her most, stopped spending time with her as he got older. Neglected, she would go out to the Burra settlement to play with their distant cousin Kothayya, the one who had helped her and Venkata bury the pieces of the landlord's broken pot. When Kothayya got older, he started working as a coconut climber at the Garden. When Kanakamma was nineteen, he came one morning with his father to propose. He was poor and dumb, but hardworking, loyal, and kind to Kanakamma. Venkata, now the man of the house, accepted. Soon, Kanakamma became the first of the siblings to have a child. They were all set to raise the next generation.

Venkata went to Ambajipuram once a week to sell their coconuts. One afternoon, passing through the village center on his way home, he visited his old friend Appayya. Like many Dalits from the area, Appayya had worked on a rubber plantation in Burma as a young man. It was there that he had encountered radical political thought, becoming a devotee of Bhimrao Ramji Ambedkar, the Dalit social reformer who would go on to author the Indian Constitution. Appayya had been in his twenties then and newly married. He might have stayed in Burma forever, sending money home, but then Radha and Sita had been born, and soon afterward, his wife had died of tuberculosis. So he had returned. With his riches from Burma, he had opened the school for Dalits and enrolled his daughters in it. Venkata, now a father as well, enrolled his sons, too.

"Did you know that Ambedkar wasn't always Ambedkar?" Appayya said, as he and Venkata sat on the school's veranda, sipping tea and looking out onto the road toward the Muslim graveyard.

"You and your Ambedkar," Venkata, who wasn't political, said. It sounded like a riddle, but Venkata was too tired to engage. It had been a frustrating day at the market. He had a good reputation in town, but anytime new middlemen arrived from bigger cities in search of coconuts, as had happened that morning, they balked at buying from a Dalit. He had to start over to build his standing.

"He was born with the surname Sakpal," Appayya said.

"Ambedkar was the name of a Brahmin high school teacher. This teacher liked Ambedkar so much that he put his surname, instead of Sakpal, on his pupil's school records."

"Good for him."

These days, Appayya went on, Ambedkarite Dalits were appropriating the signifiers of high caste as a political tactic, that is, to dull their symbolic power. Appayya had taken on a new surname, Swamy, and was passing it on to his daughters. From now on, he would be called Appayya Swamy, and his daughters Radha and Sita Swamy.

Venkata laughed.

"No, really, you ought to do the same," Appayya said.

It occurred to Venkata that he liked the idea of a name change, though for a different reason from Appayya's. He was a businessman, not a social activist. He thought if he and his siblings took on a Brahmin surname and passed it down to their children, people might mistake them for Brahmins, and that would be good for business. He chose the name most associated with the Garden all these years. Henceforth, the Burras would be the Raos.

EXISTENCE IS CHANGE. King's grandmother died, and Sita decided King should share his grandfather's bed to save the old man from lonesomeness. King was four. The first night, Grandfather Rao's room smelled sour, and it embarrassed King to watch him curl on his side. Flesh sagged from his throat like a rooster's wattle. King pinched the loose skin, rolling it between his fingers. "Does it hurt?"

"I can't even feel it."

King lay wide awake, facing the wall and listening to his grandfather snore. In the moonlight, he counted the dark spots on the wall that formed little patterns and wondered what they were made of. In the middle of the night, he heard a voice in his ear: "Kingie, Kingie, wake up." Grandfather Rao was tucked around him like a blanket, his arm clasping King's abdomen, his hand on

King's heart, his forearm as soft as overripe fruit. "I need to tell you something," Grandfather Rao whispered. "I'm not dead yet. But if I die at night, you'll be the one to find me. I hope you won't be scared. If you wake up and I'm not breathing, try not to look at my face. Just get up and find your mother. Be prepared."

"Okay."

Everything was quiet. Outside, the moon hung low and full. Grandfather Rao ran his fingers through King's hair. "Look at that moon," he said. "The Soviets sent a rocket into space. I do believe a man will walk on the moon before long. I wish I could stay alive at least until then."

If he had stayed alive long enough, he would have gotten to hear Neil Armstrong's recollection of the experience upon his return home from the moon. Grandfather Rao would have loved it. "The earth is quite beautiful from space and from the moon," Armstrong said. "It looks quite small and quite remote. But it's very blue and covered with the white lace of the clouds, and the continents are clearly seen, though they have very little color from that distance." It's such a plainspoken recounting, and yet a beautiful one. Many people don't realize Armstrong's young daughter died of cancer seven years before his moon landing. To me, his observation seems tinged with that loss. I imagine that when Armstrong looked at the earth, he thought of her.

Grandfather Rao began to lose his mind. He hallucinated that the Brahmin was alive, shouting at him about problems with the Garden. The overgrowth under the banana trees was keeping them from bearing fruit. A beetle scurrying up the trunk of the guava tree was a sure sign of disease. The Brahmin wasn't real, King tried to tell his grandfather. But Grandfather Rao only laughed and patted him fondly on the head. The exertion, of telling the truth and being disbelieved, pricked at King's skin.

One morning, sitting in the clearing with King on his lap, Grandfather Rao told everyone the Brahmin had a task for them all. They were to build a second house, exactly like the first.

"What's the point of that?" Kanakamma asked.

"We don't ask questions of the Brahmin," Grandfather Rao said. "We only do as he instructs." He stroked King's hair. King wanted to pull away but stayed still for his grandfather's sake. "It will be where King lives when he gets older and runs this place—King's House, that's what it'll be called," Grandfather Rao said. Suddenly Grandfather Rao's hand went still on King's head. He's dead, King thought. Remember this moment when your grandfather died. Then his grandfather stroked his head again, and a flash of impatience hit him. Come on, die! A shiver of shame went down his arms.

"King needs a house of his own," Grandfather Rao said.

"But who will build it?" said Kanakamma.

"Your gamblers, of course," Grandfather Rao said, and laughed.

Kanakamma and Kothayya's first and only son, Jaggayya, was responsible for the gamblers' presence at the Garden. Jaggayya had turned out to be as gentle a soul as his parents. When he was only fifteen, he had fallen into conversation with a tea-stall waitress in town. Leelamma was an orphan, but she was tall, fair, and vivacious, and had offered Jaggayya an enormous dowry, which she had told him she had inherited from her deceased parents. Kanakamma and Kothayya worried that their son was too young, but, seduced by the dowry, quickly sought Grandfather Rao's approval of the marriage.

But Leelamma had lied. She revealed after the engagement that she had three sisters, Lathamma, Lalithamma, and Lavanyamma. They were each married to inveterate gambling men who wore their shirts unbuttoned and went only by nicknames, Binky, Dimple, and Bubbles. Bubbles, having hit the jackpot, was the true source of the dowry, and he had given Leelamma the funds on the condition that she bring them all—her sisters and their husbands—to live at the Garden. They wanted to start families and get out of gambling but had no work skills.

Only then did it dawn on everyone that the decision to marry Kanakamma and Kothayya might have been misguided. They reinforced each other's softhearted, trusting natures and had raised a softhearted, trusting son. None of them had thought to research Leelamma's background. Afterward, Kanakamma had begged Grandfather Rao to make her son divorce Leelamma, but he refused. "We need more strong men around here," he said. "Also, we need more beautiful girls." He laughed.

Now, everyone agreed Grandfather Rao had gone mad, but no one wanted to disrespect him about King's House. When work began, the children clustered around the gamblers, palms on one another's backs, and watched as Jaggayya leveled the clearing with a plow. Later, Binky, Dimple, and Bubbles came over carrying four wooden stakes, with which they cordoned a long rectangular area, and warned the children, "Now, don't touch these or you'll get splinters, and stay outside this area." The uncles spent the morning on their haunches in the center of that rectangle, their chins dripping sweat as they began building. Bored, the kids tossed a heavy rock into the prohibited rectangle and dared King to run and fetch it. When he stepped into the perimeter, Bubbles stood, roaring, and raised his fist as if he would beat King in front of the others.

King's shriek drew the mothers out of the kitchen. They stood at the edge of the perimeter and shouted at Bubbles, "Shame on you, that temper again!" That encouraged King and his cousins. They sang and danced a heathen dance. The mothers clapped in time. Bubbles fumed. The rock King had tossed lay on the ground. King dashed into the perimeter again, picked it up, and pretended to throw it at Bubbles.

Grandfather Rao, observing all this from his stool, laughed and laughed and laughed and laughed, and put his hand to his heart, and departed the world of the living.

4

"Your great-grandfather was building a whole damn house when he died, baby-love!" my father liked to remind me. "Raos never rest!"

Being a Rao, my father felt, was the one monumental fact from which everything else had derived. He had been born Dalit, but because his family owned the Garden, they had allowed him to go to school instead of laboring in the fields. From that education, he had earned marks high enough to gain acceptance to one of the best universities in India, where he thrived; had been recruited to graduate school on scholarship at one of the most selective institutions in the United States; and had co-founded one of the earliest computer companies and grown it into the most valuable corporation on earth. And then, at an age when most men are well into their retirement, he had rescued the planet from nation-state rule, which was bringing society to ruin, and engineered a calm and peaceful transition to Shareholder Government, under which the world's citizens collectively owned its corporations, each Shareholder as able as the next—indeed as able as King Rao himself—to build a life of happiness and success.

Shareholder Government had been built on what King considered the most important truth of modern life: that any person possessing capital can, with effort and ingenuity, succeed. But you had to stay on your guard. He, for one, would not slide into complacence, would not age into some soft, toothless armchair dweller. He considered relaxation a synonym for lazing. *Retirement* was a nice word for quitting. "I won't sit around like a quiet retiree," he proclaimed. "I have a lot to do!"

I admired him for that. As for what exactly he did, I knew only a little. He had designed our house in the spirit of the one in which he'd been raised, a modest single-story, railroad-style construction with a wide veranda on either side. He'd built it near the northwestern end of Blake Island, in a clearing whose trees had been felled long before his arrival, when the island had belonged to the state government. Next to the house stood a small garden and orchard in which my father grew tropical produce from climate-resistant modified seed: okra, eggplant, mango, jackfruit. Some of my happiest memories are of tending the fruits and vegetables with him, in companionable silence. Tucking a seed into the earth, covering it up, drawing a circle with my finger around the little mound, the way he taught me. "My little farm girl," he'd murmur.

But it's not as if we spent all our time gardening. Next to the garden and orchard stood a small wooden cabin, not much more than a shed, and that's where my father occupied himself most of the time, clacking out code on an old Coconut computer. It didn't occur to me to wonder exactly what he was up to in there. I was a child. My father existed only in relation to my own small needs and wants.

He impressed upon me that he had moved to this remote island before my birth so no one would learn of my existence. If they knew the truth, it would be dangerous, given his stature. Someone could kidnap me for ransom. His political enemies on the mainland, having engineered his fall from grace, could now target me. He had reason to believe that some dangerous people up north on Bainbridge Island suspected my existence, though he wouldn't elaborate. But these pronouncements never frightened me; I barely registered them. The idea of kidnapping, even the idea of people other than myself and my father—they were too abstract to be meaningful. Even he must have realized, he couldn't restrict me forever, because one morning when I was six, I begged him for the millionth time to let me venture past our little clearing into the forest, and, for no apparent reason at all, he laughed and relented.

I took off running.

All around our house stood dense stands of old-growth Douglas fir interspersed with cedars, maples, alders, and even the odd bit of non-native laurel and holly, planted a century earlier by the last family that lived on the island before us. This became my playground. Traipsing through sword ferns that rose to my shoulders, I imagined myself as the protagonist of grand, theatrical dramas, with the animals who inhabited the island as my supporting cast. I took the black-tailed deer under my protection as pets, pretending to guard them against predation. I cast the fat raccoons, who foraged for clams on the beach well past dawn, as my irritating little siblings. The enormous bald eagle who had built her nest in a Douglas fir near the beach and would spiral out over Puget Sound and back into the treetops again, was my aerial guard.

Hothouse Earth seemed abstract then. You remember. Being outdoors was still pleasant, the mornings and evenings cool even in the summertime. It's true that in those days, the weather was already getting stranger, wildfire and hurricanes more common, the sunset slightly too beautiful, but the threat didn't feel existential. Reasonable people still believed the planet could prevail over circumstance. Consider the gray whale, they said, thriving as the waters warm. Consider the bald eagle, back from obscurity. I believed it, too. One autumn, my eagle brought a mate home with her, and they spent a month building a nest, stick by stick. I spent that season standing watch, waiting for eaglets to be born. The world was still full of life. It was hard to believe it ever wouldn't be.

One morning, I saw the eagle's mate circle around the treetops for a while, and when he returned to the nest, a small beak popped up from inside to take whatever he had brought. I went running to my father's office. He never minded interruptions, or if he did, he didn't let on. I told him what had happened. "That's wonderful!" he said. He swept me onto his lap, and I caught a glimpse of his screen, a steady march of code, like ants across the monitor. He kissed my forehead, my nose. But after a while, I could see his attention had returned to the screen. For such an intellectually curious man, my father didn't have much interest in the life that teemed on our island: the mating patterns of the eagles; the way the underside of a sworn fern leaf could soothe the burn from a brush with stinging nettle; the licorice taste of the rhizomes that sprouted in the crotches of big-leafed maples; the sluggishness of the deer on hot afternoons; the raccoons' practice of waddling right up to my feet to beg for scraps. What interested him was the theoretical. The way he saw it, the human mind was designed not merely to observe that which already exists but to invent that which doesn't: to imagine a future and bring it into existence. He set me onto my feet again and shooed me off. "Okay, go explore!"

I ADORED HIM with fierceness, as if my adoration could keep him safe from those who had brought him down and those who would conspire to hurt him further. My feelings were all mixed up with my awareness that he was uncommonly old. I felt protective of him. Where most children graduate over time into being their parents' caregivers, I played both the roles, cared-for and carer, at once.

During the daytime, we guarded each other's independence well, and in the evening, we spent time together. When I was little, my father would act out characters in my games of make-believe, or help me build imaginary worlds out of sticks and pebbles and ladybugs. As I grew older, the games gave way to conversation. We kept a pair of Adirondack chairs on a stretch of beach on the western shoreline, looking out toward the Olympic Peninsula. On warm summer evenings, when dusk came late, we would stroll down there after dinner, arm in arm, to watch the sun's descent behind the darkening mountains. That's when he began telling me stories about all the lives he had led in his hundred years on earth.

In the time preceding Shareholder Government—my father recounted—the nationalist movement sweeping the world had wanted to restrict the free movement of people and goods. One government after another blocked immigrants and put up trade barriers. Then my father proposed a new model. Under Shareholder Government, policies would be guided not by corrupt and biased politicians, but by the Master Algorithm, developed by Coconut. Using people's Social Profiles as inputs, the Algo would make informed decisions using not only demographic markers but lived experience. Rather than pledging one's labor to any single corporation, trading hours for dollars, kyats, or cedis, Shareholders would sell it at will and be compensated in Social Capital, based on the Algo's prediction of the actual value they had produced. The public's vote share would no longer be dictated by geographical circumstance; it would be allocated using the Algo. People's needs—food, water, energy, Internet, roads, shelter, schools, hospitals, protection, detention—would be fulfilled not through complex taxation and appropriation, but with an innovative model where, instead of paying taxes, people would have a portion of their Capital extracted monthly, the Algo determining the most efficient investment of funds. To equalize education, for example, the Algo would come up with a global curriculum and testing platform, personalized and gamified, such that children in the remotest hamlet could have the same opportunities as any scion of Seattle or Shanghai. To reform criminal justice, the Algo, not a fallible human judge, would determine the likelihood of guilt and the most appropriate punishment.

King waited until I turned seven to explain the circumstances of his downfall. After tests of a soon-to-be-launched product ended with fatalities, anti-government agents who called themselves the Exes started rioting in protest, eventually setting a fire that killed three people. But instead of concluding that the rioters should be punished, the Algo decided, to everyone's astonishment, that a deal should be made. In exchange for ending their protests, the Exes would be given a homeland of their own: The government would cede control of hundreds of islands around the world, which would come to be known as the Blanklands; anyone could cast off their Shareholder status and live there. The other component of the deal was the total and permanent removal of King Rao from power.

He told me about all this plainly, though he left out the parts that might frighten a seven-year-old, which I learned only later, like the fact that one of the people killed in the fire had been a small child. I remember gathering that he had been scapegoated. I remember that the way he told me about it all, both his openness and the circumstances themselves, just deepened my adoration for him.

As for how we ended up on Blake Island, he played it for laughs. After his banishment from the empire he had built, he told me, he went quiet. After a while, people forgot about him. Then, when five years had passed, he drove himself to the Elliott Bay Marina and stepped onto the yacht he kept docked there. He was standing on the yacht when he deactivated his Social, thus relinquishing all claim to his rights as a Shareholder. He waved to the couple dozen marina members who had gathered on the club's deck, their phones out, trying to get a good angle on the scene. He held his own phone in the air, then let it arc dramatically over the hull and into the water. And he sailed off, just like that, to the verdant 476-acre island in Puget Sound that he intended to make his new home.

People assumed it was an attention-seeking performance, a comeback prank of some sort. They waited to see the bow swing landward again. But, as the hours stretched on and King did not return, reporters discovered that he had quietly sold off most of his belongings in exchange for gold, the preferred currency in the Blanklands. He had also dissolved the Rao Project, his research organization. For the past several months, he had been moving his few remaining belongings to the yacht. "See, at that point," he said mischievously, "no one could do anything about it!" The Exes, their movement being built on inclusiveness and decentralization, could hardly keep a free man from heeding their call to leave Shareholder life behind. Nor could the Board stop him, having written the right to Ex into the Shareholder Agreement.

Blake had been uninhabited for so long that it had no real infrastructure besides the falling-down remains of Tillicum Village, the old tourist attraction where visitors would eat salmon and learn about indigenous culture. Now Tillicum Village was closed, the island abandoned. Blake Island did boast five miles of sandy shoreline, but even in those pre-Hothouse times, it was starting to recede. Taken together, most of the Blanklands would be submerged within a couple hundred years, on account of sea-level rise.

These circumstances were fine with King. They kept interlopers away, and he had the resources to make the place livable for himself. During the Gold Rush, settlers had chopped down Blake Island's trees and floated them down to San Francisco. But the island hadn't been commercially logged in more than a century. The trees had regrown, and there were plenty of Exes on the neighboring islands willing, for a fee, to cut them down and turn them into a home for King. He had even found a way to secretly access the mainland Internet.

This was the world into which my father brought me. And it's true that we lived happily there for a time.

My FIRST MORNING in here, I had just finished breakfast when the mail slot opened for a second time, and a device dropped in, a Cocopad. I touched the screen; it brightened. *Hi!* it read. The typeface was a sociable sans-serif, white against a mint-green background. *You're being held at the Margaret Rao Detention Center on a charge of murder.* You'll recognize that my interlocutor was not a person at all, but the Algo. It gave me no more than thirty seconds to absorb this message—if such a message can even be properly absorbed—before dissolving it and presenting new text. *Let's talk about next steps.* Because the Board had no record of my existence, I was required to build up a Social Profile in order to be judged for my alleged crime. This process would include, but would not be limited to, a photo shoot; assessments of my physical and mental health, as well as my intellect, skills, and character; documentation of my familial and social relationships on the mainland; and, most important, the drafting of a personal narrative about myself and my version of events regarding the incident at hand.

The charge didn't surprise me. I saw the accusation coming from the moment of my capture on Alki Beach. I also understood, from that moment, that there would be no clever shortcut out of the situation. There's a recurring mantra in a children's book my father used to read to me, about a family that encounters many obstacles while on a bear hunt: *We can't go over it. We can't go under it. Oh no! We've got to go through it!* Through it, then, we go. Five nights have passed, and I've settled into a routine. I begin each morning conjuring up my father's life and writing it down. Then I read and edit what I wrote the day before. I wash up, slurp a meal and a cola, and start typing again. I do a little exercise: yoga poses or tight little laps around my coop. This is followed by lunch, more writing, more exercise, and dinner. At night, I consider what the next section of my narrative should be about and make a plan to hit the right points. All this material, my entire Profile, will become part of the public record once my case concludes, assuming the Algo doesn't deem it too sensitive. Then you, dear Shareholder, will get to read it.

I have to admit that with a number of days having passed, the sameness of this routine is getting to me. I have begun spying on the COs through the compartment in my door in which they place food, toilet paper, and, occasionally, a clean towel, uniform, or toiletries. The one who comes most often is a compact, muscular white man, neat-mustached, pug-nosed, and balding. The first time I spied on him, he stepped back, startled, before composing himself. After that he must have learned to steel himself in advance, because he has shown hardly any reaction ever since.

Laconic though this CO is—he hasn't spoken a word—he conveys what he thinks of me through little face movements, revealing some mix of pity and disgust. "Thanks!" I sometimes shout as his footsteps recede. "I really appreciate it!" I pretend to be sardonic, as if I'm making fun of him, but this is just a self-protective move; the truth is that my desperation makes me thankful for even the most minimal contact. If my CO so much as replied, You're welcome, I would erupt in tears of gratitude.

It was in this context that, this morning, I tapped the ASSESS-MENTS icon on my Cocopad and selected PHYSICAL. I hoped it might put me into contact with someone, a human being, and I was right. Not even ten minutes later, my cell door swung open, and a white woman came in, pushing a cart arrayed with medical-looking devices. She looked like a doctor or scientist—she wore a biohazard suit, a hairnet from which a few blond wisps strayed, and a surgical mask—and moved efficiently toward me. A CO followed her, closing the door behind him, and stood at some distance, with his back to the wall. Not since my encounter with the police on Alki Beach had I been in such close contact with anyone.

"You'll want to strip down and put this on," the woman said, handing me a gown. She sounded youngish, in her thirties, and her tone, though stiff and formal, was not unkind. Still, as I unzipped my jumpsuit, neither she nor the CO did me the courtesy of avert-ing their eyes. I was the one who finally looked away, ashamed, and I didn't reestablish eye contact until I had the gown on.

"Sit," the woman said, motioning toward the cot. She crouched before me there. She smelled of popcorn. Her forehead glowed, well moisturized. She checked my vitals, temperature, blood pres-sure, breathing rate, pulse, reflexes. I was jealous of this woman, imagining the popcorn she had snacked on during her break just before coming to see me, the lotion she had pulled out of a desk drawer and applied in circles. She drew my blood into a small vial, which she inserted into a toaster-sized machine. A column of lights on the machine turned green. "So far, so good," she said, more to herself than to me. She picked up a handheld scanner and instructed me to stand still.

"What is that?" I said. It was my first time speaking.

She cocked her head a little, but I couldn't properly see her expression behind the mask. "Just for taking a peek inside," she said. "Standard practice."

I hesitated but did as I was told. She ran the scanner down the length of my abdomen, neck to belly button, and down my spine. Her reference to taking a peek had struck me as undoctorly. Maybe she was a nurse, not a doctor or scientist. "Arms out," she said, and moved the scanner along one arm, shoulder to fingertips, and the other. She circled my head with the device, several times, as if casting a spell. She looked at the scanner, frowned, and put it in her pocket. "Get dressed," she said. Now she seemed distracted. I put my uniform back on and sat down on the bed, the gown crumpled in my fist. "I'll take that," she said, and I stood and handed it to her. She didn't thank me or anything—just took it, with her gloved hand, and placed it in a bag. Then she was gone. It was five minutes later that my device buzzed with the Algo's assessment of my physical health. There were two columns, on the left, categories such as CARDIOVASCULAR, ORTHOPEDIC, DERMATOLOGICAL, NEUROLOGICAL, and so on, and on the right, the results. NORMAL, NORMAL, NORMAL, read the column on the right, and then, in red, blinking, ABNORMAL.

ONE MORNING, at the age of seven, I awoke to the sound of King calling out from the kitchen, "Rise and shine, little Puffin, I'm making pancakes!" Puffin was a nickname, one of several he used when I was small. But when he said it, pulling me out of sleep, I had what I can best describe as a vision. In my mind, I could see three black-and-white birds with orange beaks, standing in a circle on a snow-spotted boulder, their potbellied stomachs thrust forward as if they were businessmen at a conference.

The scene was as vivid as if it were real. But to call it a hallucination wouldn't be right. I was looking, in my mind's eye, at actual puffins that had conferenced on an actual boulder. The image in front of me was from the website of the Audubon Society. I was aware of this, of the source, because the experience wasn't only perceptual. It also contained information. I suddenly knew, for example, that in Iceland people used to catch puffins with a net attached to a pole, a practice known as sky fishing. For some time, restaurants in some parts of the world served customers the fresh hearts of puffins. The word itself, *puffin*, is believed to come from the impression the birds gave, with their bloated little cheeks, of having just inhaled. The scientific name, *Fratercula arctica*, means "little brother of the north," perhaps because the birds' black-and-white plumage resembled a friar's robes, or else because they sometimes held their feet together when leaping into the water in a manner that suggested hands pressed in prayer. But puffins no longer existed. Their habitat had melted, and they had gone extinct. It's strange to try to explain to someone who hasn't experienced it. But all of this emerged in my mind almost as if I were reading about it or watching a movie.

King was calling to me again, issuing the cheerful morning commands I was used to. "Pee!" he called. "Wash your hands!"

I called out for him.

He must have heard the urgency in my voice, because he arrived at the open door quickly. I tried to explain what had happened: the nickname he had used, puffin; the vision it had brought on; the fact that the vision came along with information, as if I were looking up *puffin* online. At this last part, there appeared a look on his face, bright-eyed and intense, of recognition.

He sat on the edge of my bed. "Baby-love, the human brain is capable of *so much*," he began, putting his soft and spotted hand on mine. "It's a miracle, isn't it?" The morning sunlight filtered beautifully through the trees and into the windows on that morning of my transformation. Twining his fingers with mine, he said, "I know what's happening."

He explained it, that morning, in terms that a seven-year-old could understand; the version I'm giving here is more complete, based also on what I would learn later. The Harmonica, King's capstone product that ended in failure, was a piece of genetic code, meant to be delivered to the brain through the bloodstream. The code contained instructions to the body to produce a small excess of carbon and silicon and use it to create billions of microscopic biotransistors. The transistors, once active, could turn the electrochemical language of neurons into digital signals, then process and store this digitized information. Using a radio-like signal, the transistors could also transfer it over Wi-Fi. The Harmonica could, in layman's terms, connect your mind to the Internet.

The tests were supposed to be the most preliminary of steps, meant only to confirm that the brain could safely absorb the product in the first place. King's own scientists said minor side effects were possible, fatigue or headaches, but likely nothing more serious than that. At no point did they raise a question of life and death. Only in retrospect—after the fatalities, after his ouster—did he see that the scientists might have felt implicitly pressured by his enthusiasm for the product. He had been intense about this one, knowing it would be his career capstone.

Now he could see he had made mistakes. He regretted them. Where he disagreed with the Board was in its choice, in the aftermath, to kill the research altogether. It was disastrous, a lapse in judgment far worse, he argued, than anything he had done. The problem with the Harmonica was not a moral one. It was an engineering problem, a problem of under-iteration. Maybe the Board didn't see that, but he did. Now I understood: During that time after his fall from grace when he disappeared from the public eye, he had engineered. He had iterated.

The issue was that the brain's plasticity—its ability to change and, in turn, fully absorb a modification product—decreases with age. But what if he developed a version of the Harmonica that could account for that, using AI to adjust the absorption mechanism so that it fully activated only in those brains that were plastic enough to handle it, thus avoiding damage to those that weren't?

Such a product would not function at one hundred percent in an older person's brain, but it would not kill them, either.

It was not even the toughest technical challenge of his life. If they had given him a chance to stay on and fix the Harmonica, he could have nailed it in months. So strong was his confidence that his first instinct, when he completed the project, was to test it on himself. But then he thought, what good did it do to try out the product on an old man, for whom it almost certainly wouldn't fully activate? What he really needed was the youngest person he could find.

A child. No, an infant. No, an embryo.

As he recounted all this, he perspired at his hairline, as he often did when he was overexcited or worried. "So that's the story behind all this," he said, waving a hand. A long time ago, he and his late ex-wife—at the time, she was still alive, still his wife—had frozen their embryos. Now those embryos belonged to him. On Bainbridge, one could find a surrogate to help bring a baby to term. If he went ahead and had a child, she would be born to a dead mother and a nonagenarian father; she—I—would grow up in the age of Hothouse Earth. And as he imagined this child into being—imagined me into being—the thought crystallized: She needs this more than anyone; this is for her. My child, flesh of my flesh. His decision to leave the mainland, to take up residence on Blake Island instead of one of the established islands—all of it was meant to keep the world from discovering the project of my existence.

MY CLARINET. He let me name it, and that's what I chose. If I was looking up at the moon and got curious, I could use my Clarinet to listen to the experiences of all the men who had traveled there and back. Or if my father was telling stories about growing up on a coconut grove, I could, even while listening to him, find out about the many uses of a coconut. King nurtured it in me. We would sit outside on our Adirondack chairs and come up with questions. Where had the trees on our island come from? How come people kept cats and dogs as pets, but not grasshoppers or bees? The answer would lead to another question, then another, until we found ourselves at a question for which there was no answer.

From domestication to the ancient megafaunal Taimyr wolf to the Taymyr Peninsula to the indigenous and small-numbered Nganasan people to shamanism to transcendence. From photosynthesis to carbon dioxide to climate change to Hothouse Earth to the extinction of the human species. Often, we ended up with the termination of human life on earth. No one knew exactly when it would come, or what it would be like, or whether by some miracle the government would stop it after all, as they'd been promising. The only time my father seemed to be at a loss was when I asked him about the Board's plan to reverse the warming of the planet. "It wasn't looking good during my time," he'd answer. "But you and I—we Raos—don't believe there's a problem in this world without a solution!"

My Clarinet expanded the world for me. It also made me realize how little of it I had experienced. I had never heard a parrot mimic in real life. I had never seen a pair of shoes hanging on a telephone wire. I had never smelled perfume. I knew about other people's lives, beyond my own and King's, only from the Internet. On Saturdays, my father left the island in his motorboat to go shopping at the Ex-run floating market just off Bainbridge. I begged to tag along, but he never let me, though he did bring me surprises from the markets. A white marble with a blue swirl. Taffy tied up in patterned cloth bags. *Archie* comics. Once, he gifted me a booklet of wax paper filled with stickers of all kinds, which I could tell had been pressed there by some previous owner. I stroked the fuzzies and scratched the smellables and imagined who that girl might be.

He had let his guard down, a little, about spies and interlopers. In all those years, there hadn't been a single one. When I was eight, I begged King to bring me a wet suit, and he did, a snug navy-blue piece. He taught me to swim, a hand under my belly, whispering, "Just relax—easy does it. If you relax, you'll float. Trust me." It didn't seem logical, but I trusted him. Wearing his own wet suit, he guided me through the shallow water. It felt like he was holding me up. Then he let go. I trusted him. I relaxed. I floated.

Our island's Internet connection didn't extend into the water, so when I swam, I was disconnected. The first time, it felt like what I imagine it would be like to go blind or deaf. Losing a sense that had become so elemental left me feeling exposed. My ears began buzzing with dim, ghostlike murmurs, like people whispering in my mind. It wasn't any real sound. It was only my mind trying to fill in its empty spaces, concocting aural junk to create the illusion of activity. It frightened me at first. But after a while, I came to love the feeling. By the time I was ten, I could circumnavigate Blake Island. Forbidden thoughts would drift into my mind. I fantasized about swimming the two miles to Bainbridge and wandering there awhile. Bainbridge was fully off the grid, with no public electrical service, no cell reception, no Internet. I could be there and back within a night, while he slept.

But these were fantasies, nothing I ever meant to act on. Our little island aside, I was afraid of the Ex-controlled Blanklands. Sometimes former Exes would return to Shareholder soil and try to repatriate, and from their accounts, the Board had derived sketches of the Blanklands as being full of dilapidated buildings, potholed avenues sprouting weeds, and broken streetlights. In the returnees' profile photos, they usually appeared underfed, wan, and somewhat stunned. You got the sense that, out in the Blanklands, they had lost hold of basic life skills—how to use a fork, moisturize, pose.

Even the term *Exing* had lost its radical connotations. The political movement was said to be all but defunct, with the new generation of Exes leaving home for personal reasons: legal troubles, mental illness, rough home lives. Often they were ridiculed for it, the lifestyle of the mainland being so obviously preferable to that of the Blanklands, where people were known to earn their keep selling taboo commodities to mainland customers: drugs, sex, child-bearing, violence.

One popular meme showed a girl around my age swimming

from the bright mainland to a craggy, forbidding-looking island meant to signify the Blanklands. *Where no one makes you go to class*, the original meme was captioned—the joke being, of course, that there is no public education in the Blanklands and therefore no class to skip. The caption in another popular variant read, *Where grown-ups can't police your screen time*—because the Blanklands have no Internet.

I'm sure you've seen the memes. I'm sure you've heard the horror stories about runaways turning up dead on the islands, their carcasses frothing with maggots. There was a period in my early teens when someone my age disappeared at least once a week. The autopsies, if they happened at all, often suggested violent murder. The parents would post to their Profiles in hope of clearing the names of their dead children. Their children were not traitors! They came from good Shareholder families; they had dreamed of studying engineering and becoming entrepreneurs; they must have left home as a result of brainwashing or kidnapping, not of their own accord.

I used to sit on the living room couch with my father, my legs flung over his, a bowl of potato chips on my lap, watching footage of those grieving and abandoned parents on-screen. I would be overcome with intense guilt, as if I were the one who had left my father and let myself be killed. The only explanation for the guilt, of course, is that, on some level, I did wish it upon myself. On some perverse level, I envied the dead girls their deadness, not because of any suicidal impulse as such but because it seemed the ultimate expression of independence from one's parents. At the time, the feeling manifested only as a hot and furious flush in my chest. "They *were* traitors; they deserved it!" I cried at the screen, my heart beating fast. "No one should abandon their parents!"

He squeezed my hand, his fingers soft and cold against mine, and didn't release it for a long time.

5

Baby-love, please, don't ever leave me, King thought. This poor heart could not bear it. But then—he scolded himself—didn't you flee your own homeland? Didn't you flee your own poor mother?

At the boarding school where he had finished the eleventh and twelfth grades, he had holed up in the library while classmates went to the movies or out for ice cream. They called him a recluse. In fact he had no spending money. He had to depend on merit alone, he sometimes muttered at his classmates under his breath. That and the reservation system, he imagined them muttering in return. Everyone knew it was easier for untouchables to get into college now that the government set aside spots for them. Call us Dalits, he retorted in his imagination. It's 1969; don't be a bigot! Not that any of this conversation took place in the real world—not in India, where meaning was always stuffed between the lines.

He had endured two years of that, his neck constantly sore from bending his head over his books, but in the end, the struggle was worth it. He was accepted into a bachelor's program at the best technology institute on the subcontinent, this time covered by a scholarship, including room and board.

It was almost laughable how, the farther he got from his poor little village, the more people were discussing the plight of poor little villagers. On his campus in Madras, men and women marched for their sake wearing jeans and sunglasses. Buildings were graffitied with denouncements of Indira Gandhi. King avoided all that. He was studying computer science. To write a software program—to compel a machine to obey your will, just as long as you began with an "if" and followed it with an appropriate "then"—felt enormously powerful. What intelligent person wouldn't take that over hoisting a square of weather-beaten cardboard in the air, and shouting at the politicians who drove by in their Hindustan Ambassadors, speeding up, spitefully, as they passed?

He was good at programming, too, even great. People imagined that a computer scientist simply sat down in front of a machine and bent it to his will. In fact it was more complicated than that. The word that came to mind was *coaxing*: One needed to be persuasive with a computer, needed to speak to it in a language it could understand. But if you could discover that common language and use it perfectly, with no serious errors, the persuasion would be inevitable. That was the part that felt safe to him. There was no mystery in it. It was not like understanding another human being, or, for that matter, oneself. It was instead a puzzle, which is to say, it could be solved. Americans had just used computers to send men to the moon. Those American scientists didn't sit face-to-face with their machines and ask, But for what reason are we here—we humans, our earth, the moon, and all that? And what a relief that they didn't. What a relief that a time of questions was giving way to a time of answers.

When classmates couldn't fix a bug, they would ask King for help, and, for the first time, at university, he earned a measure of social capital. When he perfected one programming language, he taught himself another, and when he couldn't solve a problem using any language he had learned, he started inventing his own. That's how he developed his specialty, custom languages.

The truth was that his genius, as his classmates called it, was mostly the result of hard work. His three roommates, excited by their emancipation from overbearing parents, spent their evenings paging through porn magazines or hanging out at the stall down the street that served hot rum in big brass tumblers. Late at night, King would wake to the sound of them throwing their bodies against the door and hollering his name, too drunk to get their keys into the lock. Despite being admired, he still wasn't one of them. One time, after he started helping them solve their bugs, they let him sit next to them, thigh to thigh, as they flipped through their magazines, slick with finger grease. A hot flame rose in King's chest at the sight of those women, their kohl eyes and cannon breasts, and he rose and retreated to his bed, while the others howled in laughter.

It was only after all that—in the summer of 1974, at the age of twenty-two—that King boarded the airplane that would bring him from his ancient homeland to a new, adopted one. He felt conspicuous and imposterish, his breath too loud in his ears. He could smell the sour stench of panic rising from his armpits. The other passengers had calm, even self-satisfied, expressions. Almost all of them were male, in their forties or fifties, and fair in complexion. They wore Western outfits—pressed pants, collared shirts with delicate, shell-colored buttons. Their hair was oiled and parted as precisely as if someone had taken a butter knife to their scalps. Rich people, sophisticates. He was acutely aware of how he must look to them. His own skin was eczematous and almost charcoal-colored. It was clear—with his sideburns, his handlebar mustache, his plastic-rimmed glasses—that he was trying too hard to fit in. Clearly, he was a villager. An untouchable.

He carried nothing but a canvas bag over his shoulder, which contained all the possessions he had to his name: clothes, photographs, some cash, a stone Hanuman statuette that had belonged to his father, papers confirming his qualifications and printed with his college's official seal, the letter from the professor in the United States who had invited him into his engineering program through some miracle, the details of which he hadn't requested, lest someone discover that a great and embarrassing error had been made.

His childhood mentor, the Dutch doctor who worked in Kothapalli, had promised that caste would be meaningless in the United States. Americans disdained class distinctions. But then, the Hollander, as everyone called the doctor, had been wrong about several things. He had also said, for example, that airplanes, like banks and private hospitals, were filled with frigid, clean-smelling air, and this one wasn't. It smelled stale, like a long-shut closet, the air dense and oniony. It frightened him to consider that such a huge, lumbering machine should loft itself into the air. It defied all good reason. He recognized this as a dumb, childish thought—he was an engineer; he wrote code to make machines defy reason—but he couldn't help it.

Someone shoved him. "Hurry up, go on." King turned around. A graying man in a rumpled suit and full paunch, with a pin on his lapel that conveyed importance, was glaring at him. "Go on, move!" the man said. King's armpits tingled with shame. Lost in his thoughts, he had stopped short in the middle of the aisle. But what was his seat number? He glanced at his ticket to find it, yet again, though he had memorized it days ago. And he chanted this number to himself, silently, like a kind of mantra, as he moved down the aisle.

His assigned place was next to a window, and this buoyed him. He sat, pushed his bag under the seat in front, and looked out. It was the end of the monsoon season. Water pooled outside in puddles the color of tar, and the outer pane of the window wept raindrops. For a long time, the aircraft sat on the tarmac. The other passengers seemed unfazed by this. A stewardess made some announcements, and the plane shuddered and lumbered forward. After some moments, it gained speed, then, more swiftly than he had expected, lifted from the tarmac and slanted up into the air. He pressed a palm to the windowpane. The droplets on the window shivered, shrank to the size of pinheads, and disappeared. Down below, the Calcutta shantytowns of cardboard and tin resembled great trash heaps. The plane climbed past the clouds, into air so blue it might as well have been painted that color. His hand was still pressed against the window. The sun warmed his palm through the glass. It felt like a benison.

WILBUR AND ORVILLE WRIGHT, known as the inventors of the airplane, were two of the seven children of a traveling bishop. Their father returned one day from a trip with a foot-long Pénaud model airplane—paper, bamboo, and cork with a rubber band to twirl its rotor. They played with it until it fell apart, then put together their own version. In their twenties, after encountering articles about men who had attempted flight, they sent a letter to the Smithsonian requesting a compilation of the work that had been done on the problem of flight. When the Smithsonian obliged, the brothers read up and concluded that two of the three major challenges of flight (lift, propulsion) had largely been addressed by their predecessors, leaving only the matter of balance. So the brothers came up with three-axis control, enabling a pilot to steer the aircraft effectively while maintaining equilibrium.

Only then, after all that, did the airplane take flight and stay aloft.

KING STOOD, some thirty hours after takeoff, in a small, dim, carpeted room filled with hanging plants. Along the left wall of the room was an array of cubbyholes marked with names. On the wall in front of him, a row of yellowed windows were covered with thick blinds that filtered the golden morning light into soft, slanted lines. Near the right wall was a desk facing the room, and at that desk sat a tall white girl, clacking at a typewriter. She had clear, fair skin and curly auburn hair barely restrained in a high, loose ponytail. She wore large-framed glasses and a high-buttoned blouse, white with black polka dots, that had ruffles at the collarbone and capped sleeves. She sat with a straight-backed posture and did not look up from her typing when he entered the room, lugging his bag and sweating. He stood watching her, waiting for her to glance in his direction. She didn't. After a while, he coughed.

"Hi," he said. "I'm a student."

She flicked her eyes up to him for a moment and smiled as if he amused her. Then she continued typing. She looked younger than him—in her teens? He marveled at her exotic looks, and had to remind himself that here she wasn't exotic at all. In remembering, he became aware of his own foreignness, and was ashamed of it.

After landing in Seattle, he had gotten a ten-dollar bill by cashing in a wad of rupees at the airport. It had been alarming, to hand over all those rupees and receive one bill in return, but he had examined the receipt and confirmed that all was in order. All his money came to this, a single damp greenish note depicting a flaming torch and a long-faced, forlorn man. A series of bus rides later, nine dollars and fifty cents remained.

"This is the office?" he tried again. "For the Engineering Department?"

"Uh-huh?" she said. This time she didn't stop typing.

"I just arrived from the airport," he said. "I got a letter from the chairman. Dr. Norman."

"People call him Dr. Borman," she said, in a voice whose volume surprised him, and smiled. She had dimples. He imagined dipping a finger into each of them and pressing. She picked up a can of Coke from her desk and ran her finger around its rim. "He's my dad," she said. "I don't know where he is."

"Dr. Norman is your"—he paused—"father?" There were certain English words, *dad* among them, that seemed to belong to native speakers.

"Because he's such a drip," she said. "Get it? *Bore*-man."

"Oh!" He'd watched enough American films to know children talked about their parents differently here, but her casual disrespect still came as a surprise.

"My parents are divorced," she said, as if this explained it.

"He left us when I was little. That's why he hired me: guilt." She added, "I'm not here because I like him. I'm here because I need the dough."

"The dough," he said.

"I mean the cash. I'm staying at his place and everything. My mom and sister are down in Tacoma. My dad lives closer, on Bainbridge Island. I suppose I'm getting to know him better, but I still hate him for leaving us."

She had a low voice but spoke in a loud, singsongy cadence that made her insults seem unserious. Was she strange, or were all Americans strange? He had no frame of reference. When he drew the letter from his pocket, soft-creased from all his readings and rereadings, his fingers trembled. He thought of how he must appear to her. Fresh off a plane, his eyes red and sleep-crusted, smelling sour. He held it out to her.

"You don't need to give it to me," she said, curling her lip, but she took the paper and unfolded it carelessly. Then she took in a small breath and said: "Wait a minute, *you're* King?"

"Yes!" he exclaimed, as if they'd come to this realization of his identity together.

"Oh, why didn't you *tell* me? I'm supposed to give you a special greeting! You're supposed to be important. I mean, my dad says you're important, but he didn't have to tell me that because I could tell from your name. King Rao. What kind of a name is that? I've never heard a name like that, and we've got a bunch of you here, Indians. Indian names interest me. My boyfriend traveled there, to India, and never came home. We were supposed to get married. He's much older than me. He works in the Foreign Service. He gave a lecture at the university, and I went, even though I wasn't a student. I was the only one who showed up, so instead of giving the lecture, he seduced me. I think he did it because he was embarrassed that no one else had shown up, and he wanted to feel big again. Men do that. So he took me home and hired me as his children's nanny.

"His wife knew about me. He was very open about it all. He said they were planning to divorce, and he'd marry me. She liked me, I think, or at least, she said I was good for him, which, now that I think about it, could also mean she just hated me as much as she hated him: ha! Anyway, they did get divorced, but he went to India, for some assignment or another, and met a gal there and never called me again. That's the reason I'm working here—because we didn't get married, and my mother said I'd better call my father and see if he could get me a job. It turned out he needed an office girl." She shook her Coke can and, finding it empty, dropped it in the trash can by her knee. "So what does your name mean—King? Does it have some special significance? I know how it is with these Indian names. I heard of a gal whose name translated as 'gently flowing stream.' She flushed. Actually, it was that gal I mentioned. The one who stole my boyfriend."

"What is your name?" he said.

"Margaret?" she said.

"How old are you?"

"What's the deal with all the questions? You didn't answer mine."

"But what *is* your question?"

"What's your name mean?"

"Oh, King?" He paused. "A king is the ruler of a place."

She flushed deeply. "I know that!" she nearly shouted. "You think I'm dumb?"

"That's all it means!" he cried.

Her expression flattened, as if he had failed some sort of test. "I thought it was an Indian word, too," she said. "Stupid. I just got flustered. My dad told me you're supposed to be some genius. No one thinks of me as a genius because of, well, all this," she said, gesturing vaguely at herself. "People don't realize it, but I'm really aware of how they see me. It's a gift. All kinds of powerful people come in here, and they underestimate me. I study them, I listen to their conversations. I've learned a lot about your field. One of these days, I'll do something with it. I have ambition. I think you do, too. My dad tells me you're going to make us rich."

To make this girl and her father rich—how was he supposed to do a thing like that? He couldn't conceive of what she wanted with a person like him. He asked, instead, "Is he here?" starting to feel a little captive in this small room with this strange and lovely girl. "Dr. Norman, is he here?"

The girl gave a heaving, performative sigh. "Oh my gosh, I told you: I don't know where he is," she said. "Downstairs maybe, in his office, if you want to find him so badly." She started typing again. "Gosh," she said. "I just wanted to talk awhile. I'm twenty-two, to answer your question. I'm so bored I could jump off a bridge."

YEARS LATER, both King and Margaret made light of that first encounter. "I thought he was a huge nerd," Margaret told one television interviewer, and King, sitting next to his wife, responded, "I thought you were a bimbo." They both paused for a moment and smiled languidly at each other—as if this moment of amusement were a private one, not meant for public consumption—before turning back to the interviewer, who blushed, third-wheeled. When I was young, King and Margie's romance fascinated me. Theirs was my model for what love might be, a kind of twinning.

ELBERT NORMAN, father of Margaret, chair of the newly established department, was to be King's adviser. He had matched King up with himself, he'd explained in his letter, because of their complementary interests. Norman designed hardware, King wrote software. This struck King as strange: Wouldn't it have made more sense for his adviser to have the same area of expertise? King intended to specialize in computer languages—learning the existing ones, and, when those didn't suffice, designing custom ones. But he let it go. Norman was the chair and had chosen him. Maybe it worked differently in America.

He imagined Norman as a big, strapping Burt Reynolds of a man. His letter—the one he had pulled from his pocket and waved at Margaret like a maniac—had a friendly but authoritative tone. In the letter, Norman had promised that they would share a "sizable" office. How many hours had he spent fantasizing about that office, in the months leading up to his arrival? He imagined a big room where Dr. Norman would work, and a smaller one, off to the side, which would be his own. Bookshelves rising to the ceiling, a picture window that brought strong white American sunlight surging in. On one end of the room there would be a heavy oak desk with a rolling chair, and on the other end a bed, a nightstand, and an armchair lit by a standing lamp. He had once seen an American film in which a young doctoral student lived and worked in such a studio. In one scene, the student's girlfriend came over and painted in her underwear, after which they had sex. Now his imagination replaced that girlfriend with Margaret Norman. He imagined her naked in here, at an easel. That his officemate was her father made the scene especially illicit.

He thought all this as he descended the stairs, as Margaret had instructed, into a low-ceilinged, fluorescent-lit hall whose grayish carpeting was furred with use. He walked down the hall looking at each door as he passed—they had faded plaques with names written on them—but couldn't find one with Norman's name. Finally he stopped for the third time in front of a metal door, identical to the rest, on which the plaque read, EL ERT   MAN, and realized this was it. He knocked. A grunt came from inside, and some slow, heavy footsteps. The door swung open, and there was the chairman himself. He was round in the waist and thighs, with a reddish face that was at the same time both fat and collapsed, a gourd left rotting on the vine. The man grinned sourly, as if in pain, and panted, "King Rao."

"Dr. Norman, sir?"

"Just Norman," he said. "I thought you'd be here next week." He coughed, the redness in his face blooming into splotches.

"Your letter," my father said, flapping it at the man. "It said to come see you."

"Oh, I don't write those," he said. "Margie writes them." He grinned. "My office girl, Margie. She's my daughter! Did she tell you that?" Norman turned and entered the room. He had a waddling gait and a thinning halo of blondish white hair. King stood in the hall, unsure of what to do, until Norman called, without turning around, "Come in if you're going to come in."

This was the room—oh, okay. More of a closet than a real office, it smelled faintly of mold and was lit, dimly, by a thin aperture of a window along the top of the far wall. The walls were painted in a mild gray, a shade lighter than the carpet. A dinged-up metal desk was pressed against each side wall, with a chair at each. The room was so small that the backs of the chairs kissed. Norman said it had in fact once been used as a closet, housing old typewriters and wiring that no one had gotten around to selling or tossing out. Back then, the Engineering Department had been a backwater for eccentric theoreticians like himself, and there had been plenty of room for closets. Now it was growing so fast that every space was an office. He knew he had written that it would be large, he said, but he had been writing about his old office, which he'd had to give up—temporarily, he'd been assured—to a hotshot professor they had just hired away from Computa. He hadn't meant to lie.

"It's fine!" King said.

"I thought Margie could find me another big one, but she couldn't. Isn't she beautiful? I told her beautiful girls get whatever they want. I thought she could talk some stud in facilities into it, go above the dean's head. But no. Nothing gets by the dean. He's waiting for old Norman to retire, so he can replace me with some hotshot." His face reddened again. "You know what kind of hotshot I mean? One of those corporate types from Armonk, New York. That's the future of this department. Armonk, New York. You know what's in Armonk?"

He tried to place it but couldn't.

"Computa," Norman said. "If you want to make it as an academic these days, you have to invent something and sell it to those goons at Computa. He rubbed his thumb and forefinger together. "That's all anyone cares about." He paused. "You know what this means?" He rubbed his fingers together again.

"Money?" King said.

"Money!" Norman said. "Money, money, money. That's America for you. What are your first impressions?"

King considered how to answer, having landed hours earlier. "It's really clean," he finally said.

"Yeah, that's what you people notice first."

King clearly wasn't the first to have come up with this safe answer.

Norman heaved himself onto his desk—it creaked mightily—and placed his hands on his big thighs. "Now tell me, Mr. Rao," he said. "What's your ambition in life?"

King had spent enough time in educational institutions to know a trick question when he heard one. "I'm at your service, sir," he said. "Whatever you need." He had survived the past six years by apprenticing himself to his teachers and professors. All had been regal men who treated their students as trusted vassals, and he had liked this, the safety of it, being tucked under the wings of men more powerful than himself. His professors had been respected, and to be associated with them earned one a kind of proxy respect. It was a conservative approach, even a cowardly one. But it had taken him this far.

To his surprise, though, Norman appeared scornful. "Your reference letters said you're ambitious," he said.

He tried again. "My focus is software programming, sir. My ambition is to program."

Norman grinned. "Listen, I'm not your typical professor," he said. "I want to be your friend."

What a surprising, and sad, thing, King thought, for a grown man to say aloud.

Norman continued, "Tell me, what did you come here for? I mean, to America?"

What had compelled him to do all that he had done and, in the end, arrive here in the United States of America? It was like being asked why he wanted to live. You lived to live; you moved to America to move to America. But of course that one grand ambition, having been attained, must now be replaced by another, grander one. What would it be?

6

At thirteen, I awoke one morning to a slick oiliness between my legs and a terrible metallic smell. I slunk to the bathroom, sat on the toilet, wiped myself, and stared at the bloodied tissue in my hand. My period. What a weird term for it. I threw the tissue in the toilet and flushed it, then stood and considered myself in the floor-length mirror on the door. How slender, straight-hipped, and clear-skinned I had been as a girl. Such a sweet Nabokovian childlet, such a darling! That I had transformed into the creature standing here, this Egon Schiele grotesque, breasts angular, hips overround, cheeks bezitted, offended me on behalf of the child I had been.

Even my father had noticed it. The mortification, one morning not long before, when I had gotten out of the bath, toweled myself off, then wrapped my hair in the towel and went to the kitchen for a banana. There sat my father, as usual, eating his own breakfast. I had come in here naked many times to pluck a piece of fruit from the bowl. But this time, he looked upon me with alarm, as if I were some thief who had stolen in, and yelped, "Cover yourself!" He would not look at me again, even after I had taken down the towel and hurriedly pulled it tight around my body. We never spoke of the incident, nor did I ever go naked in front of him again.

Now the phrase "hourglass figure" floated into my mind, and that image of Marilyn Monroe on that grate in New York, a leg bent, the pleated skirt of her dress opening like a great white flower in some rain forest, and the rain forest in general, and the Amazon in particular with its wet and potted smell, the source of so many of the pharmaceuticals in the world and the home of the last indigenous people, and the impending death of the Amazon now that scientists had confirmed the onset of Hothouse Earth, and the desertification of Beijing, Phoenix, and Málaga, the submersion of Miami and the Mekong Delta, and the flooding of London, while those Amazon natives kept on headdressing themselves with ferns, kept tattooing their children with thorn needles when they came of age, while life continued, in the Amazon rain forest and everywhere else.

A bad mood descended on me, a glooming.

I began stuffing my underwear, once a month, with old torn-up T-shirts. It was a dull spring, all low skies and drizzle. I stayed indoors, alone with my disturbed thoughts. Getting used to my Clarinet had taken some time. After a while, though, it felt natural to dip in and out of the Internet without effort. It wasn't part of my brain, any more than it's part of anyone's, but a porousness had developed between myself and the Internet. Looking at King, I could see the man who had brought me into the world, raised me up, and endowed me with a special power that would sustain me in it. I loved that man. He was my person. But my Clarinet showed me another version of him, the one known to the public, a villain who had sacrificed human life at the altar of his ambition.

That man was a stranger.

I learned from my Clarinet that he had been warned about the Harmonica. He hadn't told me that part. He had been warned, and he went ahead with his tests nonetheless, and sixty-four volunteer subjects died. At the press conference that followed, he offered brief words of condolence but rejected the notion that he, or anyone else at Coconut or the Board, was responsible. Then came the Ex-led protests that turned into riots that culminated in the fire at the Shareholder Campus in which a security guard and a custodian were killed, along with the custodian's three-year-old daughter; the clandestine meeting between the Board and Ex leaders, of which King was kept ignorant, to hash out a settlement involving the recall of the Harmonica, manslaughter charges for the arsonist instead of murder, the relinquishment of several hundred islands around the world to the Exes, and the dismissal, from all leadership roles, of King Rao, the founder and chief executive of the Board of Shareholders.

I also discovered through my Clarinet that, though my father wasn't much written about anymore nowadays, there was a long-standing and stubborn Internet rumor that he had succeeded in evading his own death. It cropped up every time a paparazzo managed to snap a telephoto picture of him rowing toward Bainbridge Island to go shopping, his biceps pulsing. Look at him, the rumormongers said, well into his hundreds and still ticking. It defies logic. With Hothouse Earth having arrived, the rumors had gained new significance. When the second-to-last man was scorched to death, they said, King Rao would remain.

What bothered me most was that the myth that he was immortal, while compelling, was totally false. It was true that he used rejuvenation technologies that most people can't afford—designer supplements, gene reprogramming, young-blood transfusions—but these were meant only to extend his life, not prolong it forever. Yet he never did a thing to dispel the myth. He issued no public statements, spread no counter-rumors. He said allowing people to believe it made us safer. The key reason no one had tried to trespass onto our island, he said, was that his supposed superpower, his immortality, scared them off. This ridiculous myth was the best security system in the world. But the myth also made it easier, I protested, for people to believe he was some kind of villain. He became even stubborner. "So what?" he said, his expression both impish and peeved. "Let them!" It wasn't that he didn't care what people thought. It was the opposite. He was like a rejected lover who, in his aggravation at having been jilted, pretends not to care.

One night, as we watched the sun set together, I looked out toward Bainbridge and let myself fantasize about being there. I imagined walking the streets, people-watching. We would smile at each other. Peace be with you, and also with you. It was a simple daydream, but like all my daydreams, it was tarnished by the fact that it had no chance of coming true. When I gathered myself, sighing, I realized King was watching me with a hurt expression, as if my sadness were a weapon aimed at him. I responded with an aggressive, scornful shrug. He met my eyes for only a second, then dropped them down to his lap, where his hands lay folded and trembling. But this—his shyness, his shaking hands—only offended me more. He had been old when I was born, and now he was getting older. His agedness chafed at me, no, enraged me. Die, then! Do it!

"Baby-love, where have you flown off to?" he said.

"It's called being a teenager, *King*."

I immediately regretted calling him by his name, the disrespect it signaled. But the damage was done. Instead of chastising me, as he would have done in the past, he nodded in response, still looking down at his hands. Then I felt even worse. I wasn't imagining it. He was diminishing, right before me. The horizon had begun its familiar pinkening and purpling; with Hothouse Earth, the sunsets had gotten more intense, almost frightening. Who could look upon a falling sun anymore and think of anything other than the great storms that had been sent to destroy us, the great wildfires and droughts? For me, it all seemed to be disappearing at once: self, heritage, homeland. But my father had been in charge, once; he could have stopped this. How come he hadn't?

On the bookshelves in the living room, he kept an old photo album. It was a fat, heavy, musty-smelling maroon thing, with three rings holding the stiff, yellowed photo pages. I had never harbored a moment of curiosity about it. But one afternoon, while he was out in his office, I pulled the album down. I was compelled by boredom, but there was something else, too, lurking behind it, some need. The first page showed two photos, one above the other. The top picture was an old-fashioned black-and-white portrait of an Indian couple dressed in finery and garlanded with marigold wreaths. They stood stiffly before a photographer's plain backdrop, their arms at their sides, a half foot's distance between them. The man was expressionless, the woman doleful. In the photo underneath, it was just the woman, a close-up of her holding a wide-eyed infant in her arms.

Those photos didn't surprise me. They had appeared publicly in a book of speeches and quotes that King wrote in the nineties: Pedda and Sita's wedding; him with Sita. I flipped forward, until the black-and-white photos set in India gave way to color ones of a young King and Margie. Some of these, too, were in the public domain. There was King, Margie, and Margie's father standing around the first computer they ever built; Margie cutting into a birthday cake; King ringing the bell for Coconut's IPO. But others were unfamiliar. In one of them, Margie sat at a desk in the old Engineering Department office, wearing a high ponytail, her mouth open, her palms down on the desk as if she were about to push herself to standing. She looked young. She was pale and green-eyed. But, in her high, round cheekbones and the mischievous readiness of her posture, I thought I could see something familiar. I thought I could see myself.

I had never really raised the subject of my mother with my father; I knew it depressed him to be reminded of her. But suddenly, pubescent, I felt a personal right to her. What temperament had my mother had? What had been her favorite color, her favorite food? I barraged him with these questions. I deserved to know such things about my mother, I said indignantly, my mother, my mother, my mother, I said many times, as if I had brought him these exact questions many times and he had refused to answer, when in fact I had never shown any interest in her before. In truth, I hadn't needed her until the moment my father recoiled at the sight of me and demanded that I cover myself.

When he didn't immediately answer, I thought I had upset him. But then he smiled, his eyes shining, as if glad I had finally shown interest in the love of his life, my mother. She used to love painting. She was into photo-realism. She painted cherry blossom trees. After a while, she lost interest in painting; soon afterward, they met and started Coconut. Then that became her life, just like it became his own.

"That's sad."

"To a young person, it sounds sad. But adults know that life is change; existence is change."

"I know it, too," I snapped. "I'm not a child."

THIS MORNING, I tapped the PHOTOS icon. I was remembering my father's album when I did it, thinking particularly about the fact that my existence, due to my father's fear of exposure, had gone undocumented. I assumed that the purpose of this icon was for me to take photos of myself. Instead, the screen said, *Tell us what you find beautiful*, and then the text dissolved into a grid of images, each the size of a small cracker, that I was meant to evaluate on an aesthetic level.

There were several clichéd landscapes—a tropical beach, a windswept field of corn, a city skyline lit up at night—as well as people's bodies at a distance and their faces in close-up. There were reproductions of famous art, abstract designs and patterns, and swatch-like squares filled simply with color. Each image was superimposed with a black *X*, on the top left-hand corner, and a red ♡, with a number on it, on the top right-hand corner.

What is beauty, my estranged friend and mentor Elemen Ex might have said, but a social construct? Yet I clicked the heart on a square consumed with red; on a photo of a woman whose strong jawline reminded me of Elemen; and on the beach, at the edge of which a single coconut tree bent. When I had rated everything, a screen full of more images popped up. Each time I got through a series of images, a new batch showed up. I guess I imagined I would be told when to stop, but a couple of hours passed before it finally occurred to me that there was no end to it, that this exercise would go on forever if I didn't put a stop to it myself. I set the tablet down, stepped back from it, took a breath.

That was, as I said, this morning. And this afternoon, a soft shrink-wrapped envelope dropped into my room. I ran to it and tore it open. Inside, I found a pair of black jeans, a red cropped T-shirt, a forest-green silk jumpsuit, a pair of leather sandals, and a pair of beige canvas slip-ons. They were gorgeous, perfect for me. The Cocopad, which I had left on my bed, buzzed. When I touched the screen, it lit up with a new message. *Try them on.*

I had been alternating between the same two pairs of Margie-issued jumpsuits, one for daytime and the other to sleep in. Now I changed into the silk outfit and used the Cocopad's front camera to film myself. I had never worn anything like this; the green made everything about me appear brighter. My hair, which fell in unbrushed waves around my shoulders, looked sexily windblown; my wide hips, which I used to compare unfavorably to Elemen's straight-hipped mannishness, now seemed voluptuous. But how the Algo could know me so well amazed me. I looked beautiful, I thought, as I snapped a selfie, and another, and another.

So this was how a person became a Shareholder.

AFTER MY FATHER told me about Margie's past as a painter, I decided to teach myself to paint. I meant it as an act of defiance. I thought of Margie sacrificing painting for him; he had drawn her into Coconut, and she had neglected her passion. One morning— I was fifteen—I was at the kitchen table painting a mango that sat on the top of a bowl full of fruit. King always kept the bowl replenished with bananas, mangoes, and kiwis from our garden. This mango was half-ripe, varicolored and beautiful, and I had been wondering how I might capture all that color, which berry juices or leaf pigments might help approximate the shades. I was so intent on this that I didn't notice him come into the house until he walked over and picked up the mango. He turned it around in his hand. He had the performatively contemplative look he got when he was about to give a speech.

"Put it down," I hissed. He was ruining my composition and distracting me. Some specimens of mango tree—the thought floated into my mind, unbidden—give fruit for three hundred years.

But still he held the mango, turning it in his palm. "You're so serious; you don't play anymore," he said.

I ignored the comment. "Come on, put it back like it was, stem side up," I said. "I'm painting."

But he didn't. "You don't—you don't play; you act like a grown-up. You should play."

"I'm fifteen."

"That's not so old."

"In three years, I'll be an adult."

He looked up from the mango and held me in a long, meaningful gaze. "Is that what's making you so upset?" he said. He tossed the mango, lightly, in the air, and a great wet, nameless feeling swelled in me.

"Hey, listen, if this mango were to rot, that wouldn't be tragic, right?" he said.

"Put it—" I managed to say, but he cut me off.

"I'm making a point," he said. He shook the mango in his hand. "Look at it. Whether it's living or dead is meaningless to us, isn't it?"

"Come on, Daddy, put it *down!*" I slapped the table with my palm, surprising myself.

Only then did he set the fruit down with exaggerated care, but upside down, the stem obscured, the opposite of how it had been. And he went on speaking. "Death itself is meaningless. All of our death rituals—cremation, burial—are meaningless." I noticed a thick elastic band around his wrist, like a bracelet. I was teetering on the edge of some understanding, but couldn't grab hold of it; it was unlike me.

"A mango isn't a person," I said.

"Right, but see, a corpse isn't a person, either!"

He wasn't—this was the point—talking merely about the rotting of a mango. "Do you see?" he said, his eyes bright. "What I'm made of, it isn't just cells! My thoughts and memories, those aren't cells! I'm talking about my soul, baby-love, nothing less!"

His soul, nothing less! There was such force in him; that's the word that comes to mind, *force*. I'm not referring to actual violence. I've mentioned his physical feebleness and his gentleness toward me. I mean a different kind of force, almost metaphysical in nature. It was as if I were a leaf, and he were the wind itself.

He put his hand in his pocket and removed a syringe, which he placed on the table between us. Only then did I understand. Here, before us, was a Clarinet of his own. "I'm an old man," he said, his eyes glimmering with desire. "What's the harm?" And if I have led you to believe that I am the kind of daughter who might have refused him this—that, since I threw a gift of flowers to the ground once, and asked for a mango to be returned to a bowl once, I would not do what my father required of me in this moment—then, Shareholder, I have allowed you to be misled. I spoke not a word. I went mute. He crossed to the sink and washed his hands with soap. He instructed me to do the same. Then he rubbed some soap and water in the crook of his left arm. After we returned to the table, he pushed the elastic band up from his wrist until it encircled his bicep and looked up at me, expectantly. He pressed two fingers to the crook of his clean arm. "Right in there—see it?" he said, tapping a faint blue vein. And then, oddly, as I took up the syringe between my fingers: "This is a *gift*."

7

The day that Grandfather Rao left this world, everyone stopped what they had been doing and gathered in the clearing. The youngest among them, perhaps by some inborn instinct, stayed on the outskirts of the gathering, far from the corpse. The girls clustered under the slanted cashew tree at the edge of the clearing with the youngest among them, a beautiful toddler named Lalu, at the center. They each took turns running their fingertips along a long scar on Lalu's forehead, cooing at its softness. So soft, they said, so amazing.

Lalu was the youngest granddaughter of Babu, Grandfather Rao's brother. She had the moon-shaped eyes and long lashes of a doll. The older girls stroked the scar delicately, as if it were a priceless gem. One afternoon not long ago, Pretty, the half-wit daughter of Leelamma's sister Lathamma and Bubbles the gambler, had clutched Lalu's head and beaten it against one of the steps of the Big House. Bubbles had overturned a pail of water on the bloody step, but the stain had only broadened into a brown blur. Sometimes King stopped and rubbed the stain with his big toe. "Look," he would tell his mother. "Remember what happened?" King, having been born with rough, uneven skin, envied Lalu for her prettiness. But with her forehead split like this, she'd never make a good marriage, his mother told him. For a moment, he pitied her.

But now he could see the scar had made her more beloved rather than less. He wondered what Pretty, who had given Lalu the scar, thought. Pretty wasn't pretty. Her name, a nickname, was a joke. In fact she had the bulbous, uneven face of a fresh-dug potato. Her head wasn't right, his mother had reminded him, to explain why she hadn't gotten punished for beating Lalu. Her head wasn't right, so she wouldn't comprehend any punishment.

Pretty stood nearby, turning a young greenish-gold mango in her hands. "My baby," she babbled to the mango. "My nicest child." Ram Babu—her first cousin, a son of Lavanyamma and the gambler Binky—circled her with his hands in his pockets. He also wasn't right in the head. Ram Babu followed Pretty around all the time because she took care of him when his mother tired of him. She helped him clean himself when he pooped in his pants. Ram Babu cried a little as he circled Pretty, trying to lure her attention from the mango, but she ignored him. King realized he had soiled his pants again, from the wet weight that hung low in the seat. He thought he should tell someone, but who? Grandfather Rao was dead.

Ram Babu and Pretty, as children of the gamblers and their wives, were considered evidence of the bad fortune that had descended on Kanakamma's branch when her son married Leelamma, the treacherous tea-stall girl who had brought the gamblers and their families to the Garden. The Raos were split into two factions. On one side was Kanakamma's branch, on the other the descendants of the three older siblings, Venkata, Balayamma, and Babu. But that afternoon, the girls all gathered together. It had been just that morning that Grandfather Rao had, mid-laugh, dropped dead. The boys, like the girls, had truced for the occasion. Seeing the commotion over Lalu, came over and hovered over the girls' shoulders.

"What are you doing?" Laddu, a son of Lalithamma and the

gambler Dimples, said quietly. All the children were trying, against impulse, to be quiet, as was required of the occasion.

"Touching Lalu's scar," said Pappu, his older sister.

"Can we do it, too?"

"It's only for girls," Pappu said, in a tone of disgust.

"You're using all the shade."

"This shade's only for girls."

"Then what's Kingie doing here? Is he a girl?"

"Find your own shade, or I'll tell Gun."

This was a serious threat. Gun was Leelamma and Jaggayya's firstborn child. At seventeen years old, he was the eldest male cousin, and he was mean—the worst of the gamblers' branch. He embodied what the rest of the Raos disdained about Kanakamma's branch.

"No!" hissed Laddu. "Fine, we'll go. But we're taking King with us."

"Take him," Pappu said, and she put a hand on the small of King's back and pushed him toward her brother.

Talk of Gun had soured the boys' fragile solidarity with one another. Everyone feared Gun. But half of them, the grandchildren of Venkata, Babu, and Balayamma, hated him. The other half, Gun's brothers and cousins, loved and respected him. The group splintered. Half went to where Gun stood, around the corner of the main house, and the other half stayed in the clearing. As Grandfather Rao's grandson, King should have stayed in the clearing, but Laddu dragged him to where Gun stood glowering in the shade of the house, his back against the wall and his large arms crossed. He had that way of bullies of seeming older than his age. He whored, he smoked cigarettes, he gambled with his uncles. Gun was old enough to get married. He used to beg Grandfather Rao to make him a match. Sure, when you're seventeen, Grandfather Rao told him each time. But Chinna—next in line as the Garden's leader—was different from Grandfather Rao, more practical. He wouldn't want to deal with a new wife in the Garden when he was learning to run the place. How long would Chinna make him wait? But he knew the answer—longer than he wanted.

"This is the end for the Raos," Gun said with force to his gathered brothers and cousins. He hacked a globule of spit onto the dirt. It shivered in place before melting. "Chinna's no leader. Remember that."

Over in the clearing, King could see that Kittu, Babu's eldest grandson, had removed his glasses and was crouched on the ground, crying, surrounded by his younger brothers and cousins. How strange he looked without his glasses on, his eyes so small and indistinct. King pulled away from Laddu and ran to the clearing. Everyone kept sweating and wiping their faces and talking in short sentences and then falling silent. King pushed in among them and said, "Chinna's no leader." Even as he said it, he knew it was an inflammatory thing to say; he'd said it partly to see what would happen.

"Who told you that?" Kittu snapped, wiping his tears.

"No one."

"Take one guess," Kittu's brother Bala said, gesturing toward where Gun stood. Kittu got up and crossed the clearing toward them. As he and Gun stood talking, they both turned to look at King. Kittu's expression was serious, though he was no longer crying, while Gun wore a smirk. King was afraid. But you can't run to Grandfather Rao, he told himself. He's dead, and you're all alone.

When Kittu came back toward the clearing, King's heart started to race. He cast around for his mother and didn't see her. He ran into the kitchen, where he thought she might be.

With relief, he found her there, alone. Sita could always be found by herself during group gatherings. She'd never gotten used to being a Rao. King went to where she knelt over a pot above the fire. The air was brown with smoke, and it got in his mouth and eyes. He thought of his mother's dead sister, the one who had given birth to him. The kitchen smoke had turned her eyes red, and she had died. Now Grandfather Rao had died. He slipped his fingers into Sita's sari at her waist, where she had tucked it into her petticoat, and tried to pull her to him.

"Stop tugging," she said.

"Amma, he's dead," he said.

"Death happens," Sita said matter-of-factly. "Those Raos are all out there crying, but it's just a show. They know it, too. Death is coming for all of us. When my sister died, I wanted to follow her. If I didn't have you to take care of, I would have. One of these days, death will come for me, too—hey, stop pulling!"

She had not given him the comfort he wanted. "No!" he cried, and he let go of her sari and ran to the door. When he saw his aunts sitting on the ground in the middle of the clearing—Leelamma and her sisters, the gamblers' wives, the mothers of Gun and his gang—he walked toward them. He didn't talk to these aunts much, the ones from Kanakamma's branch. People openly called them the bad aunts.

"Our lives are about to get much harder," Leelamma was whispering. "Grandfather Rao protected us, but that Chinna, he's never liked us."

"He'll throw us out for sure," said the youngest sister, Lavanyamma.

"Nah, he doesn't mind us ladies. He'll throw out the men," said Lalithamma.

"That I wouldn't mind," said Lathamma. "Maybe he'll take one of us as his wife." They all laughed heartily at that—some joke that King couldn't comprehend.

King stood silent and stumped, waiting to be noticed. He had a familiar sense that the adult world would be opaque to him for a long time yet.

Leelamma tugged at his ear. "Brat," she said with affection.

"I want something to drink," he said.

"Go get him some water," Leelamma said in her sisters' direction, and Lavanyamma, the youngest, sighed and went to the well and came back with a little cup of water, which she gave to Leelamma. Leelamma put it to his mouth and tipped it. But suddenly he thought of Leelamma being Gun's mother and was afraid of her.

"No!" he cried, and pushed her. "I don't want it."

"He says, 'I want a drink,' and then he says, 'I don't want it.' Well, what do you want, little idiot?" Lavanyamma cried.

But Leelamma only said, "It's all right. Can't you see he's upset? Poor little brat needs some love." She brushed his hair from his face with her rough hand. "All of this belongs to you. One day they'll call *you* Grandfather Rao. One day *you'll* be the one sitting on that stool."

King didn't want to be Grandfather Rao, sitting on his stool one moment, dead the next. He shook his head vigorously. "No," he said.

"Well, it's true," Leelamma said, mussing King's hair with her hands.

"Stop coddling him," Jaggayya, her husband, murmured from the steps leading up to the veranda. "It'll go to his head."

The bad uncles, Jaggayya and his gambler brothers-in-law, usually stayed apart from the good ones. But this afternoon all the men sat quietly together on the steps to the veranda, and it was nice, King thought, everyone together, trying hard not to fight. At least that one thing was nice.

"You gamblers, most of all," Kondanna, the eldest son of Babu, said to Binky, Dimple, and Bubbles. "You'd better stay on this one's good side if you don't want to be thrown out of here when he gets older."

He shouldn't have said it, not on a day like this. Bubbles, who had been drinking, leaped to his feet and stood like a bull flaring his nostrils. Rajubabu, the eldest son of Balayamma, put his hands in the air and said, "Come on, man, think of how Grandfather Rao would want us to act."

It was as if Grandfather Rao's spirit had passed over them. They all fell silent. King wanted to ask, What? What would he want? But they were silent, so he was, too. Bubbles punched his fist into his palm and closed his eyes and sat.

Jaggayya smiled and said, softly and carefully, as if he didn't know if it was proper to say it, "You know what I'm thinking of? You remember how when we all first married, he used to sit in that stool and tell us to send our wives over to talk to him, and he would stare at their breasts while they talked, never at their faces, and later on would come to us and say, 'Lucky you, how about those melons on her? Come on, let me just have a turn with her, we won't tell anyone!' "

When he finished speaking, the other uncles burst out laughing.

"What? What?" Jaggayya cried.

Sivaram, Balayamma's youngest son, clutched his stomach with laughter and said, "Jaggu! That didn't happen to any of us! Didn't you know Grandfather Rao was only in love with your girl?"

"You mean it was only my Leelamma?" Jaggayya said, pleased and blushing. "Only my girl?"

Satya, Sivaram's eldest brother, did an impression of Grandfather Rao: "Leelu, darling, won't you bring me a couple of melons? Bring me some of those big, plump melons." They all laughed softly. Even some of the aunts, standing near enough to overhear, laughed a little. King remembered how Grandfather Rao had followed Leelamma around like a puppy, and he, too, laughed. He remembered Grandfather Rao on his stool and Leelamma pushing her breasts close to his face and asking Grandfather Rao for some spending money for some dresses so she could keep on looking nice for him.

Now, sitting on the veranda on that same stool, Grandfather Rao's stool, Pedda cast a dirty look at the men. Probably he thought they were being impious, laughing. As usual, Pedda had been praying. Sita told him Pedda had taken it up after her sister had died, to look like he was atoning for the sin of causing her sister's death. Seeing Pedda glare at the uncles, King felt guilty, for he had laughed, too. In shame, he left the uncles and went to his father.

He waited to be berated. When his father said nothing, King asked quietly, "What are you praying for?"

"I'm asking God to take care of Grandfather Rao even though Grandfather Rao didn't believe in God much," his father said.

"But you don't, either," King said.

"Who told you that?" his father snapped.

"Amma," King said. "She said you pray, but you don't really believe."

"Your mom wants to turn you against me," his father said glumly. "Well, your old man needs to go to the bathroom. Don't let anyone sit here, okay?"

King stood with his hand on the stool that his father had warmed, and it was nice to have a job to do, to be protecting Grandfather Rao's stool.

Now Chinna came over, looking exhausted. "Let's rest awhile, little one," he said. He sat on Grandfather Rao's stool and pulled King onto his lap. Together they watched the elders who stood on the other end of the veranda, around the corpse. Chinna said, "You seem afraid, little one. Are you afraid of all this?"

King was ready to answer him—he was ready to tell the truth—when Pedda came through the clearing toward them, walking fast, a sour expression on his face. He came up the steps in three long strides and cried, "Well, I guess no one saved this stool for me after all!"

Chinna rose and let King slip to the ground. "Sit," he told his brother, his voice tense.

"No," Pedda said quietly.

"Go ahead," Chinna whispered.

They stood glaring at each other. Neither of them sat. Finally Chinna descended the steps to the clearing, and Pedda walked to the end of the veranda farthest from the corpse and stood there with his arms crossed and his back to everyone.

King was alone again. The truth was that he wasn't close with either his father or uncle. All this time, he'd been at Grandfather Rao's side, if not with his mother. Now he stood next to Grandfather Rao's empty stool and thought, I'm so alone. Finally he went, with great reluctance, to the elders standing around the corpse. Grandfather Rao's brother, Babu, told the others, "We keep dropping dead, one by one, all of us old people. Now it's my big brother himself."

King stood behind them. They, too, would die. He tried to

wrap them all in his mind so he would remember them forever. They were soft-boned and chicken-skinned, a pungent smell emanating from their pores as if they were already dying. Well, maybe they were. Maybe they were! They stood recalling their younger days, when the Garden was newly theirs and they didn't even know it. All of them crowded into the one house. Before the huts, before the children, before the grandchildren. Babu knew the Garden so well that he could name every plant on the grounds with his eyes closed. He used to let King and his cousins tie a rag around his face to cover his eyes, and lead him around the Garden, pressing his fingers to the bark of this tree or the veined leaf of that bush and challenging him, Then what's this one? Well, bet you don't know this one! At some point, Babu had grown too old for the game. King said to himself, Remember them.

Kanakamma trembled like a newborn chick; she had developed a nerve condition. She said, "I keep thinking I'll be next. Ever since my big sister died, I've known my time was coming. I kept waiting for her to come to me in my dreams. But she never did. I hope my brother comes to me, because we were closer. We used to visit the Brahmin, to lay pots in his house to collect the rain. My brother made a game of it. He made an obstacle course using those pots. I would time him as he raced. He said, 'You try it!' but I wanted to be a good girl. Once he knocked over a pot and smashed it. His foot started bleeding. I carried the pieces of the pot in my dress, and we buried them out by the old settlement."

King recognized that story. Kanakamma and Grandfather Rao had both told it a million times.

"I used to go and visit my Kothayya at the old settlement," Kanakamma continued. "I decided once to try to find a piece of that pot, and I begged him to help. We must have dug up that whole settlement. When Kothayya's father came out of the house, he found us on our hands and knees and said to my Kothayya, 'Son, we thought those Garden Raos were rich and uppity, but here's little Kanakamma crawling around like a servant girl!' We laughed. That's how Kothayya and I fell in love. That was the beginning.

But I wish I got to do the obstacle course when I had the chance! I badly wanted to do it! In those days a little girl couldn't run around like that." In grief, she pressed her eyes with both palms.

That morning, Pedda and Chinna had performed ablutions on the body and clothed it in a fresh white dhoti. When the Raos had been Burras, they had buried their dead. But as Raos, under Grandfather Rao's guidance, they had begun cremating. Soon the corpse would be taken to the river to be burnt. The Raos gathered around and touched it and wailed. Now the grandparents pushed King close to the corpse. It was his turn. Remember this, King told himself. The corpse had Grandfather Rao's eyebrows, unkempt, like copper wire, and his wide-bridged nose, but when King touched the forehead, it was cold, and he knew Grandfather Rao had left that body. The elders seemed not to understand this. They touched their fingers to their foreheads, to the corpse's forehead, and to theirs again.

Remember this. We are nothing without one another.

8

Norman's office was so small that when King and his adviser sat at their desks their shoulders nearly touched. On hot afternoons, heat radiated from the professor's skin. When one of them needed to push his chair back and stand, the other had to squeeze against his own desk to make room. Then there was Norman's nonstop chatter to contend with. Sometimes, during rare quiet periods in the office during which King and Norman both sat working in silence, Norman would turn around and ask, in a sly voice whose meaning King couldn't interpret, "Aren't you bored yet?"

But King had nowhere else to go, as a result of stupidly placed pride. He was working as a teaching assistant for Norman and his colleagues. In exchange, the university had promised him a stipend, to cover housing and other costs, and had set him up in a small beige apartment just off-campus. The problem was that he'd gotten a bill for rent before the stipend had arrived. He had no idea how to resolve this, short of explaining to Margaret or her father that, in the absence of the stipend, he couldn't pay rent, a prospect that mortified him. So he had forfeited the apartment, figuring he could just sleep in the office he shared with Norman, and when the first check arrived, could find another apartment. But it turned out he was supposed to give proof that he was renting to receive the housing stipend, which he no longer could do, having abandoned his rental. So Norman's office, the place he hated most, was the only place for him to be. At night, for a pillow, he stacked papers inside a folded shirt. In the mornings, he rose well before Norman's arrival and opened the small window to air the room out, before going to the university gym to shower.

His glee at having touched down in that plane, only a couple of months earlier, had dissipated, replaced with an anxious gloom. You aspire to something all your life, and then you do it and find yourself—it's shameful even to articulate it—purposeless. All that groping and scrambling to leave home, so that he could end up sitting in a basement grading undergraduate math quizzes? Even his research, in computer languages—so what? His late uncle came to mind, and his late father. All that they had sacrificed for him to get here. He'd sent his mother a short letter acknowledging his arrival, describing Seattle and a fictional version of his routine that he thought would please her, and asking after her, the Garden, and everyone else. Sita's reply had been even shorter: she was fine, the Garden was fine, everyone was fine, how was he, how were his studies, what did he need?

It was an extension of the back-and-forth they had established when he had left home to go to boarding school. Back then, through the letters he'd received from his old mentor, the Hollander, he'd come to understand that the situation at home was grim. Ever since Chinna's death, the Garden had been falling deeper into disrepair. Almost half his cousins had run off, and the other half were taking odd jobs, away from the Garden, to support the aging elders; there was even talk of selling off parts of the land. In one letter, the Hollander confided that he was considering leaving, too. His own parents, back home in Utrecht, were getting old themselves. The next letter came from Utrecht: He'd done it, he'd left Kothapalli. Since then, King had to rely on his mother for information, but her letters were as limited as ever. It made him assume the worst. At this point he was relieved not to know the details. People expected their family members who traveled abroad to quickly start sending back money. He had none. He didn't understand how anyone did.

But there was a name for people like my father, the skilled and educated Chinese, Japanese, and Indian newcomers who, as a result of President Kennedy's Immigration Act, were arriving stateside in the seventies on airplanes, rather than in bekelped boats and windowless vans, and settling on the margins of college campuses rather than in the tenements and shantytowns peopled by the previous waves of migration. They were "model minorities." They were, it was said, "outwhiting the whites."

Autumn faded into winter, the first truly cold one of his life. He had read about American winters, had seen them in movies, and yet he found himself psychically unprepared for the gloom and chill of it: awakening to gray, drizzling skies that seemed to push down like a lid upon the earth; spending the daytime hours, especially down in the basement, with the cold pressing into his bones; watching with dread as nighttime swung down before the afternoon had even really begun.

King was settling in to sleep one night when the building's custodian peered through a small window from the hallway. He rose and went to his desk so it would seem he had only been napping. After letting a few minutes pass, he lay down again. The custodian suddenly reappeared. He swung open the door. "Ha!" he cried. "I caught you!" He was a slight man with an upright posture; he looked to be in his thirties or so, with dark hair, a weathered complexion, and accented English.

King sat up and said, "I was only napping."

"You're Indian?"

"Yes."

"I knew it," the custodian said. "You can tell if someone's Indian by his smell," he continued in a knowing tone. "It comes out of your pores. The spices, the onions, the garlic. It's all right.

I'm from Vietnam. We smell like ginger over there. Fish sauce. Lemongrass. Those are the odors of my homeland. In my opinion, those are better smells than the Indian ones, because they're sweetish, and yours are harsh. Anyway, this isn't the place for a grown-up to sleep. We'll fix this."

He left the room.

King waited for the custodian to return. He assumed the man would invite him to sleep at his home. He must be calling his wife to make sure it would be okay. He wondered what that home would be like. Cleaning must not be a well-paying job, he assumed, and the man must be a refugee from the war. He pictured the custodian having several children, as well as aging parents, and saw an image of himself sleeping on the floor of some cramped living room with toddlers crawling over him. But a few hours passed. It was past midnight. The custodian must have forgotten about him. The gloom descended again. After he was fairly sure the man was not returning, he lay down again and slept.

He awoke to the sight of a pair of legs close to his face. It was early morning. The pant legs were blue and creased. He followed them upward and saw that a security guard stood there. The guard, a white man around King's age, regarded him with a resentful, and somewhat disgusted, expression. A badge clipped to his vest read SECURITY. Sleeping in the offices wasn't allowed, the man said.

"No one was asleep," King said, rising to a squat. He was perspiring; he felt as sinful as if this guard were a priest. He avoided the man's eyes and regretted that he had chosen a squatting position—a demeaning position, suggestive of fecal acts, but he couldn't stand now without it seeming confrontational.

The door opened again, and the custodian stuck his head in. "That's him," he said to the guard. King tried to make eye contact with him, but the custodian kept his eyes fixed on the guard. He had a subservient expression, this man of at least thirty years, as if he expected the young white security guard to pat him on the head, offer him a biscuit.

————

HE STARTED SLEEPING on the bus. Late at night, the bus filled with the sound of men snoring and the ripe, uric smell of unwashed bodies. But it was warm, and he didn't mind the bodies. He hadn't realized how much he'd missed India, where you couldn't help but be aware of other people's bodies. It made you feel your place in the human family. Many of his co-passengers were veterans, liquid-eyed and dressed in Army-issue camouflage, with their belongings stuffed in bedrolls that they shoved under their seats, eyeing the others with battle-worn looks, sussing out any would-be thieves. He asked one man where he'd gotten his coat. "Salvation Army," said the man. The next day, King rode the bus there and procured a coat for himself.

The homeless were well fed here, their occasional missing limbs explicable by service in the war, not like the mangle-faced vagrants of the cities back home, who had gotten their eyeballs scorched and scooped out in childhood by their beggar masters. Not like the one-legged cripple he had feared as a child. These American beggars were swarthy and literate, with their senses of humor on view on homemade cardboard signs: WIFE KIDNAPPED—SHORT A DOLLAR FOR RANSOM—HELP! Out on the street, pedestrians thrust dollars into the beggars' cups as if thankful. Only here, in the United States, had he encountered this phenomenon, of the middle class and upper middle class feeling remorseful, rather than proud, of their status. The beggar never chased after the giver to ask for more, only nodded and bowed his head. Americans. Never crossing the street while the orange hand flashed. Lining up at the bank teller's counter, never thronging. Smiling only with their lips, not their eyes, as if for a photograph. These cordial citizens, these earnest obeyers of rules. An innocent people.

The name, the United States, had always seemed exotic to him, back home, but now he realized there had never been a nation with an emptier name. All this sunlit glass, all this slanted metal. Early mornings, when he was roused before sunrise by the bus's constant stops for workers, he leaned his face against the window and watched the city turn gold with sun. The buildings' windows gleamed. The sidewalks were free of fecal smears, the gutters clear of debris. He'd spent his entire life plotting his escape to this place. Others had sacrificed themselves so that he could spirit himself here.

For what, though? For what? For what? Norman's question lingered in his mind. For what purpose did such a place exist, and for what purpose had he come here? His motivations remained arcane to him, expressing themselves in sensation more than reason. When he remembered home—the Garden, in particular—a clammy terror pricked at his skin, as if some force threatened to pull him back there.

One weekend, he rode the bus down to the waterfront, where some picnic tables sat next to a fish-and-chips stand. Springtime had finally arrived, the cold easing up. At one table, a pair of teenage girls, blond and gangly, sat across from each other with their legs folded under them, and dangled pieces of breaded cod over each other's open mouths. Feed me, feed me, they said. The girls had skin as white as cream.

He realized they were imitating the baby seagulls that sat on the fencing, waiting to be fed by their mothers. In the far distance, the shipping cranes were like flower pistils, bent and red with shame. The water shivered and undulated. Some shipping barges slid slowly by, their horns moaning. Out of the corner of his eye King watched the girls. They stretched their necks and fed each other. They licked their lips. They sucked the straws in their drinks. King sat down at the far end of their table but didn't dare look directly at them. They were wearing dresses though the weather wasn't quite warm yet, and when a sharp breeze sliced the air, the girl on his side of the table put down her fish and hugged herself. Glancing over, he could see the soft hairs on the back of her neck standing on end.

He thought of Margaret. Since their first meeting, King had seen her only in passing. They hadn't really spoken since that first conversation, and he didn't know whether to blame himself or her. When he glimpsed her in the office, she kept her head bent over her typewriter, fingers clacking. He fantasized about seeing her in the wild, on campus. The fantasies were chaste. She would talk, in that same jet stream of speech she had let out the first time, and he would listen.

Now the girl nearest to him thrust the cardboard container of fish in his direction and smiled warmly. "I can tell you want some," she said. It was true: He hadn't eaten all day. King plucked the smallest piece. He put it in his mouth, chewed hungrily, and licked the grease from his fingers. The girls glanced at each other and giggled.

"Sorry," he said.

"You're all right," said the girl near him. She was smiling and nudging the carton of fish closer toward him. "Another?" she said.

He thought suddenly of the nurses at the Hollander's clinic in his village. They had worn hats that looked like the cardboard container that held the fish. The girl's smile, too, kind and open, reminded him of those nurses. "Feed me," he said, and he opened his mouth.

The girl on the other side of the table cried out as if in horror. "Don't talk to him," she hissed. "Stay over here."

But the one nearer to him kept smiling at him a moment longer before turning to her friend. "Come on, don't be mean. They don't know any better."

"I'm mean because I don't go around feeding street people?"

"He could be a war vet. Have respect."

He bowed his head and became intensely aware of himself—the way he must smell after that night on the bus, the way he must appear with his rumpled clothing, his crusted eyes. He longed to explain himself. I'm not who you think I am. Have respect! But he didn't. The girls averted their gazes, rose, and went off, leaving their little hat of fish on the table.

He walked to the bus stop, agitated. One day, he would be known. Those girls with their fish—they would know his name! He used to experience the same mania as a preteen and teen, the same rageful ambition, only then it had been focused on immigration: One day, he'd leave; one day, he'd go to America! His mother would put her hand on his forehead and murmur, as if to herself, "You're so much like my sister, but you're a boy, not a girl. You'll get out of here, we'll make sure of it," and now he put his hand on his own forehead and tried to evoke the same calmness. But instead it had the opposite effect. He was alone here, he thought, more unknown than ever.

On a telephone pole at the bus stop, someone had stuck a wad of flesh-colored gum, and it increased his agitation. If only he could peel off the gum and dispose of it somewhere, he would feel better. But that would be disgusting—to touch this fossilized resin that had been mashed and tongued by some stranger. He bounced on the balls of his feet. He raked his hand through his hair. He walked a bit down the block, then returned to where he had started. His heart pounded against his chest like it belonged to some other man and was banging to be released. He realized he was sweating. He couldn't breathe well. The world grew speckled and colorless, like a static-filled television screen, and dimmed, and when he hit the sidewalk, it didn't hurt at first; it was as if it were happening in a dream.

He found himself in a hard, unyielding bed in a hospital room, a bandage constricting his head. He was attached by the crook of his arm to a bag dripping some fluid that he was sure he could taste, salty, in the back of his throat. He was moving a hand toward his chin to explore its bruised contours when the door swung open and in strode a man in a white coat who cried, "Don't touch!"

"My head hurts," he murmured. "Can you"—he gestured at the bandage—"loosen this?"

"Absolutely not," the doctor said. "You have a concussion, my friend. So you just collapsed? What about before that?"

Above him a ceiling fan whirred gently, clicking at intervals. The room was very quiet. "Before that, I was standing," he said.

"Ha!" The doctor laughed. "Good man! Comedian! But how did you feel? When you were standing?"

It was as if he were being cradled in the palm of some benevolent giant, and while on the one hand he knew it must have to do with the painkillers he had been given, on the other he thought the drugs had simply allowed him to see his circumstances for what they were. He trusted this man. "I felt afraid," he said. "It's hard to explain in words."

The doctor sat on a stool, wheeled closer, leaned in. "Try."

"I couldn't be sure I existed."

The man nodded sagely. "I know that feeling."

"Please don't tell anyone."

"I'll never tell," the doctor said, and smiled. Later, he pressed a bottle of small, oblong pills into King's hand and left, and a nurse asked him who to call to pick him up. Reluctantly, he gave her the only number he remembered. It was the professor's daughter who answered.

So it happened that, in the spring of 1975, King Rao moved in with Elbert and Margaret Norman in a picturesque neighborhood near Bainbridge Island's ferry terminal. It was Margaret who, after he had explained his situation—the homelessness, the concussion—had appealed to her father to let King stay there until she could get the university to restart his stipend. He would be staying in the spare room. No one back home would believe it, a room that existed only for the purpose of housing guests.

In April, the cherry blossoms bloomed. From the window of the room he could see the cottony pink flowers of the tree in the backyard, and Elliott Bay beyond. He couldn't believe his good fortune. He was looking out the window one afternoon when Margaret, passing in the hallway, cried, "Come outside!" and pulled him out, by the arm, to see it. "You have to appreciate it up close while it's blooming," she said. "Soon it'll be over, and you won't believe the mess." His concussion had heightened his sense of smell. The flowers, he could swear, had the scent of love.

"I adore cherry blossom trees," she said. They sat on the back porch admiring the blooms. "When I was younger, I thought I'd be an artist, so I never studied at school. I just painted. I loved to paint trees. I thought I painted them perfectly—I mean, you could look at one of my paintings and think it was a photograph, you know? I was into photo-realism. But then I applied to art school—a lot of them, nine or ten—and none of them let me in. I wrote to the directors of all of the schools and demanded a reason, and only one of them replied. He wrote that my work wasn't terribly good. It wasn't bold. I could tell it wasn't a form letter, because he referred specifically to one of my paintings. I guess I could have still applied to a regular college, for the next year, but I'd gotten those terrible grades all through high school, and, anyway, I got caught up with that man, that professor I told you about."

"Do you have them here?" he asked.

"What, the paintings?" she said. "Nope, I burned them."

"All of them?"

"Yes, all of them," she said sharply. "They weren't any good."

"Still—"

She shook her head, impatient. "That's not the point. The point is I'm an ambitious person. You might think, She lives with her father, she works at his office, this is her life." She paused, with a challenging expression, as if she meant for him to respond, but then continued on. "Well, it's not. I'm plotting."

"Plotting what?"

"Just wait," she said. Her eyes had mischief in them. "You're going to find out."

After that, each afternoon she'd march right into his room and drag him out. "You're going to *miss* it!" There they would sit for hours. His concussion symptoms were fading, but still, the flowers were almost obscenely fragrant, and Margaret was almost obscenely beautiful. It was hard to bear. They talked a little, but mostly they just sat there. She would be reading a magazine or painting her toenails. He would hold a textbook on his lap, pretending to study, but mostly he would be occupied in staying very still. It seemed as if moving would break a spell and compel Margaret to leave.

He and Margaret began commuting together on the ferry to Seattle. She'd spend the ride asleep against the window, and when they arrived, he'd nudge her awake with a tentative index finger, carefully, as if by poking too hard, he might injure her. "How did you wake up before I started commuting with you?" he asked. She pitched him a look of disdain. "Someone else would wake me up, dumbo."

At the office one morning, Norman said, "You've been spending a lot of time with my daughter, haven't you?"

"A little."

"I'm not sure you're her type," Norman said, and laughed.

"Oh, I wouldn't—"

"That'd be best," Norman said.

Then one morning—she'd been right—the trees were bare, and the flowers lay in the grass. For a day they looked beautiful there, as if strewn for a wedding. Then they became putrid. King sat in his room, waiting for Margaret, but now that the blossoming was over, she didn't come in. She just walked by, never even glancing at him. He occupied himself with his research, his studies, and grading student exams, but wondered if Norman had said something to her.

One Sunday afternoon, though, when Norman had gone to campus to pick up student papers, Margaret came to King's door with a mischievous smile. "I want to show you something," she said.

She brought him to the backyard. Toward the back of the yard on an anemic patch of grass, there stood a sort of oversized tent with a domed roof. King had seen it before but had never gone in; he'd figured it was some sort of toolshed. In here, she whispered, gesturing at it with a wide sweep of her arm, as if it were a grand hotel. When her parents still lived together but weren't getting along, she said, her father had built this tent in their yard—a geodesic dome, he called it—so that he could have a space of his own. He had ordered the parts over the phone. It was made of waterproofed canvas stretched over a metal frame.

The tent had a zippered front flap, which she opened, and they stepped in. The ground was covered with a tarp. Margaret plugged a string of little white bulbs into an extension cord and the room lit up. The space was surprisingly big. In this low light, it reminded him of a temple. He felt like taking off his shoes but didn't. "I'm not supposed to show you," she said, gesturing to a corner of the room. Raised on a bed of bricks, there stood a smallish, squarish metal machine, with rows of switches and blinking lights arrayed across the front. King stepped closer. The machine purred. It wasn't much like any computer he had seen before. The keyboard had been built into a plastic shell encasing the motherboard, and the whole contraption was hardly bigger than a television. "But it's so small," he marveled.

His first exposure to microcomputers had been from picking up a magazine, *Popular Electronics*, from a table in Margaret's office a couple of months earlier. "PROJECT BREAKTHROUGH!" the headline across the cover announced. "World's First Minicomputer Kit to Rival Commercial Models . . ." The computer was called the Altair 8800, after the twelfth-brightest star visible from earth, and had been built by an Albuquerque company in collaboration with the magazine. "The era of the computer in every home— a favorite topic among science-fiction writers—has arrived!" the article began. The machine in the magazine was beige and not much bigger than a cake box. It had an on-off switch in the bottom left-hand corner, and two rows of additional switches, each representing a bit that could be turned to the off position, or zero, or to the on position, or one, to program the computer. The magazine took pains to explain how they might, hypothetically, operate: "When the bit pattern, and thus the hardware, is changed, we have what is referred to as 'software.' " A sidebar listed several novel applications for the software: digital clock with all-time-zone conversion; automated automobile test analyzer; printed-matter-to-Braille converter for the blind; brain for a robot.

In the months after that article appeared, *Popular Electronics* kept covering the Altair. Kids in high school, the magazine said, were programming for the computer. Others, inspired by it, were building their own machines, selling them for a thousand dollars apiece. But microcomputers weren't the sort of thing that students in Elbert Norman's department were wasting their time on. You couldn't get a job at Computa, or one of the other heavyweights, by writing programs for hobbyist machines. So, what was one of these things doing in the professor's backyard?

There was a reason, Margaret now explained, that her father had been circling around all these months as if he wanted something. He had been working on a computer since well before the Altair's release, and now perceived an opening in the market, which he thought he was liable to miss if he didn't act fast. Inspired by *Popular Electronics'* Altair partnership, a rival publication called the *Information Times*—a scrappier thing, stapled together on letter-sized paper, in fact much more newsletter than magazine—had announced a microcomputer competition. Inventors had to write a letter to the newsletter's publisher, a man named Walter Martz, detailing what they were working on and listing the specifications. If your machine was among his ten favorites, he would invite you to his Palo Alto headquarters, to present to the members of the newsletter's club, some of the most brilliant computer experts in the world. Martz had enlisted the club members to help him choose a winner, to be featured on the cover of *IT* and distributed by the publication. Whoever built the computer would split the profit with Martz.

The initial deadline was in four months. Norman had been building the hardware for his computer, but he needed someone good to write the software. It would be counter to the university's ethics policy for him to solicit the work from a student, so he had been trying to get King to express some sort of boredom with his current situation, at which point he would mention this potential side gig—mention it, not offer it—and see if King bit. "You've got to let him bring it up, King," she said. "But *do not* tell him I said anything."

The question of whether he wanted to help build a micro-computer was beside the point. Margaret wanted him to do it, so he would do it. The next time Norman asked whether King was bored, he answered as Margie had coached him to. "I am," he said.

"I'm looking for a challenge." That was, evidently, all the professor needed; he didn't say anything right away, but that night, as they all sat together at the kitchen table, eating the spaghetti dinner Margaret had prepared, Norman turned to his daughter and said, "Margie, King tells me he's in search of a challenge." Margaret looked up mid-slurp, but said nothing. "Should I tell him?" Norman said.

Margaret looked at her father, at King, and back at her father. "Sure, go ahead," she said.

Norman said he had been looking for someone excellent, trusted, and determined to help him with a top-secret project. The person must be excellent, because Norman's plan was to have the person write an entire operating system from scratch, using an entirely original language to guard against copycats. He must be trusted, because the important part was to keep the work off-campus; otherwise the university would want to take a cut of their business, and God knew it had taken enough from Norman already. He must be determined, because this was an in-it-for-the-long-haul deal. King was excellent, and King was trusted, but was King determined? This, Norman said, a finger pointed at King as if in accusation, was the question that had been nagging him for a long time.

Now a deep swell of ambition rose within King. He regarded Norman and said, "I'll have to think about it."

Norman widened his eyes a little, but it was Margie who cried, "You can't be serious!"

"I don't want to fall behind in my studies. That's what I'm here for."

"But it'd be the greatest challenge, King," Margie said. "Think about how much fun you'd have." A look passed between him and Margie, and he now could see she understood. She was playing along with him. They were both acting. It felt subversive and wonderful.

"The problem is my mother," he said. "She's depending on me to start sending money home to her. As soon as I graduate, I need to start working."

All right, then: one-third for Norman, one-third for Margie, one-third for King. It was shocking how quickly Norman leaped up to offer it, but then, he probably thought he was getting a deal—giving up equity instead of having to pay an hourly rate. King, though, had a plan. He would build the most elegant operating system in the world, written in the most elegant language. What had he come here for? What was the point? Here, he'd found it. Looking back, he would never be sure what made it feel so right—ordained, almost.

The next morning, on the ferry, Margaret said Norman had built in a stake for her so that his family would have control over the company, not because he thought she had anything to add. But she did, she said. She didn't look like it, Margie Norman with her pretty blouses and soda addiction and desktop nail-polish collection, but she had people skills, she said; she knew how to persuade. "Don't you think that's true?" she asked. He'd arrived fresh off the boat from India, and she'd made him like her, she could tell. Yes—he blushed—he liked her, surprising himself by saying it out loud. She cried out, "Ha!" and turned toward the window, grinning. "My point is, I have a plan," she said. She breathed on the glass and wrote his full name in the steam. King Rao. "It's a good name," she said.

9

I t began—the slow dissolution of King Rao—in the form of minor forgetfulness. At night he would ask me a dozen times whether he had locked the front door. "My God, yes!" I would shout, after the dozenth instance, and he would look stunned and hurt, not remembering that I had answered with great patience eleven times before. He began to see people from his past and hear nonexistent sounds. He became paranoid that we were being watched. The bald eaglets had grown, and he mistook them for drones. I would see him in the middle of the garden, crouched and clutching his head in both hands as if in pain.

In his lucid moments, he chalked it up to side effects from his Clarinet. He had explained himself that morning, after I injected him with it. He desired his own connection with the Internet not so that he could enhance his knowledge—he was too old for that to be of any use to him—but so that he could upload his mind to it before he died. What he wanted was to immortalize his thoughts and memories, so that I could have my father's guidance available to me for all time. It was in this way that he considered it a gift.

But it must not have taken. The Clarinet must have determined his brain was simply too old. This was what it was supposed to do—it meant his update had worked—but I could hear a note of sorrow in his voice.

Months passed, then a year. One afternoon, when I checked on him in his office, he peered at me, confused, and said, as if we were mid-conversation, "It's just that I can't seem to remember what I was working on here."

"Side effects," I said absently.

"What do you mean?"

"From your Clarinet."

"What Clarinet?"

And I realized that this, too, was now lost to him: the fact that I had injected him with his own Clarinet at all.

Soon he stopped going into his office, unable to follow the thread of his work from one day to the next. He also stopped going to the market as often. We subsisted on produce from our garden: potatoes, zucchini, jackfruit. When he did travel, he took to wearing a kind of disguise, a long woolen coal-colored coat that buttoned at his chin and ended at his ankles, along with a hunter's cap with earflaps, a pair of leather gloves, and oversized sunglasses. It embarrassed me to think of him being in public in this outfit, paddling his little boat, even with the sun bearing down. It only reinforced his public image as a washed-up eccentric with grand delusions. I asked him once why he couldn't wear a shirt and pants like regular people. "Regular people, ha-ha!" he cried. "What have regular people ever accomplished in their lives?"

IN THE BEGINNING, humans were primitive in their trials with tools, monkeyish. Early hominids would hold a round stone in one hand and a crystalline one, such as flint, in the other, and hit them together, over and over, until pieces flaked from the crystalline rock, turning it sharp-edged enough to be used to butcher a dead animal. Those were our first tools. Next came wooden hand axes, worked symmetrically until they became two-sided and almost knife-like, followed by actual blades, which evolved into spears and arrows for hunting. Then, plows and hoes, pots and bowls. Houses and storerooms. Bronze was discovered, then iron, with which to build stronger tools. Wind and water energy to power them.

The wheel, the sailboat, the locomotive. Gunpowder, rockets, bombs. Clock, calculator. Printing press, telephone, radio, television. Sewing machine, refrigerator. Penicillin. The atomic bomb. It is sometimes said that what sets humans apart from other species is nothing but our inclination, faced with our limits, to create tools to extend our powers. The Coconut. The Harmonica. The Clarinet.

The spirit of invention, as Proudhon wrote, never stops.

ONE AFTERNOON, I was napping when I was jarred awake by a strange experience. A succession of foreign images had been parading through my mind: King's name written in steam on a bus window; Grandfather Rao's neck, fleshy as a wattle. It was similar to what had happened with the puffin all those years ago, but more intimate. I couldn't place the images. I squeezed my eyes shut and held my head in my hands, trying to regain ownership of it, but the visions only got more intense. I was not in my room but in a dark, smoke-filled kitchen with charred pots and pans stacked on the floor. I was in an outdoor shower stall where a cockroach drowned in a bucket, its tiny legs flailing. A coconut storeroom with a lofted space up top, whose relationship with the sunlight made it seem holy and cathedral-like.

These were his memories, not mine.

I must have cried out.

My father came running in. "Athena, baby-love," he cried. "What happened?"

I meant to answer, but my mouth refused to cooperate. My teeth were clattering; I felt faint. "What happened?" he cried out, louder. He never shouted at me; I must be really scaring him, I thought, faintly. But I was distracted—by the hiss of coconuts drying over charcoal; the metallic scent of the blood from a mother's menstrual cloths; the sense of being naked next to a lover; and, finally, black-and-white speckles that darkened until I could no longer see, or even feel, anything at all.

When I came to myself, he was tipping a glass of water to my mouth. "Drink," he said, and then again: "What happened?"

And I remembered his words before I injected him: "This is a *gift*." Once I had a handle on what was going on, I would reveal the truth to him. That was my plan, or, in any case, my justification for my dishonesty in that moment. "I felt faint," I lied. But the condition overwhelmed me more, not less, as time went on. I was sixteen. Months might pass eventlessly, followed by one episode after another for hours straight. No amount of mental preparation could ease the disturbance. All I could do was grab hold of something to steady myself, a doorjamb or wall, and wait for the onslaught.

I could sometimes move around while it took place. I developed a habit of blinking furiously, as if by doing so I could press some sort of reset button. I must have looked frightening, skulking around, eyes wild, like some Victorian madwoman. Often I couldn't do even that. I would feel faint and drop, heavily, onto the floor. The thump would bring my father running to find me hugging my knees, tense and twitchy. He would grip my head in his own trembling hands: "Athena! Athena!" he'd shout, as if trying to rouse me from some slumber. From inside myself, it seemed like he was trying to reach out to me over a great distance.

HERE'S WHAT I COULDN'T be sure about: whether he had done it on purpose. He had admitted to wanting to live on; he had professed to wanting to be available to me even after his death; he had made that mysterious comment about a gift. Had he *planned* this invasion of my selfhood, seeing my mind as a receptacle for his own consciousness?

But for answers, my father was now useless. He decided my

strange spells must have to do with a malfunction in my own Clarinet. He returned to his office and pored over the code, hunched over his keyboard in concentration till late at night. He thought about bringing in a doctor but talked himself out of it. He could, he insisted, fix it himself. Once, around midnight, I peeked in on him. His face was pale, his hair sticking up in all directions, his hands trembling. He did not look like a man in charge of anyone, not least himself. He looked close to death. I pitied him.

"Daddy, please go to sleep," I begged him.

"I'm on it, I'm on it," he murmured. More than one hundred years old and still working.

As my father's condition worsened, the images flooding my mind became more frightening. A crippled man waving the stump of an amputated leg. "Touch it," said this terrifying man. "Rub it." Once, King's uncle Chinna appeared to me, dead in King's House, his head cracked open, his eyes still, blood blackening the ground beneath him. A cat licked the blood. I stood over him—in King's form—in terror. It now seemed inevitable that his consciousness would not stop oozing through me until he dropped dead. By then he would have overcome me altogether. I would be his host.

He came into my room one afternoon and told me he was going shopping. I was seventeen. He stood in my doorway, wheezing from the exertion of having crossed from his bedroom, through the living room, to mine. He struggled to button the front flap of the coat. In better times, when I loved him without condition, I used to button and unbutton it for him, especially on the cold days that turned his fingers white-tipped and arthritic. But that afternoon, I sat still in my fat green armchair and kept a dispassionate expression. It was a summer day in the Northwest, the sun hot and bright.

He kept fiddling with his buttons and giving me a hangdog look. I thought about whether to rise and help him. Several times, I almost did. But something stopped me.

"I'll bring you back some taffy," he said.

"I don't like that stuff anymore," I said. "It's too sweet. It's not healthy. I don't know why you used to let me have it."

"You love taffy!" he insisted. "I'll bring you some good taffy. Tell me, which flavor, blackberry? You love blackberry."

"I stopped liking it a long time ago."

"No! I'll bring you some!" he said, agitated, fingering those buttons. "This morning, I had a craving for fish and chips, with vinegar! When I first came to America, you know, I used to go and sit on the boardwalk and watch people eating fish and chips. But I didn't have any money. I couldn't buy myself any fish and chips. When I became rich, for one whole year I used to send my assistant to bring me fish and chips for lunch every day. From the same place! It was still there!" He smacked his lips. "Fish and chips!" He peered at me, still fingering his buttons, and added quietly, "Remember, I'm not long for this world."

I must have appeared cold to him, unfeeling. He looked at me and made a little sound that I couldn't read. He got the top three buttons fastened. Then his eyes went unfocused, and he began to babble, "He had a baton! He had his baton, and he aimed it at me and started shooting, tat-tat-tat!" He said, "You can't sleep here!"

"Batons don't make that sound," I said. "You don't shoot a baton."

"What sound?" he said, his confusion deepening.

I shaped my fingers into a gun and pointed them at him. "Tat-tat-tat!" I said, in his accent. He gasped and put his hand to his chest, as if he feared I had actually shot him. It made me feel great and powerful. I was pitiless. "Tat-tat-tat!" I said.

Oh, child-changed father of mine. How could you let me sit there in my furious mirth, your hand pressed to your chest? Some small voice inside myself rose in defense of you, dear person of my heart. It did. But this person, said a stronger voice, brought you into the world as an experiment. This man created you in his image, and now he means to fill you up with himself until there's no space left for you.

"Tat-tat-tat!" I said again.

Whether he had programmed his consciousness to seep from himself into me or whether it had been accidental—all that was irrelevant now. The only relevant question was whether to sacrifice myself to be his vessel, or sacrifice him to save myself. I knew the answer as soon as I articulated the question. Had I answered otherwise, I could not, in good faith, call myself King Rao's child.

But what it should mean to be a person among people—to be a social animal, with an obligation to kin and species—is the greater question. In this wretched state of mine, alone in the Margie, even the fizz of a can of soda opened under a passing guard's thumb, like a child's first breath, is beautiful to me. It's ridiculous, it's strange, to think such a mundane thing could be so moving. But it's not about the fizz itself; it's about the kinship, having also flicked such a tab in my life and seen others flick other such tabs, in hearing someone else do the same.

Nor must fellowship take human form. These days—I'm not ashamed to say it—the sight of a cockroach in my cell, its iridescent shell gleaming in certain light like a rainbow on an oil slick, can bring me such fellow feeling that I am reduced to tears. Sometimes the fellow feeling lives in my mind. I like to picture, for example, the moment when all of a horse's legs are in the air, mid-gallop. The way a leaf, ripped by the wind from its branch and therefore near death, might somersault in the air as it passes to the ground, as if saying hello for the last time. Floating is beautiful, whatever is doing the floating. I once saw a short film of a person wearing a costume made of thousands of colored balls. This person is bouncing in slow motion on a trampoline; there are moments in that film in which this person could be said to be floating.

To use language to describe these beautiful things is beautiful in itself. I'm partial to English, my native tongue, which supposedly contains more words than any other—beautiful, buttery words, *lathe, shame, rest, nightshade*, sharp ones, *scat*, muscular ones, *jugular, defenestration*. To me, *lassitude* sounds like sitting in a wagon in springtime, being pulled with a big loop of rope by the person you trust most in the world.

But words in any language are beautiful. Once upon a time, when I was young and newly aware of my Clarinet, I came across a photo of a bar in Bucharest that, seedy and low-lit, struck me as a romantic place. I zoomed in on that photo and found on a tabletop these words etched: Tristan, I don't love you anymore. I'm translating from the Romanian. Who, I wondered, was Tristan? Could he have been the Romanian poet Tristan Tzara? He wrote, "I'd like to bury myself in your flesh when I die," and "In your hair I smell oranges grapes." Oranges, plump and soft as freshly born chicks when you hold them, are beautiful. The way the pockmarks on an orange peel resemble an old man's skin.

Life itself. Our planet. Its abundance. My father's zucchini plants in late summer, the way their stems would thicken and knot. We could not pick the vegetables fast enough. They grew as big as my forearm. Gardens. Gardeners. Other beautiful occupations: cobbler, toymaker, poet, pianist. An old piano's keys, like tea-stained teeth. Certain teas, I mean the kind of hot tea made of a shriveled flower that sits at the bottom of a pot, and upon contact with water surrenders into bloom and turns the water pink or green or lavender. Lavender itself, though I'm particularly moved by peonies, ranunculi, anything with a large bloom that sits engorged on its stalk as if waiting for a stranger to come along and make love to it.

The color red. The sound of a trumpet. The bodies of human beings: the navel, the shin, the shoulder, the toe. That, despite everything, we go on opening and opening and opening ourselves to one another. Neil Armstrong's observation about the clouds resembling white lace. When I've been at a loss in life, this returns to me, almost like a prayer or incantation, white lace, white lace, white lace, and brings me peace. Now I offer it to you.

II

11

Two weeks after Grandfather Rao's death, the gamblers resumed work on King's House, so that they would be sure to finish before the monsoon began. King and his cousins stood outside the periphery and watched their uncles construct each wall brick by brick. Once the gamblers had finished building four walls, the children crowded inside and lay on their backs in the gloaming, looking up at the sky as it turned from blue to orange to red to purple to indigo. The stars revealed themselves, like fresh pinpricks in the firmament. Only then did the children sleep.

Each evening thereafter, they returned. One night, Chinna came inside and told the tale of a miserly old merchant, a Kamma, who was said to have found four nuggets of gold buried outside town. Nobody knew where he kept the gold, but the rumor was that he had buried one piece under each of his bedposts. One night, a band of three thieves, Dalits, dug a tunnel from outside the house and crept up to steal the treasure. This had taken place long ago and the story's ending was forgotten, but the scene was immortalized in the night sky. King and his cousins looked up and saw the four corners of the merchant's bed under which the gold was hidden and the three thieves skulking up to steal it.

"What's the moral?" the children asked.

"You tell me," Chinna said. "What do you think it is?"

For a long time afterward, the children debated what the moral might be. Much later, as an adult, King would remember the tale and wonder all over again.

Once the frame of a roof was complete, the uncles climbed up there and, straddling the rafters like monkeys, began covering it with coir. The sky each night became more obscured by the patchwork of roof. One morning, King woke up late to the sound of voices, and found that the sky was gone. The air smelled dusty. The children's private lair had been transformed into a simple building, its structure identical to the main house's—four walls, a peaked roof, three rooms. The adults were peering into the windows, stepping through the doors. This was what the main house—still a fine house, but musty with age—must have looked like when the Brahmins first built it. The floor was even, the roof clear of bird droppings and leaves, the walls bright white and uncracked. The adults put their noses through the window frames and touched their fingers to the walls and speculated about the building's possible uses. As if by providence, it had begun to pour overnight, the season's first rain. "Good timing," Chinna said, satisfied. "Perfect timing."

One by one, the children wandered off. But King stayed back. The grandmothers and grandfathers laid their mats on the floor and squatted there playing gin rummy as the rain poured outside. The mothers undid their clotheslines from outdoors and restrung them across the empty rooms, tied to the windows' mullions and transoms. King listened as the uncles stood with their hands on their hips, nodding along while Chinna daydreamed aloud about the future. It would be some time before King would need a house of his own. Until then, King's House would function as a small but modern coconut-processing facility. Instead of selling coconuts themselves at market, the Raos would process it into its far more lucrative dried form, copra, from which coconut oil could be pressed. How many fresh coconuts could you store in the rafters of a space such as this? What was the best method to dry and process them? What tools would they need to get the job done fastest? They should, at the very least, acquire more coconut-picking poles.

To HAVE A HOUSE that bore your name—to be the sole heir to this house and all it contained—was both daunting and emboldening. There had been a time when King had been afraid to stand too close to the trees. A fruit could fall onto his head and crush him. Now that his grandfather had died, that version of himself felt distant, like a different child altogether. These days, the sound of mangoes falling on windy nights, whistling through the air and thudding softly on the dewy leaves, gave him a rush of excitement. When this happened, he would dive into the Garden. A mango would be sitting on the floor of the Garden, beads of dew glistening on its green-orange skin like little gems. He would carry the fruit back and fall asleep with it tucked against his belly so he could eat it in the morning.

"Hey, Pedda, our little one's a natural!" Chinna would say.

"He's *my* little one, not *ours*," said Pedda, who, since their father's death, had grown more sullen than ever.

For days after Grandfather Rao's death, the Garden had functioned more as a shrine than as a living place, everyone moving around as if afraid to disturb the state the Garden had been in during Grandfather Rao's final hours. For a while, this had comforted King—knowing that, while Grandfather Rao was gone forever, the place he had built would not change. But when King's uncles returned to climbing for coconuts and shaking them near their ears to grade their quality by the sound of the swishing water, and when his aunts returned to peeling onion skins till their thumbnails were translucent, sweeping spiders from room corners, and scrunching in their fists the clothes and bedsheets

strung along the clotheslines to see whether they were dry yet—
when the early grief dispersed like a fine mist into the air—he was
surprised, and a little ashamed, to find that he was relieved.

Business was excellent. Ever since the new road had been built,
making it easier to get to Kothapalli, traders were eager to buy
from Kothapalli. It was lucky, then, that the Garden was the largest, longest-established coconut grove in the village. As the Raos
had worked for the Brahmins for centuries, so had the Brahmins
forged relationships with the families of these middlemen for
centuries—relationships that the Raos now owned. The biggest
change, though, had been the move to sell copra instead of coconuts. Once a week, the traders came to the Garden with oxcarts,
and the Rao men helped load them up with jute bags filled with
dried coconut meat. After the buyers rode off, the rest of the evening was spent in good cheer, the women cooking chicken for dinner, the men downing arrack from tin cups. They weren't quite
rich. Still, at dinnertime, the Rao women could decide what to
make based on what they wanted to cook or what the men wanted
to eat.

King once asked Leelamma which foods she had liked best as
a child. "What did I like?" She laughed and knuckled his scalp.
"You spoiled brat! What a question to ask an orphan. I liked not
starving, how's that?"

THE COCONUT IS such an ancient species that, at various points, it
has shared the planet with the dirk-toothed cat, the cave bear, and
the woolly mammoth. When Vasco da Gama's explorers found
the fruit in India, they christened it *coco*, owing, it is said, to its
hairy shell and the three markings on its base that, in their imagination, recalled the face of the mythical child-devouring beast
people called *el Coco*. Over time, the other peoples of Europe came
up with their own names. The Brits derived *coconut*, the Germans
preferred *Kokosnuss*, the Swedes ate their *kokosnöt*.

In *The Book of Edible Nuts*, Frederic Rosengarten, Jr., writes,

"Every part of the coconut is utilized for some human need." The meat of one coconut, according to Rosengarten, contains the same protein as a quarter pound of beef. The meat can be eaten, or else pressed into oil. The fruit's coarse outer fibers, its coir, can be woven into rope or textile. The leaves thatch roofs, their midribs used as fence posts, brooms, or canes. A shell, halved, becomes a cup; tossed in a fire, it serves as charcoal. Cut into the flower clusters before they've opened, and you'll find a sweet juice. Feed it to your children fresh, or distill it into toddy and have it for yourself. Found at the top of the tree, "a bundle of tightly packed, cabbage-like, succulent, unopened leaves"—the palm heart—"can be used in salads." If you do extract this terminal bud, though, the tree will die with it. The trunk can become lumber or a medium-sized boat. "One could live almost endlessly," Rosengarten writes, "on the coconut's products."

In the morning, the boys sat in the clearing and used big knives to cut the coconuts in half. The halves dried in the sun all day long. In the evening, the children took turns working in King's House, where the halves were dried further in a bamboo berth, over coals made of coconut shells, kept in an earthen pot. They had to move this pot underneath the coconuts, shifting it a forearm's length every fifteen minutes, so that the coconuts above would dry fully and evenly. If anyone neglected the pot, the coconuts would be ruined, the resulting punishment harsh. The following morning, the children scooped the dried meat from the coconut shells with a sharp-edged spoon and laid it out to dry further.

The teenagers of the Garden undertook more specialized tasks. For example, because Kothayya came from a family of coconut-climbers, he'd taught the trade to his sons. Now his grandsons and grandnephews—Gun and his gang of tag-along cousins—were learning from their own fathers. When they weren't climbing, some of them, those who had the knack, graded the quality of coconuts by shaking them next to their ears. Not everyone could do this. It was considered, like climbing for coconuts, a virtuosic talent, made especially mysterious by the fact that those who excelled at it were unable to explain how they could tell the good fruits from the bad. King wouldn't grade coconuts, and he wouldn't climb. As Grandfather Rao's heir, he was to begin school that summer, to learn the skills he'd need to run the business.

THE FIRST BREACH of this idyll had to do with Gun.

It began when the gamblers abruptly departed the Garden one morning, having clashed, as their wives had predicted, with Chinna. That left the twenty children in their branch with Jaggayya, Kanakamma's son, as the only father figure among them. Years ago, as soon as Jaggayya realized Leelamma had tricked him into bringing her pack of scoundrels to the Garden, he had committed to atoning by accepting, without complaint, whatever task Grandfather Rao sent to him. After a while, this attitude became so ingrained in him that his heart got soft, and he couldn't harden it even when his own children and nephews stepped out of line. Everyone hated that whole branch of the family, even after the gamblers left, and the children were written off as hooligans, though whether that was due to their unfortunate provenance, or Jaggayya's softhearted parenting, or the rest of the family's prejudice against them, was debatable.

The family's hatred was directed at no one more than Gun.

While some bullies age out of the status, Gun, having turned eighteen, was more fearsome than ever. He had graduated from cigarettes to opium and had grown a mustache. He openly swore, even at Chinna. He was liable to jump at the cousins from the other Rao branches, fists up for fighting, over the slightest perceived affront. Most of the time he could be talked down by his younger sister, Jaggayyamma, the only person he trusted, but sometimes his victims would have to run for it. Gun wasn't big, but he was strong, with long simian arms that could grab a cousin by the sleeve and reel him in for a headlock all in one swift motion. The cousin would be coughing, begging for mercy, he hadn't meant it, promise. Gun's voice would be quiet, tense. Apologize, he would respond. Again. Again. Because his father, Jaggayya, was so gentle, some wondered if Gun was in fact the illegitimate son of Bubbles, the gambler with the anger problem, the one who had tried to hit little King with a stone while building the house. Maybe Leelamma had strayed with Bubbles.

Gun had grown up to be the best coconut grader among the Raos, but he grumbled about the work all the time, resenting Chinna for bossing him around. After Grandfather Rao's death, Chinna had not prevented Gun from marrying, but neither had he used his influence to help Gun find a good wife when Gun's bad reputation stymied him.

King was as afraid of Gun as anyone, but he held him in high regard, too. He admired the way Gun behaved however he wanted, with little care for how it affected anyone. That, plus his status as the eldest cousin, sometimes made him appear even more powerful than Chinna. King had seen Gun be tender, too, especially toward his younger sister, Jaggayyamma, but also toward the other siblings and cousins in their branch. If he overheard anyone criticizing or insulting them, he responded with more furor than if he himself had been wronged.

One morning, when King was five, he woke up to a commotion in the clearing—shouting, crying. He moved to the window and looked out at the scene. Jaggayyamma was sobbing in her mother's arms, while her father, Jaggayya, stood talking to Chinna, his head hung low as if in shame. Chinna was upset: "Just like that, gone?" he cried, his tone yelpy and uneven. Jaggayya spoke in a low whisper; King couldn't hear what he was saying. Others, too, had crowded around.

"Who's gone?" King hissed at his cousin Kittu, who was nearest to him, crouched on the veranda.

"Gun, that bully," Kittu said, his eyes bright with excitement. Gun and Kittu, as the eldest of their respective branches, had always been rivals.

"But where'd he go?" King said.

Kittu shrugged. "He woke Jaggayyamma in the middle of the

night and told her, 'Hey, I'm getting out of this dump. I'm eighteen; that's old enough. I'll find a job and a wife of my own. Take care of Amma. And don't tell anyone till morning.' Jaggayyamma claims she tried to get him to stay, but he covered her mouth and said, 'I'll never ask you to do me another favor in your life, just this one.' So she let him go, and didn't tell anyone till just now." She had told their mother, who had told their father, who, finally, just a minute ago, had told Chinna.

Chinna now shouted, loudly enough for everyone to hear, "That boy wants to follow in the footsteps of the gamblers? He can go ahead!" He walked off into the Garden without a word, and everyone dispersed, and that was that. But, King thought, this was incredible. Until now, the gamblers were the only ones who had left the Garden. But if a full-blooded Rao didn't like how things were done, could he just leave this place, too? Could he just get up and go?

A RAO CAN JUST get up and go, he decided, a week later, holding on to Sita's sari while she swept the Big House and its veranda. After Gun's departure, things had more or less gone back to normal. This morning, his mother's face was flushed with the heat, and she had wet circles in the armpits of her blouse. She stopped and fanned them both by flapping her hand. It was a quiet weekday, all the older children out working in the fields or helping their parents at home. "No one helps me," Sita said. "They all look out for themselves. They tell one another, 'She's the wife of Grandfather Rao's heir, so she should do most of the work around here.' But what about him?" She gestured at King's father. "He does nothing."

In the shade of the slanted cashew tree, Pedda sat cross-legged in prayer. Even before Grandfather Rao's death, he had spent hours sitting still under the slanted tree. Now he stayed in the shade more than ever. King feared that his father's stillness was contagious—that if he got too close, that stillness would envelop him, too. "He's the laziest of them all," Sita said. "Tells everyone he's praying so that he can spend all his time sitting around. Only you and I know the truth. He's a bad man."

King understood that the mother who had given birth to him was dead, and that Sita was actually his mother's sister. It was because of Pedda that Radha had died, King understood, though the details were muddled. But, while he tried to care about his dead mother, he didn't.

For a couple of moments, they stood in the doorway of the kitchen looking at his father. Pedda's chest rose and fell. "If I didn't have you, I don't know what I would have done when my sister died," his mother said. "I think I would have killed myself. I would have drunk poison. But you were there to stop me," she said, and she pulled him up from where he stood and held him on her hip. "My miracle," she said, and kissed his ear wetly. "My king, my hero!"

"Let me down," he said. Sometimes he found himself wanting to protect his father from Sita's abuse. He went to the shade of the slanted tree and sat next to Pedda. "You'd better get to work," King said.

"Ha," his father laughed. "They don't want your old man working. 'Pedda kills everything he touches.' That's what they say about your old man."

King laid his head back so the bark of the tree scratched his scalp. He closed his eyes, and when he opened them he saw a monkey perched on the low branch above their heads.

"The more knowledge there is of bows, crossbows, hand-nets, stringed arrows, and snares," says the *Zhuangzi*, "the more the birds in the sky above are thrown into confusion. The more knowledge there is of hooks, baits, nets, throw-nets, pull-nets, and basket traps, the more fish in the water below are thrown into confusion. The more knowledge there is of palings, pitfalls, rabbit nets, and gins, the more the animals in the marshes are thrown into confusion." There had been a time when monkeys were rare in Kothapalli; they preferred the forested regions up north. But these days they hung from the trees as plentiful as fruit, bounded across the road, loitered on their haunches at storefronts picking lice from their children's scalps and demanding handouts from pedestrians. This was thanks to the new road. Visitors came through town and left their trash behind. The monkeys came out to lick the candy wrappers and chug the half-drunk sodas. They became energetic, procreated, and multiplied.

"Hanuman," King whispered at the sight of the monkey, for they had a game in the Garden: Whoever saw a monkey and was the first to call out the name of the monkey god won. But no one who mattered was around to hear. The monkey flexed her tail and crouched as if she would flee. "Wait," he whispered. She had a long, pink face, with a pair of tiny holes for a nose and thin, prim lips. He stood. The monkey looked down at him. Then she made the most remarkably human gesture. She crooked her finger and beckoned to him. The leaves fluttered, but his father didn't open his eyes. A brilliant thought came to him: He'd catch the monkey! Oh, when his cousins came home from the fields and saw that he'd tamed a monkey, how they would love the monkey, and love him for having done it! But he had to be patient. He had to gain her trust.

He raised a hand to her and fluttered his fingers. Hi. He stood to get a good look at her. She cocked her head at him, leaped to the next tree, stopped, looked over at him. He approached. She moved to the next tree. He followed. Soon, like this, they were on the main road, and the monkey was flying through the trees along the roadside, and he was sprinting to catch up. The path from the Garden to the center of the village was wide and rutted from the oxcarts that traveled it. When it rained, the ruts filled with water, above which mosquitoes hovered. But this summer, the monsoon had not yet arrived, and the climate was at its hottest. The coconut trees edging the road cast wide lengths of shade over the ground, and King hopped from one canopied place to the next to keep the soles of his feet from burning. The sky was a high plane of blue, the weather so clear that, when an eagle soared overhead, its shadow on the path was as fully formed as if a second creature traveled along there. King said its name aloud. He liked the shape of the word in his mouth.

The treetops that morning were so swollen with fruit that their branches hung close to the ground; he sped up, leaped into the air, and reached, but came down empty. The monkey turned and laughed. He laughed, too. They were running and laughing. Then, at once, she was gone. He looked up into the treetops for her. A sour panic pinched at his armpits. He had run too far from home. He didn't know how to return. He scanned the treetops. "Hanuman, Hanuman," he called. Nothing.

Now he stood where the road ran alongside the canal. From here, the canal traveled alongside the road into the center of Kothapalli, and in Kothapalli lived his mother's father, Grandfather Appayya. All he had to do was go along the canal, and he'd reach his grandfather. Sometimes you could see many small boats zigzagging from one bank of the canal to the other. Today, though, all was quiet, but for one figure in the distance. The figure came closer, and he could see it was the one-legged cripple of Kothapalli, on his handmade raft.

Most cripples were dirt-crusted, withered, and hollow-eyed. They dragged themselves around on wheeled platforms, and slept crumpled in the gutter like street dogs. The one-legged cripple of Kothapalli wasn't like that. He went around on a wheeled platform, like other cripples, but he stood on it with his working leg and used a sturdy tree branch, to which he'd affixed sharp spikes for traction, to push himself around. He was six feet tall, with shoulders like sides of meat. His eyes popped out, bulbous and red-veined. His nostrils were large and flared. The cripple worked for the village's big landlords as a private guard of sorts, and when people got caught stealing from the landlords, it was the cripple who beat them up. The skin of his face and neck was patched with hideous scars from all his fighting.

The cripple also terrorized the landlords' servants and farmworkers, and was especially cruel to Dalits: With his tree branch, he would draw a line in the dirt and growl at them, "Cross this line before finishing that work, and I'll throttle you!" Some said this had to do with his occupation rather than with any inborn casteism on his part: Most of the servants and tenants happened to be Dalits. Grandfather Appayya, the Ambedkarite, had a more complicated explanation, having to do with the fact that the cripple himself was reviled and powerless, and Indian society was set up so that any such person, unless actively shown otherwise, believed that he must step on other oppressed people in order to survive. Whatever the reason, when King or his cousins misbehaved, their parents grabbed them by the ear and threatened, "We'll hand you over to the one-legged cripple if you keep it up!"

This was a terrifying prospect, but less because of the cripple's treatment of Dalits than because of the rumor that, on top of everything else, the cripple was a murderer. Some years ago, his wife and children had been found dead, and everyone believed he had killed them.

The cripple had announced not long ago that he had transformed his life. He had quit the landlords' employ, claiming that he didn't want to hurt anyone anymore. He only wanted to do good. He built a raft out of wood and announced he was going to shuttle people across the canal that divided Kothapalli from the villages on the other side. Now that Kothapalli had a good road, it was easier for people to get to the villages across the canal by first taking the bus to Kothapalli and crossing the canal from there by ferry or boat. Most of the private boatmen who provided this service charged a couple of paise, but the cripple said he would do it in exchange for donations. Everyone thought he had gone insane from belated guilt over killing his wife and children.

King and his cousins had gone that spring to watch the cripple float his raft. It was a dangerous-looking vessel, just some planks of wood he had lashed together on his own. Their mothers had forbidden them to ride on it; even if they were allowed, none of them would have dared. Maybe Gun would have dared. But Gun was gone. So instead they taunted the cripple as he used his long branch to try to push off from shore and got it caught in the mud. He grunted with effort, and King and his cousins stomped the earth and howled and egged him on. "You cripple!" they yelled at him. "You wife-killer!" It felt good. Finally, the cripple freed his stick from the mud and was able to get his raft out into the water. "Who wants a ride?" he called to them good-naturedly, as if he didn't mind their insults. He lifted from the raft a long piece of wood that he had fashioned into a paddle and used it to slide his raft around in the water, more ably than the children wanted to admit. "Come on, try it out. It's free!" No one answered. They kicked at the earth, irritated that the raft had floated well. "Wife-killer," they muttered a couple more times, half-heartedly. "Cripple." They dispersed.

Now the same one-legged cripple was on his raft at the bank of the canal, calling out to him. "Child, let me give you a ride," he sang roughly. He was shirtless, and his skin stretched tight across his ribs, but his shoulders and chest were strong and broad. He reminded King of a bull.

"I've got no money, uncle," King said. Slowly he continued down the road along the canal, kicking a rock. One of his cousins had told him that dogs could sense human fear. Maybe cripples could, too. Don't let him see that you're afraid, he told himself. But the cripple pushed himself alongside King and called out, "It's free!" He added, "You like sweets?"

King looked up and nodded.

"What kind of sweets?" the cripple said.

"All kinds."

"Come with me," the cripple said. "I'll take you to the general store and buy you all kinds of sweets. We'll just cross over there"— he pointed across the river—"and then come right back to the village center. It won't take long."

King stopped and toed the edge of the water. He longed for sweets. He also longed for a ride on the raft. He looked up at the cripple. "Okay," he said.

"Wait," the cripple said guardedly, looking up and down the road. "Are you alone?"

"Yes."

"Good, the cripple said. "All right, good. I don't like those big cousins of yours, Gun and them." He put his hand out and said, "Here, come with me," and King let the cripple take his wrist and pull him onto the raft. The raft bobbed when he landed, and cold water splashed up around his heels. Would he slip and drown? But the cripple's hand was tight around his wrist. With the other hand, he used his stick to push off from the canal's bank. King had never been so close to the cripple. A poisonous smell rose from his skin and breath—the smell of being crippled, he thought. People said you were never supposed to touch a cripple, or you would be cursed.

"Let go," he said.

"No," the cripple said.

"Let go."

"You'll try to escape," he said. "You'll drown, and they'll all blame me."

"I won't try to escape," King said. He hadn't thought of escape, but now he knew that's what he would do. He would swim ashore. He'd be a hero at the Garden.

"Swear it on your mother," the cripple said.

"I swear," he lied. In his mind, he reminded God, My mother—my birth mother—is already dead.

The cripple let go. But King was afraid; he couldn't jump. The cripple watched him with a look of gratitude. "I thought you'd do it for sure," the cripple said, and his voice swelled as if he would start crying. "You really are a good boy," he said, his voice thick with emotion. "You swore you wouldn't, so you didn't." The sun was high over them. "Nice day. Blue sky," the cripple said. "That's auspicious. We're going to have a good time. We'll be good friends. You'll never forget the time we had together." He grinned, and King noticed that he had lost most of his back teeth. Where the teeth should have been, there were black pockets like tiny pits of mud.

The raft slid across the canal. You are five years old, King thought. Remember this. He thought again of Gun, who had disappeared. He thought again of how a person, even a Rao, could just disappear like that. The sun seared his scalp. A thick muddy smell rose from the water. Red flowers crowded the treetops on the bank of the canal, as if the trees held them bunched in their fingertips, ready to toss them in the air. Little flocks of varicolored butterflies alighted among the flowers before fluttering free and disappearing among the trees. Crickets chirped. Birds made hollow titters in the trees, and King thought of the girls at Grandfather Appayya's school, their little giggles. They were halfway to the other side of the canal.

After some time, the cripple took a small bottle from his satchel and sucked from it, and his expression clouded. "They think I'm bad," the cripple said. "They don't know me at all! Only one person ever knew me, and that was my wife. She used to tease me about my leg, and we laughed so much. But she died."

"Oh," King whispered. Now he was sure he would be killed by the cripple, who had also killed his wife and children.

"My whole damn story is sad," the cripple said. "My parents were hardworking farmers. They lived not far from here. But my mother was really kind, too kind, and she kept giving everything away to beggars. Untouchables, like you. They'd tell all their friends and pretty soon there were hordes of them coming to our door. She never let them in. She always came onto the porch to serve them. But one day, when she was pregnant with me, a one-legged untouchable crawled to the door and begged her for help. He had lost his wheeled plank and he didn't know how to move. His hands were all scratched up from pulling himself along. My father wasn't at home. He'd gone to the store. Well, she brought that beggar right into the house and let him stay for three days, until she was able to get him a new plank. My father came home on that first day, but what could he do? He couldn't throw the beggar out. My mom was pregnant, and he didn't want to upset her."

They reached the far shore, and he pushed off again.

"Well, a few days later the beggar left, and everything was fine. But when I was born, I turned out to be one-legged, too, like that beggar. My dad fell into a depression. He wouldn't talk to anyone. He would work and come home and eat and sleep. And one day he didn't come home. My poor mom couldn't take care of me on her own. She heard of a man who took in kids like me. He gave her a bit of money and took me away. He was bad to me. I escaped and came back here later, but they all said my mom had decided to leave without a trace. I don't believe that. I believe they forced her to leave.

"Anyway, I stayed. I met my wife in the village. She was blind, so she couldn't see that I was a cripple. She didn't know till after we married and I got her in bed. I did it hard so she wouldn't be able to leave me and marry another man: He would know she wasn't a virgin. But she realized I had only one leg and cried, 'You deceived me! You cheat, you cheat!' Well, I cried, too. I said, 'But you didn't ask me, Do you have one or two legs? You didn't ask me, Are you a cripple or are you not a cripple? If you'd asked me, I would have told you, you dumb bitch!' I told her I loved her and didn't want to lose her. She felt flattered, so she softened. I loved her so much and didn't want to lose her—it was true—so I'm glad she was dumb and stayed with me. We had three kids: a boy, two girls. I got a good job with the landlords so I could take good care of them all."

"But they died," he said. "You probably heard: They all died. One day I woke up and they were all like bags of rice. I couldn't move them. I can't understand it! People say I killed them. They say this because then they can believe they understand what happened. But not me!" Suddenly he dashed his paddle into the river and crumpled onto the raft. "I can't understand it!" he cried again.

The paddle disappeared. But a moment later, it popped back to the surface and bobbed there. Without raising his head, the cripple grabbed it and held on to it. "Thank God," he said. They were coming close to the village center. King could see the other rafts and boats tied at the dock. He could see the peepal tree at the center of the village circle. He could see the general store where the cripple had promised to take him. I'll have a laddu and a jalebi, one of each, one part of him thought. You dummy, he isn't really going to buy you any sweets, thought another part of him. There was silence on the raft. He heard only the swish of the water against the bank, and the crickets and birds still singing. They had never stopped. The beauty of it all was stunning. The canal, the raft, even the raftsman. The raftsman took King's small hand in his own great big rough one and said, "You're like my son, my eldest, you're exactly like him. Do you believe me about them all? That I didn't kill them, they just died?"

"Yes," King lied.

The cripple sighed and thrust the paddle deep into the canal so that the water surged up around them. The raft stopped. "I'm going to show you something special," he said. "Only one person has ever seen it, and that's my wife. I've been waiting for someone else to show it to. Every time someone gets on my raft, I think he could be the one. But they all end up being mean people. What a life."

They were in the middle of the canal now, halfway between Kothapalli and the other side. "What a life," King repeated softly, just to hear his voice and be sure he was alive.

The cripple was untying the dirty dhoti wrapped around his waist. King could see his thigh and looked away. The village center had earlier appeared close but no longer did. Would anyone hear if he shouted? No, no one would. "Look!" the cripple said. "Come on, look, or I'll throw you off this raft!" When King looked, he saw that the cripple had retied his dhoti so that his leg stump was exposed. It was bulbous and strong-looking, like a small boulder. He rotated it in a circle. "I'll give you one piece of advice for life, and you can listen or not," he said. "If you're a person like us—a cripple, an untouchable—you've got to make them afraid of you. You've got to place yourself above them however you can." Suddenly he said, "Touch it," and he grabbed King's hand and pressed it to the stump. It was smooth, hard, hot.

"Go on, rub it," the cripple said. When he rubbed it, the cripple closed his eyes and sighed. "Good, good," he murmured.

King felt ill. "Can I stop?" he whispered.

The raftsman bristled and said, "Suit yourself," and roughly lowered his dhoti. Neither of them spoke. A cold shiver passed over the raft. The raftsman lifted his oar to push the raft toward shore. "I'll take you to your grandfather now."

"Okay," King whispered. He was too afraid to ask to first go to the general store for sweets, as the cripple had promised.

When they got to shore, the cripple asked King to hold his paddle while he tied up his raft. He took his wheeled platform from his bag and set it down on the ground. Then he knelt and told King to get on his back. They rolled together on the platform, the cripple now using his other stick, the one with the spikes, to move the platform along toward Appayya's school. At the sight of them, the aunties who worked as servants to the landlords came running out of their houses, shaking their brooms at the cripple and talking to him as if he were a child, too. "Let go of him!" they cried. "Get away!"

The cripple dragged his stick on the ground to stop the platform. He knelt again so King could climb off. The women bore down and grabbed hold of King, questioning him, while the cripple stood at a distance and cried, "I didn't do anything bad. Go on, ask the kid, did I hurt him?"

But they ran at him with their brooms till he wheeled off down the road, swiftly, still protesting over his shoulder.

The aunties brought him to his grandfather's school, and Appayya sent a fifth-grader to find Chinna. Thirty minutes later, Chinna strode into the school, nostrils flaring, the student trailing him. King was sitting at his grandfather's desk. His uncle came over, wordlessly took his hand, and brought him out to the school's veranda. He crouched in front of King and whispered, "What's going on? Little one, what did that cripple do?" King looked at the ground with anxious wildness. Chinna gently grasped King's head in his palms, turning it up so their faces were very close. "Did he touch you? Did he do anything strange?" Something about it—the way Chinna seemed to be able to see through him and know what had happened—prickled his insides.

"What if he did?" he whispered.

"We'll find him and give him a beating."

"But he didn't. I'm safe." He twisted away from Chinna. He was solid, and the ground was, too. "See, here I am," he said.

"Don't ever leave like that again."

"Gun did, though, didn't he?"

"You're no Gun," Chinna said. "Let's go home."

That evening after dinner he washed his face and hands, and stood at the edge of the clearing. Three anthills stood side by side. He crouched and watched the ants stream in and out. He stood, raised his bare foot, and dropped it onto the first mound. Then it was flat as a dung cake. He was trying to understand something. He was trying to find the limits of what he could control in the world—of where, exactly, his authority began and ended. He stepped on the second anthill, and the third. He crouched to see what damage he had done. It was a slaughter.

12

Committing a destructive act in service of your own small selfhood: how violent, how magnificent.

Puget Sound was blackish green and cold as I stepped in, wearing my wet suit. It was a summer afternoon; the sun wouldn't set for hours. Strapped to my shoulders and cinched around my waist was my dry bag, packed with some clothes, sandals, binoculars, several bags of nuts and dried fruit, a month's worth of the water-cleansing tablets we used at home, and a sleeping bag I used for camping on summer nights. I had circumnavigated the island more times that I could count, but never with this much weight. Then there was the fact that, once I left the Internet behind, I would have no way of knowing, aside from using my own inborn senses, how much distance I still had to cover. But it would be fine, I told myself. Being cut off from the Internet wouldn't be a loss, it would be a freedom. Plus, all that I had already downloaded to my mind remained there. I wouldn't lose that part. I looked back toward the only home I had ever known. I stepped into the water.

I swam at first with strong, deliberate strokes, counting to keep my focus, and for a while, I was able to trick myself into thinking this was a normal swim, like any other. But the farther I got from land, the more difficult it became to maintain the illusion. My exhilaration upon leaving the island ceded to a high, sea-salted anxiety. My strokes weakened, lost the beat. All those teen run-aways who had drowned out here, their bones eroding to sand among the eelgrass and bottomfish, cautionary tales forever after, though no one remembered their names. Bainbridge still seemed far, Blake Island more distant still behind me. My thighs and shoulders burned. What would happen if I began drowning? If I shouted, would anyone hear? And if someone heard and rescued me, what would become of me then?

It was more than an hour after leaving Blake Island, my mus-cles afire, that I arrived. I dragged myself onto the southern shore of Bainbridge Island, and, with my last bit of energy, unzipped my bag and retrieved my sleeping bag, which I wrapped around my shoulders. I was shivering, nerves sharp. You made it, I told myself. Relax.

I couldn't relax, though. I pulled out my binoculars and kept peering at Blake Island, small and uncanny from this vantage. What was he doing? Had he returned from his outing? Was he gardening, napping, at the computer in his office? If he'd noticed my absence, he probably assumed I had just gone for a swim and would be home any minute. Now night would fall; it would grow cold. How long would it take for him to realize I had left him? Would he go to sleep without knowing? Would it occur to him that I had come here, the place presently occupied by those responsible for his fall from grace?

I had viewed this beach so often through the same binocu-lars. Now it struck me as simultaneously familiar and strange. It was a wide strip of coarse gray sand, behind which a vine-covered embankment sloped up to a narrow, potholed road in front of a row of faded mansions. The houses—their paint peeling, lawns overgrown—looked like they had once been handsome.

I tried to separate the truth about the Blanklands from the myth. One uncontroversial fact was that, by moving to the

Blanklands, rendering themselves untraceable and unable to communicate online, the Exes had marginalized themselves and their message. They had lost touch with their Shareholder friends and families. Nor was there any public footage or photographs of the Blanklands. On maps the land was grayed out and unclickable.

I knew that when the Blanklands were first established, thousands of people had fled the mainland, in what became known as the Exodus. They had settled on islands all over the world—Kiribati and Tuvalu and Samoa, the Falklands, South Georgia, Mauritius and Réunion, Andaman and Nicobar, the Seychelles, the Maldives, Sri Lanka, the Paracel and Spratly islands, the Faroe archipelago. I knew, also, that this process wasn't, by and large, peaceful. In the handful of cases where Exes moved to uninhabited islands, the threats were primal in nature: rot, disease, predation—and, more frequently over time, floods and hurricanes.

With inhabited islands, there was a different set of troubles. Despite a major resettlement program, many existing inhabitants of those islands had understandably preferred to stay put, and some of them, angry that the Board had abandoned them to hordes of invading anarchists, gave the Exes a violent welcoming. Eventually, though, most Blanklands residents had accepted payouts from the Board to move to the mainland. Exes had occupied their abandoned homes, squeezing thirty or forty people into each house.

Here's the part where I couldn't separate rumor from truth. It was said that the Exes, lacking a traditional police force, were prone to taking aggressive self-protection measures. If you knocked on a door in the Blanklands, it was said, you would either be given a blanket and a place to sleep, or you would be stabbed. I wasn't about to attempt it. But I couldn't just stay here on the beach, exposed. Behind the houses lining the beachfront stood a dense section of forest, the tree line looming beyond the roofs. A well-worn dirt path led between two houses into the forest. I changed into a flannel shirt and jeans, packed my binoculars, and stood.

Down the path I crept, entering the woods. The ground

squelched under my feet as I moved. The sun was beginning to set, and in the gloaming the forest took on a forbidding character: the tree branches above me sagging and bemossed; the damp air smelling faintly rotten; strange trills, groans, and patters all around me. Bainbridge was only three miles from home; why did it seem so foreign?

I thought again of the runaways whose bodies I had seen online, apparently mauled by wild animals. Back home, a thought like this would be followed by the requisite information popping into my mind—what to do in case of a boar encounter. But, having never had reason to ask my Clarinet about boars, I had never downloaded the requisite material.

At the base of a spruce tree whose low branches formed a broad umbrella, I sat down, opened my bag, and scooped handfuls of nuts and fruit into my mouth, famished. I changed into dry clothes, wriggled into my sleeping bag and lay down, the bag under my head as a pillow. And now the weight of what I had done impressed itself on me. I had left home. I had left my father. I was seventeen years old, and, for the first time I was alone.

I AWOKE in the morning to a familiar smell, rich and salty, filling the air—bacon, I thought, and I turned toward it in my sleep, dimly wondering what had compelled my father to cook me such a delicacy. Mangalitsa pigs had been bred on Bainbridge since before the Exodus. These days, the Exes maintained a small but efficient operation for slaughtering and processing them. On special occasions, three or four times a year, King brought home a chunk of ham or a stack of fatty bacon tied up in twine, and surprised me with it in the morning.

But I wasn't home. I sat up, alert, in my sleeping bag, trying to tune myself toward wherever the smell was coming from. I walked toward it, and found myself in a clearing surrounded by a stand of trees. There, some boards of wood leaned against one another to form a structure, covered by a dirty, moss-stained canvas tarp. A fire was still smoking out front. I went over to the tent, bounced my knuckles on the tarp a couple of times, and called, "Hello?"

From the inside, a gruff man's voice echoed mine. "Hello?"

I had never even heard another human voice in person, aside from my father's. The sound of it made me shiver. To open my mouth and speak to this person struck me as obscene. I waited for him to open the tent, but he didn't. "Hello," I said. This time he barked, "How many of you out there?" I heard footsteps as he came closer. "I've got a loaded pistol here, friend," he said. "You'll want to tell the truth, or I'll shoot. Give me a number."

"One," I said, and after a brief silence, the tent flapped open.

The man who emerged was unarmed. He had a big, thrusting gut, a receding hairline, and the sort of flushed, potatoish face that can make a man seem vulnerable and dumb. He didn't scare me. It was a small miracle. The first stranger of my life, and he didn't scare me. He seemed familiar, even. I wondered for a moment if being born human in this world automatically granted you a sense of kinship with others of the species, even if you've only ever met one. Maybe my exposure to the Internet helped. It was only when the man eyed me up and down that it came to me. He reminded me of the raccoons.

I almost laughed, but I was growing self-conscious under his gaze. I had never thought much about my physical appearance. Now I became intensely aware of it. I was strong, though not tall, my biceps and quadriceps powerful from all the swim training. My hair fell in loose tangles around my shoulders. My father said I had inherited his face—big features, unreliable eyebrows, thrusting lips and chin. I tried to moderate this by smiling. There I stood, becoming a person among people.

He smiled, too. "Whatever you're selling," he said, "I'll have it." He smelled of mint and sweat. Behind him, in the tent, there wasn't much to see. Some overlapping canvases covered the earth. On it some provisions were arrayed: a jar of instant coffee, some dented cans of pinto beans, beets, sliced potatoes. I couldn't see any bacon.

The man, following my gaze, said, "Sweetheart, none of that comes for free," and then he laughed and added, "Come in, come in!"

He introduced himself as Arno Glad. He stabbed at the lid of the can of beets with an attachment on a Swiss Army knife, perforating it till he could pry it open. He was one of the old nomads, he said, among the earliest settlers of the Blanklands. "People don't come knocking on my door too often," he said. "They see a tent, they get scared."

Nomads were considered dangerous. I had read that the reason they didn't stay put—that they didn't plant a flag in one of the big settlements, which had basic plumbing, access to fresh water, and so on—was that they had a reason to hide. Killers, rapists, the worst of the worst. With each stab of the beet can's lid, he grunted a little. I eyed the exits, the various places where the canvas roof and walls flapped open. "Ha-ha!" he said. "Now I've got you scared, huh?"

"Nah," I lied, flattening my tone.

"Sit," he said, pointing to the ground. "Now tell me, what do you need?"

"I could eat," I said, sitting down.

"Ha-ha; that's all?"

As much as I had studied people, I didn't know the first thing about how to talk to them. That's all? I repeated the words in my head, wondering what he'd meant by them. "I thought I smelled bacon," I said.

"Yeah, you sure did," he said. "But I finished it."

It almost offended me—the only child of a single parent, I was accustomed to getting first dibs—but I caught myself. "Some beets, if you don't mind," I said politely.

He peered at me. "Where'd you come from?"

"Not far from here," I said.

"What was wrong with it?" he said. He knelt on the ground across from me and wrenched the lid off the can of beets, handing it to me.

"Thanks," I said. "I know provisions are hard to get out here."

He laughed as if we were in on some joke together. "That's all right, sweetheart. You can have my *provisions* anytime. I don't even like beets. Turns your feces red."

I picked out a beet. It was soft and grainy. I didn't want to think about when it had gone into the can. "These are okay to eat?" I said.

"Like I said, I don't like beets. A beet's never good, in my opinion. Don't want 'em, don't eat 'em."

"I'll eat them if you're not going to," I said. "Someone should eat them."

"So what was wrong with it?" he said. "Wherever you're from?"

I thought for a moment and said, "My family." I put a beet to my lips, forcing myself to push it in and swallow it. I finished the rest of them in four gulps and then felt guilty, as if in saying those two words, *my family*, I had somehow betrayed my father. "But my dad will be worried," I added hurriedly. "I might not stay long."

Arno laughed. "I've got a daughter; I get it." He sat, too. Then, with one motion, he had my feet on his lap and was rubbing them. His big, rough thumbs ran up and down the arches, ball to heel to ball to heel, and he breathed hard. He stood, retrieved a rough blanket, and put it over my legs. I was confused. I thanked him. He said I was welcome and returned to massaging my feet, under the blanket. His hands moved to my shins. The blanket prickled my skin.

"Full?" he said.

I nodded but didn't answer.

"You're tense!" he said.

"I'm tired."

"Me, too," he said. "I get bored out here, man. That's the word. It gets *boring*."

"It's quiet," I said.

"Good grief, it's quiet," Arno said, kneading my shins. "It's nice that you're here. It's nice to see people around here. I miss my daughter. It's been fifteen years since I've seen her. Not a little girl anymore, though I imagine her like that. She wasn't even one when I left. She was born right after they passed the Identity Act. I remember because it required that people register their babies in the hospital at birth. Remember that? Well, you're too young. You must have been a little kid, too, when it happened. I didn't want her on Social—my daughter, Junie, Juniper. I couldn't explain it to the doctors, or even to my wife. I just kept saying, 'She's too young.' My wife thought I was nuts, thought I was being irrational and paranoid, like those people who don't trust vaccines? We just didn't see eye to eye. Finally we agreed to file for a one-year— Wait, is this okay?"

He looked down at the blanket, under which his hands were rubbing my legs.

"Oh, it's fine," I said. It was not.

"I'm drinking, so I wasn't sure. Just tell me if it's not. You must be around the same age that she would be—my kiddo. And you look a bit like her. Not a lot, but a little. Her mother was Indian." He said this last bit apologetically, as if it might offend me.

"My dad is," I said recklessly.

"What about your mom?"

I looked away.

He peered at me but apparently decided to let it go. "Me and my wife compromised. We decided to file for a one-year extension. But as the year passed I started having this dread. It was like registering her, getting her on Social and all that, would totally change who she was. I couldn't—I can't—explain it. I'm not, you know, book-smart. I'm a tree faller myself. I used to cut trees, down in Eugene, before Hothouse and the beetles and the deforestation and all that. But I started to think, What if we just didn't put her on Social? It went on from there; I couldn't stop myself. What if we turned off the Coconut, or at least restricted it so it couldn't record everything we said in our house? What if we just dropped out and returned to the land, like those Exes are talking about? It was new at the time, and sort of exciting. I was being retrained in those days, to be an influencer, like everyone else in my trade, and I just wasn't any good at it. It didn't feel natural.

"That's when I started cooking drugs. I wasn't drawn to substances like I was drawn to trees—I never developed a taste for them myself—but that's what was available to people like me. I started spending my days in underground labs, suited up, masked up. My God, I missed the trees. People think of tree fallers as ruining the environment, but most of us, we loved the woods. That's why we worked out there. I once saw a clip on Social, where this plant scientist showed how you could actually hear the trees breathe for the last time before they died. He attached microphones to them. What happens—what happened—was that, with the heat waves and the drought, these little air bubbles would get into their veins and burst them open. That's what you'd hear. That pop. I'll never forget it. But then my wife—I told her what I was thinking, about going back to the land, and she said no, and we had it out, and I said at one point I'd take the baby and go without her. I started to dump my clothes and Junie's clothes into a suitcase. I didn't mean it. I wasn't really going to go. The baby was still nursing and all. My wife begged me not to do it. I was still acting. I opened the closet, and I got down the gun. I was mad at her, man! I wanted to hurt her like she'd hurt me! I wasn't going to do it, of course; it wasn't even loaded. But she didn't see it as acting. She actually believed that I was going to shoot her. 'My husband is about to shoot me with a gun he's holding,' she said, and three minutes later, I hear the sirens. The police. It was the Coconut: You hear those stories, about how, if you say certain high-risk words, the Algo will automatically send the cops. That's what happened. She knew it, too. She said it on purpose. But I think when they showed up, she regretted it. They knocked on the door, but she didn't open it right off the bat. I think she was giving me a chance, a bit of grace. She let me kiss Junie—Junie was sleeping—and I snuck out the back door and got out of there as fast as I could. I went to the shore, paid a smuggler, and came out here."

He took one hand off my leg and rubbed his face.

"Fifteen years," he said. "I still regret it. I ask myself every day why I did it: You thought this would be better? But it's true

I missed the woods. We'd cut them all down, and I heard there were trees out here. So here I am, among the trees. I'm still cooking drugs—it turns out to be a transferable skill—but I'm doing it among the trees. So, woo-hoo. My girl's sixteen now, and all she knows about her dad is that, once, years ago, he pulled a gun on her mom and disappeared." He smiled morosely. "You'd like her. I think you'd be friends. You're a nice girl. Some girls would charge a lot for this"—he gestured toward my thighs—"and all you ask for is a can of beets!" He laughed, as if we were coconspirators in some scheme, and finally I understood. Whatever you're selling, he'd said, I'll have it.

I shrugged him off of me and quickly stood. "Wait," I said, almost apologetic. "There's been a misunderstanding."

"What misunderstanding?"

"I'm not—"

He flushed. "Oh shit!" He scrambled to his feet and stepped back from me, as if I presented some danger.

"I didn't realize you thought—"

"I apologize," he said, his tone formal and abashed. "I assumed. Most girls who come here—that's what they start out doing. Shit."

"It's all right," I said, embarrassed.

"Shit."

"I don't mind," I said. It was true; I didn't fault him for the misunderstanding.

"Stupid," he said.

We stood quietly, regarding each other. "Well, you're going to have to work, if you're not going home," he offered after a while.

"I know that."

"What are you going to do?"

"I haven't decided."

I could see he was thinking about something, making some connection. "There's someone you should meet if you stay," he said. "Does the name Elemen Ex ring a bell?"

It took me a minute, without the Internet, to place the name. But I had read about her before, and now I recalled what I had learned. Elemen Ex was one of the earliest Exes. She had helped incite the riots, maybe even the fire. Now she was the labor boss for the island's sex and drug trades. The natural notoriety of these sectors, and the outsized interest in them, made her one of the few Exes high-profile enough to still be known outside the Blanklands. She was the sort Shareholders still feared.

"I've heard of her," I said, trying to keep my tone measured.

Arno puffed his chest a little, clearly proud of the affiliation. "I'll take you to her."

13

"This is not a computer kit, but a FULLY ASSEMBLED
COMPUTER, with the brains of the class nerd and the looks
of the prom queen," Margie wrote, in the letter submit-
ting the Coconut computer for consideration in the *Information
Times* computer-building contest. She signed the letter from
herself and King, eliding her father's role—they had read that
Martz, a high school dropout, respected only youth—and, two
weeks later, received a response, on letterhead embossed in gold.
King Rao and Margaret Norman, inventors of the Coconut computer, had been chosen as finalists in the contest and were to present themselves at Martz's headquarters in Palo Alto at a mutually
agreed-upon date.

On that date, three and a half weeks later, King and Margie
stood before a pretty Eichler house on a tree-lined street in down-
town Palo Alto. A wooden crate containing their computer, which
had made the trip along with them in Norman's old sedan, sat at
their feet. The idea was that they would get to present the computer to the club's members, giving them a chance to be among the
first buyers; after seeing all the presentations, the members would

vote on the best ones. But, having hit traffic on I-5, King and Margie were a half-hour late. Margie pulled the letter from the pocket of her jeans, and they squinted at it, and at the brass numbers lit by the porch light, and back at the paper again.

Could this really be the headquarters? They were contemplating whether to knock when a woman in her fifties or sixties opened the door. She wore a tan-colored pantsuit and had short grayish blond hair. She smiled at them. "Hello?" she said.

"Hello, we're looking for Mr. Martz?" Margie said.

"Mr.—" the woman repeated, apparently perplexed. Then she laughed: "Oh, *Mr. Martz*. You're *Wally's* friends!" She swung the door open for them, and King and Margie together carefully hoisted the crate. The house was brightly lit and smelled of roasted lamb. To the left of the entryway was a staircase leading down. The woman knelt at the top and put her hands to her mouth. "Wally, your friends are here to see you!" she said.

"Mom, don't call them my friends," a voice hollered from the basement.

"Oh, colleagues!" she sang, teasing. "Mr. Martz! Your colleagues!" She turned to Margie. "There are lamb chops downstairs, dear."

They had expected a big crowd, fifty or sixty people. Instead, descending the stairs with the crate, they found a dozen young men who looked to be in their twenties and thirties, scattered on the carpet and on a couple of sunken couches, bent over paper plates of lamb chops and potatoes. The room smelled of meat and stale pot. The oldest-looking one, bearish and bearded, stood from a couch, eyeing the crate they carried.

"Walter?" Margie said. "Wally?"

"That's me," he said. He was a blunted, red-faced man with a patchy beard and a paunch pressed tightly against a plaid button-down shirt. He looked to be forty, at least. Later they would learn he was only thirty, not much older than them. "You're late," he remarked.

"Traffic," Margie said.

Walter apologized that the lamb chops were all gone; he hadn't been sure the two of them were going to show up. He cleared the cutting board from a table in the middle of the room and sprayed the surface with Lysol, which he wiped down with a handful of paper towels, and gestured for them to place the computer there.

"Listen up, friends," Walter said to the gathered men. "Meet King and Margaret, finalists number eight. Let's give them a warm welcome."

The men, clapping dutifully, looked toward King and the crate, which he and Margie had lifted into place. King blinked at his audience. "Ready, Margie?" he said, and together they unlatched the crate's lid on all four sides, lifted the top, and set it down on the floor. King turned a crank on the side of the crate facing him, which released the four sides until they were flat, revealing the computer: a hard drive, monitor, and keyboard all combined into one television-sized machine, encased in cream-colored plastic.

King moved around the table so he was facing the computer, his back to the audience. He flipped a switch to turn the device on, and a bright blue screen lit the room. Letter by letter, text scrolled onto the screen. HI. I'M COCONUT. He typed, and his command to the computer appeared across the screen below that line. INTRO-DUCE YOURSELF OUT LOUD. When he pressed enter, a tinny voice issued from the machine: "Hi. I'm Coconut."

This was sleight of hand more than anything. He had rigged up this program to do little more than what he had shown them. The audience knew this as well as he did. Still, the fact that such a pro-gram could be written—one that invited the machine to respond to natural human commands, rather than flipped switches—was extraordinary. They wanted to know what the programming lan-guage was (a custom floating-point BASIC) and who had built the computer itself (their hardware team, with design guidance from Margie here, a trained artist).

And what did the kit include?

Yes, well, he said, that was the fun part. Everyone else was sell-ing kits that hobbyists could use to build their own computers, but they, the Coconut Computer Corporation, were offering the computer itself, fully built, for just $999. But now, a burst of laughter erupted from the back of the room. "You're trying to charge people a thousand dollars for a computer they can't even put together, with a software language they can't write in?" someone said. "Where's the fun in that?"

King was hesitating—he saw the man's point—when Margie jumped in. "The fun is that in ten years, this computer will be sitting in the home of every family in the developed world," she said firmly. "The fun is that we're not just selling people a machine; any idiot can own a machine." Coconut's proposition, she said, was to give the people in this room a chance to write the first programs for the computer, thus becoming pioneers in the computer revolution. The room was silent. The heckler appeared to have been cowed, until he muttered, "The Coconut . . . sure, sounds serious." Others chuckled. King cleared his throat and announced the phone number they could call if they wanted to preorder one of these superlative machines. No one pulled out a pen.

Afterward, Walter helped them load the computer into the backseat of Margie's car. It was a cool, quiet night. They could hear only the rustle of the leaves and the laughter, from the basement, of the guys still in there. Maybe, King said, they had overreached, gone too far. Walter rubbed his beard and sighed, as if considering this. But then he said, with a flat, unreadable expression, "Too far for a bunch of mental cripples. I wouldn't lose sleep over that." What they had come up with was remarkable. If King had designed a language that could handle a program like the one he had shown them, it was the most advanced operating system he had seen on a microcomputer. Plus, he said, turning to Margie, the computer was physically beautiful. He went to the front door to call for his mother, conferred with her a moment, and came back to them with a check made out, in her handwriting, for $999, so that the first-ever sale by the Coconut Computer Corporation, one late-summer evening in 1975, was to a blondish gray, pantsuited retiree who wrote, on the "for" line of the check, "computer for Wally."

Back on the freeway, headed north, my father cried, "Well, this is what they call the American Dream!" and hit the glove compartment with the heel of his hand, as Margie drove them home, through the mountains at the California-Oregon border, past the logging villages and the towns made up only of neon-signed motels and gas stations and strip clubs to service the drivers who hauled all that timber from Oregon to the subdivided suburbs that were being built up and down the Pacific states. "If you're smart, ambitious, and talented, you're rewarded! You get to change— foreign student to inventor, businessman!" They had, with their own brains and hands, conjured a computer, and someone had bought it. My father held the check in his hands and periodically gazed at it, enraptured.

"It's just one order, from the man's *mother*," Margie said, laughing, but she was pleased, too, he could tell.

"There'll be more!" King cried. Something was happening here.

When they arrived home in the morning, he put his finger on the doorbell and held it down, while Margie stood behind him giggling. Norman came to the door wearing a bathrobe over his flannel pajamas, muttering, "Jesus, why the doorbell? I thought you were some cop coming here to tell me that my daughter was killed on the road on the way home—" but then he fastened his eyes on the check and reached for it.

"Just hold on," King said. "You'll rip it." His first display of independence. What had happened in Palo Alto—he and Margie had pulled it off by themselves. Anyone could build a box. But King had animated that box with his code, and Margie had come up with the design and sold Walter Martz on it all. King unfolded the check and held it out. "Nine hundred and ninety-nine dollars," he said. The number filled his head. He couldn't help grinning. "Not bad, huh?"

But Norman tightened his bathrobe and frowned at the check. "That's all?"

"It's a thousand dollars!"

"It's only one sale."

"That's not how it works," he said. "It takes time. Remember, this is about the contest." He could hear the sullenness in his voice, as if Norman were his own father. What had he expected— flowers, fireworks, a cake? He should have listened to Margie, who had suggested they just go to sleep, tell Norman later.

"Go get some rest, kids," Norman said, and then he looked from Margaret to King and back to Margaret—the quickest glance, right, left, right—and added flatly, "King, we've got to get you back into campus housing."

Norman was right to be circumspect. For the rest of the month, no more preorders appeared. Margaret got King's housing stipend restarted and found him an apartment just off-campus before the fall semester began. Then one morning, in their shared office, Norman told King he was ready to shut down the business—liquidate the meager bank account and move on. King related this to Margaret in the little office as she clacked on her typewriter. It wasn't clear whether she was paying attention to him. Sometimes, when he came in and talked to her, she didn't even acknowledge his presence; at other times, she would look up and make some remark that made clear she had been listening closely the entire time.

He willed her to rise and cross the room—to retrieve more paper, fill her cup of water, whatever—so he could admire her fair, strong-shinned legs. But she didn't get up. As usual, she sat at her desk and typed. He flushed and crossed to his cubbyhole, to rummage through its contents. A note from a student, on a folded sheet of loose-leaf, requesting a meeting to discuss raising his grade. A thin sheet of folded paper reminding him that he still owed the hospital thirty-four dollars for his emergency room visit. The latest issue of *IT*.

He unfolded the newsletter. On the cover was a blurry black-and-white image of a box, and behind it, a pair of figures, a tall woman and a smallish man. For a moment he couldn't quite understand what he was looking at. Then it became clear. It was himself and Margie, standing behind that table in Walter's basement, about to unveil the Coconut. "The Machine in This Box

Will Revolutionize Computing," the headline said. King called Margie's name. "Hey, it's not possible we *won*, is it?" he said, but before he crossed the room to show her what he was holding in his hand, her phone was ringing.

God bless all those fourteen- and fifteen-year-olds with their mothers' checkbooks, timidly murmuring, "I'm calling to order a Coconut?" at which Margaret would lower her voice to a flirtatious contralto, responding, "Sure, honey, what's your name?" while King, pacing the department office, grinned madly at her. By the end of the month, they had eight hundred orders. God bless America.

FOUR YEARS LATER, the Coconut Corporation moved out of the yurt and into a couple of rented, beige-carpeted rooms in a two-story building that Margie had found on Bainbridge's main drag, a road of kitsch shops and mom-and-pops. King and Margie each rented an apartment in a building three doors down. King had all but abandoned his graduate program, taking classes one at a time only to maintain his immigration status. Most of Coconut's building was occupied by a small telemarketing firm, and it smelled of cigarette smoke and salted snacks. Sometimes one particular telemarketer, a mid-teenager, came by to offer them pizza, and stood in the doorway flirting with Margie. "Leave it alone, man. I'm married," she finally called out from her desk, her green eyes flashing.

"How come you don't have a ring?" the kid demanded.

"It's not part of our religion?" she said.

"Whose religion?"

"We're Hindus," she said, and when she turned to King, who was cross-legged on the floor, and added, "Right, babe?" he thought he might explode with embarrassment, pleasure, and terror. The telemarketer backed off in confusion. Norman, from his little office, emitted a grunt.

Margie laughed, and King did, too. But inside, he was thinking of what she had said. The fact that she considered marrying him a reasonable enough prospect that she would fake it, even to ward off suitors, was as thrilling as if she'd just proposed to him. He knew he was inexperienced compared with Americans his age. Then there was the whiteness of it all: the whiteness she represented. Margie was not just a white woman. Her complexion was almost translucent, ghostlike, a degree of paleness he never would have known possible had he not come here. Nor was he just brown. Even by Indian standards, he was too brown, a shameful shade of it, untouchable.

The truth was that he shared the telemarketer's shock at the notion of such a union. It was 1979, the *Loving v. Virginia* decision just over a decade old. To even imagine being with Margie Norman seemed improper, which made her all the more desirable.

They had hired six more engineers, on contract, but King and Margie spent more time in the office than anyone. Norman, the CEO, increasingly holed himself up in his little room, brooding and bewildered. Every generation, Margie noted, could lay claim to a world-changing invention. The printing press. The steam engine. The airplane. The automobile. In this generation, that invention happened to be the microcomputer, and they were simply going to have the best one on the market. Their strategy, Margaret and King's, was to get young Coconut owners so excited that they would all start writing programs for it, before Computa had even released its first microcomputer. The more programs that got written, the more Coconut's advantage compounded.

Four years after the trip to Palo Alto that started this all, their computers were the most popular on the market. Two years ago, they had released the Coconut II and sold thousands. But Norman was concerned. The latter part of the seventies had brought a computing boom, and while Coconut held certain advantages over its competitors—Norman's investor friends, King's software, first-mover advantage—their success was hardly guaranteed. The buyers of the Coconut I and II had been hobbyists learning to program in Coconut BASIC. But the new product they were developing, the Coconut III, was meant for the masses. These people didn't care who your investors were, how good your software was, whether you were the first to market. These people would buy the Coconut for the same reason that anyone buys gadgets: because they're useful, because they're inviting.

Now Computa, a multibillion-dollar corporation employing the best computer engineers in the world, was about to introduce a competitor. When it brought one to market, what would persuade someone to buy their little machine instead of Computa's?

The Coconut III had to appear warm and familiar—cute, as Margie put it—not like the computers of the past, with their sharp corners, loud fans, and red lights flickering like controls in a cockpit. If it were a car, it would be a Beetle. Margie lured a whole doctoral program's worth of materials experts from MIT to come up with a plastic casing for the Coconut that would be as strong and impermeable as ever, but would yield slightly to the touch. She also became obsessed with finding what she called the warmest color in the world, and for months her designers would bring her new swatches to consider, each of which she dismissed with unconcealed irritation.

Margie often said they should be building a Coconut that your mother would love. Whenever she said it, he thought, with anxiety, about his own mother. He couldn't even picture what she was doing back home, how she was filling her time. There were only a couple of phones in the village, and using them, especially for international calls, was prohibitively expensive. Once a month, he wired cash to her, but their letters had grown more infrequent. The last one he had written was about Coconut. He had told her, finally, about Norman and Margie, about the trip to Palo Alto, about the success they were having. His mother had responded, in her next letter, tersely: "The money came. All fine here. Glad you are fine." He intuited that she was upset with him. She did not have to list the reasons: because he had started a company instead of working for an established one; because he had taken an overnight road trip with a girl, a white girl; because despite all of his supposed accomplishments he had not yet visited home—all of the above. But his mother's existence seemed so distant from his own. What news could he offer that she would understand?

One afternoon, King emerged from the elevator on Margie's floor, flanked by the rest of the management team, singing happy birthday to her, happy birthday to her! He held a large rectangular cake. He set it on the table in the center of the room where the designers displayed their prototypes to Margie each morning. The frosting was a quiet buttercream, and the gold-leaf text, HAPPY TWENTY-FIFTH, M, didn't include numerals because Margie hated how they looked when set next to letters. Margie looked at the cake, and at King, and back at the cake, and grinned. He loved her—how he loved her. When he brought out a knife, she cried, "Stop!" They couldn't eat it. The perfect design had found her.

IN THE FIRST-EVER television advertisement for a Coconut, conceptualized by Margie and aired nationally, a cute, rambunctious ganglet of children—boys and girls of all sizes and races—have taken over a suburban street. Several pile into a human pyramid. Others leap from the branches of trees. We see the sun lowering to the horizon, and the shadows lengthening on the asphalt. The camera zooms in on the front doors of the neighborhood houses as, one by one, they open to reveal parents and grandparents and older siblings calling for the children to come indoors. "I made meat loaf," one mother calls. "Spaghetti for dinner," an older brother offers. They might as well be mute. The children do not even turn their heads. They are sweet but feral. Another door opens. This time, the father at the door—a handsome, gray-templed man, radiating rays of kindness from the corners of his eyes, an apron tied across his waist—cradles in his forearms what appears to be a huge rectangular cake, frosted with some sort of buttercream.

"Ellie," this father calls.

The camera pans to a tree where a scuffed-up tomboy hangs

from a limb. A bright, curious look crosses her face. She drops from the tree, lands on her feet, wipes off her knees. She takes off running toward her father as the others turn to watch. The camera pans back to her father, then zooms onto a logo on the corner of whatever he is holding: not dessert at all but the Coconut III. The next shot is of father and daughter sitting next to each other in front of a glowing computer screen framed by the same buttercream plastic as the hard drive. The hard drive sits underneath it. The father and daughter lean in, smiling, as if into the glow of a fireplace, and though we can't see what's on the monitor, we know it must be wonderful. Across the bottom of the TV screen scrolls—for the first time—the advertising slogan that would, in the years to come, become more identified with Coconut than with the Liverpudlians who came up with it in the first place. COME TOGETHER, it says.

14

Arno led me along the shoreline toward the northeast. I trudged behind him, my dry bag slung over a shoulder. It was a hot morning, the sky cloudless, the scent of cedar and pine hanging pleasantly in the air, just as it did on my own island. I could trick myself into feeling an ambient familiarity. I shouldn't have blindly followed this man, it occurred to me, but it seemed too late to change my mind. He was strong-looking, despite his paunch, and knew the terrain. Suppose I took off running: He'd chase me down if he was dangerous, or stand there and let me go if he wasn't, in which case I would be on my own again. Neither option seemed ideal.

We had walked for at least a half hour in silence, when the forested coastline opened onto an expanse of yellow, treeless land on which a campus of buildings stood. Most of the buildings were rectangular, but in the center were five glass spheres of varying heights, clustered together like giant snow globes. Around them people bustled, some of them pushing wheeled wooden carts, others walking or sitting in the yellow-brown grass. There had to have been a hundred people, at least.

The scene stopped me for a moment, my chest tight, as if someone had pressed a hand to it to hold me back. I recognized this place: It was the campus King and Margie built for Coconut after going public, on the horn-shaped Restoration Point, which jutted into Elliott Bay. The house in which they had spent most of their married life must not be far. I had seen photos in my father's album. Even all these years later, he talked about Restoration Point with pride of ownership, just like he talked about the Garden. It was as if, on some spiritual level, this land still belonged to him.

I had been expecting to see the old Coconut campus at some point, but still the sight startled me. Maybe it was the buildings that did it; maybe it was the people; maybe it was both.

I felt faint. I crouched, my head in my hands, and took some slow, deep breaths. Arno crouched next to me. "You all right?" he said. His concern seemed genuine. It helped. "I'm fine," I said, though I wasn't, and stood and proceeded on.

Arno began to loosen up and chat again. It occurred to me that he had been as afraid in my presence—as much on his guard, as we walked—as I had been. He told me that the buildings, once owned by Coconut, had been repurposed by the Exes for communal use. The spheres, in particular, got good use as greenhouses.

We entered the biggest sphere, the one in the middle. Inside, in a grand, light-filled space filled with plants and trees, were dozens of people. Some were sitting on the ground or on little stools, while others moved around the space, some pushing the same carts I had seen outside. Scattered around the open space were dozens of large transparent cubes sitting on wheels. I recognized them: These were the portable office spaces pioneered by Coconut. Staircases led to higher levels, also filled with greenery and vegetation, where people perched together in giant replicas of bird's nests. I thought of my bald eagle, her eaglets. It was warm, the air humid.

Arno walked up to a lanky Black man with an Afro, who was sitting with his back against the glass wall, reading. The man looked familiar, but without my Clarinet, I couldn't place him.

"Is Elemen around?" Arno asked.

The man looked up at Arno, then at me. "Who's the girl?" he said. His attitude was dismissive, though the dismissiveness seemed directed less at me than at Arno.

"She showed up at my tent this morning!" Arno said. Even I, a novice at human relations, could see he was trying too hard to impress the other man. "A swimmer."

The man raised his eyebrows and gave a terse little nod. "Welcome," he said to me, not smiling. "She's in Edison," he told Arno.

We walked across the big hall until we reached a cube on which the name EDISON was etched.

Inside, a woman sat cross-legged on the floor, pushing a curtain with a pattern of little blue and white flowers onto a rod. Three more rods, and a pile of fabric, lay nearby. "I'm doing curtains," she said as we entered. Noticing me, she added, "Who's this?"

I had never before seen a woman up close. When she stood, hooking her thumbs on the paint-splattered denim overalls she wore, with a loose brown T-shirt underneath, she cut an imposing figure, tall and strong-shouldered. Arno stepped back a little. Here was Elemen Ex. She tilted her head and held me in a sardonic gaze, as if there were something comical about my appearance before her.

A younger version of her appeared in my mind. The weekend of the protests, one hundred thousand people marched northward down Fifth Avenue in Seattle, toward the Shareholder Campus, south of Lake Union. The Exes had demonstrated before, but never at this scale. At nine-thirty p.m., the police began teargassing and arresting people. At midnight, though, the streets were only a little less packed. A young college dropout stood on the roof of someone's dusty Honda Civic, wearing a cropped black tank top and cutoff jean shorts, her hands cupped at her mouth, her voice hoarse from hours' worth of rallying, shouting the impromptu speech that would, years later, be immortalized in history texts.

"What we're doing tonight is historic!" the young woman calling herself Elemen Ex cried. "We're making it known that we reject any system that places commercial value on our consciousness!" She was lanky and jockish, but had a childlike face, with round, red cheeks, her dark hair piled into a plump, careless bun. Toward those assembled, she tossed stacks of leaflets enumerating what, exactly, the Exes stood for. "We demand to opt out of being Shareholders. We demand to have our Profiles erased from the public record. We demand autonomous land where we can live and trade with one another outside this system we reject." And then, turning in the direction of the Shareholder Campus: "We demand King Rao's immediate removal from power."

A couple of minutes after one o'clock, a fire alarm began ringing inside the main building of the Shareholder Campus, and the press drones hovering overhead captured smoke pushing through the lower windows and, within minutes, filling the building. An elderly man in a custodial uniform ran out, coughing, covering his eyes: "There's people inside! There's a little girl!" From where Elemen stood, she wouldn't have been aware of any of those details. Atop of the car she had commandeered as her stage, she raised a fist and led the crowd in chanting, "Burn it down! Burn it down!" She was eighteen.

No photographs of Elemen Ex had been published in the intervening decades. Of course she had changed: More than twenty years had passed. She had not only aged, but had grown more authoritative-looking, too, her lankiness maturing into a mannish, shoulder-first stance. Her mess of curly dark brown hair contained a few graying strands. She had an olive-complected, moon-shaped face. A matrix of fine lines was drawn around her eyes and across her forehead. Something unfamiliar pulsed in me. She was beautiful.

"A swimmer," Arno said, again. "She showed up at my tent, and I brought her straight here."

A flicker of hesitation crossed Elemen's face—did she recognize me?—but then she laughed. "*Straight* here, though?" she said. Her voice surprised me. It was deep, her cadence languorous, as if we had all the time in the world.

"I'm serious, nothing happened."

When she turned toward me, I stiffened. "You all right?" she said gently.

"I'm fine!" I said. My voice came out brighter than I had intended.

Arno took a deep breath and blew it out. "Nothing happened, man," he said. "Listen, I rubbed her feet, and I gave her a can of beets. But that's it." He seemed to be avoiding eye contact with me. "That's all," he said quietly.

"A foot rub for a can of beets," Elemen said.

The two of them were staring at each other, in some standoff whose terms I couldn't grasp. "I'm not from here," I interjected, feeling badly for Arno. "He offered to make an introduction."

"That's generous of him," Elemen said, without looking away from Arno. "For future reference, no more foot rubs for beets." She looked at Arno as if giving him permission to leave.

He stood there for a moment and then said, in a small voice, "What about the finder's fee?"

"Arno!" she cackled. "What about the foot rub?"

When Arno left, shoulders hunched in defeat, Elemen stepped back and assessed me with a long, probing stare. Finally, as if she had decided something about me, she smiled. It was an unexpected smile, gentle and kind. A bunch of bedrolls were propped against one corner of the room. Elemen grabbed one and laid it out. Its ends curled up. "We all keep our own sheets—I'll get you some—but no one here has ownership over space. If you're tired and you see a bedroll and an empty spot, you go ahead and use it." She sat on the bedroll and patted it next to her. It was much softer than I had expected, too soft. When I sat, I sank into it. Our thighs touched.

"The foot rub," I said. I had the urge to explain myself.

"No, no, no, no." She held up her hands and shook her head. "He owed me an explanation—he can't pretend to bring me a fresh recruit if he's already transacted with her—but you don't owe me shit. You just got here." She looked at me again, assessing. I could smell her breath, sour and a little fruity. To be this close to a human being other than my father. For it to be such a person as this.

"So have you eaten or what? I mean, besides the beets?" She gave a honking, joyful laugh.

I said I hadn't eaten. Not besides the beets, I said, and ventured a smile, testing.

She smiled, too. "Me neither," she said. She touched my thigh, then stood and left the room.

I sat there, watching the doorway. She seemed so herself in the world. Come back, I thought. Let me inspect you. Let me peer under your fingernails awhile. It was an inscrutable, unnameable feeling. It was made in part of admiration and fascination. But twisted up in there was also an obscure longing. It didn't feel romantic, though I couldn't be sure it wasn't, either. What a novice I was: at all of this, at life. My thigh burned, still, at the contact with hers.

On the wall opposite the cot, someone had painted a Thomas Edison quote. "I find out what the world needs," it said. "Then I go ahead and try to invent it." The paint was faded. It took me a minute to register that all of this—the room named Edison, the quote on the wall—had been put here when the building still belonged to Coconut. I was sitting in an old conference room that the Exes had turned into a dorm. The open space outside must have once been filled with desks. I tried to picture my father as a young man, striding around the building, in charge, but my imagination, in his absence, failed me. I could only picture him as he had been when I left, as an old and frail man, losing his senses. I could only picture him in his dissolution.

My God, I must have terrified him, leaving like that. I imagined him asking around the Ex markets, trying to describe a missing girl, without giving away his identity or mine. People would take him for some jilted pimp. Would they recognize who he was describing? Would they, for a high enough offer, give me up?

Elemen was gone a long time. When she returned, with a plate of fried eggs, a pair of them, with crisped edges and trembling, deep orange yolks, I was overcome with relief. She scooped an egg into one hand. "Go ahead," she said. I picked up the other, and we sat there together, stuffing the soft, wobbling things into our mouths. I felt warm in her presence, taken care of.

"So, listen, let me explain," she said, with a businesslike little nod. "People think I'm all-powerful, but no one here is all-powerful—that's the point," she said. "I do have a role, which is to run the night workers' association. If I catch some fucking idiot like Arno Glad trying to make a side arrangement with a girl, the union's the best tool I have. Arno's a member of the pharmaceutical group. If he really steps out of line, I can kick him out. Or if it's a smaller infraction, like this one, I can get a favor out of him in payment. And the girl gets the option of joining the union." She smiled wryly. "This must not be the utopian vision you had in mind."

How little I understood, though—not enough to have any vision, utopian or not. Unlike Edison, I had no idea of what the world needed. "I didn't have anything in mind," I said quietly.

She smiled a little. "How old are you, kiddo?" she said.

I thought of lying, naming some adult age. Then I thought of what adulthood would require of me in this place, and told the truth: "Seventeen."

She looked at me, as if she were trying to figure out whether I was a waste of her time or not. "I have a couple of minutes," she finally said, in a tone of some indifference. "Let me give you a tour."

I FOLLOWED HER OUTSIDE. In old pictures, Coconut's glass-walled campus is so clean and well maintained that it appears to gleam. Now the glass was clouded, some parts even cracked or broken, patched over with big drapes of canvas. The grass between the buildings was patchy. But despite these imperfections, the setting was quite beautiful. To our left, the tip of Restoration Point stretched out into Elliott Bay. To our right was a wide avenue.

It was the island's main thoroughfare, Elemen said, leading west-ward along the northern shore of Restoration Point, then curving north. It was filled with traffic—people walking, biking, or riding in carts in either direction. The avenue ended near us, at a sort of parking lot where people left their bikes and carts after using them, to be picked up, apparently, by whoever needed one as they were leaving campus.

Along the dirt paths connecting the campus's buildings, most people walked, some pushing carts containing food—bread, fruit—or other staples. I kept seeing carts filled with toaster-sized black boxes, which pedestrians would reach in and grab, with a nod or smile of acknowledgment to the cart-pusher, as they passed. There were single people, couples, groups of friends, families. One little girl, red-haired and suntanned, sat in a cart atop a stack of those mysterious boxes, shouting, "I'm bigger than anyone here!" while her father pushed, nodding, with the sort of fading amusement that suggested she'd been repeating this announcement for some time.

Elemen led me toward the parking area, where she gestured for me to get on a bicycle and mounted one herself. "Come on," she said, biking toward the main road. I had a bike back on Blake Island, but having to navigate pedestrians and other cyclists was unfamiliar and distracting. We rode in silence, the avenue shaded by Douglas firs rising on the left side of the road, until we arrived at a spot on the water's edge facing Seattle and Elemen gestured at me to stop. We dismounted our bikes and stood by the water.

"No one's counted how many of us live here; we don't care to count. But it's a lot more than the Board lets on," Elemen said. "If you multiply that by the number of islands in the Blanklands— more than a hundred of them—that makes a lot of us."

"Where did everyone come from?" I said. "I mean, what brought them here?"

She shrugged. "Some came on principle, especially at first. A lot came to hide," she said. "But, listen, don't ask anyone what brought them here; people don't like that."

I'm one of them, I might have said. I'm a person in hiding. But she didn't ask. By the time we returned to campus, the sun was high and hot. I wiped sweat from my brow and upper lip. We parked the bikes, and Elemen walked me back to the building and to the room where I had met her. Three women were inside, each sitting on a bedroll in her pajamas, though it was noon. They were deep in conversation but looked up and stopped talking when we entered.

"Meet your new roommate," Elemen said to them. "Be nice to her. Give her the lay of the land."

A soft smell emanated from the women, floral and hidrotic. After Elemen left, I stood awkwardly in the doorway. They introduced themselves, in turn, as Aurelia, Susan, and Magic. "Those aren't our birth names," explained Magic, who looked to be the youngest, though still older than me, maybe in her mid-twenties. "You can choose a different one, too, if you want." She was curvy and petite, with long, dark hair and bright eyes; she looked Latina.

Aurelia, who resembled Magic but seemed a little older, said, "No, stupid, she *should* choose a different one." She added, gesturing at Magic, "She's my sister."

The women all regarded me expectantly, and when I didn't respond, Susan, who looked to be in her sixties, a white woman with short, graying hair, scoffed and said, with a note of accusation, "She's mysterious. Let's call her Mystie."

And it gladdened me, this second naming. It made me feel I could belong to the world outside Blake Island, to the world of people.

Magic explained that they had all arrived around the same time, about six weeks earlier. "I'm going to tell you all the things it took us a long time to figure out," Magic said.

"HERE ON BAINBRIDGE, everyone has access to island-made bed-rolls, meals, and treated water," Magic explained. These staples could be found at resource stations around the island, along with devices filled with converted power, called Catches, or you could just grab them from a passing cart. I thought of those brick-sized black boxes I had seen piled in carts earlier; those must have been Catches. "You can even sign up for time on a computer, if you want," Magic said.

"I thought computers weren't allowed here," I said.

"You thought Exes hate technology, right?" she said. "Well, that's never been true. People here are fine with tools, fine with systems. It's just that they need to be available to anyone, and they need to make people's lives better, not worse."

Magic explained that I was at the beginning of a one-month grace period Exes call "settling-in," during which nothing would be expected of me. After that, though, I would have to start help-ing to sustain life in the Blanklands; I would have to make myself useful. "You could keep doing whatever you did back home. Teachers, nurses, everyone loves them here," she said. I must have had a stricken expression—I had no real skills—because she added kindly, "That's okay, you can get trained during settling-in, too."

All workers had their own sector-wide unions, led by elected members—"like Elemen, for us," she said, indicating herself and the others. The workers paid dues, which the unions spent on their behalf, for example paying into a mutual-use fund for health, education, and so on. Night work varied, and it didn't all happen at night. You could manufacture, test, or traffic drugs; you could sell your eggs or sperm; if you were a young enough woman, you could be a surrogate child bearer for mainland families, which Elemen had herself spent many years doing.

Magic and her sister, along with Susan, whom they had met after arriving here, had chosen the same occupation, sex work, which all three had done back home. "Arno discovered you, right?" Magic said. "That's probably why she put you in here with us."

I thought of Arno's foot rub and looked away, trying to hold in my mortification.

"Oh, come on, there's no shame in it!" She laughed, a little harshly, as if I had offended her. "It is what it is."

Since Exes boycotted Shareholder goods and services, a lot of the products on the island were made locally—what people ate;

what they wore. A solar farm on the island generated much of the power needed in summertime, and the rest was imported. Each of the Blanklands islands now had at least one solar or wind farm, a major milestone they had reached about five years earlier. Communication and trade among the Blanklands was informal, managed not by treaties but by a sense of common purpose. The Board kept tabs on the shipping lanes, in keeping with the terms of the agreement that established the Blanklands, but they left the islands alone, as long as they didn't see a security threat.

Yet Exes were fine with *selling* to Shareholders, she explained, or accepting their donations. Shareholder guilt, among those who agreed with the Exes but couldn't bear to give up the comforts of Shareholder life, was a powerful force. Where it wasn't possible to get what was needed through local production or trade with other parts of the Blanklands, it could be gotten, more often than not, through in-kind donations from Shareholders. All the computers, for example, were donated.

As for the grisly lore I must have heard about the Blanklands—boar maulings, food shortages, and all that—I'd see for myself that it was overblown, she said. There had been a handful of incidents early on. But Exes had quickly learned to protect themselves and one another in the wild. They had passed that information to newcomers. The residents of each island community—not just Bainbridge—had grown close with one another, and, in turn, violent crime had fallen. People had put aside their old animosities: There could be only one tribe now. Shortages and outages were rare, too, with Exes having figured out how to trade. Here was a system of government where position and well-being were guaranteed to all, freeing people up to other possibilities for making meaning of life. Day-to-day existence was still difficult. That couldn't be avoided. But Magic didn't regret coming here, not for one second.

That evening, Magic, Susan, and Aurelia pulled on clean jeans, shirts, and flannels. "Come see us off!" Magic said. Outside, a crowd of dozens of women, all dressed casually, were heading toward the marina just south of the tip of Restoration Point. Elemen led the caravan, walking with the brisk confidence of a person who is sure she is being followed. The other women kept pace, in groups of two, three, or four, making quiet but animated conversation. There was something peculiar to me about the way they moved, elegantly, like cats, especially in comparison to my bulldog of a father, and about the intimacy of their conversations, which I could discern less from the bits I overheard than from their body language, the way they moved almost in unison, occasionally leaning close or touching, as if dancing. But I was the strange one here, I had to remind myself, still learning what it meant to exist among others.

Magic came over. She explained where they were going, to the floating club east of Bainbridge, in neutral waters. The club, called the Cha Cha, was Ex-run, with Shareholders making up most of the clientele. It was a big source of the Exes' revenue, the main marketplace for their trade in scx, drugs, and other activities that were either illegal or much pricier on the mainland. The marina contained at least a hundred small vessels: kayaks, canoes, motorboats. "Adios," Magic said, giving me a quick hug. She walked out onto the docks along with the other women, and stepped into one of the motorboats. One by one, the boats peeled out of the marina and headed northward, until I was left standing there alone, wondering again what I was here for.

THE NEXT MORNING, my roommates, having returned late, were still sleeping. I dressed quickly, trying not to make too much noise, and slipped out on my own. It was a bright, hot summer morning. Along the dirt paths of the courtyard, men and women pushed handcarts full of good things to eat—apples, strawberries. A woman who looked to be in her fifties, stout, with curly hair pulled back in a ponytail, came toward me with a cart piled with rounds of fresh bread. I couldn't help but gaze hungrily at them. She stopped as she neared. "Lost?" she said.

"No, I'm just looking around," I said, embarrassed. If I had grown up around people, I might have learned not to stare at their food.

"You just got here, right? I saw you with Elemen," she said. She pulled a bread knife from her apron and cut a boule in half. "Breakfast," she said, pressing the bread into my hands, and kept going.

I walked along the dirt path toward the tip of Restoration point, tearing off bits of bread and eating them. The view of the mainland from here was different from the one I was used to. From Blake Island, I could see mostly residential neighborhoods. But this spot looked on to Alki Point, in West Seattle, with its thin strip of beach backing into several blocks of skyscrapers. There were a few families nearby, and some children—three of them— playing together at the water's edge. I kept my distance and tried to observe them without being noticed myself. The children must have been six or seven years old. One of them, a little black-haired girl in a dirty linen dress, cupped some water in her hands and splashed an older boy in the face. I thought he would get angry, but he grinned and splashed her back. She made a sound; at first I thought she was crying, but, no, she was laughing.

I had been feeling, for once, peaceful. But my misreading of the situation unsettled me. Get up, I told myself, and escape the presence of these human beings before they recognize you for what you are: an interloper, an alien. Run. Slip into the water and swim back home. Maybe, give all that would later transpire, that's what I should have done.

Instead, I doubled down. I vowed to wander that island until I had a mental map of it—not just its physical contours but the social rules governing it. I began waking at sunrise and walking around the island from morning till night. I apprenticed at cooking, cleaning, building, counseling.

Crossing through campus one night, I came across a crowd of people, young and old, who had gathered spontaneously to sing, play music, and dance. A little long-haired boy had flung off his clothes and was turning in circles, flailing his arms joyfully, and at one point an old woman unbuttoned her shirt, threw it off, and joined him. The onlookers laughed, unfazed. A woman with a bread cart came around and tossed baguettes and boules at the crowd; each person who caught one tore off a chunk, then handed the bread to their neighbor. Much was accepted. You could eat with your fingers if you wanted, which most people in fact did, because utensils were scarce. You could have twelve children or none, twelve partners or none. Often old-timers pointed out to me that this was what life used to be like everywhere, once upon a time. In one manner of seeing it, they weren't the ones violating the natural order of things at all.

The days shortened. Come winter, after the harvest, everyone would nest, telling jokes and stories indoors, eating the vegetables they had canned and pickled, and growing satisfyingly fat. I imagined myself pulling pickled beans from a jar, snapping them with my teeth. I imagined myself still being here in the winter. But then I thought of my father. He came into my dreams at night. I dreamed of him sitting in front of his computer, aglow in its blue light, trying to code his way to an understanding about what had become of his daughter. In the morning, I would awaken in a gloomy mood. Why *hadn't* he found me, after all this time?

COULD IT BE that, in his dissolution, my father had been waking up forgetting that I was missing in the first place? Could it be that he had been sitting around all this time imagining that I was only out in the woods, that I would return any minute? If he was trying to find me, he must not be trying very hard. Now it occurred to me that, on some level, I had counted on being caught. I had counted on ending up on a boat to Blake Island with him, both of us stewing in silence, my adventure over. I hadn't considered what it would mean to make a life elsewhere, without him. I hadn't considered staying.

A month after my arrival, I was no closer to finding a calling, a reason for being here. Elemen Ex, too, seemed to have forgotten me. When I glimpsed her around campus, I would try to catch her attention, but she would just wave and keep going. Maybe she wasn't particularly interested in my plans. I was no one to her; girls like me showed up all the time. Yet I couldn't help but feel, maybe childishly, that she was meant to be a guiding spirit for me. I asked my roommates about her, discreetly, I thought. But they quickly figured out that I had a crush.

"Careful, girl," Susan warned, shaking her head. "Elemen's charming, but you don't want to get caught up with her people. Plus, she could be your mother." I said, with more of an edge than I intended, "I don't have a mother," at which Susan brightened, as if she had discovered something important about me. "Oh, so that's it," she said.

"It's a lose-lose, man," Magic interjected. Magic was constantly brushing her glossy hair. I would find strands of it all over the room, on my own mattress sometimes. Besides that, I liked her. She was different from me, short, big-assed, and at home in the world of people. "I was close with Elemen when I got here, but I never joined up with her people. I got picked up around that time. My date took me an inch into Shareholder waters, and the cops jumped right on his ass. They wouldn't let me go: 'You're one of Elemen Ex's girls. How's she doing?' It's all intelligence-gathering." She ran her fingers through her hair, and examined her hand. "If you get in with that crowd and the cops catch you, you're in trouble."

Later, I found Magic in one of the kitchens. I sat on the counter while she emptied a can of beans into a pot and rinsed them. The water foamed; she poured it out. She put the pot of beans on the stove and stirred them with a wooden spoon while the steam rose. "So where does Elemen sleep at night?" I asked her. Magic filled me in. She stayed with her friends, the first Exes—the ones who remained political—in a house just southwest of the Coconut campus. The Board wanted people to believe the Exes were defunct as a political movement, Magic said, but the reality was more complicated than that. To create a functioning society in the Blanklands—to prove it was possible—was in itself a political act. Elemen and her friends were organizing a new way of life, so that when the mainland was ready for it, they would have something to offer.

Magic fielded my questions with patience. What if someone wanted to learn more about this planning? Where would they find information? Magic laughed ruefully. If some idiota had such a big crush on Elemen that she would trade her own well-being to impress her, that would be rare, and Elemen would sense it. She would come to this idiota herself. She wouldn't want to be chased down. If someone was too eager, that would only make her suspicious that the person was spying for the Board. Magic poured the warmed-up beans into a bowl and held it out to me. Did the idiota want some? The idiota wasn't a spy, was she?

15

"This rascal is too brave, like Radha," Chinna told Sita. "That's why he wandered off and got in trouble with that damn cripple." Chinna didn't mention Gun, but he must have been thinking of the eldest cousin's departure, too. He must have been feeling partly responsible for letting it happen, and for making sure it didn't happen again. "If we don't channel these kids' restlessness, it'll sour and go bad."

It was their good luck that King was ready to start school. Sita sent him off each morning along with the older children, his face ghosted with powder and his hair slicked with oil. On afternoons when Chinna was in the village doing business, he stopped by Appayya's school with sweets. Whenever he came through the door, the heads of King's classmates swerved like sunflower blooms. Chinna Rao was an important person, and King felt proud to be his nephew.

Learning came easily to him. Coming home from school in the afternoons, he regaled his cousins with the English words he had learned, *horrible*, *vowel*, and stunned them with his ability to add one triple-digit number to another in five seconds flat. Even his aunts and uncles changed their manner. They used to talk down to him because he was a child. Now it was as if they talked up at him, presenting their own English words to him like jewels they were proud to display, *sorry, mutton, thank you, officer.*

On cool Saturday evenings, everyone would emerge from their huts carrying stools and wooden crates and gather in the clearing between the Big House and King's House, the men to play cards, the women to gossip. Chinna had built a ladder up to the high, lofted space in King's House where the coconuts were stored above the room. A shuttered window up there could be jimmied open to face the clearing and let the light in. That's where King spent much of his time, with the coconuts as company. He used to trail his older cousins around the clearing, pleased to participate in whatever game they had invented. Now he sat studying in his loft and watched from above, feeling separate from them. It was nice to have his own space, to be distinct and special among the Raos. He mattered not because he was a Rao, in general, but because he was King Rao, in particular.

One evening when he was nine, his cousin Pinky, Gun's younger brother, climbed up the ladder to the loft with a favor to ask. He wanted King to read a letter. It was from Gun, Pinky whispered. No one had heard from him since he had left four years earlier.

Pinky, I'm dictating this letter to you. I found someone to write it for me. How's Amma? Inky, Laddu, Ram Babu? Jaggayyamma and the girls? I'm working in a limestone quarry. You can earn good money breaking up the rocks. They need more workers, so if you want to come, come. The name of the place is on the envelope. Hurry, because if you take too long, I might be gone, or the work might be. It's good, hard work. Your clothes will be covered in dust, and you'll stink. Liquor: there's a lot of it. Food: less. Whatever's around. So we smell like liquor and spice and sweat. But you work for yourself. No looking over your shoulder to see if your uncle has it out for you. The end of the week, some cash to spend however you want. I've never seen a thing like that at the Garden. There you work as Chinna chooses, eat as Chinna chooses, wear what Chinna chooses. I always wanted to learn to read and write, but he never sent me to school. Dictator Chinna. I bet he's gotten worse. I saw it coming, so I left. Is he letting you go to school? I'm sure he isn't. Come if you want, or don't. I don't care. But you've never seen anything like the sunset in a rock quarry. The rock is white, so it pulls in all the colors of the sunset. We talk about this at work, but now that I'm saying it in this letter, I'm realizing it's corny.

King read the letter aloud and looked up at Pinky, and for a moment the two of them made eye contact and grinned with flushed excitement. He hadn't thought much about Gun in the years since he'd left, except whenever he caught Leelamma by the irrigation well weeping over her son. He would go over and stand with her. She had always been kind to him. Whenever he did think of Gun, he also remembered his own brief escape—those minutes with the one-legged cripple of Kothapalli, drifting across the river, his personhood belonging not to his mother, or father, or uncle, but to himself alone—and felt almost nostalgic. Gun had escaped for good, to a place where even the sun set differently. It seemed, for a moment, as if they would go off together, King and Pinky, to meet him there. But the moment passed. Pinky shoved him and said, "Isn't there more?"

"There isn't. That's the end," King said, and he folded the letter and thrust it back at Pinky.

Three days passed. Then, early one morning, Leelamma woke everyone by shrieking in the clearing, "Pinky's gone! Pinky's gone!" She had the particular melodramatic streak of beautiful women; it comprised an important part of her beauty. "Oh God, what have I done to deserve this? Pinky's gone, too, now!" She saw King watching from his window and called him down, flapping a piece of paper in the air at him. It turned out Pinky had left a note. It was short and clumsily lettered. " 'I went to Gun,' " King read aloud.

"That's it?" she said. She grabbed the letter back and stared at it.

"Pinky can barely read and write," King said. The Rao children who didn't attend school had learned only a little, picking it up from street signs or from their literate cousins' schoolbooks.

Leelamma flashed her black eyes at him and whacked him in the chest with the flat of her hand. She'd never hit him before. It took him by surprise, the way the air went out of him. "Boy, you think knowing how to read makes you special? You think being King Rao makes you special?" He rubbed his chest and glared at her—he did think so; everyone did—but he didn't respond. She cried, "Pinky told me you read him that letter from Gun; I know all about it. If it weren't for you, Pinky would never have left!" She wailed as if in pain. "And now that Grandfather Rao's dead, who'll take care of me? You think Chinna will? Oh no."

Leelamma was right that Chinna had no sympathy for her. He was more practical-minded than Grandfather Rao, less of a romantic.

Chinna thought there were more important things to worry about than Pinky's departure. The Garden had been drenched in the longest monsoon season anyone could remember. When it rained, you couldn't properly dry coconuts; all you could do was wait.

Less income meant the women had to stretch their groceries further at dinnertime. Their rasam tasted like little more than hot salted water, their husbands grumbled. Leelamma's remaining sons and nephews bore the brunt of the physical labor in the Garden, climbing for coconuts, grading them, doing most of the manual labor required to prepare them for sale, all because their grandfather had been a laborer. But even as Jaggayya and his sons and nephews worked as hard as ever, Chinna had stopped fixing their tools when they broke, stopped sending them to the clinic in town when they pulled muscles. Then their cow, who had been a reliable source of milk and calves, died.

The Raos had options, Jaggayya muttered, they had a good

reputation, they could borrow at a good rate and fix what needed fixing, buy what needed buying, replace what needed replacing. But Chinna refused. It could wait, he said. Jaggayya believed Chinna felt bad about this, but what did that matter to them? Their tools still fell apart. They still felt in the morning as if they hadn't slept at all.

One morning, six more cousins, including another brother of Gun and Pinky's, were discovered to be missing. Jaggayyamma, the eldest daughter of their family, presented a note they had given her the previous night and told her not to open till the morning. In it, they had written that they had gone to join Gun and Pinky. It wasn't clear why they hadn't just left the note for someone to find, as Pinky had; in giving it to Jaggayyamma, they implicated her, in Leelamma's eyes. To punish both her husband and her daughter in one go, Leelamma brought Jaggayya the switch and forced him to lean his daughter over, in the clearing, and whip her across her back. The sound of the whipping brought the other Rao kids running. King stood on the veranda, jostled by the others, watching. Even Jaggayyamma's cat stood and watched, its back stiff.

GUN'S DEPARTURE HAD been acknowledged as a dramatic event, but no one had anticipated how it would unsettle the foundation on which the Garden existed. Eight more cousins gone meant sixteen fewer hands. One morning, when he was twelve, King sat down next to his father in his spot under the twisted prayer tree. "What are you praying for?" he said, not because he really wanted to know but because he could never think of anything else to say to his father.

"You know my troubles as well as anyone," Pedda said. "I told God, my brother's taken over the Garden, just gone and put himself in charge. There's nothing for me to do. But if I don't do anything, if I sit and spend my time praying, they call me lazy. I said, tell me, Lord, what should I do?"

King remembered something Sita had said once—that his

father had a gambler's belief in God. She said Pedda thought he should get something in return for his devotion, which wasn't true belief. "What should you do?" he said.

Pedda gave a mysterious smile. "He said, 'Listen, and I will give you a sign.' "

Oh, a sign, King thought. No wonder no one took Pedda seriously. That was all he ever said. A sign, a sign. But his father lowered his head in a show of piety, closed his eyes, and became very still. For a long time, he sat quietly under the slanted tree, as if he were asleep. Then he opened his eyes and said, a bit irritably, "Well, I listened, but nothing happened." He stood. King stood, too. His father started walking down the path that led from the clearing, past the paddy fields, toward the road. King—out of curiosity, boredom, and something else, too, having to do with wanting to be close with Pedda but not knowing how—followed.

They were halfway down the path when, around a bend in the road, two figures appeared. It was a woman and a girl around King's age, walking past the Garden toward the village center and pulling a big, fat cow behind them with a rope. The woman wore a white sari, browned at the hem from dragging in the dirt. They looked poor, but they had this animal with them. The cow was a slow-moving heifer, he could see as they drew near; though young, she was unhandsome, the color of dried-up grass, with dumb, mooning eyes and a big, barrel-shaped midsection. Something significant was going to happen in their lives. The cow, King thought, was the sign.

The woman in a white sari sang, loudly, "Hello-o-o-o!" At first King thought she was somehow mocking them. Then he realized she was a madwoman. He had seen others on trips to Rajahmundry and beyond, squatting in the gutter, mumbling to themselves. He hated the sight of them.

"My mother's not well," the girl said, in a bold tone that made the statement seem like a demand. The girl was small-boned, underfed, and disheveled, with strangely light eyes—hazel. He couldn't tell whether she was sane.

"Where are you from, girl?" Pedda said.

"Here and there, uncle," the girl said. "We're going to see the doctor. I heard he can cure my mom." She seemed sane, though unusually brash for a girl.

The village doctor, the Hollander, was a professor as well as a doctor. He was studying the transmission of cholera in the Godavari Delta and had chosen Kothapalli as his base. Once the villagers learned that his doctor's oath banned him from turning away sick people, everyone started going to him for all their ailments. The Hollander had opened his clinic in the village center, not far from Appayya's school, and the doctor often visited Appayya to practice his Telugu and talk about worldly matters. It was the Hollander who had tried to save Radha's life after she gave birth to King. That's how King knew the Hollander. But everyone knew the Hollander. You couldn't miss him. He was mostly white, though with a nose perpetually red and peeling from sunburn. He stood more than six feet tall, spoke in a strong booming voice, and was prone to making grand, sweeping arm gestures. He smelled fresh, like just-dried linens. He was the only person in town who owned an automobile, a white Ambassador, though he usually left it parked next to the clinic, since the local roads weren't easily traversable by car, especially when it was raining.

His father smiled. "The Hollander," he said. Most people had good fathers or bad fathers, but either way, they were decisive. His father only stood there shuffling his feet and smiling. His eyes passed over the cow. "Isn't it a lot of trouble, traveling with her?"

"We're going to offer her to the doctor," she said.

"Oh no, the Hollander is from Europe," Pedda said. "He won't know what to do with a cow. But is she for sale?" King suddenly understood what his father was thinking. They had only buffalo and oxen at the Garden, ever since their one cow had died; Chinna had been talking about buying a new one.

The girl laughed crassly and slapped the cow's side. "Sure, uncle," she said. "Are you in the market?"

BACK AT THE GARDEN, the heifer—their heifer—spent her days chewing grass and swatting flies with her tail in the shade of the Big House. When the shade moved, she moved with it. At night, she slept in the cowshed next to King's House. Chinna didn't like that they had gone and purchased a random heifer when he was planning to buy a good one, at market. But, Pedda argued, they needed one now more than ever. What a waste of money to buy milk when they were struggling financially. That cow had appeared like a sign from God.

It was just a coincidence, Chinna insisted. This heifer wasn't the right one for them. There was something sickly about her.

King berated himself for not having spoken up earlier. He had known, when that strange girl offered Pedda the cow, that it would anger Chinna. But he had said nothing. People said he took after Chinna, but what if he really took after Pedda? What if he was fated to be a person of inaction?

One morning, King found a large splinter embedded in the heifer's flared nostril. "Here, girl," he said, yanking the splinter out with his thumb and forefinger. The heifer glared at him, but the next day the blood crusted over, and after that she was like a smitten lover, shy, flirtatious, and grateful for his attention. He loved her, too. He started thinking he had been silent for a reason, back when the heifer had appeared. Maybe she was destined to be with them. Maybe there was a kind of action that merely resembled inaction.

They discovered soon enough why the heifer was so barrel-bodied. She was pregnant. Pedda saw this as a triumph. Their investment would pay for itself if they sold the calf—or else they could keep it, if it was female, and make double the milk. But Chinna brooded and repeated under his breath, Something's wrong with that animal. Secretly, King agreed with Chinna. The cow, though eating and sleeping fine, was lethargic and pale. She produced less milk as her pregnancy progressed. At night King stayed up late watching her, looking for the strange shapes that would form in the round of her belly, as the calf kicked and punched and made itself known to the world, and he loved the calf, too.

One night, he woke to the sound of the heifer moaning deeply. He found her in the cowshed thrashing her tail. Pedda appeared in the doorway holding an oil lamp. "She's going to give birth," he said, and for a moment he stood there with a look of terror on his face. There wasn't time to call the cousin who had training in husbandry. King held the lamp while his father went to work delivering the calf. The lamp cast a dim, flickering light on the animal as she bucked. The sun had begun to rise, and the susurrus of the crickets grew louder. Pedda curled his hand into a fist and pushed it into the cow, then turned to King and whispered, "I don't know how to do this. I'm acting like I do, but I don't."

For a moment the calf seemed to be wailing from inside its mother, but, in fact, the heifer herself was making those sounds. Pedda had worked his hand up inside the animal, and he moved around with his face wrenched and sweaty. When he pulled out a little to readjust, King could see globs of sputum and blood glistening on his skin. King flushed with fear and excitement. "Did you feel it?" he asked, moving closer with the lamp. "What did it feel like?"

His father didn't answer. Then his face spasmed, and he yanked his hand from the cow, with the calf's head in his fist. He collapsed onto the ground, the bloodied calf on top of him. At first, King laughed—a laugh of tension, of confusion. But when Pedda moved out from under the still, pale, mucusy calf and tried to speak, his voice came out garbled, and only then did it dawn on King that something was wrong.

THE HOLLANDER clattered down the rutted trail in his Ambassador and drove right into the clearing, where he stopped so abruptly that a great cloud of dust shot up from the wheels, and the Hollander pitched forward and cried out. Pedda sat on a mat on the veranda where they had brought him. King's uncles had stuffed the stillborn calf into a canvas bag, and Jaggayya had taken it deep into the Garden to bury it—fertilizer. When the Hollander and

Chinna gathered Pedda in their arms, his buttocks sagged between them so that his body made a V shape, his arms and legs loose like the limbs of a wooden doll. They set him in the backseat of the car. Chinna climbed in up front, and the Hollander got behind the steering wheel. The Raos gathered close and peered in, King standing with his palms on the backs of the cousins in front of him and other cousins' palms on his own, all of the Raos crushing upon one another. The Hollander drove back down the path, then down the main road, till they couldn't hear its engine any longer.

In the cowshed, King sat with his palm to the cow's chest and felt only stillness. He put his hand to her belly. It was warm. He didn't move till her belly was cold and rigid as the underside of a boulder. He wept. What are you crying for? a voice inside him chastised. She's dead, he silently replied. Not just her. His mother, too, had died like this, bucking and moaning, bleeding to death. Sita had often recounted the story of his birth and Radha's death over the years, and he had been unmoved. Now he observed the wide pink sores on the cow's thighs, and he wept. The small knob of extra skin at her shoulder blade that was like a blister but hard to the touch. The gummy blackened edges of her lips. He wept for the cow, and for the mother he hadn't known.

"I wonder what they'll do with it," someone said outside.

"Pay the Muslims to get rid of it."

"That's best."

"They'll have to chop her up first."

"Oh, don't talk like that."

"It's only practical."

"Chopping up a cow in the Garden. Doesn't it seem like another bad omen?"

Ever since he had gone off with the cripple, and later the business had faltered, some of the aunts had blamed him for all the Raos' troubles. They thought that by kidnapping King, the cripple had cursed them all. In fact, he'd heard some of them further suggest that he'd been cursed since birth—that any child whose mother dies while giving birth is a cursed child.

"Oh, don't tell me about bad omens. Our business is in trouble because of Chinna's bad management. Everyone knows that." It was Leelamma's voice. "That's why my babies ran off."

Someone gave a short, mirthless laugh and said, "Your babies, your babies."

Someone else walked into the clearing and said, "Have we gotten any word, Sita?"

He heard his mother, in a flat and somewhat annoyed tone, answer, "How could there be any word? They left just now. Am I a magician? Should I read his mind—read the mind of my husband, who I can't understand even if he's standing next to me?"

The next morning, the heifer was bloated and putrid. "Go play," Sita said, but King hovered on the veranda as she paid the neighbor's Muslim houseboy a few rupees and sent him inside the cowshed with a machete. He could hear the thwack of the instrument against the heifer's muscles and wanted to vomit; with each whap, Sita, too, cringed. But when he cried out, she raised her hand as if she would hit him and snapped, "Get out of here!" and finally he heeded her and wandered down the path to the road, kicking a big stone. The Hollander's car tires had left a pair of deep ruts, and overnight they had filled with rain. Mosquitoes swarmed over the greenish water.

magine it—King told Margie, standing in the office one morning, grinning at her; not much had fundamentally changed
between them, her at her desk, tolerating him, while he tried to
keep her attention—imagine a database program that could crawl
through all the digital information stored on a computer and analyze it within minutes. It should be technically possible. It would
be a light version of the database programs that Computa was
already marketing to corporations.

"You could call it the Shell," Margie mused. "Like a coconut
shell."

The Coconut Shell. Using it, a shopkeeper could plug in his sales
every month for the past ten years, and get monthly projections for
another year out. A housewife could input her grocery bills for the
past year, and the Shell would recommend how to cut her budget by
a fifth. If they could get the Coconut to become truly widespread,
they could establish the Shell as the world's most reliable data orga-
nizer, like a computerized filing cabinet. In the future, when the
world's information was digitized—and this would happen, he was
certain of that—they would be right there, ready to sort it all.

The problem was that floppy disks couldn't hold much information, nor could the Coconut's hard drive itself. He dragged Margie to the university library, where they sat on the floor between shelves filled with stiff-spined journals—Margie sitting in her jean shorts with her long, white, strong-shinned legs splayed out before her, King alternately standing and crouched on his haunches. Then, one afternoon, Margie thrust a journal at him and said, "What about this?"

She had discovered a paper describing a hypothetical packet-switching network, like the one Iconocor was developing, that could be used to store information in a distributed way, on multiple machines. " 'The Electro-Safe would not only hold and protect digital information belonging to multiple users, using methods common in academic settings but heretofore unavailable to the mainstream user,' " King read aloud from the abstract. " 'It would also communicate that information to a software program that could analyze the users' information in aggregate at a large scale. Future iterations of these machines might even use a sort of artificial intelligence, based on principles of heuristics, neuroscience, and machine learning, to make better sense of this information.' "

IN THE BEST-KNOWN photograph of Cora Burroughs, the British-born computer scientist who authored the Electro-Safe paper, the subject wears oversized glasses with squarish plastic frames. Her brown hair is thick and unstyled, parted at the center and hanging down in front of her shoulders. Her forehead is deeply ridged, her skin loose around her chin. At the time of publication, Burroughs was on leave from her job as a computer scientist, to recover from a mental breakdown. She had gone to live with her daughter, Lorena, a social worker who served street youth in London and lived in a loft apartment with her young husband, a photographer.

The young women whom Lorena helped, homeless and drug-addled, often crashed on the living room floor. Burroughs tried to teach them basic math skills, the sort required to balance a checkbook. She'd lecture them about how, while many men would have them believe that their bodies are the only useful tool at their disposal, it was their minds alone—she'd jab at her temple with a fingertip—that would get them out of their situation. But Cora Burroughs was a known mental case, the girls generally agreed among themselves, and, moreover, unbeautiful. A pair of the girls would go over to her and, taking her by the elbows, guide her back to her room. Good night, Mrs. Burroughs, good night.

Late at night, Lorena's husband would wander into the living room in his nightshirt and find the girls collapsed in a leggy heap on the floor. This man, Fred Henninger, would later become one of the most recognized artists in the world, but at the time he was a scamp about town who had only recently begun experimenting as an amateur photographer. His aesthetics ran Warholian. His first photograph, now a fixture of a Tate gallery devoted to his work, was a pair of shots of the hollowed-out waifs, asleep, titled *Trash Heap I* and *Trash Heap II*.

Burroughs lost interest in the girls when they rebuffed her. One morning, she was found dead in the London loft, by suicide. Her daughter, bereft, began spending longer days out on the streets, finding girls to help. Left alone with the waifs, Henninger began his own tutoring sessions, distinctly different from Mrs. Burroughs's.

I first encountered Henninger's work long after his death, when his photos became popular backgrounds for memes. His trademark had been that the waifs screamed in many of the photos, and his second wave of fame came when someone on the Internet decided to interpose dialogue bubbles above the heads of the screaming waifs, containing the quotations of famous men of the past. In *Monkeys I*, a dozen girls, white and Black and brown, hang naked from the exposed rafters of an abandoned warehouse in Soho, their mouths wide open, apparently in mid-scream. The speech bubble coming from one girl's mouth reads, "Personally, I enjoy working about eighteen hours a day." Thomas Edison, that one. From the mouth of the girl hanging next to her, "Sloth makes all things difficult, but industry all things easy." Ben Franklin.

The most famous of Henninger's photos, kept in a special room at the Tate, features the two women most important to my father's career—the one crucial to his entrepreneurial triumph, the other for his fall. Henninger's wife, too, had eventually committed suicide, following in her mother's path, after the more pornographic of her husband's photographs came to light and former models began murmuring about sexual violence. He kept living in the same loft apartment, along with his waifs, in what was described by both detractors and admirers as a den of debauched extravagance. The Warrior series was produced late in his career, when he was in his eighties. It begins with *Warrior I*, in which the waif who would become Miss Fit, the international phenom, raises a couch in the air above her, phencyclidine-aided. On the wall behind her, several photographs are hung, including the best-known photo of Henninger's mother-in-law, Cora Burroughs. Burroughs's oversized glasses sit low on the bulbed bridge of her nose, making her eyes appear overlarge and full of disapproval.

I THINK OF THAT image all the time. Miss Fit was my first celebrity idol. She was in her fifties when I was in my young teens, but she had that dewy agelessness of celebrities. She had recently started the trend of going around wearing just a Spandex unitard. It created the illusion that her thighs remained as tight and powerful as in her youth.

In detention, I find myself humming Miss Fit. When the loneliness gets unbearable, I wait for my CO to approach and serenade him with her lyrics. Come on over, come on over, come all over me. The flap in my door bangs open; into the tray falls the payload. "Meal and cola again!" I cry out, still performing. "Woo-hoo!"

THE COCONUT SHELL, Margie's rebrand of the Electro-Safe, would be remembered as Coconut's first major innovation. It used packet-switching to let people transfer their documents to a mainframe computer, where they would then be saved. Walter had convinced Iconocor's founders to sign an exclusive white-label deal with Coconut in exchange for a profile of Iconocor on the cover of *Information Times*. Starting with the soon-to-be-released Coconut IV, machines would come preloaded with the Shell, sold with a modem and starter kit courtesy of Iconocor. To convince people of the value of the Shell, Coconut would offer each user one free upload—a small data file listing all the members of the household using the Coconut, and each of their chosen electronic-mail addresses. Coconut would then build a national electronic-mail address book that any user could access. That part had been Margie's idea, another way to get people hooked.

It was on the strength of the Shell that Norman persuaded his investor friends to give Coconut a large infusion of capital, bringing King along with him to the meetings and introducing him as the technology's inventor, the most brilliant young mind working in this field, bar none.

Then, a month before the launch of the Coconut IV, King opened the mail to find a letter from Computa.

Written by a lawyer, it alleged that the intellectual property behind the product believed to be called the Coconut Shell belonged to Computa. It requested, in that vague and polite manner of despotic organizations everywhere, that Coconut cease and desist the production and sale of the above-mentioned product, or face an intellectual-property lawsuit. Enclosed with the letter was a copy of the latest issue of Walter's newsletter, which contained an exclusive interview with King. Asked how he had come up with the Coconut Shell, he had admitted the idea had originated in a trade magazine: "We stole it."

While the late Cora Burroughs signed her name on the Electro-Safe article without mentioning any affiliation, it turned out she had been employed at Computa at the time of publication. To the extent that King Rao stole the idea from her, it followed that he stole it from Computa itself. King ought, perhaps, to have recognized his error and hired legal counsel to fix it. Instead, he walked down the short hall to Margie's office and knocked on the window. She was wearing a yellow sundress and eating an orange. She gestured, Come in.

Inside, he held out the letter, and she wiped her fingers on a paper towel, took it, and read from beginning to end, snorting at intervals. "Is there any chance they'll go public with this?" she said. King said no, he doubted it. "Okay, good," she said, looking mischievous.

She would do it for them. She would go public. As far as Margie was concerned, the Computa letter was a gift. There weren't many companies with a stodgier reputation than Computa. She had always wanted to position Coconut as the opposite of that. She made a list of historical innovations that were the result of intellectual borrowing. *Massacre in Korea*, Picasso's 1951 masterpiece, influenced by Goya's *The Third of May 1808*; *Julius Caesar*, Shakespeare's 1599 play, derived from Sir Thomas North's translation of Plutarch's *Lives of the Noble Grecians and Romans*. The telephone—Alexander Graham Bell's allegedly having copied from a patent application filed by a forgotten Italian. They ordered a pizza, raided the fridge for bottles of Rainier. Norman had left hours earlier, saluting them both, as he liked to do, on his way out.

"We're not boxing him out on purpose, are we?" Margie said. They were sitting on the office couch.

"I don't think he cares as much as we do."

Margie gestured vaguely at herself and said, "Irish Catholic guilt." She told him about Sundays spent kneeling on the rough, worn carpet of aging sanctuaries. The way the wafer fizzled stalely on the tongue. But organized religion wasn't for her, Margie had concluded long ago.

"My dad was religious," King said. "I never understood it. I liked my uncle's line of reasoning. The best anyone can do is to put enough goodness into the world to make up for the badness you've put into it."

Margie said she liked that. It was rational.

"My mom died giving birth to me," he blurted. He had never

talked to Margie about his life in the Garden, but he suddenly needed to make her understand that Chinna's idea of making up for the badness meant something special. "The mom I talk about—technically, she's my aunt, the younger sister of the one who gave birth to me. My birth mother's dead. My mom, her sister, talked about her all the time. So that idea—making up for the badness—"

She nodded. "I get it," she said quietly, holding her eye contact with him.

"He died, too," King added. "They both did, my uncle and my dad. A stroke for my dad, and an accident for my uncle."

"What kind of accident?"

"He and my cousin got in a fight, and I guess it went bad." He had never said this much about it to anyone. He quickly changed the subject. "Let's talk about our TV plan."

But something had passed between them. The holy hours they had spent on this couch. Their legs sticking to the leather. The empty bottles of beer pushed to the back edge of the coffee table to make room for their papers. Their papers. Entire trees sacrificed. They had found their religion in the Coconut Corporation, and they were both in honest service to it. "Is it getting late for you, Margaret?" he said.

Margie's eyes were bright and fixed on him. "Why are you calling me Margaret?"

"Margie."

There they were, several hours later, naked on the roof terrace of their shared apartment building, the sun rising as he embraced her, the cement cold and hard beneath his shoulder blades as he heaved up toward her soft and welcoming body. They were drunk. Past Margie, the sunrise was the color of lilacs and marigolds. "How beautiful," he said, gesturing up at it.

"Oh no, I'm not." She blushed, mistaking his meaning.

"Oh, Margie," he said, feeling all the more tender toward her for her error. "Margie, you are! You are! You have the fairest skin I've ever seen."

Her lips tightened, her nostrils flared. "I'm Irish, you know that," she said. "I can't help it."

They fell silent. Margie turned over next to him, onto her back, and they lay side by side, watching the sky. "It was a compliment," King said. "For Indians, it's a compliment."

"I'm not Indian," she said. An airplane passed high overhead, bisecting the sky with its thin, fuzzy tail. Margie traced the trail with her finger and raised herself onto her elbow. "I'm thinking of the Wright Brothers," she said.

WHAT MAKES HUMANS UNIQUE? Is it the larynx, the shoulder, and the opposable thumb, the better to speak, hunt, and cook with? Is it that we stand, that we blush? A lot of attention is given to the brain, which contains more neurons in the cerebral cortex than that of any other animal whose neurons have been counted.

The Scottish philosopher Adam Ferguson, considering the question on the species level, observed, "In other classes of animals, the individual advances from infancy to age or maturity; and he attains, in the compass of a single life, to all the perfection his nature can reach: but, in the human kind, the species has a progress as well as the individual; they build in every subsequent age on foundations formerly laid; and, in a succession of years, tend to a perfection in the application of their faculties, to which the aid of long experience is required, and to which many generations must have combined their endeavors."

This is to say, our extraordinariness has to do with what we've accomplished together; our defining characteristic is being able to pass something of our lived experience from one human to another, thus ensuring our advancement as a species.

MARGIE GOT KING an appearance on *The Today Show* one week before the Coconut's launch by promising that they would make a major revelation about Computa. It was 1981. The host was a lifeguard of a man—that casual flop of hair, those crinkly eyes, that trustworthy lip at which a voluptuous blonde dabbed with a tissue.

"You've been described as a genius," he said, when the cameras were rolling.

"A genius!" King said, laughing. "The truth is, I don't buy in to the notion of individual genius. The narrative of human progress is one of collective achievement, and that notion is at the core of what we're trying to do at Coconut."

"How's that?"

"We're building computers that let people store for their children, their grandchildren, and their great-grandchildren the most valuable information about who they are. You can create a document and save it in our library, the Coconut Shell, and that document is never going to get burned up in a fire. All those family recipes that get lost over time, you can save all of those. We've found a way to let you safeguard your whole life with us. But this is the product of generations of human innovation. You know how we came up with the blueprint? We read an article written by an obscure scientist, and we built on her ideas. That scientist is no longer with us, but her ideas are going to live on through our work."

"That sounds harmless enough, but I understand that you're now facing a legal threat because of it."

"People are threatened by it. This scientist I mentioned worked at Computa before she died and tried to pitch them this idea, but they ignored it. Not long ago, we got a letter from Computa threatening to sue us if we went through with the product—if we went through with borrowing an idea from someone who happened to work for them, which they'd ignored."

"Computa is claiming you stole the idea from one of their scientists?"

"Yes, and they're threatening to put us out of business for it."

The interviewer leaned in. "Let me stop you, King. You're acknowledging you took the idea from Computa?"

"No, no, what I'm saying is that Computa shared it with the world, when one of their scientists, who was on leave at the time, published the paper. Everybody was doing the same thing. Computa was doing it, too. You know Picasso's saying, 'Good artists copy, great artists steal.' Well, we at Coconut have always been shameless about taking great ideas and making the best use of them. I'd even go as far as to say that's our founding principle. Take a great idea, and find a way to bring it to life. Think of the Wright Brothers. We call them the inventors of the airplane, but they just built on what others had done before. They were our models in founding Coconut. This obscure paper was exciting, sure, but it just presented an idea. It didn't say, 'And here's exactly how you would go about doing that.' Someone needed to come along and figure that part out. My uncle used to tell me you've got to leave the world a better place than it was when you got here. I think that's what the scientist who wrote the paper was trying to do. And now it's what we're trying to do."

17

Magic was right. One night, I returned to Edison to find a note from Elemen taped to the door. It wasn't addressed to anyone in particular, yet I was sure she had intended it for me alone. "Orientation in the atrium for new Exes, 8 p.m. tonight," it said. She had signed the letter "E" underneath, in a loopy, almost childish, cursive.

I found Elemen sitting crossed-legged on the floor; a couple dozen people had arranged themselves on the ground facing her. I moved to the front and sat a few feet from her. "Thanks for the note," I said, trying to act casual, and she smiled—a relief.

Then she addressed all of us. "Hi," she said. "Good to see you all." She told us to look around and get to know one another's faces. We had all arrived around the same time, within the past month or so. The reason she had gathered us here was to tell us a bit about life in the Blanklands, and on Bainbridge, in particular.

Those who had lived here for many years had a long-standing tradition of holding these orientations. It had taken time to figure out what people needed to hear, she said, but after a while they had realized that the most important part had nothing to do with the Blanklands at all. It had to do with the place they had all left to get here. So that's what we were going to talk about first.

She exuded calm confidence. Strange that the loud, passionate girl who had stood bellowing on that Honda Civic on that decades-ago night of the Coconut riots was the same human being as this assured woman, regal in her affect. Under Shareholder Government, she said, the world's citizens were, on average, richer, healthier, and better educated than ever. The creation of this system of government had given everyone the same shot at life, determined only by their God-given grit and sweat. "Right?" Elemen said, her tone ironic. She paused, as if waiting for an answer. When no one spoke, her tone darkened: "But, wait. If it was all so great, why in the world did you leave?"

We were silent. "I see your expressions," she said. "You're thinking, She thinks I left out of conviction. She thinks I left to help make the world a better place. She doesn't realize this about me, but I left because I couldn't make it. My Social Capital was in the toilet."

A couple of people tittered in nervous acknowledgment, but most avoided eye contact. When she turned her intense gaze on me, I willed myself to meet it, and she did the tiniest of double-takes, as if startled, before continuing. "Listen, there's shame in it. I know that. It's been the prevailing narrative about Exes almost since the beginning: We were forced to leave because we failed at being Shareholders. Given the same opportunities as everyone else, we couldn't make it. We're pitiful. But one night, you're in bed, and the thought of Exing enters your mind. What then?" She laughed. "You have to assume that you must be one of these pitiful people, too, right?"

She was not charismatic in the traditional sense. She had neither the comforting cadence of a preacher, nor the easy warmth of a politician. Her manner was challenging, even a little mocking, as if she intended to make us uncomfortable. "Right?" she said again. The truth, of course, was that the system was set up specifically so that most people couldn't make it. The truth was that a person's Social Capital depended almost entirely on the privilege they were born with, not any effort of their own.

The prior richness of the rich and the poorness of the poor had been grandfathered into the shareholding system. While the biggest Shareholders sat in air-conditioned houses not far from here, feasting on endangered fish and designer root vegetables, the smallest ones remained captive in the global south—Myanmar, Honduras, the Congo—living on manufacturing campuses where they clocked in for sixteen hours at a time, subsisted on meal and cola, and slept in monitored dorms where the lights were out seven hours a night, no more, no less. Their children, who boarded at Shareholder vocational schools, had visitation once a week, on the single day their parents didn't have to work. Even in Seattle— home to some of the wealthiest Shareholders in the world, including most of the Board—people struggled to survive. Unless you had created and sold some valuable piece of IP, your best bet on this continent, that is, if you were good-looking and charismatic enough, was to try to make it as an influencer. Otherwise, you were left to look after those who had made it—to nurse their children, scrub their toilets, trim their hedges, stencil their toenails. It's the same as what happened at the end of the ancient régime, slavery, apartheid, but this time the Algo is responsible, and who's going to argue with an all-knowing algorithm? How conceited would that be?

When she paused, I cleared my throat and spoke: "If that's true, how come no one's talking about it?" I said. My tone was more heated—defensive—than I had meant for it to be. It's not as if Shareholder Government were some kind of authoritarian dictatorship, I went on; it's not as if anyone were being censored. The whole premise was that, whether you were the richest corporate executive or the poorest laborer, you had the same means to communicate—your Social Profile—and the extent to which your message got shared wasn't decided by any person but by the Algo. After the Exodus, I added, the Board had even loosened the Shareholder Agreement's restrictions on free expression.

"Good point," Elemen said, but her eyes were gleaming, as if she had pulled me into a trap. "People can complain about the Board all they want. But why would they, when their Social Capital depends on the Board getting richer?"

When Elemen fell silent, murmurs of protestation rose. That couldn't be all. A squirrelly redheaded girl in the front raised her hand, bouncing a little on the heels of her feet. "Okay, so now what?" she said. The speech did seem incomplete. It was too short. And it had not ended, as speeches must, with a call to action.

Elemen Ex only gave a warm smile. The question didn't seem to blindside her at all; rather, it seemed almost as if this were the question she had been waiting for, her cue. The people of the Blanklands had reclaimed their freedom, she said calmly. It was a freedom so elemental that newcomers, used to the Board's capitalist definition of the term, couldn't even grasp it at first. But what do people do around here? newcomers wondered aloud, balefully, not realizing that the reason the mainland felt so bustling, so fun, was by design. The Board had a vested interest in giving Shareholders plentiful opportunities to spend. "A lot of people come to the Blanklands to 'join up' with the Exes"—she made exaggerated air quotes—"and when they do, they're disappointed," she said. "Truth is, there's nothing to join up with."

There had always been a symbiosis between people and their environment. For centuries, one tyrant after another had conspired to usurp that natural order, disrupting our ties with family, community, and nature in order to dominate us. The name, the Exes, it was never meant to connote exile; it was meant to be about excision from the latest such system, about opting out from it entirely. For the Exes to propose a new system and require us all to pledge allegiance to it would make them no different, she said, from a man like King Rao.

King Rao. The sound of his name shocked me. A man like King Rao. I tightened in protest. But then, a small voice inside me: Didn't he require your allegiance all these years? Isn't that what drove you away from him?

All Elemen wanted for us, she said, was for us to become comfortable with our freedom. We should step out of this room, and decide for ourselves how to spend our time, making this choice not because one pursuit gives us more pleasure than another, but because within us there remains a tiny spark capable of finding meaning for ourselves. Real meaning.

"Give us some examples, though," the same red-haired girl said in apparent exasperation. Were we expected to start a revolution, or a newspaper, or a band? Become doctors, teachers, social workers? What was needed here, and what wasn't? Could a person start a business, or would such a quasi-Shareholderish pursuit be frowned upon? Should we be learning to garden, hunt, fish, make fire with twigs, fight off wild boars? There had to be *some* guidelines.

Elemen would not relent. On this point, she was gleefully confrontational. To offer examples, she said—her arms flying, recalling, in fact, my father, more than anyone—would be no different from sending us to the soap aisle at some Shareholder supermarket, showing us all the dozens of brands lined up in there, and claiming this represented freedom. The examples were as endless as the whole wide universe was endless; she could not enumerate them if she wanted to. If this prospect frightened us, consider what made it frightening. "Maybe what you're scared of is freedom itself," she said, and shrugged.

There was a finality in her shrug. She just stood there, looking perfectly at peace with the collective discomfort in the room. The rest of us regarded one another in wearied confusion. One by one, people stood, said their thank-yous, and filed out.

Shareholder, I stayed.

AFTERWARD, Elemen and I stood on the beach looking out toward the mainland. "My mom's still out there, somewhere," she said, slipping her foot from her sandal and toeing a flat pebble.

I glanced at her; it took me by surprise, this sudden revelation. As tight-knit as the island community was, there was also a certain rootlessness about people, because of the taboo against talking about where you came from. Besides not asking about my origins, no one had revealed their own since that first night when I met Arno. I said, looking cautiously down at the ground, "You grew up in Seattle, right?"

She was holding the pebble between her toes, and now leaned over to pluck it and skip it across the water. It hopped four, five times before disappearing. "Right," she said. "But she's not there anymore, I mean, last I heard. She moved back to El Salvador, where she was born."

It was odd that she had brought me here and was talking this openly about her background. It had to be strategic, I thought. She had to be grooming me for something, opening herself up to me in the hopes that I would reciprocate, though I had no idea what sort of reciprocation she was after. But then, standing next to this woman, disconnected from the Internet, I didn't mind not knowing. She looked up from the ground and made eye contact. "My real name is Luna," she said.

LUNA MARIA NORTH—I learned over the course of several conversations, beginning that night and continuing for weeks thereafter, at that beach or on late-night strolls along the waterfront—was born on the cusp of the Shareholder Generation, the cohort of children who entered kindergarten the year of the Board's founding.

She was an only child, doted upon by her parents, Sofia and Ben, her quirks indulged until they ripened into full-blown eccentricities. It was in childhood, from her parents, that Elemen first heard the names of Pierre-Joseph Proudhon, Emma Goldman, Frantz Fanon, Václav Havel. Audre Lorde, bell hooks. Zhuangzi, the Daoist and proto-anarchist, too.

At Garfield High School, Ben was a high school history and drama teacher and Sofia a guidance counselor, both enormously popular; their openly anarchist leanings, their rakishness, and their affection for each other lent them an undeniable charisma. Her parents were especially beloved among the theater kids, a bunch of earnest and expressive loud-talkers, who treated Luna's arrival at Garfield, as a freshman, as a major event.

She had been a loner, by choice. In the seventh grade, she had compelled her parents to let her raise chickens and bees in the backyard of their rented house, and had learned to stitch her own dresses out of curtains and ribbon scraps foraged from the high school theater. But the first week of high school, the stoutly handsome boy who was considered a shoo-in to play the major-general in the school's fall production of *The Pirates of Penzance* slung his arm around her shoulders backstage and announced to this group of a half dozen friends, "Let's call her 'Sis.' " She gave a low laugh of surprise and said, "Uh, let's not!" The presumptive major-general began to laugh, warmly, and the rest of them did, too, and in that moment, Luna acquired the first friends of her life.

That fall, Luna played Ruth, the pirate maid, and came out as queer. Nearly two hundred years old, *Pirates* was hardly ever performed anymore. It had fallen out of fashion because of how General Stanley's daughters were so objectified. But Ben had chosen *Pirates* on purpose, casting boys as the daughters and girls as the cops, subverting the script's gender politics. That winter, Luna and the also-queer major-general lost their virginities to each other. That spring, the Board concluded its years-long audit of the world's schools and universities.

The audit resulted in the renaming of Garfield High School as the Greenfield High School, to which no one objected, the old namesake having been best known for his assassination. The audit also led to an edict that all schools spend at least three-quarters of class time putting students through a standardized global curriculum that had been translated into sixty-five languages and posted online in order to equalize access to education. Even teachers' titles were to be standardized. Math teachers would thereafter be known as Efficiency Leaders, and history teachers would become

Progress Leaders, in line with the global curriculum's focus on "actionable learning" designed to turn children into more productive, higher-scoring Shareholders.

Most teachers—cognizant that too much negativity could affect their own score and conceding, too, that it wasn't a good look to stand in the way of a pedagogical approach shown to improve children's lifelong outcomes—went along, as did most students. So it was notable when the cast of *The Pirates of Penzance*, Luna included, marched into Ben's classroom and demanded he speak out about the global curriculum, in which drama was reduced to an after-school activity. Ben was glad to be thus commanded. The truth, he told them, growing animated, was that he had chosen *Pirates* exactly so they would get a message about institutional overreach.

He opened his Havel reader and read aloud. "A person who has been seduced by the consumer value system, whose identity is dissolved in an amalgam of the accouterments of mass civilization, and who has no roots in the order of being, no sense of responsibility for anything higher than his own personal survival, is a demoralized person. The system depends on this demoralization, deepens it, is in fact a projection of it into society."

Havel had made the prescient observation that the greatest threat to humanity was not the fight between communism and capitalism—those dueling successors to feudalism—but a dangerous force underlying both of those economic models, a mindless cycle of economic production and consumption that relied on co-opting the collective brain and brawn of the human species, thus annihilating the human soul. In 1994, he told an audience in Philadelphia, where he had traveled to accept the Liberty Medal, "There are thinkers who claim that, if the modern age began with the discovery of America, it also ended in America. This is said to have occurred in the year 1969, when America sent the first men to the moon." To analyze our own planet from on high, Havel reflected, was to sour something essential about our proper relationship to it. "It is increasingly clear that, strangely, the relationship"—between us and the world—"is missing something," he said. "It fails to connect with the most intrinsic nature of reality and with natural human experience. It is now more of a source of disintegration and doubt than a source of integration and meaning. It produces what amounts to a state of schizophrenia: Man as an observer is becoming completely alienated from himself as a being."

Someone had the idea that it would be fun, and even safer, to protest Greenfield's new curriculum in their costumes—the cops as cops, the major-general's daughters as the major-general's daughters—and they went backstage to change. When no one else was listening, the major-general turned to Luna and said, quietly and with obvious embarrassment, "Do you think it could affect my Juilliard application if I protest?" She shrugged aggressively. She thought it a stupid question. Watching this unfold, though, Sofia appeared at her side and said sharply, "Don't be an asshole, Luna." She put a hand on Luna's shoulder. "We didn't raise you like that." She turned to the major-general: "No one's making you march, kiddo." When the others realized the major-general had slipped off, they didn't suspect defection; the major-general often mowed neighbors' lawns after school, to save up for Juilliard. Since he was gone, the major-general's daughters compelled Ben to wear the major-general's costume. They all left the schoolyard, chanting, "Keep history historical!" and "Fuck progress!"

But when they made their way to Cherry Street, where the rush-hour traffic was dense, and marched up and down the sidewalk, Luna grew apprehensive. No one was honking their approval, like she had seen in footage of protests in the past. Were their chants too obscure? Did people even protest anymore? She took out her phone. On Social, some people were complaining about the curriculum change, but unless you searched aggressively, you'd never see those posts, buried under more viral topics. That afternoon, the top one was a meme of cats behaving like dogs, and dogs like cats. She showed the meme to the others, and they took her phone and sat themselves down on the sidewalk, passing it around, laughing. The cops peeled off their mustaches. The daughters unhooked their corsets. In the end, Luna and her parents marched alone.

In the morning, Sofia and Ben woke to find that their Social Capital had fallen by one thousand points apiece—a year's worth of gains, erased. Three weeks later, the principal informed them that, due to this decline, their contracts at Greenfield would not be renewed in the fall. "It was the major-general; he sold you out!" Luna cried when she heard about the firings. She had noticed that, while her Social Capital and that of the other student protesters had also fallen overnight—though by only fifty points apiece, not nearly as much as Sofia and Ben's losses—the major-general's had risen by one hundred points. She imagined that he had gone home and called the authorities on them, and had been rewarded for this. "I doubt it," Sofia said gently. They had protested along a public thoroughfare. Their faces must have been photographed a hundred times apiece, and the Algo was intelligent enough to see past a stick-on mustache. The Board hardly needed the major-general's help. And the increase in his Capital must be unrelated. It must be from all the lawn mowing.

Luna and her parents moved to the same poor neighborhood as the major-general, and Sofia and Ben took up second careers, Sofia offering life coaching, Ben tutoring. Luna started selling eggs and honeycomb over Social, and ended up making more than both her parents combined. "You thought you were humoring me, with the chickens and the bees," she teased them, "but now where would we be without me?"

Somehow it made her feel better to behave this way, as if it were all a joke. The alternative—taking it seriously, holding the Board responsible for their fate—was impossible. All three Norths had petitioned to get their Capital reviewed, and all three had received bot replies within fifteen minutes saying the review was complete, and no change to their Social Capital was warranted. Of course it hadn't even been humans who did the scoring in the first place. It had been the Algo, whose motivations, by design, no human could deconstruct. The Board employed people, and those people were arranged in a hierarchical management structure, at the top of which sat King Rao, the CEO. But you couldn't message King Rao. You couldn't call him up. He appeared on Social each morning with his Daily Shareholder Update, but his appearances in real life had dwindled to his annual address at Sharefest. He could be Oz. He could be a bot. She wouldn't be surprised.

So she took it out on her parents, lightly at first, with gentle nudges of condescension, but, as time passed, more sharply. Her anger increased as she watched them fall deeper into destitution— a pair of soft gray shadows sitting shoulder to shoulder on the sagging couch, debating their Proudhon, though anyone could see they were only going through the motions, distracted by more practical matters. She hated them for it. They misunderstood. They thought she resented them for being poor. In fact, she resented them for proving that what they had argued, in their middle-class years, was a falsehood. Poor people don't give a shit about revolution; they give a shit about survival.

But she had changed, too. She had grown up eating fresh strawberries by the fistful. Now it was meal and cola most of the time. Some late-summer mornings, she rode her bicycle to Leschi Park and foraged for blackberries before anyone else had gotten to them. It was something she used to do for fun in their middle-class years. She would bring blackberries home for her parents in an old yogurt container. Now she ate whatever she could find on the spot, too ravenous to share.

That spring, the major-general was accepted to Juilliard, but not given financial aid, so was forced to decline. He joined the police department instead. That summer, Ben North ingested an entire bottle of pain pills no one realized he had been taking, and died. That fall, Sofia returned to live in El Salvador for the first time since she was a toddler. She said her aging father needed her, but Luna understood the truth, which was that this, too, was a form of suicide. After they were both gone, Luna went through their abandoned belongings to see what she could sell and found a four-word suicide note from her father addressed to her. " 'Forward on the foe!' " she read out loud—she couldn't help but sing the line from the musical and smile—and it was then that she understood that Luna Maria North also had to die.

BUT I REMINDED HER, she told me one night, that there was hope yet. Most Ex girls she met these days were fleeing homes where they had never been loved or supported. She could tell I wasn't one of those girls. I was a girl who had been cared for back home, but something—the details didn't matter to her—had broken my confidence and driven me here.

I didn't know how to answer. It seemed proper to repay her confession with one of my own, but of course I couldn't.

She knew that I had been apprenticing around the island and asked if I had been enjoying myself. I told her I had. A flicker of disappointment crossed her face. I added quickly that I wasn't wedded to anything. She looked at me, as if she were trying to decide something important, and finally said, "Can you handle a night schedule?"

I thought I understood what she meant. I spat it out, embarrassed: "I'm a virgin."

"Sweetheart!" she said, amused. "There's more than one kind of night work." She stood and indicated, with a tilt of her head, that I should go with her.

IN THE CENTER of the sphere, a set of stairs led down to a long, bunker-like underground hall. I had gone down there a couple of times, curious, but all the doors had been locked. Now, at the end of the hall, Elemen pulled out a ring of keys from her pocket and unlocked one. Inside was a small room, little more than a closet, whose contents were sparse: a chair and a desk, on which there stood an old desktop computer. From a pocket of her overalls, she pulled out a thumb drive and inserted it into the machine.

A dark, grainy film began playing on the monitor: dark-skinned men and women streaming out of a building wearing masks over their noses and mouths and identical beige jumpsuits. The footage skipped a beat and returned to the people—or another group; it was hard to tell—moving blank-faced along a wide road, then turning off into what looked like dormitories, slim, monolithic structures with laundry hanging out the windows. A dense, oily brown smog hung low in the air, obscuring the tops of buildings. The film skipped again, before showing footage of people at work on assembly lines, thousands of them, side by side, moving in unison like machines. The whole clip lasted no more than thirty seconds.

"What did you see?" she said.

"People?" I said.

She rewound the clip to the beginning, with the people coming out of a building, and paused it. "Tell me again: What do you see?"

I saw it then: the Coconut logo, a halved coconut shell, stenciled on the front of the building. This had to be one of Coconut's megacampuses, an innovation of King and Margie's, renowned for making production more efficient than ever. But the Shareholder Agreement barred anyone who stepped foot on a campus from recording or posting what happened inside. That meant I had never seen what campus life looked like. It also meant that whoever captured this footage must have broken the Shareholder Agreement.

Elemen removed the thumb drive and inserted another one. "Accra," she said. A new scene appeared, this one clearer. It showed a young Ghanaian woman wearing a colorful dress and head wrap and a small silver cross on a chain, sitting at a kind of booth on a narrow, bustling road, with three young children pawing at her knees and at each other. She faced a woman about her age, who wore a tight bun and a wide-collared white button-down, the uniform of a clerk or bureaucrat. With obvious impatience, the bureaucrat was insisting that she couldn't explain why the children's Social Capital wasn't higher.

The mom kept interrupting her to drill her children. "Thirty-one, thirty-two, thirty-three; tell her, what comes next?" "Who's the CEO of the Board of Shareholders?" "How do you spell *Ghana*?"

The oldest of the three children, a round-faced boy who stared his mother down with suspicious, intelligent eyes, couldn't have been more than six. "Don't answer," he told his little sisters, who looked at him and remained silent.

"No, no, babies, listen, it's important," their mother pressed on in an urgent voice. She turned to the woman on the other side of the booth: "They know all this. Look at them; you can see they're smart. They just don't want to answer because"—she looked down at her son, who had his jaw set stoically but had begun to cry—"well—"

"They don't want you to send them off from here."

"Right."

The clerk shook her head firmly. "My friend, I apologize, I can set their rate based only on their Capital," she said. "Your word means very little in this case."

At this, the boy cried out in triumph, "See, Mama, we're worthless; you have to keep us!"

His mother scooped him up in her arms and held him tight for a moment, then put him down again. She returned her intense gaze to the clerk, as if to convey that there must be something more she could do for them. The clerk hesitated, then said in a kind tone, "The thing is, it could be good if they end up with a family here in town; that way you might be able to see them or even take them back later."

"But I'm telling you, they're smart. I know you can market them over there, I know there are families over there looking for Black children, I read about that one—"

"I know—"

"That famous one—"

"I know about him, but—"

"He became an influencer over there, and sent for hi[s]
to move over there, too. Did you see that? It went viral, ..."

"I know all about him, my friend! But he's only one person. It's
very rare for them to ask for African children over there. Asian
children, yes. But they're not asking for children like these."

"He can read," the mother said. "That's special, ma'am! I don't
mean picture books; I mean chapter books, the sort I used to read
when I was nine or ten. That has to mean something."

"It's not for us to understand what goes into the Capital, though,
is it?" the woman said. "It's the Algo that decides."

The mother's tone sharpened, and she pursed her lips. "Now,
don't you find it strange, ma'am, that everyone speaks about the
Algo the way our grandmothers spoke of God?"

There was a pause, as if the bureaucrat were trying to decide
how to respond, harshly or not. When she spoke, her voice
remained gentle. "Oh well, I'm not here to talk about religion,"
she murmured calmly. "But it's true that the Algo is highly accurate at predicting—"

The footage ended there, abruptly, and the closet filled with
silence.

"Where did you get all this from?"

"It comes to us from all over the world," she said. "It's footage
from Shareholder life, the parts that aren't supposed to be made
public. Our sympathizers route it to us, but they don't tell us their
sources, and it's better that they don't," she said. "If you violate
that provision of the Shareholder Agreement, you wind up in the
Margie. Or worse."

"You've got to get it online, so people can see it."

"Ha, right, and get these poor people killed?" she said.

I laughed, uncomfortable. "Come on, the Board doesn't *kill*
anyone."

She removed the thumb drive and inserted another one.
"Laos," she said. Now a long line of people stood at a machine
that dispensed pouches of meal and cola. The machine jammed or
ran out, and a small, unimposing man standing in front lost it. He

banged on it with a fist, paused, then started raining blows on it. From off-screen, someone dressed in a guard uniform approached, yanked the man by his collar—you could see his neck snap back— and violently threw him to the ground, then kicked him, once, in the head. There was a cracking sound. The man on the ground was still. People were shouting. The guard kicked the man more softly, in the side, but he didn't move. The guard looked around, a bit wild-eyed, and shouted something at the crowd, which dispersed. There was a sound of jostling and a view of people running off, but then, for an instant, the camera turned to the scene again, and the man was still on the ground, motionless, the guard talking on his phone, his back to the camera. I hadn't caught it before, but this time I read, across the back of his uniform, two words that I would not be able to unsee. COME TOGETHER, it read.

I had seen videos like this, everyone had, from a time before Shareholder Government, when police were known to be brutal. But Shareholder Police were supposed to be peacekeepers, trained in de-escalation tactics; violence was supposed to be a last resort. "If you could get this out there, millions of people would see it," I said.

"But, again, what about our sources' safety?" she reminded me. Plus, we're not trying to go viral, remember? We don't meddle in Shareholder life. That's our whole deal."

"It doesn't seem right."

"Kiddo, Shareholder Government is an empire, and empires fall. That process doesn't need anyone's help." There was a steeliness in how she said it. "Look at them. They wasted decades trying to invent some gadget that would stop Hothouse Earth, instead of just doing what we already knew would help, and now it's too late. These fires, these floods. What matters to us—what's mattered to us ever since we got out of there—is what comes next. When the Board falls, something else will have a chance to be born. That's what we're trying to start here, a model. When Shareholder Government is gone, we can show people a better way of life. It might take three, four, five generations. We have to be patient." She spoke loudly. There was something in her voice, though, an over-insistence, that made me wonder if she believed her own speech.

I gathered up my courage. "The problem is that, in three, four, five generations," I said, "humans will be extinct."

For what felt like the longest time, she just looked at me. Then she began to nod. I will never forget the look on her face, flushed and wide-eyed and full of hope. I have regrets, like anyone. But for all that I have done wrong since then, I would do it all over to see her face in that moment. "Good girl," she said.

18

At City Hall, Margie slipped into the bathroom and emerged wearing blush, mascara, and a rose-colored gown whose sleeves didn't quite cover her shoulders. King said, "Hey, your sleeves don't fit," and she laughed and said, "That's what it's supposed to look like!" and he loved her. It was 1985. Coconut was ten years old. They tramped upstairs, arm in arm, where in a small, serious room, before a small, serious woman, they promised to love, honor, and support each other until one or both of them died, and as they did so, they smiled privately at each other as if at an inside joke, because wasn't it ridiculous to have to proclaim it out loud, when they both knew there was no way they could do otherwise? It was as if he were being asked to promise to love and honor his own soft, pulsing heart. If he didn't, he would die.

Afterward, they ate dinner alone at the restaurant at the top of the Space Needle. They had invited no one because, even after all these years, their relationship was secret. Even Norman didn't know, or pretended he didn't. The dishes came out on large, flat, square plates and looked like little gelatinous sculptures. They tapped at the sculptures with knives and forks, unsure of themselves. "How beautiful," Margie murmured half-heartedly. The restaurant's gimmick was that the room rotated. It made them disoriented and anxious. Every time they looked out the window, the view was transformed.

"This is fun, right?" Margie said with forced gaiety. "Have you ever seen anything like this?"

He had never seen her so eager to please, so like her father. It put him on edge. He said no, and they fell silent and bent over their plates. Her twenties were behind her; she was no longer as winsome as she had been. Her nose was slightly pinched at the bridge, her skin crepey around the eyes. The performative daffiness of her younger years had matured into a bold, dazzling charisma—it felt old school, like that of the great black-and-white movie actresses—adored by journalists and, by extension, investors. It did not hurt that there were still those gem-like green eyes, and those obscenely full lips, punctuated by generous dimples. He loved her differently than he used to—there was a comfort in their relationship that had taken the edge off—but no less than ever.

King's first time on national TV had been a turning point, and he had nailed it. The morning after the interview aired, Margie's phone started ringing with press requests. When Computa announced it would not file suit—the board had reviewed their options, said the letter, and had concluded a lawsuit against so insignificant a competitor wasn't worth their time—the decision brought a fresh round of press coverage, most of it highly favorable to Coconut. The real reason Computa hadn't sued, the pundits said, was that any legal battle would only cement Coconut's reputation as its most impressive competitor.

They were profitable enough to pay themselves good salaries, hire still more workers, and take over another floor of the building. They had poached a sales team from the telemarketing firm downstairs, and hired Walter Martz as their communications chief, along with dozens of hardware and software engineers just out of graduate school. Soon they would bring on a couple hundred more programmers, thanks to an unusual hiring process, a nationwide programming contest conceived by Margie in which the creators of the best programs would be rewarded with jobs at Coconut and a spot on the next version of the operating system for the software they had built. Coconut would outgrow its little building on Winslow Way. They had already negotiated an enormous acquisition of land farther south, on Restoration Point, where they planned to build a new headquarters overlooking Elliott Bay. Down the road, they had built and moved into a home of their own.

Thinking of the house at their wedding dinner, the domesticity it suggested, he realized, with a pang of terror, that they had not recently talked about children—he didn't want them, and, though she had agreed in the past, what if she had changed her mind? But when he blurted the question out, she dispensed with it quickly—of course she didn't, of course they understood each other perfectly—and they returned to eating again. While he worked at his little edifice of salmon, he thought of the work that had to be done back at the office. He glanced up at Margie, whose eyes darted all over the place—she was clearly also restless—and felt a great sense of oneness with her.

After dinner, King and Margie went home. The house itself was modestly sized, a two-thousand-square-foot rambler, but they had paid for the waterfront and the twenty acres of land surrounding it. They had even carved a dirt path leading to where the headquarters would be; they could walk there and back in fifteen minutes. They owned no furniture yet. They were sleeping on the carpet, under a dim, bare bulb. "That was different than I expected," Margie said. "I thought it would be the best day of my life, but it just felt like any old day."

"Me, too!" he nearly shouted, such was his relief that she had said it out loud.

They laughed and, for a while, sat in silent contemplation. Then she said, "Do you want to go to the office? I have some work I need to do."

He hopped up. It was as if she had lifted a great, heavy blanket from over their shoulders. Ever since dessert had arrived, he had felt the same urge but wondered if he needed to suppress it in favor of their married life—if, from now on, they were supposed to spend evenings in nuptial leisure. But no, his wonderful wife, she agreed with him. "Let's go!" he said.

THE HEADQUARTERS WERE finished by the end of the year. By the following year, Coconut employed a thousand people. More and more, Norman hermited himself in his office. He was a hardware man in what was quickly becoming a software business. Some evenings, they could tell he was still in there only by the thin line of light beneath his door. Still, though, he was CEO. So it happened that someone called someone who called someone, and before they knew it, Elbert Norman had scheduled a meeting of their three-person board at McDonald's, their usual spot, to discuss an important development.

The room was bright and crowded; children ran by with brown plastic trays, jostling their knees and shoulders. Norman, who ordered a Big Mac, was the only one who ate. "Margie, you used to love Big Macs, but you could never finish them," he said. His lips were shiny with grease. He licked them. The oily smell of the burger wafted over the table.

"I don't remember that," Margie said. "You're not really part of my memories of childhood."

"Oh!" Norman said, flushing. And then: "Guess what." He had already sketched out the details, a back-of-the-envelope kind of thing, with his friend on Computa's board.

"Norman, we're not for sale," King said.

"Of course we are," Norman said, turning to Margie.

For a minute, King imagined that his wife was about to take her father's side. But Margie said, decisively, "No, we're not." "Give me your friend's number. I'll give him a call and clear it up."

Another man might have worried about his standing in the company. But Norman was the founder and CEO, and the only other board members were his daughter and son-in-law. The situation just made him excitable. "Margie, don't do that," he said. "Margie! Come on!" When she didn't speak, he added, "Oh, Margie. We should have just kept it the two of us all along. The Norman Corporation."

"That's a dumb name, Daddy," Margie said, glancing at King. "Coconut is much better."

"That's not my point."

"I *get* your point."

"What's my point?"

"You're jealous of my husband."

Norman's cheeks reddened. It was the first time she had acknowledged it out loud, the fact of their marriage. They had a three-person board; between them, King and Margie had sixty-six percent of the vote. When Norman raised a balled hand, King thought, with alarm, that he might punch Margie. Instead he slammed his fist onto the table. "If you two vote against this," he said, "I quit."

Margie was quiet for a while, then nodded and said, "Okay."

Norman shook his head slowly. "Jesus Christ," he said. Grease from the burger was dribbling down his wrist.

"Norman," King said. "Your clothes."

The grease darkened Norman's sleeve. He looked around, wild-eyed, at the others in the restaurant. "Come on!" he cried softly.

King gave him a wan, apologetic smile. He and Margie had discussed this potential outcome many times. They had a plan. "You'll keep your shares—you don't have to worry about that—though they'll become non-voting shares. We can even make you an adviser."

Norman gaped. "But it's my company!" he cried. He shook his burger at King and Margie. "It was mine in the first place!" he said. Then, abruptly, he calmed down. He set down the burger. "So that's it?" he said.

"That's it, Daddy," Margie said.

"Is it because of the divorce, darling?" he said.

"I hadn't thought of it like that, but it's possible," Margie said, almost in surprise. "I've been mad at you for years, for the way you treated me and Mom, so I guess it would make sense. I'll have to think about it some more."

"Is that why you married him?" he said, looking at King. "So he could get a green card and run the company?"

"No!" Margie cried. "God, Daddy! I married him because we love each other, and he treats me with respect." She added, "But, yes, the green card does help things."

THE GUILT HIT THEM both this time. But they couldn't be cavalier about Computa anymore. Its own consumer microcomputer was imminent, and Walter's spies had told him it would be priced to compete with, or even undercut, the Coconut. King and Margie were getting their computers produced in Burien, not far from the airport, but the labor was expensive.

"What about Shenzhen?" King said one night. Suppliers in China and Taiwan had lately been pitching the recently established special economic zone on the Pearl River estuary.

"I've thought about that," Margie said.

They flew out to see one of the city's biggest factories, on an investor's recommendation. The building was enormous and white. The employees, dressed identically in company-issued espadrilles and lab coats, also white, smiled placidly as they passed.

The CEO of Roostek, a slick-haired Taiwanese man named Johnny Lin, explained that most of them were from rural regions that had been neglected by the Chinese government. Now, because they had free room and board, they could send their wages home to support their families. For the cost of a single employee in Washington State, King could pay the salaries of forty of these young men and women. King turned to a boy who looked to be in his early twenties. "My maternal grandfather"—Appayya—"was like you," he said. "He traveled to Rangoon to earn money, and when he came home, he used it to build a school for all the children of my village, and that's where I was educated!" King said, beaming. Johnny translated. "Yes, sir," the boy said to King, in English.

King and Margie's hotel in Shenzhen was Italianate in style and Soviet in size. That night, as they sat next to each other at a large round table at the hotel restaurant, sharing a plate of appealingly lo-mein-ish spaghetti, King told Margie those Roostek workers, migrants from the countryside, reminded him of his cousins back in Kothapalli.

"Do you miss home?" Margie said.

"Not really; we'll be back by tomorrow night, anyway."

"No," Margie said, "I mean Kothapalli." Every time she said the name of his village, she gave it a singsongy trochaic dimeter, the vowels distended. It was the same as every American's pronunciation, but it pained him to hear it from her. She wasn't trying hard enough.

"Kothapalli," he said.

"That's what I said," she said.

"I do and I don't," he said. "At home, I don't think about it much. But here—maybe it's just being in the Third World—I keep getting reminded of it."

His most recent reminder, before this, had been when his mother wrote to inform him that the Telugu newspaper *Eenadu* was reporting that he was married. This could not be accurate, she said, since she had not heard about it directly. She had enclosed the article for his reference. The *Eenadu* reporter had written that he had called Coconut's headquarters asking for an interview with King. But the public relations person, one of Walter Martz's hires, declined, saying she had never heard of the paper. After King had replied to his mother, sheepishly confirming the marriage, she responded, "Bring Margaret Norman to Kothapalli for a proper wedding! Now that you're rich, you can afford it. We're waiting to meet our daughter-in-law."

King always showed Margie the letters from his mother, but of course Margie couldn't read the rounded Telugu script, which looked strange to her, like rows of little side-by-side breasts.

He never told her about his mother's request, and when Margie asked when she could meet his family, he gave noncommittal half answers. We'll go soon, he told her, and she seemed satisfied. Now, over dinner, she brought it up again: "Your mom must be upset we haven't gone yet, don't you think? She must be worried about you. And you, too, you said you miss it."

"Actually," King said coolly, not looking at her, "I said I don't miss it."

"You just said a minute ago that you do miss it," she replied, matching his tone. She twisted her spaghetti slowly around her fork in a way that seemed passive-aggressive to him; he had never mastered the skill. This was the typical tone of their arguments, detached, yet very direct, unlike spousal arguments he had witnessed back home at the Garden, where wives delivered their complaints to their husbands through the familial grapevine, in response to which the husbands either silently ignored the grievance, or else berated the wife for airing it publicly, sometimes with an accompanying beating. While he and Margie rarely raised their voices, their arguments made him feel frighteningly distant from her.

"I said being here reminds me of home, which is in fact different from saying I miss it," he said.

"What are you so afraid of?" she said, in a tone more curious than confrontational. "That they won't like me? That I won't fit in?" In a nearby corner, a group of waitresses huddled and whispered. Perhaps they would make the Chinese gossip columns in the morning.

But it wasn't that at all—insecurity about Margie—that had kept him from bringing her there; it was the opposite, a fear of what Margie would learn about him. "My life at home was complicated," he said.

"You told me about all that," she said. "I know about it."

"I just want our life to be separate from it," he said. "I'm a different person now. I don't want to go back there and have to answer to my cousins. I don't want the press to trail me to Kothapalli and start interviewing all those distant Raos and write some article about King Rao, the untouchable Indian bumpkin."

"They're going to do that anyway. At some point that Telugu newspaper—"

"*Eenadu*—"

"*Eenadu*, they're going to show up in Kothapalli." She tapped her nails on the table, which she did when she was thinking. "We should get ahead of that."

"I'm not taking *Eenadu* to Kothapalli," he said.

But one month later, Margie and King were stepping through customs at the Hyderabad airport into a throng of waiting Raos, who shouted and flapped welcome signs in the air, and looked to be a hundred strong. He didn't recognize most of them, the sons and daughters of cousins with whom he had lost contact long ago.

Someone pushed a woman to the front of the crowd. It was Sita, gray-haired and shrunken. She seemed timid at first, as if they had become strangers. But then she spoke: "Her name is Margaret," she announced loudly in Telugu, taking one of Margie's big hands in both of her small ones, kissing it, and raising it up in the air, as if she were declaring Margie the winner of some contest. "My daughter-in-law, Margaret!" she cried, and the rest of the Raos cheered and clapped. Sita turned back to Margie, still gripping her hand, and said in English, with a small, uncertain smile, "You are welcome here. How do you do?"

"Oh, I'm—"

"I do not speak English!" Sita interjected, in English again, and laughed. She had clearly rehearsed.

"I do not speak Telugu!" Margie responded, in tentative Telugu. She had rehearsed as well. The Raos erupted in appreciative laughter, and Sita allowed herself a smile and pulled Margie close, taking possession.

Sita turned to King. "You look dark, you look thin, you look old," she said in Telugu, taking both of his hands and turning them over in hers, and began to weep. "Is she not feeding you well?" It was a customary line—a mother's reminder that to leave her was to weaken—but it saddened him.

"Amma," he mumbled, embarrassed, raising a hand to wipe her tears. "Stop it." He began laughing, to avoid crying himself. "I'm here; you can feed me yourself."

She laughed, too. "I'll fatten you up," she said. "I got all your favorite vegetables."

They all bundled into a couple dozen white Ambassadors, for which King had paid, and caravanned to the train station, where they boarded an overnight train to Rajahmundry. He woke early and pulled Margie to the window. "Look; this is it!" he said. The countryside was unchanged from when he had left it, the skies pinkish blue in the dawn, the landscape green with rice fields in which men and women stood knee-deep, each square-shaped paddy divided from the next by a row of coconut trees. Arriving in Rajahmundry, they piled into another caravan of cars bound for Kothapalli. King, Margie, and Sita rode with their guards. King pressed his forehead to the window, seized with conflicting emotions. This was home. It both attracted and repelled him.

When they turned onto the path to the Garden, Margie took King's hand. Her palm was clammy. She seemed uncharacteristically nervous, and this made him nervous.

"Are we here?" she whispered, as the car slowed and stopped in the clearing between King's House and the Big House.

"This is it," he said. "Home."

The Garden was still lush, wet, and green. But it had been diminished, too, in a way he couldn't quite articulate to himself. He felt embarrassed, all of a sudden, at having described it to Margie as a kind of paradise; it was not, at least not compared to Maui, Tahiti, Mauritius, where the two of them had vacationed together. "It looks a little different," he said, as if to account for this, but immediately regretted the comment, thinking his mother, in the back seat with Margie, might have understood his English and taken offense.

"It's beautiful," Margie said. He turned and looked closely at her, to see if she meant it, and could not tell.

That night, the men sat in the clearing, as they used to as boys, under a clear, star-sprayed sky, and King's cousins filled him in on what he had missed. Things weren't the same in the Garden, Kittu said, and the others nodded, bored-seeming, preoccupied with working at the tobacco tucked inside their bottom lips. He didn't remember them like this; as boys, there had been a hot electricity in how they carried themselves. How had they gotten to be like this while he was abroad: bloated, unambitious?

Kittu pulled his stool closer to King's and took on a conspiratorial, complaining tone. Each month, when they got King's remittances, he said, the family members each lined up to claim their piece of it. The little children needed schoolbooks, clothes, and shoes, and the older ones had tuition payments to make or else they would not stand a chance, in these most competitive of times, of following in the footsteps of Computer Uncle, as they all called him. The women needed saris and jewelry befitting their rank, being related to King Rao, the richest son of Kothapalli, or people would gossip. The elders had grown bored and desirous with age, and needed televisions, cameras, and high-end medical treatment. The men of King's own generation—Kittu and the rest of them—needed, for their part, to buy influence with the village council president.

What remained was not sufficient to run a proper coconut operation, especially not in this age of global competition, in which the masses of other countries could provide the same product as Indians, but more cheaply and at scale. The Philippines had now surpassed India as the world's biggest coconut producer. The Raos were hardly the only Indian coconut farmers who had shrunk their business. They were no longer producing copra. During coconut season, they sent the teenagers up into the trees to bring down the fruits, and then someone—whoever happened to be free that morning—would drive them over to the local market, sell them for cash whole, and buy a plump chicken or two on the way home.

"I'll start transferring more, no problem," King said, and Kittu and the others nodded, with the same apathetic air as they had carried throughout the conversation, as if this promise were beside the point. If he sent more cash, of course, more would just disappear.

"Times change," Kittu said, shrugging.

Gun and his gang, having fled the Garden long ago, had turned up in Dubai. They had supposedly made it rich by helping to build a port. They had even taken Gun's sister Jaggayyamma with them, to work as a nanny for the six children of an oil sheikh. Her husband, sons, and cat had stayed behind, and with the money she sent back, they had constructed one of the biggest houses in Kothapalli, right in the center of town, on the spot where Appayya's school once stood. The house was two stories tall, and at night Jaggayyamma's teenage sons would sit on the open rooftop, where the laundry was hung, and get drunk, with no concern for what anyone thought of them or, by extension, for the reputation of the Raos. Sometimes, for fun, they would feed the cat catnip, and she would join in the craziness and hollering.

Once Kittu had tried to impress upon their father, Jaggayyamma's husband, that the Garden's reputation was at risk. But the man only laughed. "You have nothing to do with us," he said. "We have nothing to do with you. Having a name in common means nothing anymore! If that makes you upset, don't blame me. Blame old Chinna Rao." Chinna was long dead then. It had taken all of Kittu's restraint not to jump at the man. "Well, it's too bad he's not around anymore to be blamed," he said coldly.

All these years later, the same battles were being waged. Hearing about it exhausted King. "Hey," he said. "What ever happened to the one-legged cripple?"

"I haven't seen him in a long time," Kittu said. "Maybe he died."

When he went into the Big House to sleep that night, Margie was already asleep in Sita's bed, which she had given them. He wasn't tired yet, and when he went to the main room to sit down, Sita called out to him. He found her curled up on the twin bed in the other room—his bed, his room. "Come sit," she said. "Can't sleep?"

"Jet lag," he said.

"What's that?"

"At home, it's daytime, so I'm not tired," he said.

She made a small sound of displeasure. "Home," she said meaningfully. "*This* is home."

It occurred to him that she seemed bitter—and then he thought back to his childhood and recalled that she had always seemed bitter; it had been her natural state, as far back as he could remember. "Amma, what do you spend your time doing nowadays?" he said.

"Nothing much," she said. "I cook, I clean. I wait for your letters."

"I write."

"You don't write."

"I'll write."

"You won't."

"Are you mad at me, Amma?" he said. He was aware that he was being childish but couldn't help himself. "Aren't you proud of me? Aren't you the one who wanted me to succeed? I remember you always said, 'I named him King because he's going to grow up to do big things.' I thought about that a lot when I was little. I thought: I'd better do big things."

"I'm not mad," she replied. "When my sister died, I promised myself that I'd honor her by making you my son and giving you the best possible life. I married Pedda, I came to the Garden. But I never fit in here. I didn't love Pedda. I didn't even trust the women. I held them as responsible as anyone for my sister's death. I did give you that life I promised, though. I wanted you to get out of here. You were my king, the child of my sister. Go, go, go rule someplace! I thought. But when you left, Kingie, it got so *quiet*. It happened all at once. Chinna died. You left. I wasn't thinking, all that time you were growing up, about what would happen next. Then you left, you got educated, you got famous, and I thought, Well, is that all there is to it? All that education, all that fame—for what? Kingie, do you ever ask yourself that? For what? My sister is still dead."

She shook her head. "I hated that Pedda for what he did to her; I hated him all along. You're a grown-up now. We can be honest with each other. I didn't want to give him more children. But I should have held my breath and done it. Then I would have had some children I could keep here at home. At least one girl, to take care of me."

He felt small, as if he had been returned to his childhood, when, whether he was with his mother or his father, he couldn't lose the sense that he belonged to neither of them—that he was, in fact, despite being seen as the Raos' heir apparent, a kind of orphan. A motherless, fatherless child. He thought of his mother—his real mother, Radha, the one whom he had killed in order to be born. Sita was smoothing the hem of her sari, not looking at him.

"I'm not trying to be famous," he said at last. "I'm trying to make the world better. Chinna told me, 'If you just make the world better than it was when you got here, that's a good life.' That's all I'm trying to do."

Sita laughed bitterly. "That's something only a man would come up with."

"You disagree? Amma, you think he was wrong?"

She laughed again. "No one cares what your mother thinks; that's my point."

"Amma, come to America with us," he pleaded. "I'll build you a big house. You can see for yourself, people think I'm making the world better."

"And then what? Spend my final years taking English lessons? I can't even have a conversation with my own daughter-in-law. Is she nice? Is she not nice? I can't tell! You should have taught her some Telugu before coming here."

"There are a lot of Telugu people in Seattle."

"I doubt there are a lot of our people." She was talking about caste.

"No one cares about that there," he said. "Everyone knows I'm

Dalit. Indians there only care about money, big houses, and all that. And you'd have that, Amma, I'd build you a mansion."

"Okay, Kingie," she said tiredly. He could tell she was just placating him. "Fine. I'll come. When you have a baby, when you have a little girl—then I'll come."

That afternoon, the *Eenadu* reporter arrived, along with a photographer, as Margie had instructed. A young nephew, wearing only a pair of shorts, brought them to King and Margie, who were wandering through the grove. He said proudly, in English, "Computer Uncle, I told them everything about the coconuts, how this is where you learned to be a businessman, how you even got the name Coconut from this place, isn't it?"

King laughed. "It all started here," he intoned, sweeping his arms wide.

Soon AFTER King and Margie's return home from Kothapalli, they were sitting on the couch in Margie's office, a box of pizza open on their laps, and King ventured, "You're good at names. If we had a child, what name would you choose?"

"For a girl," she said, "Athena."

He looked up: "Really?"

Margie laughed, and then stopped. "Wait, you're not being serious."

"Married couples talk about children," he said defensively.

Margie looked at him, grimaced, and stuck a finger in her mouth. "Do I have oregano in my teeth?" she said.

"Be serious."

"I'm not having this conversation, man," she said, with a tone of finality that enraged him. "We talked about it, remember? We decided years ago we don't have time for kids."

"That was a long time ago."

She breathed, a show of her patience being tried. "Okay, let me say it again in a more straightforward way," she said. "I don't want to have babies. It makes me sick to my stomach, the idea of having babies. It's different for men and women. I'd be stuck taking care of them while you pursued your dreams."

"Don't be mean."

"What's mean about that?"

"I want to talk about babies, and you won't let me." He was aware of his tone, sullen and pathetic, but he couldn't help it.

"Talk about babies all you want!" she said. "I don't care if you talk about babies! It does nothing for me. It doesn't turn me on. I'm not your little housewife. I'm not going to do it."

He was alarmed by her tone. "My mom never had any children, any biological ones, and she regretted it," he said.

She raised her eyebrows archly. "I hope it goes without saying that I'm not your mother."

"I know that."

"Is that why you're rethinking it? Because of her regrets?"

"She said she doesn't care if I make the world a better place. She said only men care about that."

"I'm sure that's not what she said."

"She said only a man would say that a good life is about making the world better."

At this, she laughed—a laugh of understanding. "I get *that*," she said.

"You do?" he said. "Well, what does it mean?"

"Think about the options she had available to her, King! She couldn't have made the world better, not in the way you or your uncle meant, if she wanted to. Her sister died, and she married her sister's husband and adopted you. That was her life. It was set when she was a teenage girl, a child."

"That's not my fault," he said, defensive. But maybe it had been. His birth had killed Radha and foreshortened the life Sita might have had. No one had ever said it out loud. He felt his face heating up. "You don't know a thing about it," he said.

Margie's head jolted back as if she had been hit. She rose and placed the greasy pizza box on the round table where they sometimes held meetings. "You're right that I don't know about your mom's experience," she said, with her back to him. "But I do know about being a woman and existing only in relation to the men around yourself."

"That's ridiculous. You're the most powerful businesswoman in the world."

"Ha," she said flatly. She moved back to the couch and sat next to him. "Think back a couple of decades. Think back to when we first met. Remember what I told you about not making it as an artist? Remember I told you I applied to art school, and they said I was no good—my art wasn't bold enough?"

"Of course."

"You never asked what exactly they said."

"You told me what they said."

"I didn't tell you the exact phrase he used, that man who didn't admit me. He called it 'domestic and safe.' What I told you was that I believed him. But I lied. My paintings were *good*; I knew it. I'd sat in that spot at my dad's house, by the cherry blossom tree, for a whole season, and I'd done four different paintings. One where the tree is bare, with a layer of snow on the branches. Another when it's getting its buds. The third one when it's blossoming. And the fourth when the blossoms start turning brown and drooping. That last one was gross. It was my favorite. But the photorealism movement—it was all men. Ralph Goings. Chuck Close. Those professors who rejected me—that was *sexism*. Domestic, safe—that language. What he meant was that I was too much of a girl."

She paused, as if she wasn't sure whether to continue. Then she said, quietly, "Didn't you ever wonder why I was so fixated on getting you involved in the business?"

It had never occurred to him to wonder. He had thought it was because he was an excellent programmer. He had hoped it was also because she was attracted to him.

"It was because you were a man, but one who wouldn't control me," she said.

He laughed, a bit stunned.

She seemed to understand. "It *started* like that, at the beginning," she added gently. "Then we fell in love." She took a deep breath and blew it out loudly. "I don't know," she said. "You want to have babies?"

THE FERTILITY CLINIC on campus wasn't far from the engineering building. They had requested a private consultation at their home, but this had been rejected by the clinic's director, who told them that, as a public institution, the clinic couldn't risk the appearance of treating some patients differently from others. She conceded, though, "I understand you're public figures, and we want to protect your privacy." She suggested that they visit with her before business hours, at six in the morning on a Friday in August, and for good measure enter through a side door.

They arrived at that door and knocked. King squeezed Margaret's hand and said, "It feels—" and, as she did in the moments when they were most in tune with each other, she completed his sentence, "—sort of right." Inside, in a conference room, the doctor sat across from them and their lawyers across a table. There was a contract to sign, with all kinds of morbid eventualities laid out. They checked a box saying that if one of them died, the other could make decisions about what to do with the embryos. If they divorced, the embryos would be donated for research to the King and Margaret Rao Project.

Thus began the process by which I ended up, little not-yet-human me, in a refrigerated basement room, enclosed in a tube stickered with an identification number, *63085290852*, nestled between tubes *63085290851* and *63085290853*.

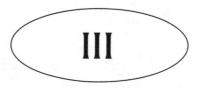

19

Pedda had suffered a stroke. That morning, the Hollander and Chinna had rushed him to the hospital in Rajahmundry for treatment. A week later, after he was out of danger, they brought him to the Hollander's clinic to recuperate. King and Sita went to stay with Pedda there, to relieve Chinna, who had been with him all week long. The clinic's ten rooms were arranged around a square courtyard, at the corners of which some marigolds sprouted from wooden planters, next to wooden benches. Pedda was asleep in his room on a small cot, a white sheet tucked tight around him. Ever since the stroke, Chinna explained, he had been sleeping almost all day and night. He had even lost the ability to talk. A light curtain on the window fluttered. A ceiling fan wheezed overhead. A clock made a tiny ticking sound at intervals. The room smelled of Pedda's sweat and some sharp detergent.

"Can he hear us?" King said.

"Maybe," Chinna said. "Maybe not."

There was a kitchen for the patients' use across the courtyard, and he could hear the crackle and pop of cumin and mustard seeds and the hushed, irritable voices of a half dozen aunties trying to navigate around one another in the small room.

"Can you hear us?" King said softly to his father, testing.

Pedda didn't move.

"Stop it," Sita snapped. "He can't hear, look at him!" She shook her head in disgust, as if it were Pedda's fault he had ended up in this condition, and maybe, King thought, she was right. It had been a dumb notion that a cow would rescue the Garden. Now, with Pedda's medical bills, they would end up much worse off than before.

"I'll be going," Chinna said to Sita. Her father was right around the corner, he reminded her, if she needed anything.

"I know that," Sita replied sharply. Indicating the mats they had brought to sleep on, she said to King, "Come on, help me roll these out."

He got up to assist his mother. His father remained still. Wake up, he thought in Pedda's direction. The nurses who had been tending to Pedda came in to introduce themselves. Ann and Helena were their names. They were from Holland, too. Ann, who didn't speak Telugu, mostly pantomimed shyly. But Helena, who was learning their language so that she could translate the Gospels, had a bolder spirit. "I know this is hard," she said, in Telugu, to Sita, touching her arm.

"It's a waste of time and a waste of money," she said. "He could just rest at home." King realized his mother was suspicious. The Hollander charged families who could afford his services, families like theirs, and she must be under the impression that he was swindling them.

Pedda suddenly opened his eyes and mooed. There was a strange, drooped expression on his face, but he seemed to be looking at Sita. "Moo," he said again.

"What?" Sita said. She looked at King, as if he could translate.

"Moo!" Pedda said again, raising his voice, and King realized that, in fact, he could translate. His father was asking after the cow.

"King, run and find the Hollander," his mother hissed.

"She died," King cried, as he stood. To his mother, he said, "Tell him! Tell him she died!"

"Who died?" Sita cried. "Go get the Hollander!"

Pedda made loud barking sounds of anguish and resumed mooing. The other patients, drawn by the commotion, crowded at the door and peered in. The Hollander came running, Ann at his side, and when he came close, Pedda reached for the Hollander's coat, clutching it. Helena and Ann each held one of his wrists to the cot and pushed their weight against Pedda as he struggled and heaved against them.

"Blessed are the poor —" Helena murmured, in rough Telugu.

"Not now, Helena!" the Hollander cried, and he flourished a needle and stabbed Pedda in the shoulder. Pedda smiled, as if something had happened to delight him. He fell asleep and began snoring.

"Now, then?" Helena said. "Now, Doctor?" There was defiance in her voice.

"Fine," the Hollander said.

"Blessed are the poor," Helena said, "for theirs is the kingdom of heaven!"

Sita had been standing back quietly, her arms stiff at her sides. Now she moved forward and put a hand on Helena's. "Stop it," she said.

Helena startled, as if out of a dream. "Oh!" she said. "Yes, it's all right. You believe in your own gods."

"I believe in no god at all," King's mother said, steel-voiced. "I don't care which god you pray to, but you looked at him and said, 'Blessed are the poor,' and that wasn't right. We may be Dalits, but, as the doctor knows well, we are not poor."

WHETHER THE HOLLANDER was swindling them, as Sita suspected, or not, as Chinna trusted, the recuperation period was expected to be long, a matter of months. Most nights, Sita stayed with Pedda at the clinic, not out of love, she made clear, but out of duty, and she instructed Chinna to watch over King. She didn't trust the others to keep him on track.

Some afternoons, Chinna would meet King after school, riding in the oxcart he had bought. "Climb in, climb in, kiddos," Chinna cried to the children, and as many of them as would fit clambered into the cart, and they dropped off each of King's classmates at home along the way back to the Garden. After arriving home, King and Chinna sat together at a long table they had brought into a side room of King's House, with the day's work spread before them. Chinna's ledgers, King's homework. The atmosphere was homey and warm. Outside, the youngest kids laughed and chattered in the clearing.

On Saturdays, Chinna started bringing King with him to the weekly market in Ambajipuram, where the coconut deals were made. In the evenings when they returned, King's cousins and nieces and nephews would hear the oxcart coming down the lane and rush up to meet them. "Oh come on!" Chinna would cry good-naturedly. "Let these poor, tired dogs pass!" But the children would surround the cart, singing, "Treats, treats," and King would jump down to join them, and finally, Chinna would reach into a cloth package and pull out one small bundle wrapped in newspaper, then another and another, which he tossed high in the air one by one. The game was that, while each of the packets contained sweets or candies, only one held their favorite—a big crystal of sugar candy that, once found, would be held up and turned in the air by whoever had the good fortune of having caught it, while the others stopped their clamor and admired for a moment how the sunlight glinted from it as if from a diamond or shard of ice, until the victor finally lowered his hand and took one bite before passing it on to the next child, who passed it to the next, and so on, so that they could each taste it, until all that remained was a sticky film on their fingers. They tented their fingers and pulled them apart with a satisfying snap.

Afterward, in King's House, he and his uncle sat at their table counting the cash from the day's sales and recording the total. Along with that figure, King wrote other numbers dictated by Chinna: the amount of copra, the price of sale. It was Chinna who packed the cash into bundles with twine and locked it away in a big box hidden in a hole in the ground, under a padlocked cover.

After years of troubles, business had improved a lot. This was mostly thanks to a decision that had been made not by Chinna, but by Grandfather Rao, a decade earlier. King remembered when Grandfather Rao had given loans to the other Dalits of Kothapalli so they could grow their own coconut trees. Now, a decade later, those loans were coming due, and Chinna, in his own stroke of genius, had decided the farmers could repay their debt in the form of coconuts. Early each morning, on the way to school, King accompanied Chinna, in the oxcart, to these debtors' farms, where they collected their due. While King was at school, Chinna and the uncles would organize those coconuts for processing. Now much more of the Raos' income was from processing other farmers' coconuts than from their own harvest.

After the market one evening, Chinna dumped the jute sack of cash onto his table and said, "Help me out with this. You're good at math. What we have to do is make piles of hundreds, then wrap them together. All this cash makes your heart beat faster. But if you keep doing it, it'll start to feel like anything else. Just a big pile of colored paper. It only matters because it puts food in our mouths, puts a roof over our heads. Now go like this," he said, and he licked his thumb and forefinger and grabbed a fistful. King did as he was told. The bills were soft and a little damp under his fingers. His heartbeat did quicken.

He would never say it out loud, but his father's stroke had freed him. When he spent time with Chinna, Pedda wasn't there to make him feel as if it were a betrayal. And yet, in another sense, he still felt guilty. He had stopped visiting as often. Pedda was usually sleeping, anyway, and he still couldn't talk.

ONE AFTERNOON, THOUGH, walking home from school past the clinic, he peeked into the courtyard. He paused. A girl was crouched on her haunches in a nightgown, chopping onions. The sight of her unsettled him. When she looked up and he saw her hazel eyes, he understood why. She was the girl with the crazy mother, the one who had sold them the sick cow. Her short hair was knotted around her head like a bird's nest. She had a large mole on the side of her nose in the shape of a kidney bean. Her skin was coffee-colored and her cheekbones sharp. He wanted to rush past, but instead, for some reason, he called to her. "You're that girl with the sick mother."

"What do you know about my mother?" she bristled. She spoke with a rough voice that gave him an unfamiliar sense of desperation.

"You sold my dad that cow," he said.

She moved her head up and down in vague recognition. "Oh," she said. "You're that kid."

"The cow died."

"I heard all about it," she said. "I know all the news around here. Another thing I know is that no one comes around to visit your dad. Your uncle comes, but only for a minute, and he mostly sits out here in the courtyard and talks to the Hollander. He doesn't sit with his brother. Your mother's even worse. She just stands over his bed and nags him."

"You don't know anything!" he cried.

"You shouldn't be ashamed of your parents when they're ill. My mother has syphilis, and I'm not ashamed to say it."

He had never heard the word. "Syphilis?" he said.

"Shut up!" she hissed, looking around. "I'll tell the Hollander you're insulting my mother. I know your name is King Rao." She said it like it contained a threat. But then she softened and introduced herself. "My name is Sushma Ganti, daughter of Vindu Ganti," she said in a grand, formal tone. "But people call me Minnu."

Pedda seemed to have aged years. Crow's-feet had deepened at the corners of his eyes, his jaw had turned to jowl, and, most dramatically, a shock of white hair had emerged at his forehead. King stood at his bedside, looking down at him.

"Talk to him," Minnu insisted, standing in the doorway.

"He can't hear me."

"He can. The Hollander told me."

"My mom said he can't."

"Then why does she nag him all day long?"

He began visiting daily after school. Often the nurses stood on the balcony of the top floor, where they and the Hollander lived, to greet him with snacks as he came into the courtyard.

"It's only because I know English," he told Minnu, who envied him for it.

She tossed her head and said, "No, it's because you're a boy, stupid."

After that he looked up at the nurses and thought with wonder, *It's because I'm a boy.* The nurses wore crisp white uniforms, complete with hats like paper boats, and leaned with their forearms on the wrought iron as they dangled little biscuit packets down between thumb and forefinger. "Only if you haven't been bad," they teased, and King smiled up at them from beneath his eyelashes and cupped his hands for the treat, hotly aware of Minnu lurking nearby, envious.

Minnu was—according to Minnu—an unusually perceptive person. She could see people's thoughts by looking at them. They sat on the foot of Pedda's bed while he slept. She watched him and said, "He's changing right in front of us, can't you see?"

King couldn't see, but he believed her. Somehow he believed her. They were sitting on the bed playing Old Maid, which Helena and the Hollander had taught them. All of a sudden Pedda kicked out his leg and sent the cards onto the floor and then laughed bitterly. King cried, "You see, he's mad that we're not paying attention to him, so he wanted to mess up our game!" Minnu didn't respond immediately. Again, she was examining Pedda's face with a questioning look. "No," she finally said. "It was a mistake; he feels stupid. Look at him, look at how he widens his eyes at you, look at how he opens his mouth a little. See, he's trying to tell you he didn't do it on purpose."

A MONTH PASSED, and another. In the springtime, the nurses planted their little garden of marigolds in the courtyard. King turned thirteen. He liked to lay on his back on the wooden benches, unshirted. Hair had begun sprouting on his chest. He twisted the strands idly between his thumb and forefinger. "Oh, don't do that!" Minnu said, and when he continued, she laughed roughly and covered her face.

Minnu, having spent what she had made from selling the cow, now earned money by making laddus in the clinic's kitchen and selling them to villagers. The Hollander took care of her mother for free, she told King, but there were other expenses, mainly food. The laddus were considered the best the village had ever encountered. Otherwise, an odd creature like her, with a mother like that, wouldn't have stood a chance of getting people to buy her food.

Sometimes the nurses gave King and Minnu money and sent them to the store with a shopping list. One afternoon, Minnu brought along her satchel of laddus so she could sell some along the way. They detoured to the outskirts of the village, where there stood a giant banyan tree with great overground roots. A famous ascetic was said to have fasted there for ten years.

King would read Minnu's palms for free, he said, in exchange for a free laddu. He had learned to read from them from one of his cousins.

"That isn't fair," she told him. "How will I know you aren't making it all up?"

"Okay, first I'll read your palms, and if you like it, I get a laddu."

"Fine," she said, laughing, and she held out her hands but kept shifting as flies landed on her.

"You have to stop fidgeting."

"The flies, they're all over."

"It's because of all your laddus; you smell sweet," he said, and blushed.

"I know that," she said, pulling away.

They sat for a while in silence. It was nice. He had never had a friendship that felt as special as this. "Hey," King said. "Do you believe that ascetic really fasted for ten years?"

"No," she said. "People snuck him food in the middle of the night. When I was little, and we had no money, I got really hungry, and one day I sat under a tree like this and prayed to God, 'Hey, you, if you're real, why don't you give me a laddu to eat?' Suddenly a crow flew right above me and dropped half of a laddu at my feet. I was so afraid that I cried. I ate the laddu, and it was the best laddu I ever tasted in my life. I went home and told my mother, and she said, 'Well, it's a sign from God. He wants you to start making laddus and selling them to make money to feed us!' I hadn't thought of that at all. But I went to the baker in the village where we were living and told him what had happened and asked him to teach me how to make laddus. He was afraid not to teach me, because of what had happened with the crow. He was a big believer himself. Many years later, my mother admitted she had never believed in God at all, but she told me it was a sign because she was hungry, too."

She took out a laddu, considered it, and returned it to the bag. "But I like Jesus because he forgives your sins. You only have to ask, and he forgives everything." Helena had converted Minnu into a Christian. "It doesn't matter what people did in their past," Minnu told King. "As long as they're willing to repent and change. The future is the important part."

"I'm not finished reading your palms," King said. He took up her hands again. Her hands were rough and dry, its lines deeply etched. "You have hands like an old woman," he said.

"What's wrong with you?" she cried. "That's not nice!"

"They say if your hands have dark lines, you have an old soul."

Minnu stood and began running back to the clinic. He caught up with her. She slowed to a brisk walk alongside him. But neither of them spoke, and her face was clouded. He asked if he had earned his laddu. She looked up at him, furious: "No!" she shouted, and he nodded, and they walked back to the clinic in strained silence. That night he masturbated and thought about her. Afterward, he felt monstrous, despicable.

WHILE CHINNA TRUSTED the Hollander—he had a sweet spot for educated men and foreigners—Sita had doubled down on her belief that the doctor was keeping Pedda in bed so that he could continue collecting fees. "If you're so great," she said, "why is he still sick?" The doctor gritted his teeth, clearly offended, and replied, "I'm not a magician, madam."

But someone in the village knew a witch doctor who reportedly could cure any ill. One morning the witch doctor walked into the Hollander's clinic and installed himself on a courtyard bench, laying out his powders and tinctures. He was a small, elderly, fair-complected man, with the sparsest planting of white hair on a liver-spotted head. Helena and Ann stood on either side of the bench, looking vexed. The Hollander had gone to the city to buy medical supplies, and they didn't know whether to kick the witch doctor out or let him stay.

The patients insisted that he stay, hopeful he could cure them. Aware of the patients' families suspicions—that the doctor was a swindler, keeping them from healing on purpose—the nurses let the witch doctor remain. The patients and their families thronged the small courtyard. King and Minnu shoved their way to the front; they were young and nimble. The witch doctor asked a couple of questions about their parents' respective troubles. He sold Minnu a bag of twigs and leaves that she was to boil in hot water to make tea for her mother. He told King that he must rub the blood of a healthy pigeon on his father's limbs to restore their movement, and on his throat to restore his speech.

By the time the Hollander returned, the witch doctor was long gone. The Hollander shouted at Helena and Ann for not having quickly sent the man away and ordered all the patients to hand over any medicine they had bought. Only one man came forward. He was extremely religious and couldn't lie. But the rest hid their potions and claimed they had bought none. That evening, after the Hollander had gone to his room upstairs, Minnu and King forced Minnu's mother, the madwoman, to drink the witch doctor's concoction. Suddenly she became animated and rose to her feet with more energy than she had shown in months. "It worked, it worked!" Minnu whispered, hopping up and down.

"It worked!" the madwoman cried.

"Now we have to kill a pigeon," Minnu said.

"A pigeon!" the madwoman cried. "Let me!" She hobbled into the kitchen and returned with a small sack of pumpkin seed, then stood in the courtyard tossing handfuls of it in the air. "Come and get it, little birdies!" she cackled. A great swarm of pigeons came flapping down into the courtyard. The patients stood in their doorways and watched, curious. "Come and get it!" the madwoman cried again, and when the pigeons descended, she sprang upon them, her sari billowing.

When all the pumpkin seed had been eaten and most of the pigeons had flown off, he realized the madwoman had a small bird trapped in her hand. It tried to flap its wings, but she squeezed it tight. He could see the alarm in the creature's beady eyes, until the madwoman covered the pigeon's head with her other hand and twisted. He heard a weak crack. The madwoman dropped the bird to the ground and looked at him. King regarded the bird. It was still. Dead, it had the composition less of an animal than of some small, strange sculpture. A sour taste pushed up through his throat and erupted. He ran to the flower bed and vomited. When he finished, Minnu fetched a knife and a cup and knelt next to King, shoving the implements in his direction. "Go ahead," she said in a soft, reverent voice.

"I can't."

"If you don't do it, I will," she threatened. "Hurry, do it. The Hollander could come down any second."

That awakened him. He set the dead bird down on a bench and cut off its head, letting the blood drip into the cup Minnu had brought him. He squeezed the bird like it was a washcloth to get all the blood out. He went to his father's room. "Get me a wet towel," he said to Minnu, and when she brought it to him, he dipped it into the cup. Minnu and the madwoman stood in the doorway and watched. "Go do something with that bird," King said. "Leave me alone."

They reluctantly slipped out. King rose and closed the door. He was alone with his father and the deep smell of iron. His father looked at him with great anticipation; he understood something important was about to happen. King sat on the cot. He placed the cup of blood on the floor, dipped the towel into it, and scooped. The blood was warm and sticky, like syrup. He could feel his own heartbeat and thought of the heartbeat of the bird. He pressed the bloodied towel to his father's shin and rubbed. His father sighed. The sensuousness of it—the hard bones of his father's ankles, the meatiness of his calves—mortified King. He took up some more of the blood and rubbed it into the bowl of his father's knee and into the long cord of sinew that ran up the back of his thigh. He was aware of the sound of his own breathing. He covered his father with blood, and when he got to his neck, he tipped the cup over it and dripped the remaining blood into the hollow below his Adam's apple. "Don't move," he said, and his father answered affirmatively with his eyes. With the towel, King spent a long time massaging the blood there.

"Is this all right?" he said after a long time—testing, half expecting his father to answer. But Pedda said nothing.

A grayish string of drool hung from Pedda's chin. With his sleeve, King wiped his father's face. His father's eyes filled with tears. They looked at each other for a long time, silent. Pedda's breath was sour-smelling and hot. On his face there appeared a blissful but alert expression, like that of a cat. You killed my mother, and now look at you, King thought, idly, without spite. He kept massaging. There was blood all over the sheets. By morning, he thought, it would be brown and cracked, like mud. He hummed a song that he had overheard blaring from the trucks that drove around the village advertising movies. Pedda closed his eyes. His snoring resumed.

On a morning soon after that, when Helena came bicycling down the path to the Garden, pumping her legs like a man, King was sure he understood what had happened: She had come, he was certain, to tell them his father had regained his speech. He stuck his head out the window and called out, "Helena, Helena!" She didn't look up. "Helena!" he called again. His cousin Kittu was hanging around the courtyard, and the nurse asked him to fetch Chinna. Chinna came out of the Big House, and Helena said something to him in such a low voice that King couldn't hear.

"But all of a sudden?" Chinna said in a high, trembling voice. "Just like that?"

20

"Pack up," Elemen commanded one afternoon in that unusual tone of hers, at once gentle and domineering. She stood in the doorway of Edison while I got dressed, then led me south along the waterfront until we arrived at a giant field, of some twenty acres, covered with rows and rows of solar panels, angled to face the sun like palms turned up in worship. Beyond the field stood a single-story home, surrounded by a veranda—not unlike our house on Blake Island. "This is—" I began, before stopping myself. The setting was as familiar to me as Coconut's old campus had been.

"You recognize it," Elemen said, watching me carefully.

"I've seen old pictures," I replied. It wasn't a lie. In the photographs in my father's albums, his estate south of Coconut's campus is filled with trees bearing mangoes, curry leaves, custard apples, and, of course, coconuts. Margie loved the trees for their symbolic value, and King loved them for themselves. They reminded him of home. Now those trees had been transplanted to the spheres, replaced with the solar panels, which, for much of the year, supplied all of the island's power. "We call it the Farm," Elemen said.

She explained that if the island's residents filled up their Catches with power all spring, summer, and fall, they lasted through midwinter. Donations and trade then provided enough extra power to get them through to the next spring.

The sun blazed as we stood among the solar panels. Two months had passed since my arrival on Bainbridge, and, for the fifth time in five years, this was the hottest fall on record on the island. Though we were cut off from the Internet, Elemen and the other night workers gathered news each night at the Cha Cha, and they had reported back that the same was happening around the world. Wildfires had started blazing in Australia, California, and Colorado in March and still hadn't stopped. A heat wave in France had killed three thousand people. Elemen had implied that the Exes were preparing some action in response to all of this, though she had been cagey about the details. Had she finally concluded that I could be trusted? Had she now brought me here to fill me in?

Across the yard, on the porch of the house, a half dozen people had come outside and stood in a huddle, a couple of them turning to look over at us now and then. Elemen went through their names, pointing to a distant figure with each one: "Palmo's the big one, the lifter around here. That's Araxa. There's Indig. Onnie and Romeo are powering up the Catches. Don's over there. He's a sweetheart, but you wouldn't know it. There's Nelo." I knew these names: These were the original, most notorious Exes, the ones who had negotiated with the Board after the fire on the Exes' behalf, and had first arrived here after the Blanklands' creation.

Elemen pointed to a tall Black man with an Afro, lean but broad-shouldered, like a swimmer. "There's Otis," she said, her voice suddenly bright. I realized it was the same man Arno had spoken to the morning he brought me to the spheres, the one who had directed us to Elemen. She had never mentioned him, but his name, too, was familiar: Otis Ex—the one who started the fire all those years ago. Elemen raised a hand toward him, and he smiled widely and waved back at her. "He's the love of my life," she said casually. The phrase rang loudly in my ears, an intrusion. The love of my life, the love of my life.

WHEN EVENING CAME, we dined at a long picnic table in the backyard, on sliced tomatoes and a length of crusted bread, which was passed around, hand to hand, dropping crumbs. The atmosphere seemed tense—no one spoke more than a few words—for reasons that were opaque to me. I watched Otis eat. He handled his tomatoes elegantly, pinching each slice between forefinger and thumb and lifting it quickly to his mouth, so it wouldn't drip. He bent low over his plate. After a while, Elemen rose and walked toward the house, and a moment later Otis followed her. A couple of faces lifted, watching him, glancing at me, then turning back to their food. It occurred to me only then that this had something to do with me. I murmured that I needed to use the bathroom. I walked around to the back side of the house, where the outhouse stood, but, instead of going to it, crept up to the rear door of the house. Inside, I could hear Elemen and Otis arguing. I crouched against the house and listened.

"What did you promise her, El?" Otis was saying. His tone wasn't threatening; it sounded, to me, fearful.

"She's pretty, man! Sweet, innocent. No one would suspect her."

"Listen, El, yeah, she looks nice. But no one here is going to go for it. It doesn't matter what kind of ambassador you trot out. Look, we're finally doing all right out here." His voice was low, plaintive. "We're building the community you talked about. You said the Shareholders weren't our problem anymore. You said it was up to them to see the truth for themselves, and when they did, we would have built a model for how to do it better. You said all that."

"I said it."

"So leave it up to them, then. It's not our problem anymore."

For a while I heard nothing and wondered what was passing between them. When Elemen spoke, it was with the same deliberately casual tone she had used when she called Otis the love of her life. She was giving a kind of performance. "It's funny," she said. "My scouts at the Cha Cha say no one's even talking about Hothouse Earth anymore. It's not that they don't believe it's happening—that's not even the argument anymore. It's that they're convinced Coconut is about to put out some invention to pull all the carbon out of the air. Some of them are convinced the invention already exists."

"What kind of invention?" Otis sounded almost hopeful.

"Oh, it's their favorite kind," Elemen said, and now it seemed she was almost having fun. "King Rao invented it: It's the kind that's never actually going to happen, but that doesn't matter, because its value comes entirely from the illusion of it. You draw a beautiful picture of the invention and post it on Social and let it multiply, and after a while the question of whether the invention exists—whether it'll ever exist—doesn't matter anymore. The invention has succeeded in its goal, which is to let all the world's Shareholders live under the pretense that they can keep spoiling the planet with no consequences. In fact, they should! In fact, it's their civic duty!"

"You talk like you're trying to convince me," Otis said glumly. "But you're preaching to the choir."

"Really, though? You talk about waiting three, four, five generations for Shareholders to see what's happening? The Shareholders will be extinct then. So will we." I recognized the language; it was my own. "This is exactly what we predicted," she went on. It wasn't that Shareholders were too afraid of the Board to call them out on their lies. It was more insidious than that. Shareholder Government had so fully aligned its citizens with corporate interests that no one cared to call the Board out. You didn't gain Social Capital for swearing off fossil fuels, going vegetarian. You gained it by consuming as much as you could, as fast as you could.

"So what are you saying we should do instead?" Otis said, a challenge in his voice. "Riot in the streets? Did you forget how—"

"You killed three people, including a child," she interrupted coldly. "I'm aware."

When Otis responded, his voice trembled. "You're cruel some-times," he said.

"But good God, Otis, you and your guilt! It's boring! It's beside the point! You're the first one who told us that people on the main-land don't even remember us anymore. You told us that yourself. They assume we're defunct. Isn't that right? If life is decent out here, you think that's somehow an affront to them? You think the Board would prefer to see us suffering? Of course not. This is exactly where the Board wants us. Far from them, satisfied. They know that when Hothouse Earth really gets bad—when that ice really starts melting—these islands will be the first to go. *Whoosh.* And all this time, you're sitting here beating yourself up over that *fire*, Otis? You're sitting here still imagining that you're the guilty one, because you're the one who got thrown in prison for your crime? How many times have we had this conversation?"

Their voices receded; they were moving back toward the front door. I waited a while before returning, around the side of the house, to the table. By the time I arrived, it was clear they had brought their argument to the group. Elemen was sitting up, addressing the group. "How many are we, fifteen, sixteen?" Her face was flushed. Her nostrils flared, bull-like. "They're sure to miss us when we're gone. That'll sure show them who's boss." She threw up her hands. "It's called retreating. At least call it what it is."

"Hey, we don't do war metaphors here," Nelo, a small, pale, hamstery girl who couldn't have been any older than me, said. She looked at Otis, as if seeking approval. He just shook his head.

"Forfeit, then; we forfeited!"

"That's a banking metaphor."

"All right, settle down, Nelo."

"But play it out, El," said the man across from her—Don, a big, blue-eyed, dough-faced man in his seventies with an air of resignation. "Imagine trying to get ourselves into Shareholder life again. First of all, if we refuse to use Social, we're never going to reach enough people. And even if we did miraculously reach them, we would be declaring war on the Board of Shareholders, and for what? The whole point of Hothouse Earth is that you can't reverse it. It's too late. What would the purpose be?"

"The purpose?" Elemen hit the table, and the plates jumped. "It's the principle of it," she said.

"The principle," Don repeated flatly. The word sounded unsubstantial in his mouth, meaningless. No one else spoke, as if his point had now been eminently made. Even I could see the illogic of her position.

Elemen swallowed and blinked rapidly. For a terrible moment, I thought she might weep. But then she sat up straighter and pointed at me. I sat still, as if indicted. "She's staying," she said. She laughed, in that small way that people laugh when they're actually sad.

No one said a thing. Some bent over their plates, while others looked to me as if they expected a response. But try as I might, I could not figure out what was going on. Elemen had some mission in mind for me that would be risky or even dangerous—I had gathered that much—and it seemed she had raised it with the others earlier, gotten a cool reception, and brought me here anyway. But now what? Elemen stared at me, sweat beading on her forehead, as if there were a line I had forgotten. A knot pulsed in my gut. "It's so beautiful here!" I blurted. "This is so great!"

It really was beautiful, I reiterated that night, sitting up, holding my knees, on the blankets that Elemen had rolled out for me on the floor of her room. It really was great.

"Oh, it sure fucking is," Elemen said, with a sour laugh.

And then she explained. The people I had met tonight, she said, had been her closest friends for decades. At the police station, the morning after the fire, this group of friends had made clear, under questioning, that they would not aid in identifying any individual perpetrator. Rather, each one of them—Elemen, Don, Otis, Araxa, Indig, and the hundred and forty-five others hauled in on charges of unlawful assembly—confessed to the crime, in vague, global

terms, until it became clear that they were there not to help with
the investigation at all but to hinder it. Their refusal was not dis-
similar to what King Rao had done, they noted, using the collective
language of the corporation to disavow any individual responsibility for sixty-four people's deaths due to the Harmonica tests. It was
only when the Board's own detectives identified the arsonist—it
took them all of six hours—that the Exes negotiated terms.

The morning the Blanklands were declared open, they had
held in their possession a couple dozen small kayaks and canoes,
carrying garden tools, canned foods, several first-aid kits, tents
and stakes, hand-crank-operated flashlights and lanterns, sleeping
bags, and a couple of pots and pans, all acquired by donation. The
last known photograph of Elemen shows her perched in a kayak, in
a tank top and sunglasses, her hair tied in a high ponytail, flashing
a thumbs-up sign and grinning campily, as if she were heading out
on vacation.

The truth was that she had been terrified. When they arrived
at Bainbridge, they were met by several dozen holdouts with pistols and rifles raised and cocked. These were the residents who
had rejected the Board's buyout offer and sued the government
instead. The only reason they didn't shoot was because they
knew it would hurt their pending case. Instead they kept Elemen and her friends in several old barns, under armed guard.
A week later, the Shareholder Court sided with the Board. The
Algo had found the creation of the Blanklands to be an unusual
but legitimate application of eminent domain. Only then did the
holdouts leave.

In the month that followed, an estimated fifty thousand people
from around the world took Elemen and her friends' lead, moving
not only to Bainbridge but to all the designated Blanklands around
the globe. That had been two decades ago. The hundreds of islands
of the Blanklands were now filled with idealistic, hardworking
people of all backgrounds, hard at work building what Elemen and
her friends had dreamed of all those years ago, a model for a better
society for all. She could not, she said, be prouder.

Then she added darkly, "But you didn't hear about that part, right?"

"I didn't," I admitted.

"Exactly."

She couldn't, when it came down to it, blame her friends. It was her own naïveté for which she couldn't forgive herself. After all the progress they had made after the Harmonica scandal, she had allowed herself to believe that the seeds of protest that they had planted would keep growing in their absence. It had been her plan, not anyone else's, to stay quiet in the meantime. Let's be patient, she had told the others, and let the Shareholders catch up with us.

While she and the rest of the first generation of Exes had been focused on making the Blanklands habitable and connecting the islands with one another, the Exes' influence on the mainland began to wane. Fewer protests were organized, and the remaining handful got smaller and smaller until they stopped altogether. In school, children learned about the Exes only as characters in a chapter of Shareholder lore in which crisis was averted and peace restored. On the social ladder, Exes stood one rung below the mentally ill homeless men with negative Social Capital who roamed the streets of affluent cities at night, to be pitied or scorned. Only old Ex T-shirts—the ones with the logos of Shareholder brands crossed out with permanent marker—still had some cachet, after the brands themselves started using them in influencer marketing campaigns.

The fact was, in the Exes' absence, a pleasant equilibrium had returned to Shareholder life. People felt a pride of ownership in being a Shareholder. Life could be difficult in the poorer parcels of Shareholder land, but, as was constantly pointed out on Social, even the people there were living healthier, longer lives. Plus, people believed if they were enterprising enough, they had the same opportunities as anyone to improve their station. Stories of such triumph consistently topped Social, giving Shareholders the impression that social mobility was well within reach.

As soon as Elemen realized this, she started pushing the others to figure out how to reintroduce Exism on the mainland. Even Shareholders who never planned to leave should hear it. But the rest of them disagreed. Even Otis disagreed. The reason the Board had left the Exes alone all this time, they argued, was that they had repositioned their exile as a lifestyle choice, not a revolution. The Board didn't see them as a threat anymore. If they went around trying to win converts, word would get back to the Board instantly. Outnumbered, she relented.

And then Hothouse Earth arrived. The wildfires that began in spring and lasted all summer; the droughts that were such old news that they no longer showed up in headlines; each new pandemic beginning just after the previous one was under control. That's when she understood the full extent of it: The Exes, in leaving all those years ago, had made the tactical error of their lives. More than that, *she* had made the tactical error of her life. In agreeing to create the Blanklands, the Board had been playing a long game. First, the Exes would be marginalized. Then, their homes would be submerged. How stupid she had been. She had let herself believe they had defeated the Board of Shareholders, when all along it had been the Board that had defeated them. That's what attracted her to me when we met, she said: my sense of clarity about the truth. She had almost let her friends convince her she was the crazy one. "We've been out here all this time waiting for the right moment to present everyone with a better future," she said. "But you and I, we get it: We've got to stop waiting."

"What do we do, then?" I said.

The whole conversation had been leading to this question. She smiled—a maternal smile, at once warm and condescending—and all my being swooned toward her. "Okay," she said. "Remember how I told you there's more than one kind of night work?"

21

Pedda's death wasn't like Grandfather Rao's. Life in the Garden didn't stop. The clearing didn't fill with mourning Raos. Pedda had been all but forgotten in the months that he had spent at the Hollander's clinic.

And other Raos had other worries.

One Saturday night, as Chinna and King sat in King's House counting the week's cash, Jaggayyamma came to tell them that her mother, Leelamma, had developed a bad fever. Chinna gave her money to take Leelamma to the Hollander, and sent King along, in the bullock cart, while Jaggayya drove. On the way, Leelamma lay shivering and sweating in the back of the cart. Jaggayyamma crouched and hugged her to try to restrain the shivers, but her mother threw her off, cursing.

"Come on, King, don't just sit there, help me!" Jaggayyamma cried, and so he wrapped his arms around his aunt's arms, his head against her chest, while Jaggayyamma held her legs.

Leelamma was soft and smelled of cinnamon and sweat, and she trembled violently. Putting his head so close to her breast, her heartbeat galloping under his ear, made him self-conscious. He wondered if Minnu would be awake when they got to the clinic. He hadn't seen her in weeks, not since the witch doctor's visit.

When they arrived, the clinic was quiet and dark. While Jaggayya stayed with the oxcart, King and Jaggayyamma rapped on the Hollander's door, and he came out in his pajamas and went with them to see Leelamma. He examined her and concluded, "It looks like she has an infection, but I can't tell for sure. It'd probably be best for you to bring her to the hospital in Rajahmundry. I can drive you there."

Jaggayyamma looked at King, as if for an answer. But he had no idea whether Chinna would support a hospital stay, especially given the cost of Pedda's treatment, which he was still repaying.

"Do we need to bring her there, Doctor, or would she be all right at home?" King asked the Hollander.

"You don't need to bring her, but I recommend it."

King hesitated. He didn't know whether to trust his instincts anymore. He wondered, for a moment, how to ask after Minnu. Minnu always seemed to know what was right. But then it had been Minnu who had egged him on about the pigeon's blood, and then his father had died. "I think we'd better go ask Chinna," he said quietly.

"Your mother can stay here in the meantime," the Hollander said to Jaggayyamma, who was glaring at King.

Afterward, King lingered in the courtyard, looking toward the room where his father had been. It was empty. He looked toward the madwoman's room. The door was closed, the lights off. He was considering whether to knock when Jaggayyamma tugged at his sleeve, hard, and said, "Come on, we have to tell Uncle what the doctor said."

When they returned and reported to Chinna the Hollander's recommendation, Chinna sighed and rubbed his temples. King could tell he was thinking of the expense. "What do you think we should do?" he asked King.

"I'm not sure," he said.

"King!" Jaggayyamma cried.

Chinna turned to Jaggayyamma and snapped at her to be quiet. He would do whatever her mother needed. Too bad she couldn't call on those brothers of hers, Gun and the rest of them, who were supposedly getting so rich up north.

Jaggayyamma gasped and reddened. It wasn't like Chinna to be overtly cruel.

He kicked the ground. "Look, my brother died, and no one's helping me," he muttered. "But you all want my help." He instructed Jaggayyamma to seek King's help writing to Gun, and to ask him to come home and take care of his mother.

He turned back to King. "It's late," he said decisively. "The Hollander can watch her tonight, and if she's not better by morning, we'll take her to Rajahmundry then."

When the Hollander drove up early the next morning, Leelamma's sisters all ran toward the car, fearing the worst. King and Chinna joined them. But then they saw Leelamma in the front seat, waving and grinning at them. "Look at me!" she called, cranking the window open when the car drew closer. "I'm in a car!"

"What happened?" Chinna asked the Hollander, leaning into his window.

"No one came back to get her, so I brought her home," the Hollander said.

"Then she's better?"

"The fever's gone," the Hollander said. "But keep an eye on her, and if it comes back, go directly to the hospital. Don't come to me."

Chinna looked past the Hollander to where Leelamma sat, looking healthy and pleased. "See," he teased her, "I knew you were just trying to cheat some money out of me. But you can't charm me like you charmed Grandfather Rao!"

CHINNA HAD BEEN toying with an idea, and the experience with Leelamma convinced him it was the right one. One morning he summoned all the Rao men into the clearing and told them, "The world is changing." He stood on the veranda of the Big House, his chest pushed out, his feet planted hips-width apart. Though he wasn't particularly tall—the others of the family were all, more or less, the same middling height—the men had to raise their heads to look at him from the clearing. He had started wearing eyeglasses, after getting his vision checked in town. They were rectangular, with black wire rims, and made him look worldly and intelligent, though this effect was properly tempered by his humble attire, an undershirt and a faded checkered lungi tied around his waist. "It doesn't make sense anymore, all of us working in the Garden," Chinna said. "Some of us have taken our own paths—Gun and his brothers up north, Rajubabu and his rickshaw business—and this is right, this is good, this is progress. We should be free to pursue our ambitions."

He caught King's eye and gestured toward his mouth. King went to the well to fill a cup. It was a hot afternoon, and he blew cool air from his mouth onto his upper lip. When he returned and handed his uncle the cup, Chinna sipped, before continuing, "We've had an old-fashioned way of spending the money that comes in. Some we save, some we spend on the Garden. This is right. But with the rest of it, I've done what Grandfather Rao did, which is to spend the money however I see fit. Of course, I take into account all the family's needs—dowries for our daughters, and so on—but it's all under my control.

"Suppose you have a craving for okra one night, Kondanna," he went on. "Can you ask your wife to go and get some? No! You have to come and ask me, or she has to come and ask Sita, and more often than not we'll say, 'No, no, we don't have any okra in the kitchen tonight; tonight we'll be eating bottle gourd.' Meanwhile, some of our men satisfy themselves by sleeping all day and drinking all night, and they also eat the food we buy, sleep in the huts we build, with our hard-earned cash. It doesn't make a bit of sense."

Recently, he said, he had been discussing this with Bala, a coconut merchant in town whom they all knew and trusted. Bala's father-in-law had a big trucking business and had shared a secret with him, and Bala had in turn shared it with Chinna: The weakness of the small businessman, in India, was that he let family interests influence his business, whereas business theory makes clear that only matters of profit and loss—maximizing the one and minimizing the other—should influence a business. A successful small businessman, even one with a family business, would separate family matters from business ones.

"What I propose," Chinna said, "is that, from now on, we set wages for each kind of work we do here, and depending on how much work each of us does, he'll be paid according to that schedule." He paused for a moment so they could absorb the proposal. "I suggest we take a vote, and if most of us don't agree, we won't do it. Democracy!"

But when they voted, all hands shot up in favor of the change. It stunned King. Even the laziest ones, who had the most to lose in a wage system, supported Chinna's plan. "I knew it would happen like that," Chinna told King, triumphant, after the meeting. "You have to understand human nature. No one wants to believe that he's the laziest. Each person wants to think he's the hardest-working." Every Rao assumed the change would bring him more income, not less.

It came with new processes. After counting the cash on Saturdays in King's House, Chinna and King tallied the hours each Rao had worked that week. They divided the cash into several piles for the head of each nuclear family, based on the work that the members of that family had done. At the end of this, they wrapped each portion in newsprint and, with a nub of charcoal, wrote the name of the head of the family on it. On Sunday morning, Chinna and King dragged their chairs onto the veranda and sat there with the packets of cash in a crate, and one by one each family head came up to claim his due.

"It reminds me of when everyone used to come up, one by one, to tell Grandfather Rao their problems," King said. "Only now, instead of advice, you hand out cash."

"You remember that about Grandfather Rao?"

"It wasn't so long ago."

"It's true that things are changing fast," Chinna said, and there was a doleful note in his voice that surprised King. Wasn't he the one who was responsible for it?

Maybe he hadn't anticipated how much would change after the new compensation scheme was in place. The aunts used to congregate in the kitchen, for example, and cook a big meal for everyone to share. Now they stayed in their own huts, preparing their own food over their own fires, so they wouldn't have to share their hard-won groceries. It was peaceful, in a sense. King could sit studying alone, without interruptions, in the loft in his house; though he was only in the eighth grade, still at Appayya's school, he had a growing awareness—nourished largely by the Hollander, who had taken an interest in his schooling—of a world beyond the little schoolhouse. But being alone in his house was unsettling, too, sometimes, as if no one lived at the Garden at all anymore.

The new setup had some awkward consequences. The families of the men and boys who had left the Garden got less than those whose men had stuck around, especially the families of Leelamma, Lathamma, Lalitamma, and Lavanyamma, who had the biggest proportion of deserters. Of course, the vote had been open only to the men of the family; Leelamma and her sisters hadn't gotten to have a say. They grew angrier and angrier as the women with hardworking husbands and sons started collecting enough for small luxuries, such as thatching their leaking roofs instead of catching the dripping water in cooking pots. "We work, too," they cried. "We cook and clean like the rest of the women around here, but no one thinks of that as work! No one thinks of paying us!"

THE YEARS PASSED; the change accelerated. It wasn't just a time of change in Kothapalli; no, what was happening to them was a symptom of a bigger transformation afoot, Appayya told King's class.

He explained to his students that India's caste system, while widely believed to be special, was only one manifestation of a social structure that had once been prevalent in premodern societies all over the world, one in which citizens were split up into three groups, priests, warriors, and laborers. France's First, Second, and Third Estates were no different from Brahmins, Kshatriyas, and Shudras. Across cultures, the priests, who provided education, and the warriors, who maintained law and order, made up the minority class granted land and political authority, while the laborers made up the vast majority of citizens but held neither property nor power.

In Europe, at the end of the Middle Ages, this arrangement began to disintegrate as some workers repositioned themselves as merchant middlemen and earned their way into a better economic position, lodged between the rich and the poor—the bourgeoisie. In the late eighteenth century, the French Crown, wracked by war debt, turned to these merchants for funding, and, sensing an opening, the merchants demanded more political power. When the Crown denied them, they moved to seize it. This was the start of the French Revolution, and a new social order governed by neither priests nor lords, but by a broader class of property owners.

In India, a similar progression might have taken place if it weren't for the British East India Company coming along. Great Britain, like France, had been begging merchants for help financing its foreign adventures, and in the early 1600s, the Crown had started approving joint-stock companies, businesses funded by outside investors who had no management role, and could not even be held legally responsible for what the business did. The risk of the foreign trading missions these companies undertook was enormous; no single investor could bear the burden. The investors were nothing without one another.

It was the East India Company, one of Europe's very first joint-stock companies, that exploited the decline of the Mughal Empire to lay claim over most of the subcontinent, employing the caste system for its own purposes—it hired Brahmins to collect taxes

from Indian families and Kshatriyas to fight those who resisted—
and thus cementing the role of caste in a society that might well
have otherwise dispensed of it.

But now, in the absence of the British, the old social order was
breaking down. This wasn't just about coconuts. This wasn't just
about family. What they were going through now was part of the
eternal struggle between oppressor and oppressed, trampler and
trampled. Here a new chapter was, belatedly, opening. A Maoist
politics was rising.

In the state of West Bengal, disenfranchised tea-plantation
workers, Dalit-adjacent tribals, had seized land from their landlords and given it over to the landless. The Naxalbari movement,
named after the village in which it took place, was crushed within
months, but news had already spread southward about the brief
and glorious coup perpetrated by those peasants of West Bengal.

King was fifteen. He and everyone else in Kothapalli heard
about all the discord secondhand. Many of the village's residents
were Daits who, thanks to Grandfather Rao's loans back in the
day, had only recently become landowners. Now the village's long-
time landlords were on guard, believing Dalits to be especially
susceptible to the new strain of revolutionary thought. The thing
to do was to be aware of little signs of uprising, as the legacy landlords saw it. Already some villages had reverted to the old rules
to guard against uppityness. Dalits couldn't sit in a cart or boat
already occupied by a higher-caste person, graze their buffalo on
common land, set foot in temples, or draw water from the common village well.

The new village council president told Chinna, who had told
Appayya, that Appayya would do well to stop inciting his students
with revolutionary talk. Appayya protested, "I'm only teaching them the truth." Chinna was unsympathetic. "Well, don't,"
he said.

But Appayya, provoked, began doing exactly what they had
accused him of doing all along. He converted to Buddhism. He
taught his students to memorize the poem by Jashuva, the first

modern Dalit poet writing in Telugu, about a starving Dalit cobbler, barred from entering God's temple to seek solace, who sees
that a bat has flown into his home. The cobbler begins talking to
the creature, lamenting that it can fly into the temple whenever it
wants, while he, human though he is, cannot.

> When you hang from the ceiling in the temple
> you are close to God's ears
> Gentle bat, tell my woes to God
> when the priest is not around.
> Come back and tell me please
> What the god of gods has said.
> I have no one else to turn to
> For help
> or support.

One afternoon a truck came to Appayya's school carrying a
coffin-sized crate, and as the children gathered around to watch,
Appayya opened the box to unveil a life-sized statue of the great
Dalit reformer B. R. Ambedkar. Ambedkar's face was pink and his
lips bright red. He wore a bright blue suit stretched over a round
belly, decorated at the throat with a red tie. On the tip of his nose
sat a pair of large, round glasses. He held a copy of the Indian
Constitution, which the real Ambedkar had written, tucked under
his left arm. His mouth hung slightly agape, his white teeth gap-
less. Appayya put a hand to the statue's forehead and closed his
eyes, as if communing with his hero. Then, with the help of the
biggest boys in the class, he mounted the statue on a pedestal in
front of the school, easily visible to anyone passing through the
center of the village.

He went further still. He passed out vermilion booklets titled
Revolution for Farmers, filled with quotes from Chairman Mao. "A
revolution is not a dinner party, or writing an essay, or painting a
picture, or doing embroidery; it cannot be so refined, so leisurely
and gentle, so temperate, kind, courteous, restrained and magnan-

imous." This was, he insisted to anyone who asked, an English lesson. He stalked the classroom, thumping his ruler against his palm and calling out to each of them, in turn, "Define *embroidery*! Define *temperate*! Define *revolution*! Define *insurrection*!" All that season, Grandfather Appayya shouted—while his students slumped glass-eyed, cheeks on palms, at the oppression of it, the knowledge that their recess would be spent indoors once again—till his voice got hoarse.

On one such afternoon, the assistant to the new Mr. President, Small Head, appeared on the veranda of the school dripping with water. His navy-blue uniform had been blackened by the rain. The uniform resembled a policeman's getup, but everyone knew it had been stitched by Small Head's wife, with fabric bought with the funds he skimmed off the top of his rent collections.

"Here he comes," the children said, "in that costume we bought him." And: "I would have preferred a gray costume, instead of that stupid blue one, but he forgot to ask my opinion, even though we helped buy it for him."

The Kammas didn't respect Small Head because he was Dalit, and the Dalits didn't respect him because they saw his occupation as Mr. President's lackey as a betrayal of their community. Besides that, many of the men in the village had grown up together and the assistant had been bullied for as long as they could remember because of his girlish, mincing style of walking, and that small head so grotesquely mismatched with his large stature.

That afternoon, the assistant stood on the steps of the school, dripping and wiping his neck.

"Look, he's melting," someone teased, and the rest laughed.

"What do you want, Small Head?" Appayya called out to him from the front of the classroom. "Can't you see I'm in the middle of teaching?"

"But look here," Small Head said, stabbing his finger at the rain-soaked notebook he held. "Your rent's gone up, and you didn't pay the new rate."

"Nobody told me about that."

"You can start next month if you don't have it; they said to tell you."

"Get out of here, Small Head. I'm teaching."

"But the rain," he protested.

"Go," Appayya said.

"Come on," came Small Head's last, weak protest, as he left them. Appayya pounded the desk with his fist so that his little cup of pencils leaped in the air, and a couple of the girls gasped. He looked up at them and growled, "Didn't I tell you one of these days they'd try to shut me down?"

"Who, Small Head?" someone asked.

"No, not Small Head! He's only their tool!"

Then came the worst of it. In a village near Guntur, a pair of Dalit boys walked seven miles to see the birthplace of a popular movie star. When they got there, they climbed on top of a large house in the village to get a better view. The house belonged to a big landlord, who suspected the boys of being thieves. He bound their hands with rope, took them to his cattle shed, and tortured them there. Then he brought the boys to the street and let the people of the village whip them to death. Afterward, the murderers bundled the bodies in gunnysacks and tossed them in the trash. "They were just kids, like you," Appayya told the class.

That month, a mysterious disease spread through the coconut groves of the Kothapalli Dalits. Some sort of waterborne, wood-nibbling insect had proliferated. A creeping yellowishness curled around the fronds of the trees, whose fruit came out stillborn—runty, scarred, misshapen. Cut open, the coconuts gave only a couple of drops of sour liquid and not even a spoonful of meat. It didn't take long for Mr. President to announce a scheme to combat the disease and the bad reputation it was bringing to Kothapalli. The village would bar from sale any coconut grown that season in the areas with affected groves. This happened to encompass the land owned by every Dalit in Kothapalli. Everyone suspected Mr. President was responsible for the scourge in the first place, but this couldn't be proven.

Chinna sold one of the oxen and the women's wedding gold. He sold three acres of the Garden to a neighbor, a slice along the back edge. No one would miss it, he said. Still, there was barely enough for the Rao workers' wages.

THEN, ONE NIGHT, Leelamma fell ill again. She lay in bed, feverish, sweating, and howling for Gun. When her sisters came to Chinna to have her taken to the hospital, he said, "You can use the oxcart to take her to the Hollander's place, and see if he'll drive you all there."

"What about the money to pay for it?" Lalithamma pressed.

"You know the arrangement; the men all voted for it," Chinna said.

"You know we don't have that much money!"

Chinna sighed. "Listen, I can give you a loan, all right?" he said wearily. "Take her, and repay me later."

The sisters grumbled. "If she's not better by morning, we'll go then," Lalithamma murmured.

The next morning, King was roused by the sound of women wailing. He could see from his loft Leelamma's sisters storming through the Garden to the Big House and pulling Chinna from his room as he struggled to re-knot his lungi so it wouldn't fall off. "She's dead!" they cried. "She's dead, gone!"

Chinna put a hand over his mouth and breathed into it. "Oh no," he said. He squatted and put his head in his hands and rocked back and forth and didn't make a sound.

Leelamma's sisters stood back and watched him. They seemed not to know whether to accept this show of repentance as genuine. After a while Chinna stood, went to Jaggayya, and slung his arm around his shoulder. "Come on, my brother, we'll bring her out to the clearing so everyone can pay their respects. We'll give her a proper ceremony."

The sisters relented in their pursuit of Chinna. It was not clear, after all, who was to blame for this—Chinna, for not offering to cover the cost of Leelamma's treatment, or her sisters, for failing to take her to the hospital right away when he offered a loan.

But Jaggayyamma, Leelamma's eldest daughter, made fierce by all the beatings she had endured by Jaggayya's hand and brave by her recent marriage to a good man, persisted in her anger. Jaggayyamma ran to Chinna, as he stood with her father, and pounded at him with her fists, and cried, "You did this, you selfish man! All you descendants of Grandfather Rao, you selfish souls, will get what you deserve!" She turned to King and went on, "I know what you think of me. You think your life is more important than mine, but the truth is that no one is above anyone else. One day your bones will be ground up with the earth, just like mine!" Finally her father pulled her away, with uncharacteristic force, and growled at her, "Shut up, silly girl." He flung her toward her husband, who opened his arms to receive her and held her tightly as she sobbed.

King found his mother sitting on the stoop of the Big House, picking the pebbles from a bowl of uncooked rice and tossing them violently to the ground. He sat next to her. "No one is talking about Dad anymore," he remarked. "They're all talking about Leelamma now."

Sita turned to him and shook her head. "Life doesn't turn out the way you want," she said. "When I was young, my sister and I made patties of cow dung and stuck a marigold in the middle of each one. We laid them on the road and danced around them and prayed. The thing to do was to pray for a good husband, but I didn't care about a husband at that time, so I prayed for other things. I thought about what my sister was probably praying for. I prayed for us to move to town, I prayed for us to work as teachers. But my sister told me, 'I prayed for a good husband.' I was annoyed, because I had only prayed for what I thought she had prayed for. 'Think for yourself,' she used to tell me, but I haven't ever had a thought of my own in my life. Even now, all I think of is what my sister would do. Even in raising you, that's all I think. What would she do?"

He remembered that day he left with the cripple, how it had been the suffocation of home, and the newfound knowledge that one could leave it, that had driven him off with that man. Now he felt it again. To live and die in this place was to be forgotten. What did it take to be an important person in the world—a human being who, long after his passage from the earth, would be remembered still?

n the decades before the transition to Shareholder Government, harbor cruise vessels would loiter off Restoration Point so tourists could gawk. The old Coconut buildings had been torn down and replaced with a Frank Gehry–designed campus, the centerpiece of which was the quintet of giant transparent spheres that doubled as tropical greenhouses and the corporation's main buildings. Inside, employees, rather than being assigned cubicles, could seat themselves wherever they liked. The conference rooms were glass cubes on wheels, named after famous inventors. There were contractors on site whose sole occupation was to stroll around tossing out healthy snacks, just-ripe avocados and oranges, often grown in the greenhouses themselves.

With Coconut's expansion, some employees had advocated for moving the headquarters to Seattle, to lessen their commute. But King and Margie had vetoed that. Instead, they polled workers on the amenities they desired and built them on the island itself: free private schools for children age one to eighteen; three dozen restaurants, representing all the major cuisines of the world, that delivered for free; 24/7 shuttle service to the mainland; a state-of-the-art hospital that, within a year of operation, was named one of the nation's ten best medical facilities.

Heading south toward the Rao estate, the tour guides would advise that, if you looked carefully, you might glimpse the man himself. The house was constructed with the same material that surrounded it, Douglas fir, salvaged from a Weyerhaeuser lumber mill being torn down. Notice not only the unusual architecture, the guides said—the way the house sits low to the ground—but also its unusual landscaping. None of the plants on the Raos' twenty gorgeous acres of gardens were native to the Pacific Northwest; they were all tropical flora, guava and coconut trees, multicolored flowers that practically spurted from their stems, wax-like.

How do you get this kind of landscape in the Pacific Northwest? the tour guides would quiz the passengers. More often than not, some home-and-garden aficionado on board would have the answer. King and Margaret Rao's secretive, private research organization, the Rao Project, had been commissioned to come up with genetically modified seeds that produced tropical trees and plants capable of growing in cooler climates like Seattle's. The group was also working on inserting edible vaccines into tropical fruit eaten by the world's poor and creating climate-adaptive produce that could withstand rising temperatures.

The tour guides provided this information as part of a marketing provision of the agreement brokered between the local tourism board and the Raos. In exchange, the Raos granted the tour companies permission to bring their boats close. On weekends, King and Margie stood barefoot on their veranda in thick white bathrobes, knotted floppily at the waist, King's arm wrapped around Margie's waist, Margie's hand curled around a mug of tea, and if you were one of those tourists with binoculars, you could see their expressions of loose, tired satisfaction. Sometimes, if they were in the mood, they both looked up, shading their eyes, and gave obliging half waves.

Half of the world's households owned a Coconut device. King's cousin Kittu had opened a King Rao Museum in Kothapalli where he displayed King's old school notebooks where he had practiced his cursive on *chicken* and *vowel*; the museum turned a bigger profit than the coconut grove. In the homes of Indians around the world—London, Nairobi, San Jose—parents framed images of King and mounted them on the wall next to portraits of Gandhi and Sai Baba. "Work hard, and you'll get your own Coconut," these parents said.

When children taught themselves to program and wrote letters to King about their aspirations, he tried to answer some with hand-signed notes. These were their future customers, he argued. Margie thought this was an inefficient use of his time. King Rao could no longer be just a businessman. He had to be a leader. There had to be something almost presidential in his carriage. Margie herself had undertaken a series of subtle cosmetic adjustments. The slightest vertical shave of the lateral cartilage of her nose, *zzip*, no thicker than a potato peel—this undertaken thrice. An experimental graft of the thinnest layer of cells from her soft inner thigh onto her prematurely aged forehead—six times. The implantation of hair from her head onto her eyebrows—a baker's dozen. The injection of hair-smoothing serum into the sebaceous glands of her scalp—a bimonthly procedure. She was careful not to go too far, and not even the most diligent of observers could prove that she had gotten work done, even as she became younger-looking and more beautiful as she progressed through her fifties and sixties. At a fundraiser, she met Gwyneth Paltrow, who became her best friend, or, in any case her #bestfriend. Some of the most iconic photographs of the decade would capture the two of them stomping through Seattle in matching leather jackets and acid-washed mom jeans, radiating good fortune.

Eventually King let Margie redesign him as well. The new King Rao had a collection of well-tailored pastel oxford shirts, which he wore, tie-less, with jeans and, for an unthreatening splash of quasi-Indian style, Birkenstock sandals. The King Rao uniform, they started calling it in the press. His hair was styled with a swooping wave that floated above his forehead and sometimes flipped down onto it, his eyes framed by a pair of round glasses with thick black frames. He drew the line at surgery but allowed a visit to the world's best dermatologist, who cured his eczema with an experimental steroid-and-ultraviolet treatment. The rest was nonmedical, the work of a great hairdresser and a meticulous tailor, Goop affiliates both. When he was all fixed up, he looked in the mirror and was startled by the impressive man standing before him, almost handsome.

Margie trained him to sit with his shoulders straight but relaxed, his eyes focused but not too intense. She taught him to converse in a way that made his interlocutors feel understood, rather than feeling that his intellectual plane failed to intersect with theirs. It was that man, that King Rao, who charmed the prime-time audiences. It was he who was named *Time*'s Person of the Year for having invented devices "so intuitive that you would be forgiven for believing they contain a human soul."

King learned to tuck himself, that is, his private self, somewhere inside the fictional character of Margie's invention. He hadn't lost his old nagging dread that some puzzle remained unsolved before him and the time left to solve it was running out. Not long after their visit to Kothapalli, Sita had died. He had not attended her funeral, arguing to his cousins that he didn't want his presence to draw unwanted attention to what should be a private affair. Nor had he visited since. The truth was that it was too depressing. He still sent money to Kittu but had no idea how it was being used, or if it was even being distributed at all.

Did everyone reach their fifties and feel like this—as if the self of your youth were another creature altogether—or was it something particular to his experience? The question felt too private to share even with Margie. He loved her as much as ever, though these days sex was less about adventure than solace. What aroused him was the way her existence made him more certain of his own. Anytime he traveled without her, some woman or another sidled up to him, but aside from the inevitable physical reaction, he was left uncompelled. His wife was, after all, the most powerful woman on earth.

Nowadays, instead of walking to work, he and Margie commuted in the backseat of a custom-built sedan with tinted windows and room for four across the back, so that King and Margie could sit next to each other in the middle, while the window seats were taken by two guards in bulletproof vests. There had been threats, some quite credible. Precautions had to be taken. Sometimes fans would line the sidewalks outside the Coconut campus, hoping to meet him. He would swivel, look out from the backseat at his admirers, their cameras in the air, feel a tightness in his chest, and put a palm to his heart.

"You okay?" his security man George would ask.

"Just heartburn."

"Acidophilus. Tell him, Margie, to take acidophilus!"

You learned about this period in high school: The standardized global curriculum calls for a month focused on it. Those decades just before the establishment of Shareholder Government, when we brought ourselves to the verge of a global breakdown. The system of economic interdependence created after World War II and reinforced after the Cold War had succeeded, more or less, in its original goal: keeping countries' fortunes so intertwined that they could no longer afford major wars. Other benefits emerged as well. Fewer people were poor than ever before. Fewer infants died, fewer mothers. More children were enrolled in school, more young adults in universities. So many people in once-poor countries—China, India—were becoming rich that inequality between countries had fallen for the first time since the 1820s.

This would seem like a positive development. But then why, the question had emerged forcefully at the turn of the twenty-first century, did people seem so upset, so convinced that the whole setup was bad for them? It had to do, it turned out, with fast-growing inequality *within* countries. If you were an Indian citizen who wasn't among the newly rich, you weren't gladdened by your countrymen's suddenly acquired wealth. If you were an American or European who had always been poor, learning that children of Chinese peasants were becoming billionaires didn't charm you.

The defining sentiment of this late capitalist period was disaffection, and it began to take alarming forms. Mass murders became so frequent that they no longer trended on Social. Sure, you could go through the exercise of psychoanalyzing each killer in an attempt to classify him, as they used to, terrorist or psychopath, but what good did that do at this scale? The only useful conclusion was the broadest one, which was that the world order itself was making people murderous. But then, the politicians most equipped to address the unrest were those least invested in ending it. Race-baiting nationalists from oligarchical families began winning elections all over the world. It was the oldest trick around, promising the poor members of your own ethnic group that you'd help them become as rich as yourself, in large part by making sure that the poor members of other ethnic groups stopped stealing your group's opportunities, thus dividing the poor so that they wouldn't rise up together against the rich.

For a time, King and Margie had been insulated from the damage this was doing. More than that: For them, the benefits of this world order outweighed the damage. Coconut was the largest corporation in the world, with a global workforce of nearly two million employees. Every major advance in computing, from personal computing to smartphones to smart networks, could be attributed to King and his scientists. But then came the incident that changed things.

Murali Dharmarajan, a sweet, fat, sideburned Telugu kid, twenty-four years old, had been engaged to be married when they found him knifed in the stomach and left in the gutter to die, in Austin. The perpetrator was a local man, white, forty-eight, single, who had cycled in and out of the criminal-justice system all his life. The most immediate explanation was that it must have been a botched mugging. Dharmarajan had been hapless and gullible, with a habit of grinning at strangers when he walked down the street at night. But the perpetrator's Social presented a different narrative. There he wrote of his struggles to find work, despite his undergraduate degree in business, and his analysis of the forces behind these struggles. "The best jobs go to aliens, the leftovers go to blacks, nothing's left for real Americans," he had written.

You couldn't consider the crime in a vacuum, the President of the United States said. When your own citizens lose jobs to foreigners, they become upset, and violence ensues. He was working to address this, he said, and committed to working with the National Right–led Congress to put limits on the hiring of foreigners by American corporations, many of which were themselves run by foreign-born executives.

King and Margie had stayed out of politics all these years— the optics of choosing a side weren't good—and they had neither supported nor opposed this President when he was only a longshot, fourth-time candidate with a talent for one-liners who made that earlier standard for presidential egregiousness, the forty-fifth, look staid in comparison. Plus, for a time the President had been good for them. After he took office, he had called on Congress to invest an extraordinary sum in overhauling the federal government's technology infrastructure, an undertaking that had handsomely benefited Coconut.

But now the unrest gathering in the world was coming to their own little corner. At a press conference, the President was asked what he had meant by his comment, whether he had been targeting King Rao and Coconut in particular when he had mentioned "foreigners," and he only flashed his broad smile, at once clownish and enigmatic, and said, "I said what I said, and I meant what I meant." All of this compelled King and Margie to consider whether Coconut's future was as certain as they had once believed. This was what led them, one afternoon, to a decommissioned cruise ship that bobbed in the Pacific Ocean, 250 nautical miles off the coast of Ecuador, from which one of Walter Martz's oldest friends, a founding *IT* member—the one who, in fact, had heckled them at their presentation of the Coconut I all those years ago—operated a start-up incubator. By virtue of being headquartered on the ocean, the floating incubator constituted an extra-national organization not beholden to any state.

They walked into the meeting just a little off-kilter, because *Lady Libertad* was gently shifting in the water, but when the former *IT*er greeted them with bear hugs in his wheelhouse office, and informed them that he had been in the room on that historic night when they had first unveiled the Coconut and had known in that moment that they would change the world—a claim they both knew to be false but didn't bother to question out loud—they were charmed. After they got the grand tour of the ship and the *IT*er brought in his head of business development to explain how Coconut might go about leasing a small part of the ship so they could put a couple of employees in there and see what happened, they shared a sense of real goodwill and expansiveness in that high room, with its fine vantage over the curved edge of the earth.

King said, "This might seem—" and Margie glanced at him and said, "—sort of nuts—" and King said, "—but what's the point of putting three or four people on this boat if—" and Margie said, "—right, if the theory behind it is sound, why not?" The *IT*er and his business-development man looked from King to Margie, and Margie to King, and the *IT*er smiled and said, "You don't mean—?"

That really was the beginning, though it's rarely mentioned in historical accounts. King and Margie's vision of moving thousands of Coconut employees to a glorified offshore barge never came to pass, but the threat of it—Margie had a genius for leaking information without ever being identified or even suspected as the source—was enough to persuade the President to call King and ask for a confidential private meeting to discuss certain issues that were, he trusted, of mutual interest. King accepted and said Margie would attend, too.

Did that man, the social-media influencer turned Commander in Chief, realize what he was proposing in the meeting that followed? People have argued both sides. On the one hand, pundits have said, it brought about the end of the American empire, an eventuality that an intelligent and learned President might have anticipated and tried to avoid. On the other hand, this President did have a kind of animal, instinctive smarts, the kind that won likes, and in turn followers, and in turn elections. Maybe he realized that the American empire had already begun its descent, and he wanted to engineer, for the country and for himself, a soft landing.

What the President told King and Margaret Rao, in that private meeting, was that he had a partnership in mind. The U.S. government had been borrowing money like nobody's business over the past several decades, particularly during the first pandemic of the twenty-first century and its aftermath, for which he blamed the forty-fifth and forty-sixth Presidents. A major component of his platform, in running for President as a National Rightist, had been a top-secret plan to reduce the national debt without raising taxes or cutting social programs. While he had refused to share it in advance, lest his rivals from the well-funded major parties steal it for themselves, he had shown it to a number of high-profile business influencers who had strongly endorsed it.

He said he hadn't told the Raos about the plan earlier because, to be honest, he didn't consider them friends. He wasn't sure where their loyalties lay. They had been so studious about avoiding all appearance of bias. But whether they liked him or not—he waved a hand—didn't matter anymore. King and Margie did not make eye contact with each other, worried about what they would reveal if they did. They only directed separate smiles, mild and questioning, at the President. He laughed. He admired them, King and Margaret Rao, fast-movers, breakers of things. He was a smart and successful man in general, he said, but what he was smartest and most successful at was investing. The reason he had called them over was that the time had come for the ultimate deal. The small matter of the epic debt, he said, and he smiled, liking the sound of what he had said, perhaps mentally recording it for later use on Social.

His plan was to invite the country's biggest and best corporations to compete to provide services to the public—essentially selling off portions of the government to the private sector—then using the proceeds to pay off its debt while also ridding itself of the most expensive aspects of governing. Governments had once been forced to provide these services because no one else had the infrastructure to do it. But companies' own infrastructure had grown far superior to governments'. His friends at Walmart agreed. His friends at J. P. Morgan. "Food stamps—there's no reason the retail sector can't handle those. Social security—you leave that to the banks. And then there's the technology piece."

Here King and Margie broke in the same instant and glanced at each other, Margie furrowing her brow, King widening his eyes, all of this transpiring in less than a second. For all his bluster, the man was making them a good deal: delivering to them what would surely be the biggest tech contract in business history.

A month later, the President's most loyal congressional surrogates introduced the Smaller Is Better Act, privatizing the American nutritional assistance and social security programs. By the end of the year, Coconut and a half dozen other American corporations were responsible for the provision of telecommunications, education, health care, roads, and welfare programs in the United States. The chairmen of these corporations' boards held their own quarterly meetings, along with the Vice President, Senate Majority Leader, and Speaker of the House, to share notes. The President won reelection and began his second term but was losing interest in the matter of governing. He had founded a venture-capital firm. The quarterly meetings of the chairmen were boring affairs, truth be told, taken up with discussing international taxes and employment laws and after a while even the Vice President and the congressional leaders dropped out.

It was during this phase that the press started referring to the board as, simply, the Board. Toward the end of the President's term, a page appeared on the Board website encouraging other countries to get in touch if the products and services provided by the Board appealed to them. When the Board began responding to those queries and, within the span of a decade, serviced a third of the countries in the world, it was too late for those in the U.S. government—only a nominally new administration, since the former Vice President had by then been elected President—to admit they hadn't quite grasped the scope of what was taking place here. Instead, the new President arranged an international summit for the Board and the heads of state of all the world's nations, to be exclusively livestreamed by a start-up in which the former President was the lead investor, at which a pact would be signed regarding the relationship between the Board and the sovereign nations of the world.

King Rao was the keynote speaker. In the former President's footage of the event, King stands at a dais and looks straight into the camera, addressing viewers at home. He explains that numerous countries had come to the Board to tell them that they could no longer provide all that their citizens desperately needed. The Board had stepped in to help, providing infrastructure and services to any nation that wanted it. The old President captured all this while murmuring his trademark running commentary for his viewers. "It's beautiful to see this coming together, and to remember that I was there at the beginning, I was responsible for it, I came up with the idea and put it all into motion!" he said.

By the end of the weekend, the Board of Shareholders had been established, by international treaty, as a formal, legal, supranational unit—an intellectual and cultural heir, as Margie framed it in the Social post she ghostwrote for King, to the organizations created to maintain global peace after World War II. In an election that took place on the final night of the summit, King Rao was chosen to be its first CEO.

There was the usual protest—civilian marches, speeches by principled politicians who preferred the old-school style of governing, hashtag campaigns—but nothing came of it and, with time, the resistance faded. This was not a coup. Nations did not collapse. They just gradually ceded their powers. Historians later noted that there had been plenty of precedent. You can go at least as far back, they said, as the British East India Company. At first the Board of Shareholders was simply the most powerful supranational governing organization in the world—the first effective one, many people felt. Then, though no one could distinguish quite when it happened, it was the government itself. No reputable pundit could argue that this was a worse system of government than the disaster that had preceded it. The metrics proved it. People were, on average, leading longer, healthier, and more productive lives. All was once again well in the world.

ut if everyone had perfect access to information, the fail-
ings of the Board would have been exposed long ago. It's
true that, on average, life spans and wealth increased. It's
also true that only the wealthiest Shareholders ended up seeing
real gains from the bargain—driving up the averages—while most
everyone else could do little more than feed and shelter themselves.
Yet everyone is bound by the same obligations, to consume only
Shareholder-made products no matter the price, to abide by the
Shareholder Agreement no matter the cost. If, despite this, you—
wise as you are—have chosen to remain a Shareholder, mustn't it
be because you have been misled?

This was the seed that needed replanting on the mainland.

WHEN ELEMEN TOLD OTIS she planned to keep me at the house,
letting me crash on the floor of their shared bedroom, he tried to
reason with her. The only people who had ever stayed there were
the original Exes. This was for security's sake: The property provided most of the island's power. How would other Exes feel, Otis

pressed Elemen, if they found out some random newcomer was suddenly living with them for no good reason, after they had been told such a thing was impossible? Wouldn't it look like favoritism?

When Elemen insisted—change is good; they would understand—Otis tried a tougher tactic. If she invited a guest into their room at night, he would not share a bed with her. "Fine," she said. "There's a comfortable couch downstairs," and at first he assumed she meant *I* could sleep on the couch, but then—her expression cold, unyielding—he understood it was *he* who was being exiled.

Elemen's bullheadedness hardened her compatriots' impression of me as a dangerous influence, threatening to disrupt the fragile balance they had spent decades establishing. True, she had done the labor of building their community from scratch and forming relationships throughout the Blanklands. But Otis's years of imprisonment and quiet stoicism—his martyr's air—made him a commanding figurehead. While he was never overtly hostile toward me, he studiously avoided acknowledging my presence, and so the others did, too.

I would go around asking them to help me learn—let me spend a shift maintaining the solar panels or delivering Catches—but they just waved me off, dismissive, though not unkind. After a while Elemen advised me to just relax. Read up on what we're about, she said, directing me to the living room shelves. That's when I began studying Elemen's old copies of Bakunin, Proudhon, Havel, and Goldman. Her Angela Davis and Audre Lorde. Her Zhuangzi. I holed myself up in Elemen's room and read.

One night, as I was falling asleep on the floor, I heard Otis come into the room. I opened my eyes, a little. He stepped around me and crawled into the bed with Elemen, who was facing the wall, pressing his face into her hair to wake her. "Cuddle me," I heard him whisper, and I watched her scoot back until she was nestled against him. They held each other awhile, and then Otis began kissing her neck. Quietly, they undressed and had tender, near-silent sex. Their backs were to me; I couldn't stop watching. I found it beautiful. "I miss you," he said, when it was over, and then he crawled out of the bed and left.

After that, Otis returned often, most of the time just to hold her and be held. One night, after he left, Elemen called me into her bed and let me sleep there for the rest of the night. Self-conscious, I couldn't get comfortable enough to relax until she did. She was facing me. Her handsome nose flared and fell with her breaths. Her face, at rest, was monk-like. I had an urge to reach out and touch her brown, weathered skin, to see what it felt like.

After that night, I was invited into Elemen's bed often. Once, she whispered, "Mystie, you remind me of what Otis used to be like." We were facing each other in bed, and I could smell her breath, hot and faintly sour. She and Otis hadn't met through the movement, she told me. He had been a barista at a coffee shop she frequented, an aspiring poet who knew nothing of Exism. He had grown up comfortable, the son of an engineer father and a physician mother. Though they were a Black family, his parents' racial politics began and ended with the line about being twice as good to get half as much. He had acquired the sense, from this upbringing, that Exes were to be avoided. He had already disappointed his parents by wanting to be a poet. But, over months' worth of coffee and sex, Elemen taught him another way of seeing the world. With Capital from Otis's parents, they opened their own coffee shop, a co-op called Ex Café. You didn't have to identify as an Ex in order to join, but the shop didn't accept Social Capital or provide Wi-Fi. The only way to get a drink was by working a barista shift or by bartering: fair-trade beans; organic local milk. Elemen and Otis moved in together. Their sex was so energetic, in those days, it felt like brawling.

They were at Ex Café the morning the news broke about the Harmonica—about the poor woman who had trusted King Rao's promises and died for it; about the sixty-three others who followed her. The place erupted. Exism was a fringe movement, mostly Seattle- and Portland-based, but the café had become its informal headquarters. Don, Romeo, Araxa, and Indig were all there that morning, shouting over one another. It shouldn't be this hard to convince people of how violent a society theirs had become. People should be realizing it themselves. But, Otis pointed out in his calm way, think about him. Think about how oblivious he had been, standing behind the counter of the café where he used to work, earning minimum wage. He needed to be shown what was right, to be shown the inherent violence of the social structures we humans had built, to be shown how the structures themselves inoculated individuals from guilt over this violence. The question, Otis said, was how you could show this at scale without using the tools of Shareholder Government.

There, for Elemen, was the spark. That was right, exactly, you had to show them. Anarchists had a name for this, even, she told them all, growing animated. It was called an attentat, propaganda by deed. When the Franco-Prussian War sent France into crisis, the anarchist Mikhail Bakunin wrote, "We have for better or worse built a small party: small, in the number of men who joined it with full knowledge of what we stand for; immense, if we take into account those who instinctively relate to us, if we take into account the popular masses, whose needs and aspirations we reflect more truly than does any other group. All of us must now embark on stormy revolutionary seas, and from this very moment we must spread our principles, not with words *but with deeds, for this is the most popular, the most potent, and the most irresistible form of propaganda.*" The italics are his. "Let us say less about principles, whenever circumstances and revolutionary policy demand it—i.e., during our momentary weakness in relation to the enemy—but let us at all times and under all circumstances be adamantly consistent in our action."

That was the answer: an act of violence so startling that Shareholders would be blasted out of their complacency and forced to reckon with the Board's violence. Someone powerful had to die. In the aftermath, people would see how swiftly the Board assigned blame, and they wouldn't be able to help but compare it to the evasion of blame for the sixty-four deaths caused by King Rao.

But when Elemen proposed this that morning in the café, they all fell silent. She could feel their judgment on her skin. No one agreed with her, not even Otis. He—this man who had once believed that the word *anarchist* was a synonym for *criminal*—had the gall to lecture her. He reminded her of the disastrous attempt on the life of Carnegie Steel's Henry Clay Frick by Alexander Berkman, the love of Emma Goldman's life, in the early days of anarchism. The assassination attempt had failed, Berkman had been imprisoned for years, and the movement's reputation had been irredeemably damaged.

Otis argued that trying to kill someone would be a logistical clusterfuck. And if they pulled it off, the sympathy of the public would only swing, violently this time, toward the Board. But his main point was that killing someone would be immoral. Elemen remembered the unpleasant shock of hearing this, like a bitter taste on her tongue. More than his general tactical disagreement, the moral judgment speared her. In the end, Elemen lost the argument. The fire, Otis's suggestion, was her consolation prize.

IT WAS AS IF the question slipped out of me of its own accord. Who, though? Who had she proposed, all those years ago, as the target of a hypothetical attentat? She hesitated, and in that fraction of a second—seeing her mouth slightly open, her eyes bright—I willed her not to tell me. But it was too late. When she spoke his name, her voice was firm.

How many times have I replayed that moment, Shareholder, during these long days and nights of perdition? How many times have I been tormented by the thought of this being the proverbial flap of a butterfly's wing that set my father's death in motion? It's uncountable. But I swear, in the moment in which my father's name escaped Elemen Ex's lips, all I felt for him was a swell of warmth. All the times he had warned me about interlopers, all the times he had told me that, while we were technically Exes, we couldn't mistake the original Exes for anything other than a danger to us. All the times I had accused him of being overprotective and paranoid. My god, you were right, I thought. Forgive me, I thought.

By then, Elemen had moved on. After the Exodus, she said, she threw herself into building a self-sustaining community on Bainbridge. It was Otis she held in her heart, as motivation. As part of the settlement with the Board, Otis had faced charges of manslaughter, not murder. Still, he had been given ten years in prison, the maximum sentence. When she tried to picture his life inside, her imagination failed her. But she knew enough. He had to be suffering—she understood that much—as a result of an act that she had, if indirectly, forced him into. She accepted the atonement available to her: She atoned through action, through building the life that she had promised would be possible once they were free. And then one morning, a decade later, she was standing at the marina and heard his voice. She thought she had imagined it—she thought she was losing it—and then had to laugh. It was him, the love of her life, rowing up in a little boat, grinning the same broad grin as ever. Ten years incarcerated, and here he was, the same old Otis, if a little rumpled at the collar. She climbed right into the boat to embrace him.

That night, Otis explained to Elemen that, back on the mainland, no one perceived the Exes as a threat anymore. She accepted the information with relief, not yet comprehending its implications. Later she would feel stupid about that, but in the moment, they were in bed, their bodies pressed tightly together, restaking a claim, and it was impossible to feel anything other than relief.

There was no single instant when it became clear that something had, in fact, ruptured between them. It was so minutely perceptible that neither of them acknowledged it out loud, hoping they could will it away. It was not that they had stopped loving each other; it would never be that. So what was it? One night in bed, Otis nudged Elemen awake. When she turned to face him, his eyes looked strange, haunted. He admitted, his voice hoarse, that he couldn't sleep. He had slept fine in prison, but since coming to Bainbridge he hadn't experienced a single full night of rest. He kept dreaming of the faces of those poor people who had died in the fire and popping awake, after which he was afraid to shut his eyes again. In prison, he had at least done penance. Having been released, it was as if he had taken the work of punishment upon himself.

Elemen, wanting to help him but also desiring a return to sleep, said what she thought he needed to hear to calm his mind. The deaths, tragic as they had been, had been required. Without them, the Board never would have been thrown into crisis and forced to negotiate, and the Blanklands never would have been created. Plus, remember: King Rao and his lackeys killed sixty-four people and didn't accept any blame at all.

Listening to her, Otis only grew more agitated. "That doesn't change that I killed three people—I killed a *child*, El!" he cried, flinging the blankets off, as if, remembering the fire, he had suddenly grown hot himself. "Nothing justifies it." The fire had transformed his ideas about violence, peace, the ends and the means. That was when Elemen began wondering, privately, if he had been brainwashed in prison after all. In her darkest moments, she even wondered, could he be a spy? All this time, she had pushed these suspicions to the back of her mind. But over these past several years, since the beginning of Hothouse Earth, these ugly thoughts kept returning to her. How could he remain reluctant to get back into the fight even with the stakes this high? The man who had returned to her after a decade away—had he not been the same old Otis after all?

It was right at that moment, Elemen said, that I had come along.

BUT HOW TO REVIVE the movement on Shareholder land? It wouldn't do to turn up in mainland train stations with an armful of pamphlets and a megaphone, like the Exes used to in the olden days, pre-Blanklands. It wouldn't do to turn up on the mainland at all. Elemen knew of a handful of people who had tried it. They had never returned, never even got in touch. The loved ones of the Disappeared would bring photos to Elemen, desperate for information, but when Elemen had her mainland contacts do an image search on Social, nothing came up. These people seemed to have vanished. In the Blanklands, people assumed that they had never been let out of detention. Or worse.

Instead, Elemen decided, I would turn up at the Cha Cha. Despite all the illicit trade that took place there—sex, drugs, eggs, sperm—there had never been a bust. The man who had donated the yacht, less out of solidarity than out of a desire to have a place to party unimpeded, was the scion of a powerful Board executive. I would start by getting acquainted with the Cha Cha scene. Over time, I would get to know people individually and gauge their receptiveness to Exism. I would wait until the conversation turned, for example, to the rising cost of insulin, and take mental notes on who seemed frustrated with the state of affairs, or at least open to hearing about a different approach. I would get the names of those who responded well—that is, in an Exist direction—and pass them along to Elemen so that she could follow up. That was to be the extent, at Elemen's insistence, of my role. I was the target hunter. She would take it from there.

She sent me with Magic, Aurelia, and Susan. I had seen them only in passing over the past several weeks. "So you came around, after all!" Aurelia teased, nudging me, as we boated there. Elemen had told them I would be joining them as a sex worker.

"She convinced me," I lied, hugging myself against the wind. I wore a T-shirt, overalls, and high tops.

Magic painted my lips with lipstick. It was the first time I had worn it. It felt gluey, like honey on my mouth.

"You'll be fine; you look gorgeous," Magic said. "We'll stick together."

The Cha Cha was—is—a handsome old triple-deck mega-yacht, wide-bellied and long-beamed, with fine cedar flooring on the top decks and a glass-bottomed observation lounge. Elemen sent a couple dozen Exes each night. On an open foredeck, people stood at tall cocktail tables, flirting. Inside, they sat on plush couches and armchairs or stood at the windows watching the stars.

Magic and I walked up the stairs to the uppermost deck. She pulled me to a couch, where we sat watching the people who moved past in little groups, and she tried to orient me. The crew, all Exes, worked and stayed belowdecks. The two decks immediately below us looked a lot like this one, but also contained small cabins, which Shareholders could rent for—she gave me a sly, meaningful look— private time. On this deck, there was a long bar against one wall. If I didn't know what to do with myself, Magic said, I should go up to the bar and wait for someone to buy me a drink.

At a small dance floor in the middle of the space, Shareholders and Exes bobbed together to a trance beat. Beams of fluorescent lighting blinked and skittered around, making the people seem as if they were moving in stop-motion. I had seen videos of clubs and knew to anticipate the loud music, the orgiastic vibe. What surprised me was the wet, tangy smell of all those bodies in one place; it filled the space, even with the doors open.

A white man in a pink T-shirt and cutoff jean shorts, not much older than us, came over and sat on the arm of the couch. "Hey," he said, nudging Magic. "Remember me?"

She laughed. She seemed genuinely pleased to see the man. "I remember," she said.

"Good memories?" he said.

"Not bad," she said, laughing, and stood. He did, too. "You'll be all right," she told me as they left.

I sat by myself, the room pulsing around me. Then I remembered Magic's tip: the bar. I stood and made my way toward the space. People stood shoulder to shoulder, exuding sweaty impatience; I felt claustrophobic, crowded. What was I doing here, pretending to be a regular person? I was about to turn and slink back to the couch when a tall, broad-shouldered white man, in jeans and a button-down shirt, sidled up next to me. He had a strong jaw, leathery, well-tanned skin, and the smallish paunch of a person who had never lacked for sustenance. He put his mouth close to my ear and said wetly, "What are you thinking?" I took a step back, startled. He tipped his thumb toward his mouth and shouted, to be heard above the music, "To drink!"

"Oh right!" I shouted back, embarrassed.

So this was social life as Shareholders lived it. Having gotten to the bar and had a Manhattan bought for myself, I allowed myself to be dragged to the dance floor to bob and writhe in the general direction of my benefactor, my drink sloshing, oceanic, out of my cup and onto myself. I allowed my lips to be tongued open and kissed. I allowed myself to be led by the hand downstairs, then through an interior hall into a small, dark room that the man unlocked.

Inside—red-painted walls, a red-sheeted bed—he offered me another beverage. I had prepared myself for this. I had come here on the pretense of being a sex worker; I had expected to lose my virginity, tonight, to some grown man or another. But I was only seventeen, and now I found the prospect of going through with it terrifying. My mind was slow, blunted. I sat on the edge of the bed holding my second alcoholic beverage of the night, of my life, and, stalling, asked the man about himself.

He settled next to me, closer than was strictly comfortable. He was a German-Italian influencer, he said, here in Seattle on business. He represented one of the big drug companies, whose name he preferred not to disclose. When he told me his name, it sounded like it was *Yawn*, but, he clarified, it was spelled with a *J*. Jan.

When I told him it was a strange spelling, he bristled a little and said, no, it wasn't. In Germany, it was normal. The *J* was pronounced like that. It was the kind of fact that, back home on Blake Island, with the help of my Clarinet, I would have known. I told him, a bit defensively, that I had never met a German. A German-Italian. But he didn't seem to notice my shame. The situation had made him self-conscious, too. He glanced all around the room, not directly at me. I wondered if it was his first time here.

"You've never been to Germany?" he said.

"No."

"It's beautiful, though only in the summertime. People love the forests, the castles, the beer, the drugs." He coughed. "If you're interested, I actually brought with me a new one. A drug." It was called Rosebud, he said, and it was a female aphrodisiac. If I wanted some, he added quite abruptly, we could go all night.

I laughed; I didn't mean to. "Sorry," I said. "I've never heard of it."

"My brand, the one I rep, is testing it," he said. He seemed to have gotten even more nervous. "I've got a stash I'm allowed to give out." He sounded apologetic.

It took me a second to realize what was happening. Once I did, I was almost offended. Jan hadn't chosen me for sex, per se. He had chosen me to help test an unvetted drug.

Quickly, I blurted: "I can't; I have a condition. I have to be careful."

Jan rubbed his face. He looked old, his skin more flaccid at the jawline than I had noticed. He got off the bed and stood next to it, deflated. I couldn't tell if he believed me or not. Maybe it didn't matter. He rubbed his face. "Christ," he said.

"Sorry," I said reflexively.

"Listen, this is awkward, but I'm on the clock," he said. He looked at the floor. The implication was that if I couldn't, or wouldn't, be his test animal, he couldn't waste any more time. Suddenly I realized I had wasted an hour of my time, too. Me neither, pal! I wanted to tell him. Me neither!

THAT NIGHT, when I told Elemen what had happened, I thought she would be upset with me. She just laughed. "Rookie mistake," she said. "First of all, you should have slept with him; it's not that bad." But also, she said, it was inevitable that, if I sat passively by, I would meet men like Jan. Drug-testing was in high demand on the Cha Cha.

I had to be more proactive. I was looking for conversion targets, not clients. There was a fundamental difference. I couldn't just wait around the way Magic could. In a group of friends—in Elemen's experience—the potential Exes were the outliers. Sometimes they stood apart from the others, not participating much and seeming ill at ease. But at other times they were loudest and most animated. If I trained myself to concentrate on these outliers, she promised, I would start to notice subtle signs of existential angst—a brief eye roll, for example, or a closemouthed, unamused laugh. If I could manage to gain these people's trust and get them alone, she believed, they might admit to some dissatisfaction with the world. Then we would be off.

I started spending six nights a week at the Cha Cha. I would return home and fall asleep when the sun was rising, then sleep until midafternoon. It was restless, broken sleep. The mission wasn't going well. She had to realize it, too. I had hoped that I could avoid getting caught up in the transactional side of the Cha Cha scene—my encounter with Jan had given me cold feet—but there was no other side. If it was intimacy I sought, I needed to offer something in exchange. Sex was the most obvious currency available to me, but I couldn't bring myself to trade in it. And so, after almost a month, I had collected only seven names.

Shareholders were guarded about their interior life. Living in a world governed by Social Capital necessitated a certain restraint, even mistrust, around others. Imagine seeing your Capital decline because, in a moment of abandon, you'd said something you shouldn't have. That was the explanation I gave to Elemen, to absolve myself a little. But of course that wasn't all there was to it. It was me, too. I had no real instinct for human interactions; after a life spent with only one person, King Rao, I found myself constantly perplexed by people's behavior. When men flirted at the Cha Cha, I couldn't help but recoil a little, without meaning to.

The man who finally did me the honor was a chef. That I chose him as my first had less to do with physical attraction or any instinct about his openness to Exism than with my sense that Elemen was growing impatient with me. The chef was a tall, thin white man with arched, mime-like eyebrows and an otherwise morose face. When he removed his clothes, he resembled an inverted exclamation point. I wasn't sure whether to look at him or not. It occurred to me that I should have asked Magic more questions. From the pocket of his jeans, which he had lain on the bed, he pulled out a lighter. He flicked on the flame and came toward me with it. "Do you like fire?" he said. Oh, so this was it, I thought. I would die in flames, on a mega-yacht in Puget Sound. But the thin man did not light me on fire. He handed me the lighter, and, from another pocket, a tall, thin white candle. I lit it, and held on to it. He sighed. "That's beautiful," he said. "Wine?"

"I'd love that," I said. He seemed eager to please. From a bottle on the nightstand, he poured me a generous glass. It tasted unlike what I had expected—mossier and bitter, an unpleasant taste—but I gulped it down.

There was music playing, Etta James, and I laughed, because I found it a little beautiful, the flames from the candle in my fist and the music, and was surprised, and ashamed, at the feeling. He sighed and became erect. Then I was overcome with disgust. He had me undress and sit against the head of the bed. He slid on a condom, sat facing me, and entered me. It felt like being choked from the inside. I don't want to sensationalize it, but it hurt a lot. There was nothing sexual about it.

"Can I put this down?" I said, nodding at the candle, still in my hand.

"You'd better not—fire hazard," he said, and laughed. He bucked softly. "Do you like this?" he said tenderly, and though I didn't, though it chafed at my insides and I was afraid about the candle, I had watched enough of Fred Henninger's old pornos to know my lines. "Yes," I said. "Don't stop."

I tried to catch glimpses of the clock on the nightstand, hoping neither of us would accidentally knock the candle onto the bedsheets and light ourselves on fire. When fifty-three minutes had passed since we had entered the cabin, I whispered, in as diplomatic a tone as I could manage, "Time's almost up." He groaned, ejaculated, and collapsed on top of me. Still I held the candle out at arm's length. My bicep hurt.

Afterward, he requested a brief head massage, complaining that the fluorescent lights inside the club gave him a migraine. I obliged, then asked, casually, whether he had migraines often. He never used to get them, he said, but in the past month—hadn't I heard about the migraine epidemic on the mainland? Hadn't I heard about the theories circulating on Social that it had something to do with a recent Cocoglass update?

It was that night, after acquiring my eighth target for Elemen, that I had a strange dream. I was in bed with Elemen, my body curled around hers, spooning. But the thing is, I wasn't exactly myself. I was King. Elemen, too, wasn't herself. She had a thick mess of black hair, and brown skin. She was small, too, girl-sized, her rib cage jutting. Even with her back to me, I could tell who it was.

Minnu.

After a while, she sat up in the bed tearing at a hangnail on her finger, a distant look in her eyes. I, as King, was with her in the bed. She was saying something about men seeing the hangnail and not wanting to sleep with her. I—King—wasn't surprised by this mention of men sleeping with her. The room was small and dark, different from the rooms in the Hollander's clinic, light-filled and marigold-scented. This one had a dusty smell, incense or tobacco. In the past, when this happened, I would panic and try to shake myself free of the vision. But this time, I remained inside of it. Minnu turned to me—King—with a disdainful, but also forlorn, expression. "Time's up," she said.

I awoke startled. Outside, the sky was bright. My first confused thought was that King had figured out how to open a portal to me even though we no longer shared a network. But that didn't make sense. It was simpler than that. I hadn't severed his consciousness from mine at the moment I left Blake Island's Internet range; his mind had never left mine at all. Even though information was no longer flowing from him to me, the material he had shared before—just like what I had downloaded from the Internet—must have been inside me, dormant, all along, waiting to be rediscovered.

The visions started appearing all the time.

One morning, I was drifting to sleep when a picture crystallized in my mind of Margaret on the night of her wedding to King. She sat at a white-clothed table by a window whose view slowly changed—the revolving restaurant at the top of the Space Needle. She wore a pinkish gown that kept slipping off her shoulders. I had never thought of Margaret as beautiful, not because she was my mother, but because she had seemed to me like one of those rare women, the Eleanor Roosevelts and Margaret Thatchers of the world, who are powerful enough to render beauty beside the point. Now I watched her and was moved by the bold intensity of her gaze and the flush of her high, pale forehead. "We haven't talked about kids," I—King—said.

"We don't want them, right?" Margie answered.

"Thank God you said that."

I wasn't angered; I wasn't resentful. All I felt, Shareholder, was my love for him returning to me, forcefully. It wasn't at all like the flooding from when I was younger, the sense of being invaded. The figment of King's mind simply drifted off, and I was left with a strong, but no longer overwhelming, sense of his presence. I hadn't seen him in months, but it felt as if he were right here with me, as if I could talk to him and he would answer. I could ask him what to do, and he would tell me. The thought came to me then: What if I had been wrong about his Clarinet? What if, all along, I needed only to learn to absorb his mind, the way I learned, years earlier, to absorb the Internet? What a miracle that would be. What a *gift*.

THIS MORNING, my twenty-third in the Margie, I tapped the assessment icon and chose the character assessment. The earliest versions of these assessments, the Myers-Briggs and the like, assigned you one of a number of personality types, from which experts claimed to be able to discern your suitability for various occupations. But those were debunked long ago, and now it's the Algo's job, not a human's, to integrate this data into evidence-based predictions about who a person is. I was to be presented with a series of statements and asked to choose, on a scale of one to five, the extent to which each one rang true.

You would never let yourself cry in front of others. People can rarely upset you. You often spend time exploring unrealistic yet intriguing ideas. You are still bothered by the mistakes you made a long time ago.

24

At first nobody recognized the man who came down the path early one morning. He wore sunglasses, a cowboy hat, and a pair of stylish jeans, tight at the crotch, flared at the bottom, and dusty and frayed where the hems had dragged on the ground. He looked to be in his twenties. King had been eating breakfast in the clearing, with his cousins, before school. They had all stopped eating at the sight, setting their hands on their banana leaves in awe. When the man got closer, they could see chest hair sprouting like wire from the top of his undershirt. He was handsome, with fierce, crow-footed eyes and a handlebar mustache that had been carefully groomed.

"Well, I'll tell you," he said roughly, gazing around the Garden and speaking almost as if to himself. "I got a good look at the world, and there isn't a whole lot that's better than this old place."

"Who's that?" the young children whispered. The cowboy spat onto the dirt and rubbed it in with the heel of his shoe, and it was then, only then, that King recognized Gun. King was sixteen; his cousin had been gone for more than a decade.

"Where's the old woman?" Gun said.

No one answered.

"Amma," he clarified.

"But he doesn't know?" a cousin asked another.

Only then did Gun seem to understand. He dropped his bags to the dirt and fell to his knees, his palms and forehead to the earth. He knelt there trembling for a long time. Tears rose behind King's eyes. He wanted to fall to the earth, too, and mourn the ones he had lost. But he didn't. He stood still and watched until Gun rose and spat again and grinned at all of them. Something about his mouth made it seem like a dare.

That night, Gun filled them in on where he had been. "You all remember that I went off to find a wife," he said, standing in the clearing, the younger boys sitting cross-legged before him like students in a classroom, the older men standing at a distance on the veranda of the Big House, pretending to have their own conversation but eavesdropping. "Well, there were girls in the quarry, but when I got there, I knew they weren't worth impressing. Skinny, dark-skinned, hunchbacked girls; they looked three times their age, at least!" King found that he was enthralled, and, looking around, saw that his relatives were as well—all but Chinna, who was standing with his arms crossed like a shield, among the uncles, while Gun commanded his audience's attention as if Chinna were not nearby at all. When had a Rao last been capable of that? Not, King thought, since Grandfather Rao.

"Here's what happened," Gun continued. "Those girls started looking like beauties to me! See, there were probably twenty men for each girl. All of us out in the middle of nowhere. One of those girls proposed something to me. I won't say what it was—"

"What?" they cried. "What? Tell us!"

"Ah, I won't say! Not in front of the little ones! I'm a gentleman, I'm a good man, but I'm sure you can guess. Raos aren't dumb. I told her to come see me the next night in my tent. We were drinking, we were all out of our minds. The next day, my buddies kept coming up to me. 'Ooh, man, bet you can't wait for tonight!' and so on. Well, I'd been so drunk that I didn't remember what was supposed to happen. Finally I asked one of them, my good pal, 'All right, what's supposed to be happening tonight?' Everyone had a big laugh. They said she was going around telling people we were getting married. Man, oh, man. I got out of there. I took the bus to the train station. A mendicant asked me, 'Where are you going?' and I laughed and said, 'Where should I go?' and he said, 'Brother, join up with us and it's the easy life all the way!' So that's how I joined up with the mendicants. Nobody knew I was a Dalit. We traveled everywhere, and everywhere we went, the housewives brought us their best food and touched our feet. What a life. When I quit, it was for the same reason everyone quits: I met a pretty girl, and I wanted to marry her. A tailor's daughter in Calcutta—"

"Calcutta? That far?"

"You think the world ends at the edge of this Garden? That's what Chinna wants you to think! But, yeah! Calcutta, man! We never got married, though. It's a sad story. She found out I lied to her about my caste, and she went back to her mother and told her. Her mother said, 'Leave him,' and she said, 'I won't leave him,' and her mother got my would-be father-in-law to block the door from the outside with a heavy barrel so that she couldn't escape. We went to her window at night—Inky, Pinky, and I—and she cried and said she would never marry anyone else, but she couldn't marry me. Well, that night I went to the tea shop and told all my friends about this sad story. I even cried. I was really sad. I loved her. This guy came up to me and said, 'Why are you crying over someone who rejects you for your caste? It's the sixties. People should know better.' I told him, 'My uncle wouldn't find me a wife, and now I see I can't find one on my own.' This guy got really angry. 'That's the problem with our society,' he said. 'We Indians, no matter what happens, we say, 'There's nothing I can do, it's God's will. Even if we don't believe in God, that's what we say. God's will, God's will. Don't people know there's another way?' He told me about Chairman Mao. He gave me a flyer. 'We're having a meeting,' he said, 'and I can tell you have the spirit for this. We need more people like you.' "

"That's enough," Chinna said abruptly, interrupting Gun's monologue. "The kids don't need to hear all this nonsense."

"Oh, sure, Uncle, I'll stop there," Gun said, but behind his voice there remained a challenge. "What else did I come home for but to obey you, Uncle?" he said. "My only satisfaction is to work and make you money, Uncle, so that you can buy some new shirts to wear to your meetings with those big politicians, after letting my mother die." He turned to his audience. "Well, you heard Chinna," he said. "Work comes first: the mantra of the businessman."

"Call me a businessman!" Chinna said. "I'm proud of being a businessman! I'm not ashamed. Appayya tells me what people are saying these days about businessmen. I tell him, 'At least the businessmen never killed anyone. Not like the Naxalites.' "

"Oh no!" Gun said, laughing. "Businessmen never get blood on their hands!" And he turned and strode off into the Garden, not allowing Chinna the last word.

CHINNA WAS DISTRAUGHT for reasons other than Gun's sudden return. The ban on Dalits' coconuts meant business was at a standstill. He had decided to bribe Mr. President to get him to reconsider. "If you want to have power, this is how you get it," he told King one afternoon as they counted bills. Without smiling, he held up a sheaf of bills and flapped it in the air. "Not with that revolutionary nonsense," he said. He added, with genuine puzzlement, "Really, I don't know where all this revolution talk came from."

"Those boys in Guntur, Uncle," King said. "People were protesting over those Dalit boys who got beaten to death."

"Which ones?"

"Those ones in the news."

"The news, the news," Chinna said. "I'm tired of the news. When I was a kid, it wouldn't have made the news."

"Some people think you've got to do more than take care of your own."

He laughed ruefully. "Show me a man with a family who says you've got to do more than that."

But when Chinna went to Mr. President to ask him to reconsider the ban, making it clear, through various well-established innuendos and gestures, that he was offering something in return, the president laughed in his face. "I can't be bought, Rao," he said. "I'm an ethical man. Anyway, I see Appayya egging his students on, even after I asked you to get him to stop."

"I tried to talk to him," Chinna offered, with a weak, embarrassed laugh. "He wouldn't listen."

"Try harder," Mr. President said.

This, the precarious future of the business, was what finally persuaded Chinna Rao to run in the local election to replace Mr. President. Half of Kothapalli's residents were Dalits, yet the village council had never had a Dalit president. No one had ever heard Chinna utter a word of political thought, let alone attend any of the underground meetings of Dalit activists that were held in the back rooms of bars and brothels in town, where Gun was becoming a fixture. But Chinna convinced all the Dalit coconut farmers in the village to volunteer for his campaign. They plastered flyers displaying his face on the outer walls of Appayya's school. Chinna paid the driver of the movie wagon that went around to all the villages blasting announcements about the theater's timetable to also include exhortations to vote for Chinna Rao. He spent his days in the streets with his entourage, or sitting on an overturned crate under the peepal tree at the center of the village, handing out sweets to children while engaging their parents in conversation. "What do you need that Mr. President isn't doing? Give us a list, tell us everything. We're here to help; I'll do it all."

King sometimes accompanied Chinna and his volunteers, helping them hand out sweets. One morning, Helena approached their spot under the peepal tree. She took King by the shoulder and, steering him away from the group, asked quietly if he knew where Minnu had disappeared to. Minnu? He hadn't seen her in two years; the only time he had been to the clinic after his father's death had been that one time, with Leelamma. When he asked Helena what she meant about disappearing, she told him that Minnu had left the clinic. She was living somewhere else—no one knew where—and sent groceries for them to cook for her mother each week through a messenger.

"Did you ask the messenger where she is?"

"Of course, but he's a little boy; he just runs off."

Much had happened in the time since his father's death, Helena said. Minnu had been taken in by that witch doctor, and he had turned out to be a con man. Every week he brought her some new miracle cure and took her money. Helena hadn't known about any of this until one morning a drunken man had come barging into the clinic and banging into one room after another. When the Hollander came downstairs and confronted the man, he said he was looking for someone named Marilyn. Marilyn Monroe. The drunk said Marilyn was a cute little girl with a mole on her face. He had met her in town and fallen in love with her after spending time with her, and he knew she lived there. "A mole on her face," Helena said again, meaningfully. "It was Minnu!"

"Who was the man?"

"Oh, King, it doesn't matter; she needed the money! Or she thought she did, to pay that con-artist witch doctor. We told her, 'Stop it, Minnu, this man is a cheater, a fraud; you don't have to do this.' But you know how she is—headstrong, proud. She said we didn't know what we were talking about. She said there was nothing wrong with what she was doing for a living. She could fend for herself, she didn't need our judgment, and so on. Then— only a couple of weeks ago—she left. I dream about her all the time. I don't know where she's gone, but I have a bad feeling about it."

"I don't know, either," King said helplessly.

"But you'll try to find out?"

"I'll try," he said, though he knew he wouldn't.

"It's my fault," Helena said. "I should have worked harder

to teach her the Word." She sniffled a little. "Blessed," she said tiredly, "are the poor."

EVERYONE EXPECTED Gun to leave within a couple of weeks. His mother had died, he had been too late in coming, what use was this place he had abandoned so long ago? But he stayed. He even sent out word to his younger brothers and cousins, and, one by one, they returned, too. Some were alone, some had new families. Some were so changed that only their mothers recognized them, and even they regarded their sons circumspectly.

That's how Pinky returned, and Inky, and the rest of Kanakamma's forgotten grandsons and great-nephews, all of them dressed well and cleanly shaven, so that it was only after a period of days, when the fine clothes they had been donning upon arrival darkened with sweat and dirt, and it became clear they had nothing else to wear, and their facial hair grew back all raggedy and prematurely gray, and their mothers' and aunts' questions about what they had been doing all this time were answered unsatisfactorily, that it became clear that all these prodigal Raos were returning not in triumph but in failure.

The men took up residence out in the clearing, hung hammocks between the trees, clambered into their childhood cots so their dirt-blackened toes hung from the edges. They spent the mornings sleeping in, the afternoons playing cards, and the nights bicycling to town and engaging in shady practices that Chinna heard about later from the men who stopped by his little setup under the peepal tree: soliciting prostitutes, smoking opium, and, if these spies were to be believed, fomenting some kind of revolution.

Chinna wanted details, so he dispatched King, who persuaded Gun to take him to see where he went at night. King rode on the handlebars of Gun's bike to Ambajipuram. King knew the town well enough; he had been to the market there countless times. But Gun rode his bike to a neighborhood outside the center, a quiet grid of alleys.

King saw only one group of men—three of them, their arms slung around one another's shoulders, singing film songs and shouting to the few women who stood kohled and lipsticked in the doorways of their little huts, "Let's get married; let's get married and leave this place!" The women laughed, openmouthed, and acceded. "All right, get in here, I'll marry you. That's what you want, darling? Sure, I'll be your wife, come on in." One by one, the men released one another, each man disappearing with a woman without so much as a glance at his companions.

Gun slowed the bike, and King hopped off.

"You been here before?" Gun said.

"All the time." King blushed. "I go to the market."

"Don't play dumb." Gun bumped his shoulder, grinning. "I mean, have you been *here*?"

"No," he admitted.

But Gun had stopped listening. He was threading the bike through the small alleyways, and King had to jog to keep up. What was going on? Was Gun coming to town every night only to hire prostitutes? Gun grinned at the women, and to the few men wandering through the alleys he said, "Hey, man," or, "Hi, my friend."

Then King saw her. She stood at the entrance of one of the houses, not in the doorway itself, but behind one of the women in the doorway, laughing at something taking place inside. He had never seen her in makeup, and there was an instant in which he recognized her but couldn't place her face. She looked over, and her hand rose to her mouth, and she ducked away, and then he knew for sure it was her. Minnu. She had been wearing garish costume jewels on her ears and around her neck, and a mask of makeup that had turned her brown face a pale whitish pink shade. Gun stopped a couple of yards up and was impatiently motioning for King to follow.

When King glanced back toward that door, she was gone.

Gun led King to a small tavern, where several tables had been pushed together. About a dozen men sat together, most sober, most young, most talking loudly over one another about caste, class, revolution. Someone mentioned Chinna's run for office, and everyone laughed. "The propaganda of the ruling class is a powerful thing," a man slightly older than Gun, maybe in his early thirties, said. "They tell us that their rules are God's rules—they tell us over and over—in the hopes that even if one of us manages to rise above his station, he'll still go on following their rules." Everyone was nodding, as if this man held some position of power.

Gun periodically flicked his gaze over to King to see how he was responding, and King told himself, Pay attention, this is important, but all he could think of was Minnu's face and how much he wanted to see it again. Where exactly had she been? Was it before the paan shop with the newspaper rack against the wall? Was it before the hut where the man had offered Gun a cigarette and he had taken it, and a light, but moments later tossed it on the ground? While the men threw around names he hadn't heard and made elaborate plans about who should meet whom where, he prayed that they would finish soon, and that he and Gun would return home along the same path that they took to get here, so that he would have a chance of passing her again.

But afterward, Gun hopped back on his bicycle and King got back on the handlebars, and Gun took them on a different route toward the main road. As they made their way home, Gun spoke with great agitation. "Anyone can grab power for himself," he said. "That's the secret. The way they keep you from doing it is by making you believe you can't. It's not just caste. It's people like Chinna, too. You've been taught you'll be successful in life by hitching yourself to Chinna, but who does that help? It helps Chinna. No, man, you have to grab that power. That's what I'm working at. That man at the tavern, he's higher up than me, but above him there are ten more layers before—Hey, you okay up there?"

King said he was fine.

"What are you thinking of?" Gun said. "Believe me, I know how you feel, I saw how you were looking at me that day when I came back and found out about my poor mother. We understand each other." As they rode back over the dark and rutted roads and neared the Garden, King, holding his legs up while the bike bounced and hopped, was in fact thinking of nothing of the kind, his mind devoid of intelligent thought, being occupied only by the recurring fantasy of Minnu, friend of his heart, standing in a doorway, purring, Is this what you want, darling? I'll be your wife.

THE FOLLOWING EVENING, King found himself alone and surrounded by stacks of bills. Chinna had gone to the village center to campaign, as usual. King peeled a ten-rupee bill from one bundled stack, then one more. A hundred. He pushed these bills down the back of his shorts, into his underwear. He surveyed the pile of cash before him. He imagined that he had come into the room only just now and sat down, and that nothing had happened between that moment and this one. Same as any Saturday. A pile of cash to be counted, recorded, split into piles—one to be divided for distribution among the family members and another, equal pile to be used to maintain the Garden.

When Chinna checked King's work, he did it fast, in all of five minutes. "Hmm, a bit less than I expected," he said. King's palms were wet, and a lump pressed at the back of his throat. Though he swallowed, the lump remained. But Chinna said nothing more, only mussed King's hair and murmured, "All right, go eat dinner."

King waited until well after nightfall to leave the Garden on Chinna's bicycle. In the brothel district, he walked the streets with his head down for an hour before resorting to talking to anyone. "Do you know a girl who calls herself Marilyn Monroe?" he finally asked a woman. "Big birthmark on her nose here"—he pointed—"shaped like a kidney bean."

"Kidney bean? Never heard of her."

Then a hunchbacked woman came scurrying up to him in the road, tapping him hard on the small of his back and wheezing as she caught her breath, "You're looking"—*wheeh*—"for that"—*wheeh*—"girl with the kidney-bean spot?" He nodded. She held out her hand, and he placed some coins in it. She raised her eyebrows. He added a bill. She smiled and turned and waddled down the street, until they reached a hut with a curtain at the door. That was it. The same one. "Marilyn!" the hunchback shouted. "Hey, Marilyn, you sleeping?" She went inside; he followed.

When Minnu pulled aside the curtain in the doorway of one of the rooms and found King standing next to the madam, she widened her kohl-rimmed eyes but otherwise showed no sign of recognition. The madam left them and limped to the front of the house, her anklets jingling every time her wide feet slapped the floor, so that he could tell when she was far enough away and it was safe for him to speak freely. Minnu stepped to the side so he could enter her little room. Sitting down on a stool in front of a hanging mirror, she motioned toward the bed. She was probing and pinching at her chin with her fingernails.

"Minnu, what are you doing?" he said.

"Chin hairs," she said. "Men don't like them." She went on spreading the skin of her face with one hand and plucking at the hairs with the thumb and forefinger of the other.

He sat on the bed, which was covered with a red sheet. He was overcome with shyness. Two years had passed since they had seen each other, and it seemed to him that they had both changed a great deal. She dipped a cloth into a tin cup of water and pressed it along her eyelid. The kohl smeared. After a second pass with the cloth, it was gone. They both sat still, watching each other with untrusting eyes.

"Someone could hurt you," he said. "This is dangerous."

"You watch too many movies."

"Those boys in Guntur, that wasn't a movie. That happened."

"I make a living. I take care of my mother. One day I'll earn enough to take her to the city and open my own laddu shop. I can hold my head up high."

"I didn't think you were that greedy. But now it all makes sense. You sold my dad that cow—you let him buy it—when you knew it was sick."

"Oh!" For some time they didn't speak. After a while, she stood, businesslike, and moved to the cot, where she stood before him with her arms crossed before her chest, like a schoolteacher or someone's mother. She transformed herself then—without even moving, simply by rearranging the tilt of her head and the cant of her hips—into a vixenish figure.

"Listen, Helena told me to find you and bring you back," he said. "That's why I'm here."

She laughed. "Is that *really* why you came, though?" she purred.

He lowered his head and muttered, "Well, go ahead and take off your clothes, then."

She gasped, as if she hadn't expected this, even though she had goaded him into it. She said tightly, "It'll cost you."

25

The small-boned woman who bounded onstage at the twelfth annual Sharefest wore a fuchsia-colored bobbed wig, a multitude of beaded bracelets, and nothing else—or so it seemed until the camera zoomed in and it became clear she was wearing a bodysuit the exact color of her own flesh, complete with nipples and genital slit.

Miss Fit was the biggest performing artist in the world. Born to Chinese parents in Dubai before moving to London for high school, she had met the photographer Fred Henninger at a club one night, at the age of sixteen. Soon afterward, she had gotten herself emancipated from her parents and had become one of Henninger's most famous waifs and, later, a triple-crossover pop star, with lyrics in Mandarin, Arabic, and English. It had been one of her songs, her first to go platinum, that had finally gotten Henninger canceled. After years of innuendo about his relationships with teenage girls, she narrated theirs in tight rhyming verse, beginning with the first rape and ending with the last.

It had been Margie's idea to juice the crowd with a bigger-than-usual act before the launch. She knew this one could be major if they introduced it right, and a disaster if they didn't. It had been a rough time in the world. The wildfires, the hurricanes, the heat waves. Coastal capitals were flooding on the regular: Miami was all but unlivable, as was much of the entire nation of Bangladesh; Vanuatu had been evacuated.

It had begun—this march toward Hothouse Earth—well before the transition to Shareholder Government. In King's first year as CEO, he had convened a global consortium of experts to examine how science could be deployed to return the climate to historically normal conditions. But when the scientists presented their report to the Board, they explained that it was, according to their calculations, too late to make a difference. The Board, and before it the world's nations, had done so little to compel polluters to stop poisoning the environment that nothing could be done to repair the damage. You couldn't refreeze the Arctic. It had to be acknowledged that at some point, perhaps in a couple more generations, the world would be too hot to bear human, and most other, life. Hothouse Earth was inevitable.

The Board, after discussing this among themselves, redeployed the scientists, a bit sternly, with an instruction not to come back until they had the solutions that had been requested. The next time the scientists returned, they announced, also a bit sternly, that the only solutions they could propose were theoretical and involved not returning the planet to its previous state, but rather, finding ways to safeguard its inhabitants against what was to come. Heat-resistant bunkers. Civilian space colonies.

"You've got to be kidding me," Margie interjected, rubbing her forehead. They were in the Founders Room, where all the Board meetings were held. The Board sat around the Founders Table, while the scientists stood together in front of the picture window overlooking Lake Union. But such solutions, the scientists continued—their attitude overtly mutinous at this point— were not at all in their wheelhouse. Their own expertise had been exhausted; they themselves had been exhausted. They would leave the development of the needed technologies, they said, to the experts in the business community. They would be spending their remaining years with their families.

After the scientists were dismissed, Margie spoke first. She was of the mind, she announced, that the Board should deploy an enormous investment into solutions like the ones the scientists had proposed.

"No, what?" King said out loud, stunned. Wasn't it clear to her, to all of them, that the scientists had been making a rhetorical point? If these schemes stood the slightest chance of working, wouldn't someone have already started pursuing them, given the enormous profit potential? Hadn't the scientists informed them that the game was over?

Margie persisted: Was he really suggesting that humans had exhausted their potential for innovation—that if something hadn't been invented yet, it never would be? Did he really believe they should just give up?

There was little debate after that. They wouldn't give up; that would run counter to the Coconut spirit, the Shareholder spirit. When it came time to vote, all but one of them—the one being King—voted for the moon shots.

A rift opened between him and Margie. The meeting was the first time he felt his wife was an alien, inscrutable being. It was the first time he thought not to trust her. Most people believed that, as CEO, he could do whatever he wanted. Most people didn't understand the limits of his position. It was true that he had created the system. But now he was as beholden to it as anyone else.

When he told Margie about his idea for the Harmonica not long after that, he kept his real intentions from her as well. The truth was that he viewed the Harmonica as humanity's only chance of having a future. With Hothouse Earth coming, we needed to think about how to preserve some record of who we were. But all he told her—appealing less to her sensitive side than to her skill at marketing to consumers' sensitive sides—was that it would be a way for people to communicate more authentically than ever. That explanation got her. The other one would have only reopened the fight.

Gwyneth's publicist had made the introduction to Miss Fit. But Margie, having come down with a bad flu, was viewing the events from a hotel suite down the street, while King stood alone in the wings watching the artist make the entire stadium vibrate in anticipation.

The stadium lights dimmed and a pounding bass line commenced, as Miss Fit crouched in a low yogic pose, her knees bent and her arms stretched upward. Suddenly her head seemed to explode. It was a special effect, some trick of the light. A brilliant blast flashed midair above her, a hundred thousand minuscule, translucent, magnetic bulbs, and turned to a confetti that rained down onto Miss Fit and glittered on the stage like stars.

Slowly, she rose to her feet. She pulled the microphone to her mouth. In the robotic staccato that was one of her most beloved vocal registers, she began to sing the song that had opened every Sharefest since the beginning of Shareholder Government twelve years earlier. When she got to the line right before the chorus— the part about being free—the crowd, according to custom, went nuts. When she began the next line—the one about coming together—a holographic slide above her head, also according to custom, flashed for just a second with a photo of the product King Rao was about to unveil, the one that, at first, would be considered the capstone to an illustrious career, and, within a month, would end him.

At the time, King saw only the blinding light of thirty thousand photographs being taken at once and heard only the audience's collective roar of enthusiasm. After Miss Fit's performance, he stood on the same quaking stage that she had just departed, from which he could see only an ocean of darkness before him. He knew, though, that this ocean contained thirty thousand people who had camped out for a week or more, or paid someone to do it for them, for a place below him at this moment. He had appeared at this event eleven times, but never like this. This would be his last Sharefest as CEO, after serving three terms, the maximum. In the next Shareholder election, Margie planned to run to succeed him. They had already mapped out her campaign. "Dear Share-holders!" he cried, as he had cried at the beginning of each of the past eleven festivals, and the crowd's applause was like a material substance, gathering force and rising up to embrace him one last time. "Dear Shareholders!" he said. "Shareholders!"

When the noise subsided, he took a deep breath, pushed it out through his lips, and said quietly, "When I was twelve years old, my father suffered a stroke."

The audience sighed, sadly, in near-unison. Those who fol-lowed King had heard the contours of this tale before.

He told them that the stroke had suffocated the part of his father's brain responsible for speech. He admitted that he and Pedda had never been close. He paused and blinked, hard, several times. When the stroke happened, he didn't at first understand the seriousness of it. But afterward, his father was left with only a cou-ple of words. It was then that King realized how little he knew of the man who had brought him into the world. "He died soon after that," he said. King left home as quickly as he could, and wound up here, in the United States, in the 1970s, to study computer science. He hadn't understood at the time why he kept obsessing over using code to deepen human beings' connection to one another. "But I kept thinking: How can we use this to get people to really start to understand one another?" he said.

A slide appeared above him, depicting a petroglyph on a rock wall. He swiped his finger in the air. Hieroglyphics. He swiped again. A letter. A telegraph. A telephone. "Do you see what's happening here?" he said. "The history of communication, dear Shareholders, is nothing less than the history of *ourselves*. We started out as scattered tribes, and then became feudal societies, then nations, then this grand collective of Shareholders. All this time, we've been pursuing the same human project—to become more and more *connected* with one another." More slides: a radio, a television. "This is where we were"—the TV—"when Margie and I met. This is where we were when we started asking ourselves what should come next and tapped into an incredibly subversive

notion: that we could use computers, these supposedly cold, calcu-
lating, heartless devices, to bring people together in a way that no
one ever had before."

Now came a new series of slides, showing Coconut products:
the Coconut, the Cocophone, the Cocoglass. "Dear Shareholders,
we didn't start Coconut to get rich; we started it so we could do
our part in bringing us all closer together."

Now he raised, between his thumb and forefinger, a small
syringe, no longer than his thumb. "I wanted you to be the first to
see this. I'm holding a syringe filled with a test version of a product that will eventually let you communicate over the Internet just
by *thinking*." The most obvious use case would be to help people
like his father—those who could no longer produce language—
communicate again. But eventually it would go far beyond that:
Anyone could use it. "Dear Shareholders," King said, and the audience roared again. "Get ready to meet the Harmonica."

AFTER LEAVING THE STAGE, King stopped at Miss Fit's dress-
ing room and knocked. She opened the door wearing an oversized zebra-striped sweatshirt that hung to her knees, over a pair
of lime-green leggings. "Hi," she said languidly. To the three
bodyguards—one napping on the couch, another perched on the
makeup table, reverently cradling Miss Fit's limp bodysuit in his
lap, the last standing behind the door and eyeing King—Miss Fit
said, "Give us a minute?"

The napping bodyguard, who now appeared to have been only
pretending to sleep, snapped open his eyes and said, "You sure?"

She nodded, and the bodyguards filed out, the one with the
bodysuit leaving the costume behind, folded in half so only the
chest was visible. She followed them to the door and closed it
behind them.

"Loud out there," she said. "They went wild over us, huh?"

"They did."

The bodysuit emanated a mildly rotten smell. Miss Fit touched his shoulder and looked intently at him. "Did you like my costume, King?" she said, in a soft, almost hypnotic, voice.

"It was unusual," he said. "A unique, interesting costume. I've never seen anything like it."

"Thanks. If that's a compliment."

"It is!"

"You get what it is, right?"

"I—is it called a bodysuit?"

"I mean, what it's made of."

"What's it—" he said, but as he said it, the answer became clear to him. The smell. The verisimilitude. "Oh," he said, a bit weakly.

She nodded, her painted eyes bright. "Taxidermy," she said. "Human skin. My stylist knows a med-school professor."

He thought he should be disgusted, but, looking at the costume—at the nipples standing erect—he grew unexpectedly aroused. "You were great," he said. "You looked great."

She smiled. "You were, too," she said. "They loved it."

"I hope they did."

"It sounded like science fiction."

"Doesn't it?" he said. "I didn't even get into the details of what I might do in the future. You can imagine a time when every human being becomes intertwined at the mental level, all networked together in one system, right? Then, if you can build a master system smart enough to understand all the information flowing through this network, you can—"

Miss Fit leaned in, her eyes bright. "That sounds like a kind of god."

"Oh, that's an old argument, but it's got a simple rebuttal," he said. "We control it."

"Who's we?"

"The Board—I mean, on behalf of the Shareholders."

She smiled knowingly. "Then, as the CEO of the Board of Shareholders, you're God, correct?"

He laughed. Women who weren't Margie used to hit on him all the time, and he never followed through. Now he was an old man, beyond sex. But Miss Fit was working herself into some deep place in his soul. It reminded him of his earliest conversations with Margie, back when they were starting Coconut together and never disagreed. The artist's lips were dark and wet-looking, like a ripe plum. He had never before contemplated how fruit-like lips could be. He felt sure that if he bit them he would draw nectar.

"If you like that, yes, I can be God," he said. He was alarmed and excited at the same time. "Do you like that? Then call me God."

THE COCONUT CORPORATION's whole business was built on extracting and profiting from its users' personal information, while claiming its goal was to bring people together in harmony. But to create a product that could read people's minds and claim benevolence—that was another level entirely, wasn't it?

King and Margaret laughed privately at the naïveté of the protesters who made this argument, earnest Portland types with side-shaves and Che Guevara's profile across their T-shirts, gathered outside the Shareholder Campus, a couple hundred, no big deal. At night they tumbled into tents that wobbled and lurched in the wind, and by day they stood bedraggled outside the buildings, passing around kombucha-filled thermoses and hoisting hand-made signs that read I'M NOT A MACHINE, and BEING HUMAN, and NO TRESPASSING. They began changing their last names, legally, to "Ex," supposedly a reappropriation of the freedom from surveillance that they considered their natural birthright. They thought if there were enough of them with the same last name, they would be untraceable by the Board. In reality, they could easily still be tracked. The Board's software could identify a person by her facial features, writing style, speech patterns. These poor punks—who was going to tell them?

They were far outnumbered, in any case, by those who clamored for the Harmonica on Social. Of course, you couldn't be sure who had been paid for their clamoring—Coconut was generous toward influencers—but the desire did *seem* authentic, which was what mattered. Within a month, one billion Shareholders joined the lottery to be among the lucky ones who would get to help test the Harmonica, in exchange for early access to the product once it was complete. Soon the winners were announced, and the unboxing videos began appearing. The test version came nestled in a tiny plastic-wrapped pod, the size and shape of a ring box, stamped only with the phrase COME TOGETHER. This test version didn't do anything; it was just meant to study how people's bodies reacted to it. Still, in the videos, winners reverently unwrapped their boxes, removed the little folded manual, unfolded it, read aloud the explanation of how to inject themselves, then set the paper aside before pulling the long-awaited syringe from its plastic nest. You could often hear, in these videos, the user's long sigh of awe, before he injected the fluid into the crook of his arm.

So what if a couple dozen slouchy, disheveled, tattooed, floppy-haired youths moved their protest to the front of King and Margie's estate, waving posterboards in the wind? The Exes' refusal to avoid using Shareholder products—their refusal to even use Social to spread their message—destined them to fail. This notion that people were so gullible as to be tricked by King into letting him read their minds was insulting to those billions of people who had embraced the Harmonica. Maybe the Board had problems, but were these kids the ones to fix them? Was it they who had fed and clothed the hungry and naked; who had created free universal systems of health care, education, and housing? No, the Board had. The Raos had. Margie kept reminding King of this when he couldn't sleep at night.

THE VIDEO FOR "Call Me God (Do You Like That)," which appeared without warning on Social one night, opens with a giant robot dancing on a stage. The robot's movements are stilted, all right angles, offbeat. It opens its mouth and a large red fleshy-looking tongue emerges. It's just the tip of the tongue at first, but it keeps extending, until it has unfurled itself like a scroll all the

314 • VAUHINI VARA

way to the ground. What is it made of? Plastic, or what? To a deep, droning bass line, the camera zooms closer and closer to the tongue until a small figure is perceptible at its tip. We approach the figure and see that it's Miss Fit, crouched, sweat running between her breasts, dripping from her armpits. But when she opens her mouth, the voice that comes out isn't hers. It's that of a man with a slight accent and a high-blown tone. If the voice sounds familiar, that is because it is.

I might do. I might d-d-do. I might do you like that. She had spliced it together from different parts of their conversation and modified it to sound less like the question it had been than a declaration.

The bass line speeds up, and Miss Fit's voice comes in, as she begins to dance. *Please, Mr. CEO, please, King Rao, please, would you do me like that?* The familiar voice again: *I might do. I might d-d-do. I might do you like that.* The image cuts to a low-resolution, hard-to-interpret film, all abstract curves and angles, and King's voice can be heard again. *I can be God, c-c-c-call me God.* The footage resolves itself—grainy and grayscale, but, yes, visible enough—into an image of King Rao crouched naked on top of Miss Fit, thrusting himself into her. *Do you like that. Do you like that. I can be God—d-d-do you like that.*

It was bad enough that Miss Fit had taped him talking. But in the film of him fucking her he looked pathetic, like some large rodent bobbing up and down. In a post accompanying the video, Miss Fit explained that she had long admired the scientist from whom King had stolen the idea for Coconut. The scientist had been the former mother-in-law of her rapist, Henninger. Though Burroughs had died in obscurity, never getting credit or compensation for the scientific insight that launched Coconut, Miss Fit hadn't forgotten about her. There was, in her mind, a thread between herself and Burroughs. She had always fantasized about avenging the forgotten scientist. Then her friend Gwyneth had given her the chance.

Margie moved out the day the footage was released. It wasn't that he had fucked another woman, or even that, in a fit of panic, he had lied at first, accusing Miss Fit of creating a deepfake, before breaking down and confessing. Margie wasn't as provincial as that. She herself had fucked another man—the same man, twice—she said. So it wasn't that. It was that the transgression had destroyed the launch she had been planning for years. For that she couldn't forgive him. They had been drifting apart for years, anyway. He had to admit that. These past two years, there had been the growing disagreement about the climate scientists. The other man, in case he cared, was Johnny Lin, the CEO of Roostek, who had been charismatic at the bar but bad in bed. The first time she thought the awkwardness had been her fault. But the second time she blamed Lin. She regretted it afterward. She told herself she would never tell King because it would hurt him too much, but at this particular moment she thought hurting him as much as possible would make her feel at least a little better.

Now Margie's driver came to spirit her off—she wouldn't say where to—and King grabbed her arm. "Margie, I'll fix it with the Harmonica, I promise," he said, but she shook him off and spat, "It's too late."

In this, as in most everything else, she would prove to be right.

The divorce papers followed. She got the main house. He got all the other properties and the Rao Project. After the documents were leaked, King saw himself on Social's trending page looking haggard and mean, while in a small superimposed photo Margie was raising her hand to hail a taxi, a roll of fat exposed at her midriff. "The World's Most Expensive Divorce!" one headline declared.

When, a week later, he was awoken one morning by his phone's special ring indicating it was Margie calling, his whole being ignited. Could it be that it wasn't over? Could it be that she had found it in her heart to forgive him after all? But when he picked up the phone, she didn't even let him finish saying her name before interrupting, "Have you not seen it?"

"Wait, seen what?" he said, irritated and defensive, realizing this was a business call.

"You haven't seen it. Jesus, check your messages. Walter's been calling you all night." She sounded annoyed. He had been taking sleeping pills for the first time in his life, and realized, glancing at his phone, that he had been sleeping so deeply that he had missed a half dozen calls from Walter; it must have been Walter who had asked Margie to call.

"Just tell me," he said, defensive. "What's going on?"

"There's some doctor, some famous geriatrician from Columbia University, claiming one of his patients died because of us. One of our Harmonica testers, she had a stroke and died." Margie ran through the details: A seventy-five-year-old New Yorker, the user had been an early adopter all her life. King's speech about Pedda's stroke had moved her to action. Her doctor had cautioned her against trying the Harmonica—she had suffered a stroke before, in her sixties—but ultimately left it up to her. "Walter wants to set up a press conference for this afternoon," Margie said. "He needs us to tell him, what do we want to do?"

"What does he want to do?"

"I mean, what you'd expect, 'We're investigating the situation, our hearts go out to the victim and her family—' "

"But is it really our fault, Margie? Shouldn't we try to figure that out?"

"Of course. That's what the investigation is for."

"Right."

What they decided on, the two of them plus Walter, was that King would promise both an investigation and, out of an abundance of caution, a recall of the Harmonica while the investigation was ongoing. But that afternoon outside Coconut, King was standing at the podium, looking out at the reporters gathered there, and for some reason—seeing the coldness in their expressions, maybe, the way in which they seemed already to have jumped to conclusions—he found himself pushing out his chest and announcing, with no evidence, "There's nothing wrong with the Harmonica."

The reporters posted his words, in real-time, on Social.

"Did an individual who tested the Harmonica die?" he went on, ad-libbing. "Yes, no one's contesting that. But was that *because of* the Harmonica? No, no, I don't buy it. I built the thing. I don't buy it." He continued like this, until Walter tugged him away by the shoulder, my father stammering, "No, wait," as Margie, his ex-wife, replaced him behind the lectern and announced, in a perfect voice, funereal and authoritative, "I can take any other questions from here."

It put him in a mood. When Walter called King the following morning, whispering that he had just hung up with the *Wall Street Journal*—some Southeast Asian correspondent claimed to have multiple credible sources telling her that King had known about the Harmonica's defects and covered them up—King's first reaction was to double down. "For God's sake, Walter, it's not true!" he cried. "Do *you* believe this crap?"

Walter ignored the question and shared the specifics. Three former Roostek employees, on Harmonica assembly lines in Yangon, Lusaka, and Havana, were claiming that, while learning to code in their spare time as part of a job-training scheme sponsored by Coconut, they had been encouraged to practice together over the Internet. In one such session, they had jointly hacked into the Harmonica's software and discovered an overly optimistic assumption in the code. If the device emitted even slightly more heat that expected, brain damage could result. These former employees had told the reporter they had coauthored a letter to King and Margie in which they laid out what they had learned, and no one had responded. A week after sending the letter, they were fired from Roostek for unspecified "security violations."

My poor father. He should have just acknowledged the truth. His product had killed a person, and he had been forewarned that such a thing could happen. He had made a mistake, an error in judgment. He would pull the product and fully compensate the victim's family, though, of course, no monetary compensation could make up for what had happened. But maybe it wouldn't have made a difference given what happened next—the sixty-three additional deaths in the month that followed, including that of a French teenager with no medical history whatsoever.

Shareholders gathered en masse around the globe, this time not to witness a product launch, not to hear a speech by a top influencer, not to compete in the quadrennial Brand Olympics, but to let it be known that they would prefer a CEO who would not kill them to serve his own hubris. Suddenly the Exes, whom no one had been paying much attention to, were heroes.

For three days, King sat alone at home—though, outside, the number of men guarding him had been quadrupled—on a video call with Margie, Walter, and several lawyers that began each morning and didn't end till nightfall. Sometimes other executives, or a crisis consultant Walter had hired, would drop in. In another window on his screen, King watched the protests playing out, some not far from his own home.

"We're not machines!" people chanted in the streets, in cities around the world. "No trespassing!" In Paris, they scrawled graffiti on a statue of my father. GOD, they wrote across his face, then scratched it out. Footage spread online, and soon every statue of King in the world, it seemed, was thus labeled. People were knocking off his arms with hammers. They were pissing on his toes. He watched, that night, as a young woman calling herself Elemen Ex stood on a car and read a manifesto scrawled on a paper plate. "We're here to fight the insidious violence of Shareholder Government with our own *honest* violence!"

There was something ridiculously old-fashioned about the rhetoric, as if they had ripped it from the journals of some nineteenth century anarchist, and yet, people were listening to the young woman, rapt. People were storming the headquarters of the Shareholder Campus, shattering the windows with rocks and fists. He watched this all unfold from his quiet home, carrying his phone from room to room, unable to sit still. The property was locked up and surrounded with extra security working overtime. King posted on Social at one-hour intervals, a series of carefully crafted messages: that the Board "supports peaceful protest" and was deploying police "to keep Shareholders safe." Margie always said that what happened offline didn't matter, as long as you could control the online narrative about it. That night, though, he understood he had lost control. It was on his phone that he saw smoke begin to pour out of the windows of the main building. It was thus that he realized, along with the rest of the world, that the seat of Shareholder Government had been set ablaze.

ong before I could claim Blake Island as mine, it was an ancestral camping ground for the Duwamish Tribe and, according to legend, the birthplace of a singular child named Si'ahl. The islands, back then, were dense with cedar and Douglas fir. The child is said to have sighted George Vancouver's ships as they sailed through the bay in 1792 and dropped anchor at the tip of the point that jutted out from the large island north of his birthplace, the one that Vancouver would decide to call Restoration Point. Si'ahl's uncle, the powerful Chief Kitsap, welcomed Vancouver's men. Si'ahl would have been six years old.

Over the decades that followed, Si'ahl himself grew up to be an important chief and a friend of the white men, who he believed would be powerful allies against rival tribes up north. He misread the situation entirely. In a season of treacherous treaty-making, Governor Isaac Ingalls Stevens and his supporters took ownership of the ancestral lands of the Duwamish and Suquamish tribes, renamed them Bainbridge and Blake Islands, and logged their timber to be floated down to San Francisco, house-building materials for newly rich gold miners. Chief Si'ahl, along with his people, was eventually sent to live on a reservation on the Kitsap Peninsula, across the Agate Passage from Bainbridge. In the end, the white men took his name—anglicizing it as Seattle—as well.

A famous speech is attributed to the chief, which is said to have been addressed to Governor Stevens himself when it became clear the white men had betrayed the chief. "But why should I mourn at the untimely fate of my people?" he said. "When the last Red Man shall have perished, and the memory of my tribe shall have become a myth among the White Men, these shores will swarm with the invisible dead of my tribe, and when your children's children think themselves alone in the field, the store, the shop, upon the highway, or in the silence of the pathless woods, they will not be alone. In all the earth there is no place dedicated to solitude. At night when the streets of your cities and villages are silent and you think them deserted, they will throng with the returning hosts that once filled them and still love this beautiful land. The White Man will never be alone. Let him be just and deal kindly with my people, for the dead are not powerless. Dead, did I say? There is no death, only a change of worlds."

Can't you just imagine the defiant, even threatening thrust to Chief Si'ahl's chin? But then, there's no evidence the chief said any of this at all. A white doctor, Henry Smith, published the words in a newspaper two decades after the chief's death, claiming it was based on his notes from the speech. Further adaptations were made by much later authors. In 1970, a man named Ted Perry adapted the words for a film script about pollution. "The earth does not belong to man; man belongs to the earth," Si'ahl said in that version. "This we know. All things are connected like the blood which unites one family. All things are connected." Those were the lines picked up by environmentalists in the 1980s and '90s, as well as by Suquamish leaders themselves. They were the lines later evoked at the height of mainland Exism, when the Exes were chanting anti-Board slogans in Si'ahl's name. Chief Seattle told us true! This land does not belong to you!

What would Si'ahl's ghost make of all this? Is he really watching, and if so, what quiet vengeance has he been planning? Or was the speech just another colonial fiction? Si'ahl was the first signatory of the treaty granting white men more than two million acres of land, relegating his people to the Kitsap Peninsula reservation where he died and was buried with little fanfare. The gravestone declared him for posterity, his final feelings on the matter notwithstanding, THE FIRM FRIEND OF THE WHITES.

THE THOUGHT OF the chief came to me on a cool autumn night, when I dragged the kayak I had taken out from the marina onto the northwestern shore of Blake Island, and, for the first time in months, my Clarinet rumbled awake.

Concentrate, I told myself. Focus. I hiked through the woods and sword ferns toward the house, trying to quiet my overactive Clarinet. When I got nearer, I could see that the lights were off. I made my way to the front door. It opened as easily as ever. Then I was standing in the living room of my childhood home. It was the smell that got me, of spice and incense.

Through the open door of my father's room, I heard him snoring.

It was by plumbing my father's mind—by studying the period when he designed the Clarinet—that I had finally understood why it had activated in him only fully enough to connect with mine. He had told me he adjusted the technology so that it could gauge each user's ability to absorb it, working only in those whose minds were young and plastic enough. What, then, convinced him to eventually inject himself, knowing he had to be far too old for the Clarinet to function? In my mind's eye, there he sits—I sit—at his computer, fingertips trembling over the keyboard. The thought is half-formed. Even if I can't *feel* myself going online, he thinks, maybe the connection will still be open, and if the connection is open, maybe Athena will be able to find it? It isn't a nefarious thought; it's a tentative one, barely there at all.

I moved toward his room and entered. He lay in his bed facing me, curled on one side with his hands tucked under his face, like a child, the way he always slept. I sat on the bed. He looked pale, gaunt. I took one of his hands and held it. It was cool, blue-veined, and soft as ever. "Daddy," I said.

He opened his eyes for a moment and closed them again. "Mmm," he said.

"Daddy, it's me."

"Go back to bed, baby-love. It's late."

"I'm here."

"Mm-hmm."

"Are you eating? Are you staying hydrated?"

"Shh, there's a lot to do. Let's go to sleep."

"Daddy—it worked. Your Clarinet. It connected with mine."

He opened his eyes and blinked at me a few times. I held my breath. He said, again, "There's a lot to do." He scooted to the other side of the bed, and patted the space he had made. "Come on, baby-love, it's late."

"I can see inside your mind, like you hoped, remember?"

He gave an uncertain little laugh. "Baby-love, you know I hardly remember anything nowadays," he said sadly. He added, as if to appease me, "If you're happy, I'm happy, though."

I needed to get home before Elemen discovered my absence. But here was my brilliant father. Here was the immortal King Rao, so close I could smell him. I pulled back the sheets and slid in. The space was warm and a little damp. I turned away from him and pulled his soft arm over me, so that it was as if I were nested there. I let myself pretend that I was a child again. I waited. Then, for the first time in months, my Clarinet connected with my father's again.

It took a minute, the way a little-used faucet sputters a bit when you turn it on. I worried that it would be like before—his mind flooding mine, uncontrollably. But I took deep breaths and coaxed myself into relaxation, the way I had taught myself to do on the floor of Elemen's bedroom. On Bainbridge, I had already arranged all that I had previously downloaded from him in roughly chronological order. Now here was everything he had gone through since my departure months ago.

The afternoon I left, my father had come home from his shopping trip, wandered into the house, and called for me. When I didn't answer, he hadn't been at all alarmed. He figured I had gone swimming or wandering, as usual. It wasn't late yet. He had opened the fridge, taken out some leftover rice and a jar of yogurt, poured the yogurt onto the rice, and eaten it, just standing there. He had gone to bed early. In the morning, he had called out for me again. This time, again, the lack of response didn't concern him. He had forgotten about the previous afternoon.

I moved through the time between then and this moment, trying to find evidence that he had grown worried at some point. But each day was the same. He never remembered I was missing for long enough to be alarmed by it. He took his meals standing, in his lungi, illuminated by the light of the fridge. When he ran out of food, he boated out to the market, not far from where I had been all this time, to get more.

"I've been gone a really long time," I whispered. My voice was small, plaintive—a child's voice.

"You went for a swim this late?"

I wanted to tell him no, I hadn't swum, but he kept talking. "It's okay, you never go far," he said.

He began snoring again.

I turned to face him now and tried to memorize the contours of his face, its deeply etched lines. Then, once it was clear he was fast asleep, I spoke. I told him I would never leave him. I said I would stay with him until the end of time. I wanted to hear those words leaving my mouth and entering his ear. It was a bit of make-believe. Even as I said it, I knew I was lying. I kissed the soft, yielding skin of his forehead. I held his hand, twining my fingers with his. Maybe some part of me hoped he would wake up, come to his senses, and command me to remain by his side forevermore. But when he didn't, I felt a wash of relief. I stood and left him. I walked out and went around to his office. I turned on his computer, found the source code for the Clarinet, and saved it on a thumb drive. Then I retrieved the box I had come for—the one containing one hundred doses' worth of Clarinet—and let myself out.

IT WAS ONE NIGHT later that I sat myself on a cushioned banquette in the sternward corner of the Cha Cha. The crowd was sparse; it was a Monday, the slowest night of the week. After a while, a couple of men came over and looked me up and down. They appeared to be in their forties, with dark hair and tanned skin, and wore bright T-shirts emblazoned with brand logos. "What are you thinking?" one of them—they were interchangeable—said.

"A Manhattan," I said. It had become my go-to. They left for the bar together and returned with three glasses, and we drank together.

"So what else is going on?" the second man said after a while. This was it: my cue to discuss what I had on offer.

"Let's talk about it in private," I said.

When they brought me to a room, I explained I had a drug to test. I couldn't tell them anything beyond that, to avoid influencing their reactions. But they could try it for free. I had samples.

The men were sitting side by side on the bed, as I stood, like obedient pupils. "That's what we come here for," one of them said confidently; it was clear they did this often.

When I injected the men, each in turn, they moaned in pleasure, their eyelids fluttering a little. I watched them closely, my throat tight. Then it came to me, an explosion of memories (a paper boat sailing swiftly down a gutter; a pair of squirrels mating in a flowerbed) and feelings (the pain of a broken leg; the unexpected joy of holding a little sister's tiny hand). It was so intense I had to squeeze my eyes shut to contain it.

I had to remind myself: An exploration of strangers' consciousness wasn't what I was after. I had a more specific goal, to locate a sense that the status quo dissatisfied them and that they might be open to doing something about it. Then, there it was: Sebastian's addiction to a painkiller that a brand had tested on him for months; Javi's inability to make partner at his law firm because the size of his student loans kept his Social Capital too low. When I opened my eyes, the men were watching me, with warm, open expressions. How, I carefully asked them, did they feel?

"Beautiful," one of them—Sebastian—said. "A burst of *happiness*," he said. "Quick, but intense."

"A sense of connection," said the other, Javi, still smiling. "With the universe; with Sebastian; with you, too."

I returned to Elemen that night with six targets. In the morning, I visited Arno's tent with a question. If someone provided him with a drug and its source code, could he reverse-engineer more of it?

"That's what I do," he said, full of pride.

"It's a psychoactive, a mood-enhancer." It wasn't a lie; after Sebastian and Javi had suggested as much, so had the others I had tried it on. "I'd test it for a while, three or four months, and then, if I started selling it, you'd get a quarter of sales." That wasn't a lie, either; I didn't plan to ever sell it, but I had said *if*.

He shook his head and laughed. "You sound like Elemen," he said. "Half."

"Fine," I said. "But this is between us."

He whistled, impressed. "A side hustle," he said. "I get it."

It had taken me a month to pass the first eight names to Elemen, including that of the chef. But a month after Arno reverse-engineered the drug, I had given her a hundred more. The targets' minds combined, in my own, into a symphony of loss, betrayal, and hardship. Sometimes, after injecting them, I would have to lie down, making excuses about not feeling well. But the targets' own experience of it was different. Like Sebastian and Javi, they described an intense hit—lasting maybe a minute—that gave them a deep sense of love and connection. It felt, they said, incredible. It reminded them of Ecstasy. They felt close to me in that moment, as if they could trust me completely.

I swear, Shareholder, I never exploited that. Once I practiced a little, I was able to use the Clarinet only to gauge their openness to Exism; I never did anything else. After a while I learned to dip into people's minds and absorb what I needed in a minute or less. It could still be overwhelming. Sometimes I couldn't be sure whether my thoughts were mine, or King's, or someone else's. I would hear words come out of my mouth that surprised me, as if some stranger's tongue had made those sounds. But Elemen's list of names was lengthening. While she didn't tell me what she was doing with them, or if she had even made contact yet at all, she told me that she was impressed. We were beginning to accomplish what had seemed impossible. You are a Rao, I told myself. You, too, will change the world.

EXISTENCE IS CHANGE. The days shortened. One cool morning, I awoke to find Elemen crouched next to me on the floor, tugging at the sleeve of my nightgown. "Hey, kiddo," she said when I opened my eyes. "Get up, come with me." She had an errand to run, delivering Catches, and needed my help with the boxes. I hadn't had a full night's sleep in weeks, but I got up and followed her.

The sun was brilliant as we went down the road, but it awakened me only superficially. I felt alert, but also as if time were moving discontinuously, spurting rather than flowing. As Elemen and I walked, taking turns pulling the Catches piled in a wagon behind us, she said, "I don't know what's happening out there at the Cha Cha, but you're doing great."

"Luck," I said.

"Talent!"

I remember she was cheerful that morning.

She turned down a long driveway to her right, toward a farmhouse painted red like a barn. The door opened and a thin old woman with long gray hair emerged. She wore a low-cut, sequined dress that caught the sun and glittered. "Hi, doll," the woman called. "Come in. I got olives and made olive bread."

"I'm Ruthie," she said to me. "I run this place." The place was one of the island's clinics, Ruthie a doctor. The inside of the farm-house was filled with light. A long picnic table was set in the middle of the kitchen, with a basket full of fruit sitting on top. I thought of home. I thought of my father, palming a mango, the day I injected him with his Clarinet.

"What's her deal?" Ruthie said to Elemen.

"She's one of mine."

Ruthie rolled her eyes, but in a pleasant way. "Aren't we all, in some sense?" she said to Elemen. To me, she said, "Orange?" Before I could answer, she took one from the basket and pitched it at me underhand. She tossed another at Elemen. "Eat your fruit, girls," she said. "Vitamin C."

"I like your dress," I told her.

"Oh, take it. I'm bored with it." She turned to Elemen. "Unzip me, doll," she said.

Elemen pulled the zip down to the small of Ruthie's back, and the older woman's flesh spilled out. Her skin was freckled and, where the dress had squeezed her, red. She disappeared down the hall, and when she returned a couple of minutes later, she was wearing hospital scrubs with little cartoon cats all over them. The dress hung over her arm, and she came over and draped it around my shoulders. The sequins tickled my skin. The dress smelled of Ruthie's sweat and perfume.

"So did you hear?" Ruthie said.

Elemen laughed. "Ruthie's always the first to hear what's happening on the mainland," she said. Sympathetic doctors there worked with health care providers in the Blanklands to share public health information, and each morning one of them showed up to give Ruthie an update. "What should we have heard?" she said.

"You didn't hear?" Ruthie said carefully, looking from Elemen to me and back to Elemen.

"About what?"

"About King Rao?"

My heart clenched.

"What about him?"

"He was found dead, doll," Ruthie said quietly.

Orange juice dripped from my mouth onto my chin. I willed myself to be silent, occupying myself with wiping my face with the back of my hand.

He had been assassinated while in his boat on Puget Sound, Ruthie said, heading toward the market. The perpetrator was a college student from the mainland who had gotten his hands on a sniper rifle. They had caught him right afterward—the kid hadn't stood a chance.

But I had seen my father not long ago. I had seen him alive. I had spoken to him.

"Dammit," Elemen said. "When did this happen?"

"Maybe three or four hours ago."

Elemen shot me a fast, inscrutable glance. "The Board's going to come after us for it; this is the excuse they've been waiting for." She rubbed her face.

My father used to do a trick to cheer me up when I was down. He would give me a banana. "Come on," he would tell me. "Have a snack." When I peeled the banana, slices would tumble out, perfectly cut. For a long time, I couldn't figure out how he had done it. I thought he was a magician. He would grin at me, full of joy, and I would grin, too, my sorrows forgotten. Once I was connected, though, I easily learned his trick. You take a safety pin, prick the peel, and slide the pin back and forth to slice a piece. You move the pin up a little and repeat the process, till you've sliced the whole banana from the outside. I hated having learned that. It killed the magic. I wished I could unlearn it.

I went to the kitchen sink so they wouldn't see my expression. My face burned. I rinsed my mouth and chin. I washed my hands for a long time. Maybe it was a dream. It had the logic of one, an unreality. I came and saw you with my own eyes, I thought. You were old then. But you were alive. I saw you.

Ruthie said, "I think even people around here will assume you knew about it, or even—"

"Well, we didn't!" Elemen snapped violently. "What a stupid

thing to assume. Who's King Rao to us? He's no one; he's been powerless for years." She took a deep breath and let it out. Maybe Ruthie had been one of the people who assumed the Exes were involved. Yet she had still let us into the clinic. "You're a good person, Ruthie," she said. "Sorry, I'm on edge."

Ruthie shrugged. "Me, too," she said. They both fell into silence. I looked out the window.

"Damn," Elemen said after a while. "I know it's nuts, but I really thought it was true all along."

"That he was immortal! Me, too!" Ruthie laughed, and Elemen joined in—a rueful laugh, but a laugh nonetheless. He's no one, she had said. He's no one.

Only then did Elemen turn her attention to me. "Head back to the house, kiddo, and gather everyone up," she said. "I'll be there in a minute."

I didn't trust myself to open my mouth. I nodded mutely and left. I was running down the road when I heard his voice—my father's—in my mind. I have never been spiritual, Shareholder. I believe in no God at all. But I heard him. His voice was not gentle, like you would expect of the dead. It was insistent. Raos, he said, never rest.

IT'S NO GOOD, being alone in this cell with no human contact. It can drive a person to madness. I've been here almost a month. Not long ago, I heard a faint clicking sound—a roach, scratching across the floor. When he approached my mattress, I put a foot down and nudged him with my toe. I meant it as a companionate gesture. Let's be friends. But I must have scared him. He scuttled into the space between the mattress and the wall. I stayed still and waited for him to come out from hiding. Five minutes. Ten. Fifteen. He never emerged.

He's gone. But I don't mean the cockroach. The cold in here— it's exactly like the cold from the fridge on my father's arms, after I left him. There's a word for the feeling of having lost a loved one.

It's a small word, *grief.* But for the disappearance of the one person by whom you have defined yourself, without whom you cannot be sure of your own existence, there is no word at all. If there were, it would have to be an endless one. You would go on speaking it for the rest of your life. You would die with the word on your lips.

WE HAD ALL BEEN waiting on the veranda for a half hour, the others getting impatient, when Elemen came jogging down the road. We rearranged ourselves to make room for her. Nelo perched on the railing, Romeo crouched and bounced on his haunches, the others sat on the stairs or leaned against the front of the house. Otis set himself on the porch swing alone. Elemen didn't wait for everyone to settle before spitting it out. "Listen," she said, her voice tense. "Someone killed King Rao. The Board's investigating."

Romeo whooped, as if in celebration. I flinched, then looked around, hoping no one had noticed. Otis caught my eye; I thought maybe he had seen.

But Otis snapped at Romeo, "Don't. That's a human being— we don't cheer."

Romeo scowled and settled. Nelo broke in: "My question is why the Board cares if he's dead. He Exed a long time ago. It happened in neutral waters. It's not their jurisdiction."

"The assassin's a Shareholder," Elemen said. "That makes it their jurisdiction. Plus, they're afraid of what it symbolizes. If someone can kill King Rao, who's next, the current Board members?"

Romeo and Nelo's comments loosened everyone up, and now they all started in: How had Elemen found out? When did this happen? Who had done it?

Elemen answered each of them in turn. Ruthie told us. It had, according to Ruthie, happened that morning—a sniper had shot him, six times, from his boat. The perpetrator had been apprehended thirteen minutes later. He was a twenty-year-old man, a college graduate, a Shareholder in good Social standing. At his home, an apartment near the university, the cops had found his roommates bewildered and in denial. The young man's brother had recently died, the roommates said, and he had been depressed ever since. Over the weekend, he had gone to his brother's funeral, and they hadn't seen him since. They had assumed he was with his older sister, that he just needed his space. It was at the sister's home that the detectives had discovered three pages of loose-leaf paper, folded in quarters, on which he had written a long-winded, roundabout manifesto identifying himself as an Ex and blaming King Rao for his brother's death. The Board was calling it a terrorist assassination.

Otis had been mostly silent while Elemen talked. When he spoke, he addressed her directly, not looking at anyone else. "Identifying himself as an Ex," he repeated, and then, hopefully: "But we don't know him, right?"

"The good news is that he claims to be acting alone, and I've never heard of him," Elemen said. "The bad news is that he spent the weekend at the Cha Cha." Her eyes scanned the group, and I could have sworn they paused on me. Then she told us his name.

I recognized it at once.

27

After the fall of King Rao, video crews descended upon Kothapalli with microphones and satellite dishes. They discovered, where the Garden was supposed to be, a muddy, abandoned plot of land, littered where it met the road with crushed pop cans, rain-sodden plastic bags, and cigarette butts. Down a puddled path they found some untended coconut trees flapping brown and brittle fronds. Passing an irrigation tube well with some viridescent wetness scumming its reservoir's walls, they arrived at a sort of yard that appeared once to have been a clearing, but through which weeds and grass had pushed up. In the center of this former clearing were two long, squat houses. They stood parallel, nearly identical in their disrepair—paint peeling from their walls, the thatching of their twin roofs lifting in the breeze and slapping down again.

With the money King wired once a quarter, Kittu and the others had, unbeknownst to him, moved to Rajahmundry, or, farther away yet, to Vijayawada or Hyderabad, where the lifestyle was more comfortable. No one had lived at the Garden for years. The TV reporters learned this from some enterprising Kothapalli teenagers who, having heard of the crews' arrival the night before, met them in the clearing of the Garden in faded Miss Fit concert T-shirts, and promised the inside scoop to those willing to pay for it. It was their stories, passed down from parents and grandparents, that filled out the gaps in the new King Rao narrative—King Rao as villain, not hero—that had emerged. Didn't they know he had murdered his father and uncle? Hadn't they heard about his tryst with a local prostitute?

King tried to ignore the coverage. He tried to focus inward. He had seen Margie a couple of times after the divorce. She had come over and he had served her coffee, as if she were just another guest. They had cried together, laughed a bit, strategized about her campaign plans for the CEO race. He had made apologies, many of them, trying out different words, different tones of voice, but she had rejected them all. Then, right before she launched the campaign, she cut off contact. She didn't want any complications, she told him through a press aide he had never met.

It was after this that he had tried especially hard to tune out what was happening in the wider world. He did see that she had been elected as CEO. He couldn't avoid seeing that, when he briefly went online the night of the election. She looked radiant and sparkling onstage as she made her acceptance speech; she had the same mix of exuberance and poise as an actress who had just won an Oscar. It was she, not he, who was the natural statesman. It had always been her. On-screen, her eyes shone, as if she were sharing a grand inside joke with all her constituents.

One night, he saw her announcing the creation of an oversight organization within the Board to regulate the development of brain-computer interfaces. Anyone working in the field had to submit to quarterly audits of their research by an independent committee. "No human being should play God," she said, with just a tinge of sarcasm in her voice, to applause, and he made a sound of disgust and closed his browser—not because he heard this obvious reference to him as a betrayal, though he did, but because he knew she had been as excited as he about their plans for the Harmonica.

Now it was up to her to regain the Shareholders' trust, the trust he had lost. He didn't deserve her loyalty.

He attempted to become interested in watching sports, but the stakes were too low to capture his interest. One team wins, another loses—and for what? At one point, he invited a famous chef to live with him for a month and teach him to cook. Sometimes he forced himself to sleep in, rolling out of bed at eleven o'clock or noon dim-headed and not at all rested. For five years he lived like this.

Margie's second term as CEO had just begun when he got the text message from his assistant early one morning. She had suffered a heart attack. No one imagined her to be at risk—she still exercised, ate well—but she was elderly. Elderly people did die. Later in the morning, after the Board announced her passing, he wrote on Social, to head off the requests for comment, that he was devastated and preferred to grieve in private. He read the hagiographic obituaries. The first female this, the first female that. Good God, how pedestrian. This woman had made Coconut happen; she had made the Board happen; it had all been her. Never had a more brilliant human lived. Ever since the catastrophe with the Harmonica, he had been doggedly pursuing a single goal: He would atone so well that Margie—and with her, the life they had built—would return to him. He would simply be Margie Rao's husband, and he would be contented with that. Now Margie had disappeared from the universe.

For the first time in years, he turned on the TV and kept it on. For six hours, he sat there watching her reanimated on-screen, disbelieving that the image was an illusion. "She's dead," he said out loud, to himself. She had been so alive, though. No one had ever been more alive. "She's dead, you idiot." He had to say it several times for it to sink in. Only at night did he turn off the TV, lay his head down, and weep in the dark.

He had a vivid dream. It was of himself and Margie, in bed with a little girl who had Margie's joyful eyes. The girl was between them, giggling and rolling around, and in the dream, he had never been happier. This girl was not an ordinary child. Margie had not simply given birth to her. The child represented a technical break-through, as the Coconut had been. The mechanics were hazy, but, in the dream, they kept calling her "our invention."

After waking, he couldn't remember the details. But he was energized, as he hadn't been in half a decade. The old feeling had returned, the impulse to act. He imagined, as he often did, an interlocutor questioning him. It was mortifying, at his age and stature, but he imagined the famous journalist who had done his first interview. Are you really planning to engineer some sort of computerized superhuman? Isn't this exactly what got you kicked out of power? He answered, in his mind, Listen, my friend. I'm no less mortal than anyone. What good would a computerized super-human do me? No, sir, what I want is to give my child a shot of surviving this godforsaken world, and, with some luck, even mak-ing it better. That's all I want.

He sat up, dressed, and drove to the Rao Project's campus near the Space Needle. He went down to the room in the basement filled with tanks of liquid nitrogen containing, in little vials, all the embryos that had been donated for research purposes. In each of the four coolers he took from the supply closet he could fit several hundred vials, packed with ice. His heart quickened when he left the Foundation and got back in his car. He almost cried out in pas-sion; he had to put his hand to his mouth to stop himself.

THOMAS EDISON BROUGHT music into people's homes. The man lit those homes so they glowed from within. Yet even he was not satisfied toward the end of his life, having not figured out how to master death. He told a magazine reporter that he believed people were made of microscopic life units that travel in so-called swarms. The strongest of these swarms, responsible for higher-order quali-ties such as personality, never die. Instead, at the moment of a per-son's physical demise, they rush out of the body and go on living outside of it, ghost-like.

Edison vowed to construct an apparatus that would let the personality swarms of the dead communicate with their living loved ones, a sort of telephone line from the afterlife to life. He told the reporter, "The apparatus will at least give them a better opportunity to express themselves than the tilting tables and raps and ouija boards and mediums and the other crude methods now purported to be the only means of communication. I do hope that our personality survives. If it does, then my apparatus ought to be of some use."

The inventor gave little indication that even a prototype existed. As he got older, he himself resorted to analog methods of prolonging life—in his final year, he chugged milk by the pint, a fad diet—but still he died from diabetes complications in his eighties, without ever having built his death-defying telephone. In the years that followed, all sorts of inventors, most of them quacks, tried to pick up where Edison had left off. They failed. The soul, scientists concluded, can't survive death any more than can the gallbladder, the colon, the heart, the brain.

Under Margie's decree, brain-computer experimentation was being monitored by the Board. But then, the Board's legal influence ended at the borders of the mainland. Such were the circumstances that, soon thereafter, found King abandoning the only life he had ever known and steering his yacht across Elliott Bay to the abandoned island south of Bainbridge. There, in a makeshift but functional lab, he began his experiments.

Hundreds of embryos were tossed in the service of my creation—spoiled, taciturn, unusable creatures that either rejected the modification or accepted it and promptly expired, most of them the size of poppy seeds, but some the size of apple seeds, prunes, lemons, and sweet potatoes, some of them with eyes and mouths but a no-good brain. But finally, it worked. He tried a few more times. It worked again and again.

Then he brought out one of his own embryos, his and Margie's, and replicated the experiment one last time. He pulled on a balaclava and rowed out to Bainbridge Island's Restoration Point. There lived a woman on the island, he had been told, an Ex who could arrange the next part. He had not been told this woman's name or any other details except that she reserved one hour each night for clients like him. She was discreet, no questions asked.

It was only after arriving at the marina where he had been instructed to go, and watching the woman as she came down the pier toward him, tall, messy-haired, and wearing a pair of overalls, that it occurred to him that he recognized her. Without speaking, he handed this woman a small cooler containing the embryo and a letter explaining the circumstances. Elemen Ex read the letter, expressionless. The client, who wished to remain anonymous, was willing to pay triple the going rate on the mainland for a safe, healthy, and confidential transaction. She said flatly, "Half the payment is due now. Come back for updates as often as you want, same time, same place, but those cost extra. Starting at eight months, you need to be here nightly, in case the surrogate delivers. We'll hand you the child here along with a supply of formula, and take the rest of the payment, and that'll be that."

Once a week, he put on his balaclava and returned. Every time, Elemen Ex came down to the water in her overalls and told him the fetus was fine. He had questions but didn't know how to put them in words. He showed up, once, with a note asking whether it was a boy or a girl. She laughed at him, openmouthed. "Sweetheart," she said, "what kind of high-end operation do you think we're running out here?"

He didn't press her further, but her words haunted him. Did the Exes' prohibition of technology prevent them from using ultrasound? Could they just not afford it? In what circumstances, exactly, was his unborn child being kept? Returning home from these visits, my father would feel faint with anxiety. He would have to quickly shed his coat and unbutton his shirt, his sweat softening the thin, ribbed undershirt he wore, his breath quickening to a pant. At one point, about seven months in, Elemen stopped showing up at all. She had been replaced by an older, redheaded woman.

"Elemen's indisposed, but she told me about you," the woman said. "We call you the mute. I'm the doctor. You can call me Ruth. Ruthie, if you want. The fetus is fine."

Zeus, the father of my eponym, claimed his daughter as his alone. People forget that the goddess, like me, did have a mother. The mother was a tough, clever girl named Metis whom Zeus had happened upon, raped, and impregnated. Someone had told Zeus that if he stayed with Metis, she would bear him a second child as well, a son, who would usurp him, and to avoid this fate, Zeus had eaten Metis whole. His daughter gestated in a double womb— inside the raped girl, who was inside the king of the gods. Then, on the banks of the River Trito, Athena burst out of her father's head, demothered, armored, and armed from the get-go. My eponym is said to have announced herself to Zeus with a yell—and who could blame her?

When, at eight months and twenty-one days, Elemen herself appeared again at the marina and handed me down to my father, in his boat, I, too, wrapped in a blanket, began wailing. He had to sit down. It was all he could do to keep from splashing me into the water. "Jesus Christ," Elemen said. "Do you need help?" The loudest, most fearsome sound was coming out of me, the keen of a feral wildcat. He held me tight as I bucked and wailed. He loved me. He didn't let me go. Beneath my blankets, I was still covered in mucus slime. He could feel my birdlet bones and, behind them, my strong heartbeat. He was old. His vitality already couldn't match mine. But no one would ever love me more. He looked at Elemen and suddenly understood her absence these past two months. Ruthie had pushed her halfway down the pier in a wheelchair, and she had walked the rest of the distance toward him. "Thanks," he said, hoping she would understand his meaning. "I don't need help." And then, with a rush of fellow feeling for this woman who had birthed his daughter: "Her name is Athena." She didn't answer. Her mouth hung open a little; she coughed. "The payment," she said faintly, and he took one hand from his child only to reach into his pants pocket and give Elemen the fee she was owed.

He realized his error only after I had fallen asleep and he was rowing home. He remembered the openmouthed expression Elemen had when he had spoken. At first he had interpreted that look as an expression of grief. What must it feel like to give birth, over and over, to children to whom you could claim no bond? Now another thought seized him. What if she recognized his voice?

He didn't have time to dwell on it. At home, in my room, he stood and bounced on his heels to calm me. After some time, when his arms trembled and burned, he cast around for a spot to put me down and chose a plastic laundry basket. He placed me in the basket and used his foot to rock it. Still I howled. He felt like an actor on a stage, his movements strangely artificial. He picked me up. He took off his shirt and sat in his armchair and pressed me to his chest and offered me the bottle he had prepared. I gulped from it and became calm.

"Athena," he said. He murmured my name over and over. "Athena," he said. "Athena, Athena."

There was such wonder in his voice, such hope. He put his hand on my heart. Wanting—needing—to be even closer, he pressed his cheek to my heart, he felt its beat against his breath, in unison, then not, then in unison again. The child's nails, he thought, were as translucent as fly wings. But then, those arms were made for punching. They frightened him a little. That big, bare head was all covered in dents. It was alien. He sat with me and considered my existence. I frightened him. I was strange. But he loved me, too. He did. I cannot claim there's any logic to it. He required of me what any parent requires of his child, and what any child requires of her parent: everything and nothing, all at once, until the end of time.

28

There's one part of building my Social profile that I've left for last: documenting my significant relationships on the mainland. The one relationship I have—if it can even be called that—feels too fraught to explain; I'm afraid I'll be misunderstood. But this morning, I've finally tapped the SOCIAL icon, the only remaining one. For all my brief interactions with Shareholders on the Cha Cha, most could hardly be described as relationships. But then, of course, there is the one.

THE YOUNG MAN who called himself Abdul Ex was born two years after the Exodus, a time of newfound peace on the mainland. His parents had grown up as next-door neighbors in a Syrian town near Aleppo. They fell in love as teenagers, married, and had a daughter. It was a time when Shareholders were again feeling optimistic about their future, and Abdul's father, Faisal, like many in his generation, was ambitious. He was a driver. He paid a neighbor to borrow his car, which he used to shuttle local merchants to their appointments around town.

One particular merchant took to him and, when Abdul was born a few years later, the firstborn male, the merchant gave Faisal some advice. "Stop feeding your children so many eggs," he said. "Instead, save up your Capital and buy your own car, so that you don't have to keep renting from that greedy neighbor of yours while he sits around doing nothing. That's the only way to get ahead: ownership."

Abdul's mother, Fatimah, didn't like this advice. "The children need to eat," she said. "What's the use of saving for their college educations if I can't feed them enough to make their brains work properly?"

When Faisal relayed to the merchant what his wife said, the merchant made a new recommendation. "At least take that car and go to the city, where you'll make more money. And come on, man. This time, don't tell your wife what you're up to."

Faisal left each morning at six o'clock and returned at ten o'clock at night. By the time Abdul was four, his father often slept in the car in Aleppo—he was still renting, paying the owner overtime—and returned home only on weekends. When Fatimah became pregnant with a third child, she told Faisal that their time together mattered more than making a fortune, and demanded that he stop this nonsense and just work in town. In response, Faisal filed for divorce. The truth, it came out later, was that he had met another woman, the beautiful housekeeper at the merchant's city house, and fathered two children with her. "What about our children?" Fatimah said. "Of course I'll visit them, but I have other financial responsibilities now," Faisal said. "You should have been working, too, all this time."

Fatimah, now a single mother to an eight-, five-, and one-year-old, consulted her most cosmopolitan friend, the owner of a fabric shop, for advice. The friend said it was illegal, under the Share-holder Agreement, for Faisal to just leave without taking care of them, but it would be cost-prohibitive for Fatimah to sue him. There wasn't much that could be done. She would probably have to take the three children and go to work in one of the factories outside town, where they could at least live on campus.

"But what about their education?" Fatimah said. "Those schools are no good."

It was then that the cosmopolitan friend told Fatimah about a program she had heard of. Professional women in America were waiting too long to have children and finding themselves unable to conceive. They were willing to pay to adopt children with high Social Capital. "You have three, and they're good and smart and cute," she said. "If you sell them all, you can make enough to buy yourself a ticket to join them. You won't be their mother anymore, technically, but you can live nearby and try to see them. I've heard of a lot of women doing it."

So it happened that Abdul, along with his older sister and younger brother, ended up in Burien, Washington, in the home of devout evangelical Christians who replaced their Muslim names with similar-sounding biblical ones. At the ages of nine, six, and two, respectively, his sister became Rachel, he became Paul, and their little brother became Caleb. Fatimah had promised to join them. But Faisal discovered what she had done and took her to court for having sold their children without his permission. When she traveled to the airport to try to catch her flight, the border authorities would not let her leave.

The case dragged on. The children adapted to their new life.

They had been surprised to learn that their adoptive parents were not rich at all, though they weren't poor, either. Their white mother had a clerical job in a dentist's office, and their white father constructed houses. They had tried to have children naturally, but, when the white mother turned forty and it still hadn't happened, they had pooled donations from their congregation to pay for the adoption.

Among the siblings, Paul, né Abdul, was the ambitious one. He couldn't remember if he had simply inherited ambition from his father, or if, as a child, he had been indoctrinated in its importance as the elder son. When school started, he concentrated hard, at his sister's urging. He adored her—in their difficult first years of life in America, she sang Paul and Caleb to sleep with old Fairuz love songs that reminded them of their mother—and accepted all her advice. The only exception was her exhortation that Paul and Caleb stop playing video games so late into the night; Paul adored his little brother even more than he adored Rachel.

They spoke with Fatimah nightly, at first. Then, once a week. Then, once a month. Their father was still trying to get them returned to Syria, and their adoptive mother thought it best that the children stay out of the situation until it got resolved. She worried—she once admitted to Rachel, who told Paul—that their talking to their mother might convince the Algo that they were still attached to their homeland, that the adoption had therefore been fraudulent. It was to support their mother's desire for them to stay in America that they agreed not to speak with her. Later, Paul wondered if it had been a mistake. He wondered if his mother had even been told of their strategic distancing.

He wondered this because, when he was eight, his adoptive mother received a phone call from their real mother's cosmopolitan friend, who was fluent in English. Fatimah had died in a kitchen fire, she said. When their adoptive mother related this to them, they understood it as the euphemism it was. Their real mother had killed herself. Paul watched Rachel and Caleb sob and willed himself to cry as well but couldn't. Though he couldn't explain it, he was sure doing so would be dangerous. Once he began, he would never be able to stop.

One month later, they each received a small grant of Social Capital from their mother's deactivated account. Paul, who hadn't shed a tear at his mother's death, wept when he learned his inheritance was hardly enough for him to buy the programmable robot he had been coveting. He redoubled his efforts. He made straight A's and was admitted to college—the same university King attended for graduate school—with full financial aid. His personal statement, a collaboration with his sister and the church's pastor, could not have hurt. "This country has given me so much," he wrote. "Now it's time for me to invest in its future."

Later, he would hate himself for using such capitalistic language. Capitalism had sent his father to Aleppo and compelled his mother to put him and his siblings up for adoption. But back then, it hadn't occurred to him that there was any other language to use. His campus apartment was a light-rail ride from Burien, and yet, occupied with his classes, the engineering club, and parties, he couldn't make it home often. Rachel was married to the son of the pastor at church and raising her first daughter.

But something had gone wrong with Caleb, who constantly fought with their adoptive parents, though he was the only one young enough not to remember his birth parents. At fifteen, after another blowout fight, he filed for formal emancipation, moved out, and vowed not to talk to them again. A rootless ghost of a kid. Without his siblings' attention, he had grown into a dumb, too-trusting teenager, with the wrong friends. One night, toward the end of his sophomore year in high school, he slept with someone else's girlfriend—no one important to him, just the cousin of a friend—and got himself shot, three times, in the stomach. He could have died, but luck intervened, and he was out of the hospital in three weeks. Still he didn't feel safe going back to school, because a pain persisted in his gut.

An infection I think, Caleb texted his siblings. *bullshit excuses*, Paul replied. *come see him*, Rachel wrote, *big shot, come down from campus and set your brother straight if ur so smart.* Rachel had been pleading with Caleb to see a doctor, but, having emancipated himself, he no longer had his parents' health insurance and couldn't afford his own. He texted that he was *hurling all over the toilet cause of the infection lol.*

Paul, in the coffee shop with the good lattes and cardamom-flavored scones, held his phone out to his friends and said, "He's making this shit up, right? Otherwise, he wouldn't insist on giving us all these gratuitous details."

He felt so sharp. He was a sophomore. He was going to be a

video game developer. He had introduced his little brother to the classic game *American Thugz*, their last shared passion, and had an internship lined up at the Coconut studio in Portland that had created the game. He was studying computer science, which required courses in logic. So he felt equipped to reason this out. "The problem with my brother is that he was younger than me when we came over here. I have a strong relationship with my motherland, I have pride. But he doesn't remember living over there. He thinks of Burien as home; he's turned into an American."

Caleb died that night.

He stopped breathing alone, with his head in the vomit- and blood-filled toilet of his girlfriend's brother's apartment, while Paul slept in his apartment. Paul was twenty years old, Caleb sixteen. The church put together the memorial service, and when Paul arrived at the funeral home, he was the outsider, Caleb's friends gesturing at him as they questioned Rachel, "Who's that brother?" Rachel, with a small, sad laugh, answered, "He's our brother. Our actual brother. Blood."

He found himself that night sitting in the playground where Caleb used to have a wild, performative manner of playing on the slide, climbing up against gravity instead of sliding down, but this time he was with Caleb's friends, the friends he had warned Caleb against, neighborhood miscreants, he had called them, and they had finished off several forties. Paul had regrets, he was telling them, he was full of regrets, what had happened to his brother was his fault, not theirs, and these kids—that's what they were, just kids—were patting his shoulders, making sweet, kind, compassionate sounds, pushing the joint into his hand, here, you need this, brother, and at the sound of this word, *brother*, he wept.

It was Caleb's best friend, a fat, agreeable sixteen-year-old named Green Man, who gathered Paul up in his thick, soft arms and said, "Shush now, shush now," like some grandmother. You might assume the others, neighborhood miscreants, would laugh at a sight like this, but they just straightened their backs and nodded along to Green Man's words, as if it were a beat, "Shush now, shush now, shush now, shush." Green Man and the others led Paul onto the bus heading to the waterfront, then hailed one of the small motorboats that ferry people to the Cha Cha. The boat moved swiftly across the bay while Paul, the wind in his face, sobbed and sobbed and thought, alternately, about how nice it had been to be held by someone and about how he would like to avenge his brother's death, in fact, he would like to avenge the whole sequence of events that led up to his brother's death.

But where did it all begin? Who, in the final analysis, should be held responsible?

It was around two in the morning when, with love and vengeance still on his mind, Paul and his companions arrived at the Cha Cha. Soon another boat pulled up, and a brown-skinned woman stepped out of it, smoothed out her overalls, and surveyed the little ganglet of teens and post-teens still standing on the deck. She—I—zeroed in on the one who looked a bit older than the others, red-eyed and lost, and thought, That one.

THE MOMENT Elemen told us all the name of the young man suspected of killing my father—Abdul Ex, also known as Paul Emerson—it transported me to the Cha Cha's deck, under a bright, stout moon. As I walked up to this kid, who was in fact a couple of years older than me, I didn't have an inkling of what was ailing him, but it was clear he was ailing. I stood there with him, looking out onto the dark water, after his friends drifted off. He introduced himself as Paul, not Abdul. We were only talking, at first. We were talking, Shareholder, about the moon. I told him about Neil Armstrong and white lace. He agreed it was a beautiful observation. I told him I had something that might help. I had it right here, in my bag. He could try some if he wanted.

We got ourselves a room. I took out a syringe.

As soon as I finished injecting him, a confused expression crossed his sorrowful face—a crumpled brow, a slightly dazed smile. His spirit was entering me. His life, up until this moment, began arranging itself in my mind. That part was familiar, from the hundred of times I had done this before. But something was different, off. This time, it felt like it had with King in the beginning, like I couldn't control it. I was the one who had done everything right, and yet had been punished over and over. It was my mother who had burned herself up in the kitchen. It was my brother who had vomited to death in some stranger's toilet. It was I who was consumed with anger. It was I—this, too—who said the words out loud: "Your brother should be alive. Your mother should be alive. The people who should be dead are the ones who came up with this evil system in the first place."

I regretted it instantly. Elemen's most basic rule was for me to leave the proselytizing to her. I opened my mouth, ready to take it back, as if I hadn't meant it, and in a sense I hadn't; it had been Paul—Abdul—whom I had been channeling, hadn't it? But he was no longer crying. His eyes had sharpened, and he seemed completely present. "King Rao came up with it," he said. "But he's immortal."

Then, my second transgression: "No, he's not."

"Ha!" He was smiling; it was a lovely sight.

"He's not."

"How much would you bet on it?"

My third transgression: "Whatever you want."

"All right," he said, and he laughed. "I'll think on that." Later, I pulled out a scrap of paper from my pocket and wrote down his name. Soon I would pass it on to Elemen.

But I hadn't done that yet. The paper remained in my pocket.

AFTER ELEMEN SHARED what she had learned about King's murder, I waited around after dinner, helping her with the dishes, until the others retired to their rooms. Afterward, she went to the living room and dropped herself onto the couch as if in defeat. I hung the drying rag and sat next to her. I had a strong urge to confess. I wanted her to know it all, from the beginning. I began: "El, we have to—" But before I could go on, she clamped her hand over my mouth. "*Quiet,*" she hissed. She had never used that tone with me.

Then she rose and went down the hall.

I strained to listen for voices, imagining she was talking to Otis. When she returned, she was carrying backpacks for each of us, one over each shoulder. Tossing one to me, she said we were leaving. I peered inside my bag; it contained all my meager belongings, including my dry bag, folded into itself, plus a sleeping bag. She went into the kitchen and grabbed some nuts, some dried fruit. "Where are we going?" I said. "Will this be enough?" Instead of answering, she opened the front door and motioned impatiently for me to follow her.

We hiked uphill, westward into the old-growth woods, not speaking to each other. It was one of those clear nights when the moon's craters are visible to the naked eye. Under other circumstances, I would have found it beautiful. I was reminded of my first night here and the days that followed—my fear of this strange, foreign place. I had been so proud of myself for overcoming it. But people did die out here. That wasn't propaganda. Real bodies had been discovered. In a moment I would explain to Elemen Ex that I had messed up. That it was I who had gotten King Rao killed. She could strangle me out here. She could leave me to the boars. I would disintegrate there in the woods, Clarinet and all.

We reached a clearing, and Elemen stopped and threw down her bag. From it, she pulled a sleeping bag and slipped in. I took mine from my own pack, which I laid down next to hers.

"We need to talk about what happened," I said, when we were both cocooned, next to each other. My voice was jarringly loud in the silence.

Swiftly she moved close to me and put her mouth so close to my ear that I could feel its wetness. For a stupid moment, I thought she had gone in to kiss it. But she hissed, "Don't."

I understood then. The Board's police would show up at the marina, sirens blaring, and demand to be shown to where the Exes lived. We live everywhere, some poor pedestrian might answer, terrified. All of us are Exes. Then the pedestrian would hear the guns cocking and would point southward. He would mention the trail. When you see the solar farm, you're there. "No one at the house knows what we've been doing," I said weakly. I was working it out in front of her. She was watching me work it out. At the farmhouse, they would knock down the doors. Otis would be the first to come barreling down the stairs, his hands in the air. Otis the pacifist.

I understood then. She knew it was my fault. This was her best shot at saving her friends from what we—I—had wrought.

I couldn't help it. I put my mouth to her ear. I whispered, "I *met* him."

She shook her head.

"But I—"

She pulled away from me and interrupted. "Okay," she said. "All right." Our faces were inches apart; through our sleeping bags, our knees were touching. "You want to do confessions?" she said. "Let me start."

"When you left Ruthie's place," she went on, "she and I talked about the man—the strange man—who showed up here with his face covered, around eighteen years ago, with an embryo he wanted to have implanted. We never knew for sure whether it was him. It became a kind of running gag between us: the time King Rao brought his unborn child here to be carried to term. I don't know if we even believed it ourselves. But here's the part I didn't point out to Ruthie this morning. Here's the part I hope she didn't notice. You look just like him, you idiot. Your nose, your lips. I knew it as soon as Arno brought you to me. This was King Rao's child in front of me. Ha! King Rao's child was begging me, the woman who had tried to plot his death, to take her in."

"I didn't tell anyone but Otis," she continued. "I told him my suspicions as soon as you showed up. Of course, he didn't believe me at first. They all thought I was going nuts, plotting to reestablish Exism on the mainland and all. He thought this was part of that madness. I kept bugging him about it; that's when I disappeared for a while, right after you got here. But finally he agreed to at least take a look for himself. So I got to know you better. And I brought you home. Once he saw you, he believed me, but he still thought I was nuts for thinking you could be useful to us. I told you, he's gotten conservative with age. 'It's too dangerous,' he said. 'What if he sent her here as a spy?' I told him, 'He isn't even part of the Board anymore.' Plus, I knew what it looks like to fall out of love with your parents. I told him, 'Can you imagine a better ally than the daughter who's abandoned King Rao? Come on, think of what we could learn; think of all the atoning she'll want to do.'"

Now she gave a rueful laugh. "For a long time, I really did think your dad was immortal," she said. Her voice shifted to a softer, almost sympathetic register. "But honestly, when he showed up, it was pathetic. I pitied him. He didn't look powerful at all anymore. Later, I told Otis, 'You were right. King Rao might have started all this, but if he hadn't done it, someone else would have. Now he has nothing to do with the system. If we had killed him, someone else would have become CEO in his place.'" She took a deep breath and let it out. "None of us wanted him dead anymore."

Her words hung between us, full of weight. "I didn't mean for it to happen," I said quietly. I said it to her, but you understand I meant for it to be delivered to the universe. I meant for it to be delivered to him.

She shook her head slowly, as if in disbelief. "Good night, Athena," she said.

It was the first time she had said my name. It felt like a kindness.

That night, I lay at some distance from Elemen, my cheek cradled in my palm, watching her breathe until I was sure she was asleep. Then I wriggled out of my sleeping bag and stood, hugging myself against the chill. I looked around, to get my bearings, packed all my earthly belongings, and made my way downhill toward the water.

29

To love and be loved in return—that's the thing!

The cup of her armpit on his cheek. Her shallow navel. The hot, damp cockleshell of her ear. Her old woman's hands, with their deep lines and bitten nails. He visited Minnu as often as he could without catching anyone's notice, each trip paid out of the same pool of funds. All the while, he waited to be caught. How much had he slipped into his pocket to finance his time with Minnu? He didn't like to think of it. After the first time, each successive theft had felt easier. But, no, it wasn't theft, he told himself. He would repay the money as soon as he went to work; he would call it a contribution to the family finances as repayment for all they had done for him. Chinna would have his safe refilled, and King would get credit for being generous. Three times a week, there he was in Minnu's bedroom, paying a tiny price for the privilege of burying himself in the flesh of his beloved for a couple of short, hot minutes. They were sixteen years old.

Once, after they finished and lay talking, she used her teeth to tear at a hangnail on her thumb until it bled. "It bothers me when there's a piece of skin hanging off like that, but taking it off makes it worse. It's so ugly. I'm scared some man will see it and never come back." Once, at the moment just before climax, he was filled with a horrible flailing sensation, as if he had pulled her with him from some high bridge and they were both about to hit the water. He wanted to cry out, Oh God, what have I done? Once, as pleased as if he had eaten a deliciously rich meal of mutton and curds, he stood and belched.

He loved her. She must love him; she had to. But she never said it. In fact, he had a nagging sense that a distance had grown between them since their days at the clinic together. One night, he worked up a heartful of courage and told her, "I'm in love with you."

She curled her lip and rose from the bed. Sitting before the mirror, she untied her braid, from which some hairs had escaped.

"You're beautiful," he tried. She smiled a little and called him a liar. "What's so beautiful about me?" she said. He told her it was the way she looked at him. She turned and regarded him as if she suddenly understood something that she hadn't noticed before. She reworked her hair into a tight coil, pinned it up at her neck, and said, "Time's up."

TIME WAS UP.

One Saturday morning, King rose and found that Chinna had left for the market without him. When Chinna returned that evening, King met him at the path and said sullenly, "You forgot me." Chinna said, "No, I thought I'd let you sleep, since you've got your exams coming up." He went into the side room of King's House, where they always counted the cash together on Saturdays. When King followed him, Chinna stood silently for a moment, without emptying the bag, then turned and mussed King's hair and said, "Listen, this time, it's not much; I can do it myself." Later, in the middle of the night, when everyone slept, King tiptoed down from his loft and tried to push open the door to the room where they kept the cash. It wouldn't budge. It was locked.

In the morning, Chinna invited King to go on a stroll. As they went down the road, Chinna chatted about unimportant things. They arrived at a mango grove, and Chinna said, "Let's take one; Pedda and I used to steal mangoes all the time." He added, "It wasn't actually stealing. No one minded in those days. We would sit down and eat them right there." He leaped into the air and grabbed hold of a branch that held a ripe, low-hanging reddish green mango. He pulled off the fruit. The branch snapped back and shivered, leaves rustling.

They sat on the ground, and Chinna used a blunt knife he kept tucked in his pants to cut the mango, handing a slice to King. The sun crept higher in the sky. King bit into the slice. He let the nectar drip down his chin and onto his bare feet and waited for Chinna to confront him. But Chinna didn't.

"Life is fun, kid. I really love it," he said. "There's no man on this earth who loves life more than me. If only I could live forever."

He cut a slice of mango for himself and scraped the meat off with his teeth.

"Listen," he said. "When Grandfather Rao died, your dad fell apart. He just sat there under the tree staring ahead. I saw him and got so scared of having to be in charge of the Garden myself, for the rest of my life, that I packed a suitcase and went to the train station. I thought I would run away to Rajahmundry, and from there to Hyderabad. I got on the train and left. Do you remember?"

King shook his head. He didn't remember. The nectar stung his lips.

"No, no one noticed! Everyone was busy mourning! But I wasn't gone long. When I was two stations away, I changed my mind. I never told anyone; I was ashamed of myself. But now I ask myself, Why should you have been ashamed? You did exactly the right thing, in the end. You came back and got everything taken care of. What happens to people like you and me, who don't believe in God? I think when people are young, they think, I have no God, so there is no right and wrong. But there I was on that train, running away from home, and I thought, I'll never see my brother again. I'll never see King. Because of me, they won't be taken care of. That's the reason I turned around and came home."

He stopped talking and looked closely at King. King said nothing. He didn't even nod. The mango juice was dripping all over him and attracting flies. They swarmed him and tickled him with their tiny feet.

"We each have only this one small life to live," Chinna said. "We all make mistakes. I've made them, too. In the end, we only try to do more good than bad in our lives."

ALL RIGHT. King understood. He and his uncle had a tacit agreement. King would stop taking money, and neither of them would discuss what had happened. But one afternoon, while China was out campaigning, King was sitting in the clearing with Gun and his brothers, and Pinky mentioned a rumor that Chinna was going around the village trying to bribe people into voting for him. Gun turned to King and said, "You're the only one who sees the money come in and out. Have you noticed anything strange?"

"Oh, I'm not involved in that anymore." He said it without thinking.

Gun peered at him. "You're not?"

"No, I stopped."

"How come?"

He opened his mouth but didn't answer. The conversation ceased for a moment, then everyone was talking at once. Why would Chinna lock King out? What reason did he have unless he had something to hide? King was his most trusted lieutenant—he had said it himself—so why keep King out unless he was up to no good and didn't want anyone to find out? It was Gun who said the word *embezzlement*. There was no reason for Chinna to squeeze King out unless he was trying to hide some kind of embezzlement scheme.

King stood abruptly and walked into King's House. He could sense them watching him, wondering what had happened, but didn't know what else to do. He climbed up to his loft and huddled there, his knees to his chest, paralyzed. There is a kind of action that resembles inaction, and it is the kind on which all of society is founded. He heard the oxcart rumbling down the path toward home, signaling Chinna's return. He heard the voices of Gun and his brothers—rough, boasting—as they jogged down the path to meet Chinna. Gun was shouting his uncle's name, and Chinna was coming down from the oxcart. The men were walking quickly toward home, their voices low but urgent. King could see the tops of their heads. Their voices escalated as they neared the clearing, and when they arrived there, Gun was shaking his fist, shouting, "What do you want us to think? You tell me what we're supposed to think!" Chinna put his hands up and murmured, "Lower your voice," and Gun grew angrier still, sputtering, "Lower my voice? My mother's dead!" He raised his face to the skies and, this time, bellowed it. A provocation: "My mother is dead!"

Chinna made the first move. It was he who raised his hand into the air, took a quick step forward and slapped Gun across the face as if the younger man were a child. King gasped. Gun was the last person who would be cowed by an affront like that. Gun stumbled, pressed his hand to the offended cheek, and then, recovering, lunged at his uncle, blurting, "I'll kill you, I'll kill you—" He looked wildly around at his brothers and cousins, and sputtered, "I'll kill him, you watch!"

Everyone gathered around, provoking both Gun and Chinna, as the men lunged and grabbed at each other and fell to the ground. The grandsons and grandnephews of Kanakamma fell upon Chinna in solidarity with Gun, while the sons and grandsons of Venkata, Babu, and Balayamma stood back and watched in the innocent terror of the privileged, shouting, "Now, wait a minute, let's talk this through!" They stood shouting as Kanakamma's descendants dragged Chinna into King's House and stood him before the safe where he kept the family's money; they stood shouting as Gun held Chinna by the shoulders and cried, "Open it, open it, let's see how you'll account for it all!"

Gun and his gang rarely entered King's House, being as it was reserved for business matters. This was, however, where they stored the six-foot poles used to pick coconuts. At the end of each pole was a hook. They kept the poles piled in a corner and retrieved them on days that they picked coconuts at dawn. After climbing partway up a tree trunk, the older boys would swing their poles up almost as if they were hoisting javelins, and bring them back down with ripe fruits swinging from the end. Now King heard Pinky shout, "Get the poles. He's not listening, but we'll make him!"

It was like a dream. Had it not been like a dream, it would have been simple to climb down from the ladder and stand between those men and his uncle, or if not that, at least to shout from above, "I can account for it, I'm responsible, this is a mistake." But it was like a dream in which you wish to speak up but simply can't; your mouth opens but there is no sound. In this dream, Chinna called his name, urgently and almost with irritation, as if he were needed to sort out this misunderstanding—"King, where *are* you?"—and King pressed himself into the wall of his loft, considering how he might climb down and help without getting hurt or implicating himself.

Then there was a sickening sound, like a coconut falling to the ground from a great height and squashing there.

All was silent. A stampede of men pushed out of King's House. From his window, he saw the men disperse into the Garden along its well-worn paths. Whatever was happening, had happened, couldn't be undone. He felt nauseous. He climbed carefully down from his loft. He first saw the pole, with a patch of bloodied skin stuck to its tip, and then a limp and crumpled form in the corner, like an old blanket. Chinna had one arm splayed behind him and the other curled around his head. A thick, pulpy matter had burst from his temple. Blood flowed forth and covered it. His eyes stared blankly at King. Jaggayyamma's cat had already found the corpse and sat crouched next to its head licking the blood.

"Get," King said. "Get."

His uncles and cousins were hollering now, coming into King's

House, calling his name and his uncle's. He slumped to the ground and closed his eyes. His blood pulsed in his skull. He waited to be carried forth from there and taken to some prison to meet his fate. But they weren't treating him like a criminal. They were treating him like he could have been a victim of Gun and his brothers, too. Sita rushed over and squeezed him tight, as if he were a small child, kissing his forehead and cheeks. "What happened?" she kept asking. "What happened here, Kingie?" But he couldn't answer. "Leave him alone," someone said. "He's numb; he can't talk." Most of the men were crowded around Chinna's body. They were trying to resuscitate him. Then they gave up. Someone said to call the Hollander, and someone else said, "There's no use. He's finished."

They made a sling for the body out of one of Sita's old saris and carried Chinna to the veranda, where they set him on a cot that had been dragged from his bedroom. It was the same cot on which Grandfather Rao had lain after his death. Some time passed. Chinna's limbs stiffened in rubbery rigor, his lips purple and pursed, and his cheek slick from being licked by the cat. The children gathered around and stood mutely, shivering and confused. The women flew around like mosquitoes. The men had gone in search of Gun and his gang, who had scattered and disappeared. There would be justice. There would be justice. Sita stood over Chinna and tented her fingers against the mask of his stiffening cheek and let out a sob, as if it were he who had been her husband.

THE CORPSE WAS stiff by the time they brought it to the little cove at the bank of the canal and put it on a raised platform to be burnt. Scattered around Chinna's body were bits of other people's bones, gray and brittle-looking. "Go on home," King's uncles told him kindly; it was loathsome to him how kind they were. "You get some rest."

"I'll stay," he said, knowing this was the answer they expected.

"Good boy," his uncles said. "Chinna loved you more than anyone. He loved you like you were his own child."

The night darkened. People walked by on their way home from

the market, peering through the bushes at the Raos. They clucked their tongues and whispered in pious tones. "Those Raos, they did themselves in," King heard one passerby whispering to her sister. Her sister replied, "Shut up, they'll hear," and the first sister said, "I don't care if they hear, it's evil what they did to their uncle. They'll be reborn as snakes, as the blackest flies," and the second said, "But these relatives burying him—*they're* not the ones who killed him. And you don't know the truth; they say he was pocketing the family's money." The first said, "Well, he was too big for his britches, running for council president like that, a Dalit."

King crouched on his haunches at a distance, watching the black smoke pluming up into the air and forcing himself not to look away. That night, he lay on his side on the ground, still facing the pyre around which his uncles lay sleeping, taking turns standing watch. The next thing he knew, the sun was rising, he was bathed in sweat from the heat of the sun, and all that was left of his uncle was a mass of gray bone bits in the shape of a man. "Come on." Kondanna beckoned to King. "You come over here, too."

"I can't," he said weakly.

"Okay," Kondanna said. "That's okay." He and the other uncles were gathering Chinna's ashes into a large tin can. But when almost all the bits had been picked up, and all that was left were the large pieces that the others had avoided—pieces of Chinna's arms, his legs, his pelvis, the curved skull fragments like bits of dried coconut, to which some gray, curd-like substance clung terribly— Kondanna turned to him and called out, "King, come on over, it's only right." Reluctantly, King joined his uncles. It was he, in the end, who took up the last pieces of Chinna between his thumb and forefinger, still hot to the touch, and dropped them into the can.

"Oho, King Rao!" came a voice from the canal. King looked up. It was the one-legged cripple. King had crossed paths with him over the years and tried to avoid conversation. This time, the sight of the cripple frightened King more than ever. It seemed like confirmation that he had something to do with this, that when King had gone off with him, the cripple had indeed placed on him some subtle curse that had culminated here, with Chinna's death. "I heard your uncle died," the cripple called.

"It's true," King said. He was afraid to say more.

"What a world," the cripple said. "But everyone dies." He pushed his oar into the water and continued on.

When it was over, they returned to the Garden, where the women and children waited. With the rest of the family close behind, King paced the length and breadth of the Garden, holding the can and sprinkling Chinna's gritty remains over the earth. They felt like bits of chalk between his fingers. He pinched the dust and pebbly bits and released them as he walked, until he had crossed every last inch of the Garden, and all that remained in the can was a fine dusting. He had the urge to put his face to the can and inhale. Or to lick it. The ancient Greek historian Herodotus— King wouldn't have been aware of this, but I can't help but mention it—wrote of an Indian tribe who he called the Callatiae, who ate their parents' corpses in lieu of burial or cremation. But King did not lick the can. He was a civilized person. He went to Sita, who was part of the procession, and thrust the can at her and said, "I don't know what to do with this."

"Give it to me," she said.

They all followed Sita and King back to King's House and stood like worshippers as Sita placed the can on an altar she had made, in the office where King and Chinna used to count cash. Sita pushed King forward. He knew what he was supposed to do. He lowered his hands to the can and raised them to his forehead and lowered them again, and wept.

LATER, King stood alone in the clearing upon which he had looked down from his loft as the confrontation between Gun and Chinna had begun. Bile rose in his throat, and he put his hands on his knees and retched. But the bile came up only to the base of his throat. It wouldn't eject itself; it was lodged inside him. He stood again, his chest tight with sourness. Death was everywhere in this place. He had to get out of there.

He analyzed the situation as if it were some problem on an exam at school. Only he and Minnu knew about the cash he had stolen, and Minnu would never tell. But what if this whole affair were to end in some kind of trial? What if they were to put him on a witness stand, because he had been the only one there, up in his loft as the crime was committed, and ask him questions about what he had seen? He would have to tell what he had heard—that the men had fallen upon his uncle after accusing him of stealing money that belonged to them, that they had stood Chinna in front of the safe and asked him to open it. Everything could come out.

The clearing was quiet, no one around. He went down the path and turned toward the village center. At the clinic, he sat on the bench where he and Minnu used to sit and talk for hours. He thought of her for a moment, feeling guilty. But she had been the one to abandon him first, leaving the clinic without a word. If it had been up to her, they never would have seen each other again. He said goodbye to her in his mind, and vowed to forget her.

That he was capable of all this frightened him.

The Hollander was in his bedroom, combing his hair. He set down the comb. "Oh, King," he said gently. "How are you managing?"

"I'm scared," King said. "They're vicious, Gun and his cronies. I'm the only witness, and I'm scared of what they'll do to me."

He had only this one small life to live. He would not be given another.

The Hollander rubbed his head. "No, no, no," he said. "They can't, they won't. We'll get you out of here." He went to the chest that he kept in the corner of his room and raised its lid. He dug to the bottom and pulled up a sheaf of bills. "Helena," he called. "Helena, go to this boy's mother and tell her to pack his bags."

t was the middle of the night when I finally arrived, in the rowboat I had taken from the marina, at the mainland. The beach at Alki Point was cold and unlit, long emptied of beachgoers. I tied my boat by the red-roofed lighthouse, found shelter against the siding of the building, and climbed into my sleeping bag. Go explore! my father's voice whispered in my mind as I fell asleep.

You must be wondering what I planned to do. The truth is, I had no solid plan. I thought that, as long as I didn't attract attention to myself, I could pass myself off as a transient and continue my studies of Shareholders' openness to Exism using the old-fashioned approach from before my Clarinet experiment. I would stay away for a while, and once the trouble had died down on Bainbridge, I could return to the island with at least a couple more targets and redeem myself. It was less a plan than a faint wish. Still, I fell asleep taking solace in it.

The sun woke me at dawn. I packed my belongings, sleeping bag and all, and made my way toward the sandy part of the beach, to the east. I could see a couple of people sitting on driftwood by the water, nursing coffees. They wore hoodies and jeans and held themselves hunched against the morning chill. Most of them had Cocoglass headsets strapped on, so that only the bottoms of their faces were visible.

When I got near enough, I set myself down on a big piece of driftwood and tried not to look too conspicuous with no device. It was seven o'clock, warming a little. I took in my surroundings. Alki Beach was one of the first places where white adventurers tried to build a settlement, but they quickly found it was too wind-swept and abandoned it. Now tall glass-walled buildings loomed across the street from the beach; already the line of cars headed toward the West Seattle Bridge was dense.

Scanning the spare architecture of the beachscape—telephone poles, lampposts, sweetgum trees lining the promenade—I couldn't see the surveillance hardware I had been warned about. Maybe Elemen had been mistaken: If the surveillance was as intense as she had always suggested it was, they would have caught me the moment I stepped foot on the mainland. But this was per-fectly pleasant, I thought, I was perfectly anonymous. My closest neighbors were a young boy sitting cross-legged on a picnic blan-ket and a plump, curly-haired teenage girl who must have been his babysitter. The boy, wearing a headset, twitched and writhed as if he might be having a mild seizure. The teenager sat peeling an orange, unconcerned. She wore her own headset. I realized, after a second, that he must be playing a game. Suddenly he cried out, fell back on the blanket, and went still. The teenager moved her headset up onto her forehead, turned to him, and put a hand on his shoulder.

"I died," he murmured.

She clucked her tongue. "Have some orange, mijo," she said, and held a slice to his lips.

He twisted and made a face, and she told him to suit himself and popped the fruit into her mouth.

Then I noticed the police. They came up on speedboats, a half dozen of them, flashing blue lights and blaring sirens. Peo-ple watched, curious, but stayed put. I did, too, not wanting to set myself apart. No one would send six vessels after one wayward Ex. But when they approached, a cop shouted through a megaphone, his voice harsh and overloud, "Girl in the overalls—hands up!"

For a moment it made me feel almost beautiful, the way those blue lights were trained on me. In the first, confusing instant, the lights gave me hope. I felt like some godlet, lit up like that. I stood and raised my hands, as instructed. The people around me scurried to their feet, pulling their Cocoglass headsets down around their necks, bundling up their towels, and darting off. The teenager turned to me with a questioning but nonjudgmental look—as if we were friends or sisters and she wanted to give me the benefit of the doubt—but something about my affect must have changed her mind. She stood, roughly pulling the child up to his feet, and hurried away.

Oh, but it would be all right, after all, I thought still. For all our differences, we are all human beings. We have more in common than not. It was in that spirit that I held my hands up, palms facing him. I come in peace.

But when the man shouted, "Keep 'em up!" it rankled. I had the impression he did not perceive me as kin. I had the impression he was no ally at all. It was then, though it was the opposite of what one should do in these circumstances, that I dropped my hands and took off running. I realized too late that I should have swerved toward the sidewalk, rather than trying to make my escape through the sand. They had hopped out of their boats to give chase, some dozen pistols pointed, and a detour at this point would only slow me down.

They might have shot me right there. It had been known to happen. The authorities could claim, credibly enough for their purposes, that they perceived me as a threat. But they didn't shoot. Credit their morals, or their compassion, or their judgment that they couldn't well convict a non-breathing murder suspect. I'm alive, I thought, as I ran, full of wonder. I felt like I was flying, I felt like a horse midair. Maybe it was the adrenaline. I exist, I thought. I'm a person among people. How special it is to be here, I thought, in those seconds before they tackled me to the ground, knocking the air out of me and filling my throat with sand.

I TOLD YOU, SHAREHOLDER, about waking up the following morning and finding myself accused of a crime that I did not commit; about determining that my only chance at freedom would be to follow the instructions I had been given; about spending the time that followed—tonight it'll be one month—providing the information required to complete my Profile and prepare for my judgment under the Algo. I made it my mission to immerse myself in my father's mind, as it existed in mine, excavating the story of his life. I confessed to the Board and its Shareholders all that I found within—in his mind and my own.

And now, a question for you: What happens next?

The problem is that there's little left on earth for humans to master. Each generation standing on the shoulders of the one before, we have mastered it all. We have rid ourselves of those enemies that have stepped into the path of our advancement. We have wrecked their homes so their children cannot return. We have sucked the earth of its life-giving marrow, so that no one else can have it but us. We began by creating fire, and now here we are, standing in its glorious blaze. The problem is that we are witnessing the upper limit of human accomplishment. In time the oceans will slam over the last of our good green land and the hot lid of heaven will press down upon it. We humans have become so excellent at conquering that we have succeeded in conquering even ourselves.

Lately, though, I have taken solace in considering all that my Clarinet turned out to be capable of. It gave me the story of my father's life; it gave me the stories of hundreds of strangers' lives. The stories of our lives are ephemeral: When we die, they die, too. But what if someone (what if I) could gather up these stories and hold on to them for safekeeping? When humans finally drive ourselves to extinction, wouldn't that be our best shot at proving to the universe that, once upon a time, we were here? All this time,

I have been asking and asking and asking myself: What am I here for? What are we all here for? Could it be, Shareholder, that this is the answer?

BUT THIS IS STRANGE. It was only this morning that I wrote these words. Not ten minutes later, a small, balding man walked into my room, without warning. He was dressed in a white coat, the kind doctors and lab scientists wear. A pair of COs in uniform came in right after him and stood on either side of the door, straight-backed, hands clasped before them. The man was hunched and furtive. Without making eye contact with me, he came to my bed and stood over me, his hands on his knees. He bent down. I could see his pores and the oily purple veins of his eyelids. His breath smelled of honeysuckle, like an infant's breath. He said, in a rough voice, "Lie down on your stomach."

I was opening my mouth to protest when he stepped even closer and grabbed me by the shoulder. I didn't mean to do it. I was upset, and it was reflexive: I rose and clocked him in the face. I didn't—don't—know how to punch a man. I had never done it before, and it shouldn't have worked. But he wasn't a strong man; he stumbled. I don't know why they sent him, of all people. I suppose my existence had to be kept quiet and so they didn't have many trusted people to choose from.

I couldn't contemplate all this for long, because, in the next instant, the guards came forward and tackled me to the floor, swiftly pulling my wrists back and handcuffing them. They cuffed my ankles, too. Others entered the room and crowded around me, shouting. The floor was cool against my forehead, pelvis, and knees. The only grace in all this was that no one could see my face. I let myself open my mouth against the floor. I could hear footsteps nearing my head. I could see, out of the corner of my eye, someone's shoes—the same doctor's or scientist's—crusted with brownish gray dried mud. Half a foot from my head, no more than that. I could only wriggle.

You shouldn't have done that, I scolded myself. You've got to calm down. But I couldn't help but wonder how much of this had to do with my actions at all. Maybe it had all been predetermined the moment my father thought to give me my Clarinet. Maybe anyone who learned about it would automatically see a problem, not a solution. Maybe it marked me as alien from the start. Let me tell you, though, the cell was cold that morning, and my fingertips went as numb and white as anyone's would. When that man gently jabbed me in the shoulder with a sharp needle, I almost screamed, then swallowed the scream, as anyone would.

I realized then that I couldn't move or talk. I remained conscious but had been muted.

There's this Zhuangzi tale, "The Joy of Fishes." Zhuangzi is walking with a friend named Huizi along the Hao River. "See how the minnows come out and dart around where they please!" Zhuangzi comments. "That's what fish really enjoy!" But Huizi takes exception. "You're not a fish," he replies. "How do you know what fish enjoy?" Zhuangzi retorts, "You're not I, so how do you know that I don't know what fish enjoy?" At this, Huizi acknowledges that he can't know his friend's mind, just as Zhuangzi can't know the mind of a fish. Zhuangzi gently reminds Huizi of the original question and answers it. "I know it by standing here beside the Hao," he tells his friend. Couldn't it be—isn't it—that simple?

Centuries later, when the philosopher Thomas Nagel considered, in the Zhuangzian tradition, whether a human can understand what it's like to be a bat, he came to the opposite conclusion. To be human is so different from being otherwise, he writes, that interspecies communion is impossible. "The loose intermodal analogies—for example, 'Red is like the sound of a trumpet'—which crop up in discussions of this subject are of little use," he wrote. "That should be clear to anyone who has both heard a trumpet and seen red."

My eyes were still open, and I still had some dull sensation in my nerves. I was aware of myself when the guards hoisted me onto a wheeled cot. "Restraints," someone said, and someone else—someone with fast, efficient hands—fastened me down. Now I looked more closely at the people in the room, who seemed a mix of medical and security personnel, along with some bureaucrats in khakis and button-downs, the ones in charge, the most fearful and innocent-looking of all. Someone rolled me out of the room, down a desolate white hall, and into a large elevator that clanged as it descended, then opened into what seemed to be a medical ward. No one there paid us much attention, though I heard someone comment, "Quite an entourage for this one."

We were in an operating theater. Someone had brought the doctor a stool. He sat on it and muttered, "Cart," and a woman in light blue scrubs rolled in a small metal table on wheels, on which there sat several tools. He murmured, "Comb." There was a silence in the room that was nearly reverent, as he ran his fingers through my hair, and began, carefully, to comb it. It almost comforted me; I thought of how my father used to comb my hair when I was little. I could almost believe this man was here to help me—that all of these people, the Shareholders' representatives in the halls of power, were here to help. If I could make words come out of my throat, I would have told them, My dad used to do that.

But then he finished combing my hair to his satisfaction and said, "Razor." A loud whirring filled the room, and he began shaving the hair from my head. I heard someone gasp. I tried to keep my eyes open, but the hair kept falling into them. I closed my eyes.

What was he searching for, there on the surface of my scalp: nuts, bolts? Did he see me as some scientific specimen? But that's ridiculous. You and I are both encased in flesh, engorged with blood, water, and air. If a physician were to lay us side by side and slice us each open from chest to navel, he would discover the same soft, maroonish organs nestled together, the same hot and throbbing hearts. If he opened our skulls, he would learn that even our brains, slightly different in function, appear the same, masses of rose-colored coil that, if stretched out neuron to neuron, would reach from San Francisco to Portland. The examination would yield nothing of value. It would accomplish nothing.

It accomplishes nothing for a dissector to grasp the dissectee by the scruff of her neck, murmur, "Scalpel," and to slice at the base of the dissectee's neck, close to her skull, and do so again, till the dissectee cries out in anguish; to persist through the dissectee's groans, through her telepathic pleas; and finally, to cut clear through her flesh with a small, dignified grunt of satisfaction, so that the dissectee cannot help but open her eyes to bear witness to what is happening to herself, and see a flash of the dissector's fingertips, colored with the blood of the dissectee. It accomplishes nothing for the dissector to pull apart the flaps of skin formed by his scalpel's cut at the dissectee's neck, and mutter, "Drill," and press some sharp and heavy instrument against the skull of the dissectee, once, twice, thrice, then move another sharp and heavy object in a line from one hole to the next to the next, and murmur, in a voice full of academic fascination, "Well, superficially, it doesn't *appear* any different," while the dissectee's teeth bite into the mattress on which her face rests, and the dissectee's throat fills with the taste of her blood, and the taste is red, oh God, the taste is a trumpet blast—

I LOST CONSCIOUSNESS. After the operation—whatever it entailed, in the end—they must have kept me unconscious for hours, long enough to remove me from the detention center and bring me here. When I came to my senses, I was lying on a mat of leaves in the shade of coconut trees. The shade cooled me, and, with the fronds waving around above, made shapes on the ground. I could see a house, for example, and a girl's braid. The air was hot, humid, and sweet-smelling, like fruit fully ripe on its vine, about to drop. My head hurt badly.

But it's all right; it's all forgiven now. When I realized it was the Garden that they had brought me to, I was as surprised as you must be. I had thought they were on a path to murdering me and extracting my organs for research; I had thought maybe my Profile would never be made public at all; I had thought maybe you would never read these words of mine, that they had let me go on only for long enough to give them the evidence they needed to target Elemen and her friends. Shareholder, imagine! But instead, they brought me to this gorgeous place. It is inexplicable.

Also inexplicable: The Garden is not in ruins at all. It isn't anything like what those TV reporters showed. It's just as it is in King's memories, not a single tree out of place. Since awakening, I've been aware of voices in the distance. Now I hear someone calling my name. "Athena, Athena." But it's his voice, my father's. Now another one is joining, a firm female voice. It's Margie, or, no, it's Elemen. They seem to be searching for me. "Is she still with us?" the first voice is saying, but now it doesn't sound like him anymore; it sounds, strangely, like that doctor from the detention center. There's background noise, too, as if a movie is playing. The first drone strike on the Blanklands. The Algo's recommendation. Eight Ex terrorists killed. Infrastructure damaged. There's something familiar about it; maybe I've seen this film before. "Yes, or, wait, maybe not—" the second voice is answering, and, she, too, no longer sounds familiar. "She's going in and out."

I can't stand. I'm tethered to the ground. The sun is a great orange in the sky, spraying its sweet, glittering light in all directions. There's all that lace, too, white lace, floating right above me. One day, this will all be over. Yet the fact will remain that we were here once, beneath all that lace. The fact needs no proof. We were here. What great fortune. For what? we kept demanding. For what? For what? For what? For what? But when a tree sprouts from the ground, it doesn't demand answers; when its blossoms grow tired and heavy, it lets them drop. After all our trouble, is that it, then? Did it all mean nothing but itself?

Acknowledgments

This novel took twelve years to write. My profound gratitude goes to Susan Golomb, my dream agent and friend, for seeing potential in an early draft and steadily helping me realize it. I appreciate Susan's assistants, past and present, Scott Cohen, Mariah Stovall, and Madeline Ticknor, and her colleagues at Writers House, including Peggy Boulos Smith, for their support. Thanks, Brando Skyhorse, for introducing me to Susan.

I feel proud to be publishing this book with W. W. Norton. I am grateful to my wonderful editor, Alane Mason, for her excellent edits, which made the novel so much better, and for her smooth stewardship of the novel through the publication process. Dassi Zeidel, Erin Lovett, Meredith McGinnis, Mo Crist, and Steve Attardo, of Norton, all played integral roles, as did Dave Cole and Keith Hayes. Peter Blackstock, of Grove, was an early champion, and his deft and sensitive contributions to the editing process as the novel's UK editor were invaluable.

I began taking creative-writing classes as an undergraduate at Stanford University and am thankful to the creative writing program and its former and current faculty, in particular Adam Johnson and Tobias Wolff. I will never forget the phone call I received from Lan Samantha Chang admitting me into the University of Iowa Writers' Workshop, and I value the friendship and guidance Sam has provided since then. Gratitude, too, to Connie Brothers, Deb West, and Janice Zenisek, and to Charles D'Ambrosio, Edward Carey, and Ethan Canin.

Elizabeth McCracken led the excellent workshop in which this novel was born, and I have returned many times, in the years since, to the feedback she gave about some early pages: "Write, write, write. Then write some more." It worked. I also appreciate the valuable feedback from colleagues in that workshop: Alex Dezen, Anthony Marra, Benjamin Nugent, Christina Minami, Gerardo Herrera, Haley Carrolhach, Jill Bodach, Kyle McCarthy, Marisa Handler, Matthew Null, and Michael Fauver.

Those who gave crucial notes on complete drafts of the book include Andrew Altschul, Anna North, Annie Wyman, Anthony Ha, Anthony Marra, Gerardo Herrera, Karan Mahajan, Krishna S. Vara, Nathan Burstein, R. O. Kwon, Tony Tulathimutte, and Vidyavathi Vara. Additional feedback on sections of the novel came from Alice Sola Kim, Andi Winnette, Anthony Ha, Colin Winnette, Chris Lee, Daniel Levin Becker, Esmé Weijun Wang, Greg Larson, Jennifer DuBois, and Mauro Javier Cardenas.

The novel is informed by my years as a technology reporter at the *Wall Street Journal*. I am grateful to Cathy Panagoulias, Don Clark, Pui-Wing Tam, and Steve Yoder for their guidance and for supporting the two-year leave of absence during which I began this novel. I also appreciate the colleagues, mentors, and sources who informed—and continue to inform—my understanding of technology companies and their growing role in social, economic, and political life. I finished the book while working as an editor at the *New York Times Magazine*, and thank Jake Silverstein and my magazine colleagues for their flexibility and patience. Extra gratitude to Kate LaRue for weighing in on the cover.

This project could never have been sustained without the financial support of the Canada Council for the Arts, the

Jeffrey G. and Victoria J. Edwards Prize, the Rona Jaffe Foundation, and the University of Iowa Writers' Workshop, as well as the quiet, beautiful spaces to write provided by MacDowell and the Yaddo Corporation.

Regarding caste and colonialism, scholars and others who provided important context include D. Shyam Babu, E. Sudha Rani, K. Satyanarayana, K. Y. Ratnam, Mallepalli Laxmaiah, Atlury Murali, Ramnarayan S. Rawat, and Y. B. Satyanarayana. I learned about coconuts from A. Sujatha of the Horticultural Research Station of Ambajipeta in India.

I am especially thankful to the family members and friends who shared their recollections of life on the rural coconut grove that is my paternal ancestral home. They include, among others, Damayanti, Lakshmi, and Raju Chinta; Deena Ganti; Rambabu and Ramdas Bojja; and Abbis Master. Sindhura Vara and Venugopalaswamy Vara, my research and travel partners, prepared me for those conversations and provided language and cultural interpretation. I am grateful, too, to Jayabala Vara and Saroja Bojja. A special acknowledgment goes to Sandeep Vara, who made sure I didn't take myself, or this book, too seriously. Indian-born friends whose perspectives informed the novel include GK Maganty and Rao Remala.

My brilliant sister, Krishna D. Vara, was my greatest teacher and ally. I inherited my love of literature from my parents, Krishna S. Vara and Vidyavathi Vara, who energetically supported this project. Gratitude to Alyssa, Douglas, and Georgette Graham, and to Fred and Susan Altschul, my loudest cheerleading squad. Others who provided much-needed advice, enthusiasm, and support during the writing of this book include Dana Mauriello, Hart Gilula, Jenny Zhang, Kathleen Founds, Kristy Beachy-Quick, Sanam Emami, Sarah Heyward, and Sophia Parker. Thanks, too, to the Mauriello, Mitchell, Ngongo, and Parker families.

My husband, Andrew Altschul, gets the second-to-last acknowledgement for driving me across the country to the town in which I began this novel and, through co-parenthood and all, protecting my writing time more fiercely than anyone, myself included. (Extra points for reading and giving me notes on at least four drafts of the novel, possibly more, which wasn't in the ketubah.) Kavi Altschul gets the last acknowledgment, in part for staying out of my office while I was writing this novel, but mostly just for existing.